From an iso[illegible]rn Hundred came Tol, a peasant boy whose great deeds would resound from one end of the Ergoth Empire to the other.

Called upon again to rid the empire of the evil sorcerer Mandes, Tol—ennobled as Lord Tolandruth—exacted justice on the sorcerer for his many crimes. But forces greater than Tol stirred in the imperial capital, and all his honors and alliances were swept away in a single night. Exiled and humiliated by the new emperor, Ackal V, Tol vanished into the primeval forest, the Great Green. For six years his whereabouts have remained a mystery.

The Ergoth Empire, once all-conquering, now faces two grave threats: an invasion by nomadic tribes on its eastern border, and a destructive rampage by a hundred thousand lizard-men, the *bakali* of ancient times. Army after army is smashed by the invaders, and Tol's hometown, Juramona, is sacked and burned. The bakali threaten Daltigoth itself. From every corner of the realm a call goes out, first whispered, then shouted: Where is Lord Tolandruth?

No one wants Tol back more than Empress Valaran. Shackled to a brutal husband, she dreams and schemes to find her lost love. Vastly rich and profoundly conniving, the empress enlists the best trackers and spies in the empire to find Tol. The College of Wizards likewise seeks him, for Ackal V decimates their ranks every time their magic fails to defeat the invaders. Old friends and old foes scour the world for Lord Tolandruth.

He will be found, and the ensuing events will forever change the Ergoth Empire.

# The Ergoth Trilogy

Paul B. Thompson & Tonya C. Cook

Volume One
A WARRIOR'S JOURNEY

Volume Two
THE WIZARD'S FATE

Volume Three
A HERO'S JUSTICE

# A HERO'S

The Ergoth Trilogy
volume three

# Justice

## Paul B. Thompson
## Tonya C. Cook

**A HERO'S JUSTICE**
©2004 Wizards of the Coast, Inc.

Distributed in the United States by Holtzbrinck Publishing. Distributed in Canada by Fenn Ltd.

Distributed to the hobby, toy, and comic trade in the United States and Canada by regional distributors.

Distributed worldwide by Wizards of the Coast, Inc. and regional distributors.

Printed in the U.S.A.

Cover art by Daniel R. Horne
Map by Dennis Kauth
First Printing: December 2004
Library of Congress Catalog Card Number: 2004106793

9 8 7 6 5 4 3 2 1

US ISBN: 0-7869-3397-6
UK ISBN: 0-7869-3398-4
620-17666-001-EN

U.S., CANADA,                                EUROPEAN HEADQUARTERS
ASIA, PACIFIC, & LATIN AMERICA              Wizards of the Coast, Belgium
Wizards of the Coast, Inc.                           T Hofveld 6d
P.O. Box 707                                    1702 Groot-Bijgaarden
Renton, WA 98057-0707                                  Belgium
+1-800-324-6496                                     +322 467 3360

Visit our web site at **www.wizards.com**

For my mother,
Anita A. Thompson

PBT

# A Hero's Justice

N

Hylo

Sancrist

Ergoth

Hylo

Juramona

Caergoth

Ackal Path

Dom-shu Village

Daltigoth

Thorngoth

Bay
of
Ergoth

Tarsis

Gulf
of
Tarsis

------ Invasion route of the Bakali

---·---·--- Invasion route of the Plains Nomads

# Avalanche on Level Ground

General Lord Relfas, mounted on a massive roan gelding, watched six streams of dust rise into the warm
morning air. Widely spaced in an arc from north to
south, the six dust streams were converging on his
position. His aide, Lord Fracolo, spoke the obvious:
"Scouts returning, sir!"

Relfas didn't bother to reply. Fracolo might be a Rider of
the Great Horde, but he could make no claim to nobility,
while Relfas was of the wealthy house of Dirinmor. Instead,
Relfas turned to stare at the view behind him. It was a sight
to stir the blood, and one he never tired of.

Fifty thousand mounted warriors were drawn up in
perfectly ordered ranks, iron armor gleaming and crimson
cloaks spotless. The First Fifty of the Great Horde of Ergoth
filled the bottomland of the Solvin River, as far as the eye
could see to the north, south, and west. So named because
they were the first to be summoned in time of war, the First
Fifty comprised the cream of Emperor Ackal V's fighting
men. None was younger than twenty, nor older than thirty.
Relfas, at forty years of age, was the oldest among them.

Horde standards rose proudly among the shining host.
Each flag bore the symbol of the fighting men behind it.
There were thunderbolts, stars, skulls, axes, and a veritable
menagerie of animals: dragons, panthers, bulls, bears, and
serpents.

Directly behind Relfas was the greatest standard of all,

1

the arms of the House of Ackal. The crimson banner emblazoned with a golden sun over a pair of crossed sabers had a proud history. First carried by the empire's founder, Ackal the Great, this emblem had journeyed into the far corners of the land, always returning in triumph. Those enemies who survived their contest with Ergoth said the banner's color came from the blood of the untold thousands slain by the Great Horde.

To be here, leading such an army into battle, was the dream of every Rider of the Great Horde. Even before his days as a shilder, training with blunted weapons, Relfas had never doubted he would attain this pinnacle. Such accomplishments were nothing more than his due.

The scouts arrived, hauling their foam-flecked horses to a stop amidst clouds of thick yellow plains dust. The first man to reach Relfas was a Rider from the Stone Shield Horde, a contingent well known for its elegance and dash. Since all the scouts were covered with yellow grime, this particular Stone Shielder hardly lived up to that reputation just now.

"My lord!" he cried. "I beg to report the enemy has withdrawn!"

"More than a league beyond the riverbend!" added a second scout, arriving hard on the heels of the first.

"So, the lizards are running," Relfas said, a smug smile on his handsome, red-bearded face.

He had brought the army here in a rush to contest the invaders' crossing of the Solvin River, some twenty leagues east-northeast of the city of Caergoth. The news that the enemy had fallen back, even before his men could engage them, only confirmed what Relfas had long believed. The invader host might terrify peasants and nomad barbarians, but it stood no chance against the trained hordes of Ergoth.

Raising his voice he declared, "We will pursue!"

His subordinate warlords, gathered behind him, exchanged looks. Hojan of Hobor, who knew the Eastern Hundred well, urged caution. "We should not rush blindly into a fray," he said. "There are other scouts still out. We should wait and hear from them."

"Other scouts? What other scouts?" asked Relfas.

"He means the nomads, my lord," said the Stone Shield rider, lip curling in disdain. "Curs! They take our coin, ride out, and don't return!"

"The ones I hire do," Hojan replied.

Relfas had no interest whatsoever in nomads, scouts or no.

"The first law of war, as set down by Ackal the Great, is to pursue a fleeing enemy until they are utterly destroyed," he said. "Is that not so, Lord Hojan?"

Hojan grunted an affirmative, but added there was no proof the enemy was fleeing. They might simply be leaving the flatlands around the river, to take advantage of the better position provided by the Solvin Hills.

Relfas shook his head. "You give them too much credit. They're little better than beasts."

The casual dismissal left Hojan and several other warlords staring.

"My lord, in olden times the *arkudenala* nearly overran Silvanost!" Lord Dukant said.

The name, bestowed on the invaders by displaced nomads, meant "sons of dragons." The arkudenala had landed on the empire's north coast seven years earlier and begun driving inland, slaughtering all who opposed them. Peasant refugees, driven before the invaders like the bow wave of a great ship, made for the presumed safety of the empire's southern cities, bringing with them confusing tales of their inhuman attackers. However, it soon became clear these arkudenala were not some new, draconic evil, but *bakali*, a reptilian race once thought cleansed from the world.

"Elves are not Riders of the Great Horde," Relfas stated. "What overran them, *we* shall destroy! The order is: pursue the retreating foe!"

Most of the warlords, fired with pride and eager for battle, saluted their general and rejoined their respective hordes. Hojan and a handful of skeptics departed with more deliberation.

Lord Relfas's command echoed through the lines. Drawing their sabers in one long thunderclap of iron on iron, the Riders roared, "Ergoth! Ergoth!"

Fifty thousand horsemen trotted out of the bend of the Solvin, advancing straight ahead. On either wing, Riders fanned out, opening the interval between them and breaking into a canter.

The river bottom, lush with newly leafed willows and a rampant tangle of blooming vines, gave way in less than a league to grassy land that rose in a series of low, step-like ridges. The sod was trampled and torn in a swath five leagues wide. The sheer breadth of the trail caused the Ergothian advance to falter.

"How many lizard-men are there?" asked Lord Fracolo, staring at the scarred ground.

"What does it matter?" Relfas snapped. He rose in the stirrups, lifted his saber high, and shouted, "Whether they be ten thousand or a hundred thousand, the lizards are showing us their backs and we shall sweep the land clear of them!"

He ordered the pace increased to a gallop. Most of the First Fifty surged forward, supremely confident of their own invincibility.

Before Relfas joined them, Lord Hojan steered his mount next to the general's and spoke quickly. He reminded his leader of another time-honored precept handed down by Ackal the Great: when the enemy's strength is unknown, hold men in reserve.

Although he did not share his warlord's caution, Relfas ordered Hojan to proceed. Then the general galloped away.

Several warlords had held back when the rest increased their pace. At Hojan's command, these formed up around his own Golden Helm Horde. Six hordes in all, the reserve continued to move forward, but at a walking pace.

Far ahead, the Riders galloping in the forefront of the charge reached the lowest step of the hills without catching sight of the enemy. They'd covered a thousand paces, and their mounts were winded. They slowed, and the formation became confused as faster riders trod on their heels. Still, the throng of mounted men continued their forward motion, beginning the climb up the first slope.

At that instant, a shrill screeching filled the steamy summer air. The Ergothians reined up, unable to trace or identify the bizarre sound. From the army's edges, solitary riders broke off and rode swiftly away. They were clad not in iron armor, but buckskin or homespun. These were nomads, hired as scouts by the Ergothians, and they alone recognized this sound, knew exactly what it meant.

All along the rim of the ridge ahead, dark figures appeared. With the late morning sun in their eyes, the Ergothians could make out no details, only bulky, shapeless silhouettes, but the clatter of arms was unmistakable. Horns of warning bleated along the imperial line.

Relfas saw his men hesitate. Warriors of the Great Horde feared no mortal foe, but a charge up a steep incline at an entrenched enemy such as this was not a thing to be taken lightly. Relfas took personal command of the vanguard and roared the order to charge. Weary horses panted and gasped, fighting their way up the slope already torn up by the enemy's passage.

Atop the ridge loomed a wall of green and dull metal. Spears swung down from the front ranks of the bakali host. Behind them billhooks and poleaxes cleaved the air in menacing circles. The enemy himself was not quite visible, only the seemingly impenetrable phalanx of shields and protruding spears.

Standing in his stirrups and whipping his saber around his head, Relfas led his men into the first clash. He was promptly unhorsed when his mount reared to avoid the spiny greeting the bakali had prepared. The animal toppled, and Relfas tumbled ignominiously down the slope. Around him, smarter horsemen kept low over their mounts' necks and struck at the spearpoints with their sabers.

While the front ranks jabbed at each other, the second rank of bakali waded in with hooks and axes. With these they snagged unwary riders, dragging them onto the waiting spears of other bakali.

For most of the Ergothians, this was the first time they'd seen the enemy. It was a sight not easily forgotten.

Standing two paces tall, the bakali were roughly human-shaped, with narrow, protruding chests and heavily muscled arms and legs. Brow ridges and upper lips lined with yellow horns lent them a beaked, almost bird-like appearance. Eyes were either yellow or pale green, with black, diamond-shaped pupils. Ears the bakali had not; only a hole on each side of the head. Likewise, the nose was nothing more than a small bump, with two slit nostrils, above a lipless gash.

Hands and feet were enormous, and sported four thick fingers or toes, all far longer than any human's and tipped with yellow talons. For battle, the bakali draped themselves in loose coats of tiny iron rings, which were secured by leather belts around their narrow waists. Weapons were oversized and crude, made for hacking and slashing, and horribly effective against soft-skinned enemies.

Perhaps even more unforgettable to the Ergothians than the first sight of their inhuman enemy was the smell. Acrid and fetid at the same time, the bakali gave off the stench of a viper's den. The odor hung over the enemy host like an invisible fog, stinging the eyes and clogging throats.

Lord Relfas, unhurt by his embarrassing fall, had remounted and returned to the fray. He and the vanguard continued their attempts to come to grips with the enemy, while the main body of Riders maneuvered around the struggle and fell upon the bakali flank. The lizard-men turned left to face this onslaught. Before the sun reached its zenith, three-quarters of Relfas's army was furiously engaged. Only the reserve—Hojan and the other more prudent warlords—remained out of action, awaiting orders to join the fray.

By sheer weight of numbers, the imperial army forced its way onto the lowest hill. There, they beheld the bakali host in its totality for the first time. Relfas reckoned the number to be forty or fifty thousand strong, about the same strength as his own army.

The creatures were proving to be unexpectedly tenacious. As their front line was hacked apart, the lizard-men stood back to back and fought on, selling their lives dearly. Ergothians who'd considered them little more than animals were shocked to see the bakali resist charge after charge. Great quantities of their dark, purplish red blood flowed, mixing with the scarlet gore of men and horses. Still, the bakali did not give up.

With the vanguard attacking head-on, and the main body assaulting their flank, the bakali were forced back to the base of the next hill. Hard-pressed, the lizards did not try to retreat up the slope, but remained where they were, fighting furiously. Relfas sent word to his main force to withdraw just enough to gain room for a full-fledged charge. Such a strike on the flank would, he was certain, roll up the bakali line like a rotten carpet.

As the Riders formed up for the charge, a chorus of intense, metallic screeching rose over the battlefield for a second time. Relfas, enjoying a brief lull in the action around him, gave a shout.

"They're begging for mercy!" he exulted.

His feeling of triumph was short-lived. On the ridge behind and above the hard-pressed bakali a whole new host of the creatures sprang up. These lizards had been lying concealed in the tall grass. In the space of two heartbeats, the enemy force had doubled in strength.

Relfas stared at the new foe in frozen shock, but only for a moment. Boldness, not timidity, won battles and brought glory. Ignoring the chatter of his subordinates, he ordered the charge.

The tired Ergothians surged forward. The fresh wave of bakali ran down the hill to reinforce their comrades, then the entire bakali line began to push forward. Charging Riders ran straight onto a wall of lethal spearpoints. Their comrades, blinded by fury and foolhardy courage, came on. Line after line of horsemen threw themselves against the resurgent lizard-men. Line after line perished. The bard Aylimar, writing of one of Ackal Ergot's battles centuries before, had likened a similarly futile charge to wax soldiers flinging themselves against a red-hot anvil. For Relfas's men, it was like being fed into a horrendous threshing machine. The whirling blades, wielded with terrifying skill by the bakali, tore them to pieces.

Continuing their slow, implacable advance, the bakali line pushed the Ergothians off the lower hilltop, retaking the ground Relfas had earlier won at such cost.

At last acknowledging the danger, Relfas summoned the

reserves. They did not come. Instead, a Rider arrived, bearing dire news from Lord Hojan.

The enemy was behind Relfas.

Facing west, his back to Relfas's position, Hojan battled a new army of bakali that had appeared seemingly out of nowhere. Although a smaller contingent, perhaps twenty thousand lizards, it far outnumbered the six hordes under Hojan's command. The first tendrils of despair chilled Relfas's proud heart.

"Rally! Rally to me!" he cried, parched voice cracking.

The mass of confused Riders around him slowly dissolved. Some men rode hard to join Hojan. Some remained with their commander. Others—more than a few—did something thought inconceivable for Riders of the Great Horde. They fled. Wanting nothing more than to put distance between themselves and the remorseless inhuman killing machine they faced, they rode away.

His army disintegrating, the bakali before him still advancing, Relfas had only one goal left: survival. The lizard-men were far stronger and more numerous than anyone had guessed. His Majesty Ackal V must be told. Therefore, the imperial army would fall back to the city of Caergoth and replenish its ranks there.

He gave the order, then realized no one was left to relay it to the warlords. He was standing alone. The bakali line was eight paces away, and coming toward him fast. Bent-kneed, the creatures ran with a strange hopping motion that set their ring-armor coats jingling.

Lord Relfas yanked the roan's big head about and drove his spurs hard into the animal's sides. The battle of Solvin Hills was lost. His duty now was to warn the empire that this threat was far, far graver than anyone had imagined.

❦ ❦ ❦ ❦ ❦

Hojan's ranks swelled as warriors from the rest of the army sought refuge with him. With eight thousand men, he organized a fighting retreat northward, away from the bakali's westward line of advance.

Although the Ergothians were defeated and disorganized, the bakali did not press their advantage. Instead, a league from the battlefield, the lizard-men gave up the pursuit and returned to the main body of their army.

From a distance, Hojan watched as the departing enemy was joined by even more bakali. These newcomers were not warriors. Unarmed, they were burdened by baggage, or dragging heavy sledges. A veritable river of scaly lizard-men flowed through the Solvin valley.

This wasn't an army on the move. It was a nation.

Once the tide had passed on, Hojan sent scouts back to the battlefield. They found it picked clean. Every broken sword, every fractured spearshaft had been taken away. Far more disturbing was the fact that the slain—men and horses alike—were all gone. What the bakali wanted with them no one dared contemplate.

# Chapter 1
## A Visitor for Uncle Corpse

T he stone canyons of the city channeled sound in odd ways. Sometimes an altercation in the next street might be inaudible, but a catfight six blocks away sounded like it was happening next door. Tonight's commotion was loud enough to hear anywhere in Daltigoth.

Rumors of meat for sale had drawn a hungry crowd to a shop in the butchers' lane. The rumors proved false, but the angry crowd would not be denied. They began to ransack other shops in the quarter. City guards moved in to stop them, more hungry residents turned out, and a major riot erupted. Emperor Ackal V sent troops to quell the trouble, but the fighting continued. Confronted by armed warriors, the rioters hid, only to reappear when the soldiers had passed on.

The rioting was useful cover for the stranger in the fawn-colored cape who moved carefully through the dark alleys. The streets were alternately crowded with looters, or empty of all but wreckage. The way had been impeded only once, by a large ruffian with a cudgel. Spying the slight figure drawing near, the man thought he'd found easy prey. A fast stroke of the knife left him with his throat slit, dying while still on his feet. The caped stranger quickly wiped blood from the knife blade and moved on. The Empress of Ergoth could not be kept waiting.

The Inner City gate, flanked by burning braziers, was

manned by two dismounted Horse Guardsmen. They crossed their spears, barring the stranger's way.

"What business d'ya have here?" one soldier rasped.

The cape flipped back to show one hand holding a silver disk. Engraved on it was a coat of arms known to all. Both guards stiffened respectfully, and stood aside.

Beyond the gate, the fabulous mosaic that paved the wide plaza was nearly invisible, covered by the crowd of imperial guardsmen who stood ready to fend off any attackers who dared approach. The stranger walked boldly across the torchlit plaza. None of the disciplined soldiers broke ranks, but all eyes followed the figure's progress across the vast courtyard. By firelight the palace's marble steps resembled gold. The visitor nimbly ascended the broad stairway.

In all, the stranger was challenged six times. Each time, the silver seal turned aside all questions. Once inside the palace, the caped figure kept to side passages as instructed. The blaze of light coming from the audience chamber meant the war council was in session. Voices, loud and profane, rang through the open doors. No doubt Emperor Ackal V was busy haranguing his beleaguered warlords about the invasion.

Lesser corridors of the palace stood in startling contrast to the splendor of the public chambers. Devoid of decoration, the plain stone halls were musty and smoky, as though not recently cleaned. The stranger's supple deerskin boots made little sound on the flagstone floors. Servants had no warning of a presence until the fawn cape swept into view. Trained not to wonder at odd goings-on, they waited silently, eyes cast down, until the phantom was gone.

The stranger's destination, the solarium, was not easy to find. Located deep in the heart of the sprawling palace, it was guarded by hidden doors and misleading passages. Twice the stranger went astray and was forced to backtrack. At last, the solarium doors came into view: twin portals of blackwood, inlaid with the bold crest of the House of Ackal in solid gold.

The solarium housed a magnificent sunken garden. The splash of water in the fountains echoed off a corbelled ceiling twelve paces above the floor. By day, isinglass panels let in sunlight. Now, at night, hooded lamps lit the scene like ruddy moonlight.

Murmuring voices, barely audible over the play of water, reached the stranger's keen ears. Following the sound as easily as a hound might follow a scent, the visitor soon arrived at a pool by the base of an artificial waterfall. Five women sat on a low stone bench there. All were identically garbed in pale green, loose-fitting robes, hoods drawn up to cover their heads. Four of them turned toward the newcomer, their wide eyes showing white in the dim light. The stranger advanced to the fifth woman and knelt on one knee.

"Your Majesty."

The woman stood and unhooked her robe. The garment fell, pooling on the gold-streaked white marble tiles. Beneath it, the woman wore a close-fitting velvet gown the color of old blood. A matching headdress, stiffly starched, pulled her chestnut hair back from her face, allowing it to fall in a rich cascade to the middle of her back. She regarded the visitor with vivid green eyes.

"How did you know me?"

"Your companions were alarmed to see me. You were not."

Valaran, chief consort of Emperor Ackal V, nodded once and dismissed her ladies-in-waiting with a wave of her hand. When she and her visitor were alone, she seated herself again on the stone bench.

"You are called Zala?" The stranger nodded, and Valaran added, "Let me see you."

The cape was removed. Of medium height, with a lithe build, the visitor had chin-length black hair which she tucked haphazardly behind her ears.

Taking note of those ears, Valaran asked, "Which of your parents was an elf?"

"My mother was Silvanesti, Your Majesty."

"You had no trouble reaching me?"

"No special trouble, Majesty. A riot rages in the New City."

Finely shaped eyebrows knit in confusion. "Another one? Why wasn't I told? That's the third in ten days!"

"Have you not seen the fires, Majesty?"

"I rarely leave the palace's inner core. I must get to the battlements more often." Velvet strained through her fingers as Valaran clenched a hand in her lap. "By custom long established, the empress of Ergoth resides in seclusion. It is a custom my husband delights in enforcing."

At the empress's request, Zala told what she knew of the riot and its cause. "No fresh meat has come to the city for four days," she finished. "It's said the cattlemen up north are holding onto their herds, lest they fall into the hands of the invaders."

"All the more reason your mission must be carried out without delay," Valaran said. "You're said to be an expert tracker and huntress. You'll need all your skills. The country between here and where you're going is no temple garden."

Zala gave no response, since none had been requested, but her journey here from Caergoth hadn't been exactly easy. Although the bakali invaders had not penetrated as far south as her native city, their approach had driven desperate refugees there to rob and kill. And there were nomads, plainsmen from the east, rampaging though the border provinces. Most of the once peaceful roads and fields were now highly dangerous to traverse.

From beneath her stone bench Valaran produced a small roll of parchment. She tapped it against one palm, regarding her visitor in frowning silence. Finally she asked, "Can you be trusted? If I give you a task to perform, will you carry it out?"

"I live by my word and deeds. I am known for this. Why else did you choose me?"

The slightly arch tone caused the empress's eyes to narrow. "I chose you, half-breed, because I am forbidden to receive any male but the emperor, and you are the best of the few female rangers I could find. But know this: fail me, and your head will gather crows atop the Inner City wall!"

Zala knew the truth of that. One did not fail the House of Ackal.

Valaran rose. She continued to tap the small scroll against the palm of her hand as she studied the half-elf. In addition to raven-black hair, Zala had dark eyes, a pointed chin, and a short, straight nose. Her skin was fair, with a spray of tan freckles across her nose.

At last, Valaran said, "You'll do. You seem strong. I imagine you look fetching enough without your hunter's togs."

Zala's face grew hot. "What exactly is Your Majesty hiring me to do?"

"Find a man. One particular man. When you find him, you must convince him to return to Daltigoth. You will offer him whatever it takes—gold, honors, yourself—anything." Valaran held out the scroll. "This is a description of him. Study it well."

Zala tucked the parchment into her belt.

"Begin your search in Juramona, in the Eastern Hundred," the empress said. "That was his home once, and the best place to seek clues to his current whereabouts."

She removed a narrow gold ring from her finger and pressed it into Zala's hand. "This was a gift from him to me. I had a wizard place a spell of finding on it. The power of the spell is limited to the width of the horizon, so don't use it until you think yourself close to him. Once you find him, give him the ring and he will know that I sent you."

Zala couldn't help asking the obvious question. "Majesty, what of the imperial mages? Surely they could find and summon this man much more quickly than I."

The empress's forthright manner became suddenly evasive. "He cannot be moved by magic," she replied, looking away. "Even the ring will fail if . . ."

Her voice trailed off. Zala waited patiently. The empress shook off her odd mood and added, "He must be found the hard way. Rely on your own wits and skill."

Zala vowed she would. She always had.

The empress explained that ten thousand crowns had been deposited with Zala's partner in Caergoth. When the huntress returned with her quarry, another twenty thousand would be paid to her on the spot. The sum caused Zala's jaw to drop. She'd never dreamed of such a commission.

"What man is worth thirty thousand crowns?" she blurted.

"His name is Tol, once Lord Tolandruth, general of the Army of the North and champion of the late emperor, Ackal IV."

Zala knew the name. Tolandruth had been an important warlord once, winning many battles against the Tarsans, but six years ago he'd fallen afoul of the current emperor and gotten himself banished. He must've done something pretty bad to lose his titles and position. No wonder the empress wanted their business kept secret. The emperor would not be pleased to know his chief consort was searching for a disgraced former hero of the empire.

"He may be dead, Majesty," Zala warned.

"He's alive," was the unhesitating response. "I know it in my heart. Bring him to me. Quickly."

Zala took her leave. Once out of the empress's presence, she drew a deep breath. She was sweating beneath her deerskins, though the palace was cool enough. Here was a chance to make more money with one job than she could in fifty years of ordinary tracking. Her partner in Caergoth—her human father—was old and sick. Thirty thousand gold pieces would ease his burdens immeasurably.

However, the empress's threats, delivered with practiced ease, were very real. If Zala failed, she would die; of that she had no doubt. The empire was broad, with many places to hide, but the Empress of Ergoth had a long reach. She must find this Tol swiftly and get him back to Daltigoth.

She pulled the hood over her head again before she exited the palace. Leaving the unnatural calm of the Inner City, she merged into the turbulent night.

❦ ❦ ❦ ❦ ❦

The forest rose ahead, seeming solid as a city wall. The sun, playing hide and seek behind ragged clouds, would alternately illuminate the trees in golden light, then leave them again in shade. Thick undergrowth made it impossible to see more than a pace or two into the forest.

Egrin Raemel's son sat on horseback a dozen strides from the edge of the Great Green. The former Marshal of the

15

Eastern Hundred scratched his chin through a beard mostly
gray; very little of its original auburn color remained.

Two decades had passed since Egrin last had entered this
forest. Sword in hand, he'd followed the trail broken by his
commander, Marshal Odovar. Only a few score paces inside,
the dense undergrowth vanished as the branches of the
majestic trees formed a dim, leafy canopy. There were few
landmarks; one enormous tree looked very like another to
open-country Ergothians. Within half a day, tribesmen had
fallen upon their rear, driving them deeper into the woodland, and away from any hope of rescue.

But rescued they were, by a force of one hundred foot
soldiers led by Tol, Egrin's shield-bearer. The boy was barely
seventeen. Born to farmers so backward they didn't bother
keeping track of birthdays, Tol didn't know his precise age.
His people moved to a different set of rhythms than town
folk. A boy was old enough to do a deed when he was big
enough and strong enough to accomplish it. Even after
coming to Juramona and training as a warrior, Tol lived that
way. More often than not, he succeeded.

The sun came out from behind the clouds again. Egrin
mopped sweat from his brow. He didn't relish entering the
Great Green again. This time, it wasn't forest tribesmen who
worried him. There had been peace between the Dom-shu
and the empire for years. These days, worse things than wild
woodsmen inhabited the world. Inhuman things.

Although born in a wooded area himself, Egrin had been
forced out at an early age. The small settlement of humans
and elves in which his family lived was destroyed by raiders.
His human mother was killed and his father, a Silvanesti elf,
had vanished. Egrin had been left with a sympathetic human
family at a settlement far from the woodlands. His new
family insisted—for his own safety—that he hide his mixed
lineage, going so far as to have his upswept ears cropped to a
more "normal" shape.

He had been concealing his parentage ever since. He had
told the truth to only two people: a wife, long dead, and Tol,
the farm boy who had become like a son to him.

The broad meadow at his back, known as Zivilyn's Carpet,

was alive with spring wildflowers, just as it had been that day twenty years ago when he'd entered the Great Green with Lord Odovar. This time Egrin had traveled alone, and this time he had no Tol to come boldly, foolishly, to the rescue.

No, that wasn't strictly true. Tol *was* going to rescue Egrin again—Egrin and everyone else in the Ergoth Empire—if only Egrin could find him. It was for that reason the former marshal had left his small, comfortable home in Juramona to undertake a journey for which he was, he admitted frankly to himself, getting much too old.

Well, he wasn't getting any younger, or any closer to finding Tol, just sitting here staring at the trees.

He dismounted and led his horse forward. The sway-backed beast was the only horse he'd found for sale for a dozen leagues in any direction. All decent animals had been rounded up and sold to the imperial army. As many horses as men had died in the last three battles—and men were more easily replaced.

Once he'd entered the shade, Egrin hoped the heat would abate, but it did not. The trees grew so close together they shut out any breeze, making the air stifling and oppressive. He'd forgotten that.

Further in, the tangled undergrowth thinned enough to allow him to ride. Brownie—the illogical name his gray-coated mount bore—sighed as Egrin settled on his back again, but the beast moved readily enough when Egrin tapped heels to his ribs.

They picked their way carefully through the great maples and broad oaks, until Egrin found the beginning of a trail. A less experienced eye would not have seen a trail at all. It was no more than a scuffed area of moss, a few rocks worn free of dirt, and the suggestion of an opening in a tangle of windfall trees, but Egrin knew someone had trod this way before.

Unable to get more than a general glimpse of the sun, he could only guess how far he rode that first day. Eight leagues, maybe nine, passed beneath Brownie's hooves by the time daylight faded and the first mournful call of the whippoorwill echoed through the trees. He saw little game. Although a deft tracker, and considered stealthy by his comrades in arms, by forest standards Egrin was a great lumbering oaf, tramping and crashing through the woods like a rampaging bull. Wild beasts and forest folk easily kept out of his way.

On the second day, he found more trails, some quite obvious now that he was deep in the forest. Artifacts turned up. Small things, but the bits of woven cloth, tufts of fox fur tied to twigs, and shards of unbaked clay, indicated people had passed this way.

That night he heard distant drums, and a strange humming sound rising and falling through the black trees. The noise was eerie, like nothing he'd ever heard before, and he slept with his sword by his side.

First light of the third day brought visitors. Four brown-skinned foresters stood in plain view on the trail ahead, watching him. They wore buckskin vests and long, floppy trews. Tufts of animal fur on loops of fine cord hung from tiny holes punched in their earlobes. All four carried deeply curved short bows. The stiff bows could easily put a flint-tipped arrow through a man's leg. If they were still getting bronze and iron from the Silvanesti, their arrowheads would penetrate his mail shirt.

Moving with great deliberation, Egrin packed up his meager camp. He lashed his bedroll across the horse's rump, mounted, and rode toward the waiting men.

The forester on the far right held out his hand. When Brownie's nose touched the fellow's hand, the aged horse shuffled to a stop.

"You're a long way from home, grasslander," said the forester on the far left.

Egrin ceased his fruitless efforts to urge Brownie into motion. "Peace to you," he said. "I'm alone, and I'm looking for someone."

The fellow who'd halted Brownie muttered something in his native language. The others grunted. The mistrust in their eyes needed no translation.

The man on the left said, "You've found someone. Now go back."

"I seek Voyarunta."

Two decades earlier, Tol had bested the Dom-shu chief

Makaralonga in battle. Ergothian custom obliged him to ex-ecute the man. Unwilling to kill an honorable foe who'd sur-rendered on promise of clemency, Tol and the healer Felryn had conspired to fool their superiors and allow Makaralonga to go free. To help keep their deception from becoming known, Makaralonga had chosen a new name, *Voyarunta*, meaning "Uncle Corpse" in the Dom-shu dialect. It was his joke on the mighty Ergoth Empire.

The fellow's dark eyes narrowed. "We are Karad-shu," he said.

Egrin silently cursed his luck. Voyarunta's tribe was friendly with the Ergothians, because of Tol's wisdom in sparing their chief. The Karad-shu were another matter entirely. Reputedly allied with the Silvanesti, they were no friends of Ergoth.

"It is important I get to Voyarunta," Egrin said calmly. "The lives of many foresters and grasslanders depend on it. Where can I find him?"

The tribesman regarded him in silence. Egrin waited, drawing on the legendary patience of his long-lived Silvanesti ancestors. His calm persistence was rewarded.

"The chief of the Dom-shu is at the Place of Birthing." Twitching his head slightly over one shoulder to indicate a northeasterly direction, the Karad-shu added, "Two days on two feet."

A day and half by horse. Egrin thanked the tribesmen. He had no idea what the Place of Birthing might be, but decided against questioning the foresters further. He was too relieved to see them go.

That day and the next night were full of portents. Drums beat far away; the whistling, humming noise continued to wax and wane. Egrin found totems and fetishes erected next to the trail—skulls on posts, carved boulders, and the skin of a bear tacked to a maple tree. As he rode by the latter, hornets erupted from the dead bear's eyes and mouth.

He was instantly engulfed by a cloud of huge, stinging insects. The stings felt like a red-hot iron wire stabbing into him over and over. The attacking hornets caused the aged Brownie to dance sideways. Lashing the reins, Egrin drove

Paul B. Thompson and Tonya C. Cook

the terrified horse away from the swarm. He slapped insects out of the air with his gauntleted hands, and the ferocious creatures tried to sting him through the heavy steerhide.

The insects pursued them only a short distance, but Egrin's danger wasn't done. Once stirred to action, Brownie was not easily calmed. The sway-backed horse barreled ahead, heedless of the branches that threatened to sweep Egrin from the saddle.

Galloping down a hill, the horse stumbled, throwing his rider. By the time Egrin sat up again, all that remained of the horse was the sound of his hoofbeats fading rapidly into the west.

Egrin cursed as he slowly sat up. Most of his gear had gone with the horse. All he had left were the sword and knife he wore. Ignoring his various aches and pains, he brushed dirt from his clothing and continued on foot.

The eerie whirring, humming noise was growing louder, sounding like a chorus of dragon-sized crickets. Distracted by the noise, stumbling a bit on tired, aching legs, Egrin found himself surrounded by a score of tall foresters.

They were armed with spears, most flint-tipped but a few sporting tarnished bronze heads. More startling than their arms was their attire. Each forester wore a long skirt made of strips of red bark. Breastplates of white whittled sticks, knotted together with cord, covered their chests. Any exposed skin was hidden beneath a paste of grease and ashes, and their heads were encased in fantastic masks made of clay, leather, animal teeth, and horns.

Before Egrin could speak, two tribesmen came up behind him and shoved him to his knees. A quartet of flint blades ringed his face. A forester with a pair of boar's tusks protruding from his mask uttered a sharp phrase. It did not sound kindly.

"I am here on a mission," Egrin said, keeping his hands out to his sides, away from his weapons. "I seek Voyarunta."

Boar Tusk spoke again, a longer speech, but no more helpful.

"Makaralonga," Egrin said carefully. "I have come to see Chief Makaralonga."

Even with their faces hidden, the tribesmen's suspicion was plain. Two of them hauled Egrin to his feet, taking his sword and knife.

A newcomer arrived, and the foresters parted ranks for him. His mask was of a particularly hideous mien, with protruding eyes, a sunken, twisted nose, and the tongue of a buck deer hanging from between its bared wooden lips. The entire mask was painted dead white.

White Face eyed Egrin up and down. "I will take you to Makaralonga," he finally said, his words muffled by the grotesque appliance.

He addressed his comrades in their own tongue, and an argument broke out. Boar Tusk seemed strenuously opposed to the plan. White Face's reply was to rap his spearshaft over Boar Tusk's head. The blow likely would have felled a bareheaded man, but Boar Tusk staggered, merely stunned.

White Face turned to Egrin. "Do not speak, and when I hold up my hand, look at the ground," he ordered. The lolling-tongued face came close. "Disobey, and you die."

Egrin nodded, and they departed.

As they traveled, a quarter-league at least, the throb of drums grew more distinct. Glimpses of blue sky ahead revealed they were approaching a clearing. The redbud, dogwood, and other smaller trees disappeared, leaving only the widely spaced giants of the forest. The ground around the massive tree trunks was bare, packed by the tread of many feet over many years. They reached the edge of a ravine and halted.

The narrow, bowl-shaped gully was lined with crudely cut blocks of native stone. The stones were set in horizontal rows along the ravine's sides, and these benches were crowded with tribesmen. Hundreds of the Dom-shu, all garbed and masked like Egrin's captors, sat and stared at a ceremony taking place on the floor of the ravine.

Their attention was focused on two concentric circles of foresters. The outermost ring was made up of drummers, beating a regular one-two rhythm on pairs of skin-covered drums. Within arm's reach in front of them was a circle of flame, a ring of wood stacked waist-high. Inside this marched a circle of tribesmen, wearing tiny breechcloths and a thick coating of ash and grease. They moved in single file. Following the east-to-west motion of the sun, they lifted their knees high and drove their heels hard into the cindered soil. Each dancer whirled a length of cord over his head. At the end of each cord was a slat of wood. This whirling slat was the source of the weird humming Egrin had heard. This close, the sound was deeply affecting. Not just the sheer volume of it, but the quality of the noise. The bass note seemed to penetrate the chest and make the bones shiver.

In the center of these circles, a lone figure squatted. Alone of all the tribesmen present, he was not covered in ash, nor masked. He was naked, his long gray hair falling past his shoulders. Skin browned by years of forest life stretched tautly over his sinewy frame. On his back, scars stood out white as paint.

"Makaralonga," said White Face, though Egrin already had deduced as much.

The Place of Birthing, the Karad-shu had called it. Egrin understood a little better what the forester had meant. The chief wasn't witnessing the birth of a child or grandchild; it was Makaralonga himself who was being reborn.

At some unseen signal, the seated onlookers rose in a body and shouted. White Face lifted a hand. Egrin dropped his gaze to the ground, covering his eyes with his hands for good measure. The shout resolved into a chant. Only four words, the chant was repeated again and again. Egrin felt the hair on his neck prickle. Sweat beaded on his brow.

"Do not look, if you value living." White Face punctuated his words with the point of a metal dagger in Egrin's ribs.

By regulating the whirling of their sticks, the dancers produced a concerted pulse, matching it to the machine-like regularity of the drummers. To Egrin's surprise, he felt his own heartbeat quicken to match the rhythm. The blood pounded through the great vein in his neck, as though he was engaged in strenuous exercise. Even more astonishing, he realized he could feel White Face's heartbeat as well, transmitted through the blade of the dagger he still held to Egrin's side. The forester's pulse matched Egrin's own. He had no doubt the heart of every soul present was hammering now in perfect unison.

Gradually, the dancers allowed their music to slow to a less frenzied tempo. The drummers changed their rhythm as well. White Face's dagger was withdrawn.

Given leave by the forester, Egrin looked up. Makaralonga stood in the ravine below, donning a deerskin robe. Pale wisps of fog drifted around him.

The flaming ring of wood was no more than glowing embers, and the scene was washed in the ruddy light of the setting sun. Egrin was puzzled. He was certain only one mark had passed since his capture, yet if sunset had come, half a day must have elapsed.

White Face guided him away from the Place of Birthing. They followed a wide, well-marked path eastward, deeper into the Great Green. Scores of masked Dom-shu trod silently on either side. It wasn't until they reached the foresters' village that the masks were removed and the foresters began to speak among themselves.

Egrin was taken to a sod hut of considerable size, with a steeply pitched thatched roof. The top of a boulder by the door had been hollowed out to serve as a lamp, the hollow filled with burning animal fat.

A boy came out of the hut. About seven years old, he had curly dark hair, a high forehead, and skin paler than most Dom-shu.

Nodding toward Egrin, the boy asked, "Who's the old grasslander?"

"Mind your tongue, Eli!" White Face snapped. "He is an Ergothian warrior of great renown."

The boy's face showed skepticism, but before he could say more, White Face removed his fearsome headgear and Egrin's mouth fell open in shock.

"Kiya!"

Eldest daughter of Makaralonga and a warrior of the Dom-shu, Kiya had been given to Tol years ago as hostage and wife, along with her younger sister Miya. The formidable pair had never been wives in the usual sense, but looked after Tol, his household, and his affairs. When Ackal V drove Tol into exile, Kiya and Miya were the only ones who dared go with him.

Egrin's head was reeling. "By all the gods, Kiya!" he exclaimed. "I never suspected it was you in that getup!"

Kiya pulled her long horse-tail of blonde hair from the neck of her tunic, where it had been concealed. She and the old marshal clasped arms, warrior fashion.

"I could not reveal myself until now," she explained. "You entered a sacred area at a most critical time. If I hadn't come along, you might be dead in the greenwood now. Why do you seek my father?"

"To ask his help in finding Tol." He gripped her shoulder. "Where is he, Kiya? Where's Tol?"

In answer, she held up the leather door flap and gestured for him to enter the sod hut. The boy Eli scampered in ahead of them.

The long narrow room within was smoky and ill lit by a fire burning fitfully on the rock hearth in its center. Egrin scoured the shadows, looking for the face he so longed to see, but it was Miya who emerged from the rear of the hut.

"Egrin!" she cried. "You look older than dirt!"

"He *is* older than dirt."

The comment came from a blanket-draped figure stirring by the hearth. Egrin saw brown eyes gleaming through a long shock of dark brown hair.

"Egrin Raemel's son," Tol said and extended a broad hand.

Abandoning restraint for once in his life, Egrin sank to his knees with a glad cry and embraced his friend.

## Chapter 2
# Waves Breaking on a Distant Shore

**T**ol sat silently by the fire in the sod house, listening to Egrin's recital of the grim events engulfing Ergoth. This deep in the Great Green, news of the outside world was scarce. A refugee talked to a traveler, who exchanged news with a roving hunter, who brought information to the land of the Dom-shu. Not even this hearsay reached Tol's ears. He had only superficial interactions with those outside his family circle. The Dom-shu respected him, but even after six years among them, he was still an outsider.

Miya passed around more food, a simple meal served in gourd bowls, as Egrin related the bakali's defeat of the First Fifty Hordes at the bend of the Solvin River.

Swallowing a mouthful of smoked venison, Tol asked, "Was Relfas killed?"

"I'm certain he will be," was Egrin's grim reply.

Relfas and a handful of his warlords had survived the battle and returned to Daltigoth to report on bakali strength and tactics. Egrin expected they would not long outlive their men. Two centuries before, Ackal Dermount had created a law stating that no warlord could live if his horde was defeated. Seldom applied back then, the harsh decree suited the current wearer of the Iron Crown. Ackal V had employed it before, and there was little hope he'd be inclined to leniency after such a stunning defeat.

"Your emperor had best take care, or he'll run out of

generals," Miya said. Motherhood and village life had rounded her face and figure, but her brown eyes were as penetrating as ever.

Remnants of Relfas's army, led by Lord Hojan, had retreated to Juramona. As Hojan recruited more soldiers and prepared for an attack, the bakali instead struck southwest, toward Caergoth, second largest city in the empire. Its governor, Wornoth, owed his position to the emperor's patronage. Although an imperial lackey, he tried to do the right thing, summoning all the hordes in his domain. Seventeen thousand Riders mustered outside the walls of Caergoth, under the command of General Bessian.

Tol knew Bessian; his reputation as a fine soldier was well deserved. Unfortunately, Bessian's horsemen faced over one hundred thousand bakali—nearly six times their own strength. The Ergothians caught the enemy host while it was divided by the East Caer River, and many lizard-men fell to their sabers, but the bakali eventually regrouped and surrounded Bessian's army. Not a man had been left alive.

Silence descended as Egrin finished his account. For a time, the only sound was the hiss and pop of the fire as Tol and the Dom-shu sisters took in this second disaster. The First Fifty, the cream of Ergothian warriors, defeated at the Solvin, and Bessian's seventeen thousand wiped out completely.

Egrin explained that the bakali, having no weapons with which to destroy Caergoth's walls, had simply marched on, desolating the countryside in their path. What they could not carry off or consume, they put to the torch.

"With no warlords surviving the second battle, I suppose the emperor had to settle for taking the governor's head," Miya said with gallows humor.

Egrin replied, "Wornoth survived."

Desperate to deflect his patron's wrath, Egrin explained, Governor Wornoth had sent General Bessian's entire family, in chains, to Ackal V. Shocked by the twin disasters, and placated by the arrival of the slaves, the emperor had thus far neglected to order Wornoth's execution.

The last Egrin had heard, the bakali were ensconced in an

enormous camp north of the Ackal Path, halfway between Caergoth and Daltigoth. Nearly every warrior in the western half of the empire had been called to battle, including garrison troops. As a result, one hundred and eighteen hordes had mustered on the west side of the Dalti River, and stood ready to defend the capital.

"To defend—he doesn't plan to attack the invaders?" Tol inquired sharply. Egrin's silence was reply enough. Tol shook his head. "He's ceding the richest half of the empire to them!"

"He fears losing his remaining loyal warriors in another battle. You know how he mistrusts the landed hordes."

Ackal V had summoned only the western hordes to defend the capital. Living in the east and north were the so-called landed hordes, comprising warriors, retired for the most part, who had been granted estates by Ackal V's predecessors, Pakin II and III, and the short-lived Ackal IV. As they did not owe their positions to him, the current emperor did not trust the landed warriors. Steeped in the intrigues and plots that were a part of everyday life in the capital, Ackal V was certain these "provincial lords," as he termed them, would like nothing better than to plan his downfall. He preferred that they and their armed retainers remain scattered on their holdings.

Kiya and Miya argued strategy, while Egrin finished eating. He listened with half an ear to the women, but most of his mind was on the man who sat quietly next to him, by the fire.

Six years was a brief span to a long-lived half-elf like Egrin, and even for a human it was not so great a length of time. Yet, the six years that Tol had passed in the Great Green seemed to have wrought many changes on him, Egrin thought. Some were physical. Tol seemed bigger. Not taller, but broader in the chest and shoulders. He'd allowed his beard to grow and it now reached his chest. His hair, likewise untrimmed, hung loose past his shoulders and was threaded here and there with gray. New lines feathered out at the corners of his eyes, and bracketed his mouth. His eyes, however, were just the same. In them, Egrin saw the memory of the boy he'd watched grow into the finest soldier in the empire.

Other changes were less obvious. Tol seemed somehow quieter than Egrin remembered, less given to speech, more introspective. As the Dom-shu sisters enjoyed one of their all-too-frequent arguments, Tol sat and stared into the fire, giving no sign he even heard the sisters. It was as though he had withdrawn into himself.

Egrin ate the last of his meal and set aside his empty bowls. "There's more," he announced.

The Dom-shu ceased their wrangling and Tol looked up from the dancing flames.

"There's been a second invasion."

Miya swore. "More lizard-folk?"

"Nomads. The bakali invasion displaced tens of thousands of them. Having lost everything to the lizard-men, they formed an army and now they're trying to seize as much Ergothian territory as they can. The Eastern and Mountain hundreds are crawling with their warbands, and Hylo is threatened. Some isolated garrisons sent out small detachments, demi-hordes, to stop them, but these were swept aside."

Tol shrugged, saying, "Who can blame the nomads? For centuries Ergoth has taken their land and slaughtered them in battle."

"They're savages!" Egrin exclaimed. Miya snorted, and Kiya gave him a dry look. Embarrassed, Egrin cleared his throat. "Beg your pardon, but the plains nomads are far more barbarous than any forest tribe."

"Grasslanders," said Kiya, shaking her head. Egrin didn't know whether she meant the plainsmen or himself.

Soft snores from Eli, who had fallen asleep with his head in Miya's lap, recalled them to their surroundings.

Tol rose and carried Eli to bed, a pile of furs in the darkest corner of the hut. Rejoining his comrades, he said, "The chief will have supped by now. He should be told of these events. Let's pay a visit to Uncle Corpse."

Kiya and Egrin preceded Tol out, but Miya remained where she was. Only warriors could enter the chief's great hut. However, Tol gestured for her to accompany them.

"You fought beside me for twenty years, Miya. That should

make you warrior enough. If anyone protests, we'll fight them. That's tribal law, too."

Miya stood, hitching a patterned shawl up around her shoulders. "That's my old husband!" she said, grinning down at him. "I've missed him!"

Tol gave her a friendly shove through the door flap.

The Repetition of Births ceremony was the Dom-shu's most important ritual, celebrated every three years once the chief's hair turned white. The rites would continue for nine days, with exhausted dancers and drummers being replaced by fresh ones to keep the spirit level high. Voyarunta's great hut, six times the size of any other structure in the village, was crammed with sweaty, noisy warriors. Most were seated on the hut's blanket-covered floor. When Tol and his companions entered, the sight of Miya brought the revels to a sudden halt.

"Son of My Life, why have you come here?" said the chief, peering through the haze of hearth smoke at the newcomers arrayed inside the door.

"Father of My Life, a visitor has come from Ergoth. He seeks to deliver a message to us," Tol answered.

Several of the warriors called for Miya to be sent out. She didn't budge, but cast a wary sidelong glance at Tol. With his own gaze fixed on Voyarunta, Tol declared, "All here are warriors. Both of the daughters of Makaralonga have fought at my side. Does anyone care to dispute this with me?"

He shrugged off the bearskin. His shoulders, arms, chest and stomach were impressive, rippling with muscle.

Noting Egrin's wide eyes, Kiya whispered, "He chops wood every day."

"A great deal of wood, apparently," Egrin muttered.

Voyarunta, looking very hale despite his mane of snowy hair, waved away his warriors' objections. "Miya fights better than most of you. She may stand by the door."

It was a great concession, and the Dom-shu woman swelled with pride. Tol introduced Egrin, and the old warrior moved further into the room and saluted the chief.

"I know you!" Voyarunta said. "You were in the battle where the chief of the grasslanders perished." He meant

Paul B. Thompson and Tonya C. Cook

Lord Odovar. "You were the one whose sword struck twice for each blow!"

It was an apt description of Egrin's fighting prowess. Egrin inclined his head in gratitude. The chief bade him speak his message.

Egrin shared the tale of the bakali invasion. He held nothing back, recounting the twin defeats of the imperial hordes in grim detail. A few Dom-shu expressed dry pleasure at their old enemy's plight, but when Egrin mentioned the second menace—from the plains tribes—the foresters erupted.

"The men of the plains are our brothers!" declared one. "We should stand with them!"

"Death to the iron soldiers!" shouted another.

One particularly tall fellow with bronze skin and yellow hair stood and addressed his chief.

"The gods are punishing the grasslanders for their pride," he intoned. "Great Chief, will we leave our forest and fight alongside our plains brothers?"

Voyarunta leaned back in his blanket-draped chair. His penetrating blue eyes were fixed on Egrin. "I do not think Twice-Strike came here to rouse the Dom-shu against his own people, Turanaki."

"No indeed, Great Chief!" Egrin said quickly. "I came to warn the Dom-shu of this peril. No one knows where the host of lizard-men will strike next. It could be the Great Green!"

The blond warrior, Turanaki, made a sound of disgust. "They will not come here! The forest would swallow them. There are richer takings in the west!"

As the foresters debated the merits of aiding the plainsmen in ravaging the Eastern Hundred, Egrin finally realized just how much hostility they felt for Ergoth. Anger held for generations now blazed forth.

Voyarunta silenced them after a time. The chief looked beyond Egrin to where Tol leaned against the doorpost with Miya and Kiya.

"Son of My Life, what say you?"

Tol paused, allowing an interval of silence to pass to dampen the echoes of the heated argument, then he said slowly, "For twenty years, the Dom-shu and Ergoth have had peace. In that time, have the Ergothians ever broken their word to the Dom-shu?"

His gaze traveled around the room. No one spoke because all knew the answer.

"Has trade with the empire enriched the Dom-shu?"

Another question with an obvious answer.

Tol came forward, standing shoulder to shoulder with his old friend. Egrin was still the taller one, but age had begun to whittle down his frame.

"The emperor now reigning is a cruel man, and he never forgets an insult, however slight. If you go to war against the empire, Ackal V will not rest until he has laid waste to the forest. He will kill not only you who fight, but your children, the old ones—all who bear the name Dom-shu."

Turanaki opened his mouth to speak, but Tol went on, raising his voice. "It may cost the emperor the life of every Rider in his hordes, it may swallow all the gold in the imperial coffers, but he will not stop. He will drown you in the blood of his own warriors if no other means of vengeance remains to him." Tol shrugged his broad shoulders. "This you should know."

"We would not be warriors if we lived in fear of what others might do to us!" Turanaki exclaimed.

Egrin ignored the hotheaded forester and addressed Voyarunta.

"Great Chief, I did not come here to incite you against the empire, but to warn you, as a friend and neighbor. I also came to ask Lord Tolandruth to return home."

Miya drew in a breath sharply, but Kiya nodded with satisfaction. She had guessed as much.

Voyarunta pondered what he'd heard. No one, not even the fiery Turanaki, interrupted the chief's cogitations.

"The Dom-shu will keep to their forest," Voyarunta said at last. "As for the Son of My Life, he will do as the gods guide him."

"I will listen for their counsel," Tol said, giving the expected answer. Under his breath, he added, "Though I doubt they will speak to me."

He picked up the bearskin and took his leave of the chief. Miya and Kiya followed. Egrin departed more slowly, as dignity demanded. It would not do to appear to be fleeing the unfriendly climate.

Outside, the cool air was balm to the old warrior's sweat-drenched brow. Fog was rising in the clearing, and the glimmer of firelight from the surrounding huts looked like amber stars in the mist. Arriving at the sod hut, Egrin found Kiya sitting on the split log that served as a stoop. She barred his entry.

"Husband's gone to bed. Don't wake him." She cut off his protests, saying, "He sleeps so little and so poorly, rest is a treasure to him."

Giving in, Egrin seated himself next to her. He asked how she had fared over the past six years of Tol's exile.

Kiya was a formidable woman. She had grown up in a tribe that trained her to fight and suffer without complaint. So when she did not reply right away, Egrin did not press her. He adjusted his position slightly so he could rest his back against the hut, and waited. She would answer in her own time.

The story was a painful one. Miya, Tol, and Kiya had departed Daltigoth in the depth of winter and in the teeth of a snowstorm. Miya was ill with milk fever, and the newborn Eli was no more than a mewling newt wrapped in furs. Tol had sustained terrible injuries at the hands of Nazramin's personal gang of thugs, the Wolves. Kiya managed to bring them all across the snowy land to the Great Green. Once they reached the Dom-shu village, she'd slept for two days and nights.

Tol was shamed by the beating, and grieved the loss of Valaran, now consort to the new emperor. He remained indoors for many days, but as winter grudgingly relinquished its hold on the forest, so too did Tol emerge slowly from the white silence of his despair. He hobbled around the village, loosening muscles stiff from disuse. His terrible bruises turned yellow and faded. Unwilling to live on the charity of the chief, Tol sought a home of his own. The repair of an empty hut gave him purpose, and once it was done, the sisters and Eli joined him there.

His injuries healed, Tol took up a stone axe and cut firewood. Every swing of the axe made his arms and back sing with pain, but he would not stop. Each blow was a strike against Nazramin. Every cord split were Wolves' heads cleaved by his sword. After he had killed his enemies many times over, the silent rage in him began to pall. It was too bitter a flavor to nourish Tol. He had purged the fury in his heart by this regimen, while he built his body up even stronger than before, and for a noble reason: bettering the lives of the forest folk.

The Dom-shu had always fed their fires on windfall limbs or punk wood, neither of which burned very hot or long. Tol introduced them to hardwood, cut green, dried, then split. Heat was no longer a rare luxury for the Dom-shu. Cold retreated from the village. Disease, fostered by poorly cooked food and damp living conditions, was greatly lessened by the simple introduction of good firewood.

Tol also planted wild onions, strawberries, and rabbit-cabbage in a small but neat garden plot beside his hut. The tribesmen, who normally hunted game or combed the forest for berries, roots, and nuts, were puzzled by the grasslander scratching the raw earth, but before long, Tol was gathering food not ten paces from his hut. The Dom-shu had thought farming something that could be done only on broad, open spaces. Tol showed them they could grow food in the forest.

Younger Dom-shu men sought his knowledge of war, but this Tol would not share. They already knew how to defend their homes. To know more would only tempt them to fight beyond the forest, and that was the path to destruction.

One warrior tried to goad Tol into fighting, hoping to make his own reputation by besting the grasslander champion. Tol endured his many insults in silence rather than kill the fool. Unhappily, the warrior would not give up. In the village square, he made the mistake of tormenting young Eli, injuring the boy in the process, and the foresters finally glimpsed the warrior Tol had been. He slew the foolish challenger with a single blow of his axe. No one ever challenged Tol again.

When Kiya finished her tale, Egrin weighed what he'd heard against the memory of the man he'd known.

"Is he happy here?" he asked.

"He is calm. He is not happy."

Tol did not sleep well, Kiya explained, but often roamed the woods alone at night. No Dom-shu would ever do such a thing; they feared the spirits who walked abroad by night. And Tol sometimes stayed away two or three days. He would never say where he went during these extended absences.

"It isn't the honors or wealth he misses," Kiya noted. "It's her. She belongs to his enemy, the man who had him beaten and humiliated, and it eats at him like a festering wound."

"He must return with me. There's no one else who can lead the hordes to victory against the nomad and bakali. No one else commands the respect he does. No one has his vision, or his . . ."

Egrin groped for the proper word. Kiya supplied it: "Luck. He's lucky."

"No longer."

They turned. Tol stood in the dark doorway behind them.

"My luck is gone," he said flatly. "I used it up when I left to pursue my private vengeance against Mandes. I was the Emperor's Champion, but I abandoned Ackal IV to the evil plots of his brother. Nazramin staged everything like a playwright, and I handed him the throne of Ergoth as if I'd been magicked to do so."

Egrin rose and gripped Tol's shoulder. "Luck isn't wine, drunk up then regretted! Come back with me, Tol! Only you can save Ergoth. Do so, and the emperor will have to make amends!"

Tol removed his old friend's hand. "It's not my fight any more. Let the empire fall."

# Chapter 3
## The Unsightly Gardener

From the sparse woodland, the town of Juramona wasn't much to look at. An agglomeration of buildings, some stone but most wooden, clustered around the base of a large, man-made earthen mound on which stood a palisaded citadel. The town wall was weathered timber, strengthened at intervals by squat stone towers. Here and there outside the walls were piles of rough-hewn granite blocks. Grass grew tall around the stones. While marshal of the Eastern Hundred, Egrin Raemel's son had begun to convert Juramona's wall to stone. After he was forced from his post by Ackal V, his successor allowed the ambitious plan to languish. Given the current state of things, no one was likely to disturb the blocks any time soon.

Crouched at the base of a leafing poplar, Zala surveyed the scene. Her journey from Daltigoth had been nightmarish. The countryside between the Caer River and Juramona was infested with roving bands of nomads. Too many times she had to watch from concealment as marauders laid waste to farms, sacked caravans, and put hapless Ergothian captives to the sword. It grieved her, but she could not risk entanglements that would delay her progress.

She stared at the gates of Juramona and pondered how best to enter the town. Night offered the best concealment, but it was only now midmorning. She dared not waste an entire day waiting for darkness. Not only did her commission require speed, but the nomad warbands were gathering nearby. Juramona might be attacked at any moment, making her mission that much more difficult.

Eventually fate, the gods, or sheer luck provided what she needed. A convoy of wagons came thundering down the western road, together with an escort of half a hundred cavalry. The wagons were drawn by teams of horses rather than the more usual bullocks or oxen. Horses meant speed. The convoy must be carrying something vital. Zala noticed the escort was bunched together at the head of the caravan. No one was paying attention to the rear of the procession.

When the last wagon passed her, Zala raced from cover and swung herself into its canvas-shrouded box. She was under cover again in the space of a few breaths. The wagon was filled with assorted casks and crates, all firmly nailed shut.

Once the speeding caravan was inside the city wall, Zala's wagon pulled hard to the left and stopped, throwing her to the floor.

"Close the gate! Close it!" bawled a hoarse masculine voice.

Zala peered out. Clouds of dust, churned up by the wagons, roiled high into the air. Taking advantage of this cover, Zala slipped out of the wagon and quickly vanished into the unfamiliar streets.

Juramona was preparing for a siege. Lanes nearest the walls had been cleared of obstructions, and the roofs of the houses were covered by green cowhides that could resist fiery arrows. Buckets of sand or water were placed at every corner, and everyone—men and women, youths and oldsters—wore helmets, but there seemed to be few real warriors present. Zala kept her own head firmly covered by her hood, to conceal her upswept ears. One never knew how humans would react to the sight of even a half-elf.

The skills she employed to travel invisibly through field and forest worked just as well in town—perhaps even better, because the town-dwellers were not so in tune with their surroundings as country folk. Many humans credited elves with the ability to make themselves invisible. This was legend, but enjoying the advantage such beliefs gave them, no elf would deny this supposed power.

Zala's techniques were simple, but required great dexterity. To follow someone unseen, she matched their footfalls so no stray noise would betray her. When standing still, she turned edge-wise from people and, whenever possible, moved toward the left. Most folk, being right-handed, tended to look to the right first before setting out. Taking advantage of this habit allowed a stealthy tracker to keep from being noticed. When looking around trees (or here, the corner of a building), she kept low. People expected to see heads or faces at their own eye level, not close to the ground.

In this way Zala passed like a ghost among the anxious Juramonans. Not till she reached the location described by the empress did she relax her woodland stealth.

The house before her was old and looked long abandoned. Shutters were closed, and crossed timbers were nailed over the front door. Concealing her true purpose, Zala hailed a passing laborer and asked if the house was available for rent.

The youth shifted the hod of bricks he carried off his shoulder and regarded her in wide-eyed astonishment. "The barbarians are coming!" he cried. "Who needs a house at a time like this?"

"I do. Does anyone live here?"

"No! No one's lived there since Lord Tolandruth left it, before I was born!" The fellow hurried on, shaking his head at the stupidity of strangers.

By such oblique queries, Zala gleaned information about her quarry's rumored whereabouts. In one street she pretended to be a soldier's wife seeking news of her husband. In another, she was a peddler trying to collect a debt, and further along, a healer searching for a delirious patient.

As Empress Valaran had surmised, Tolandruth was not in Juramona and hadn't been for years. However, an intriguing bit of gossip kept coming up. Several people mentioned a man who was said to know Tolandruth well. No one spoke his name; he was referred to as "Tolandruth's captive," "the special prisoner," and most frequently as "the unsightly gardener."

Inquiring into this mysterious person's whereabouts, Zala was directed to a rather squalid part of town. She arrived at a row of houses buried beneath the frowning shadow of the High House. Although the day was waning, a few shafts of sunlight still pierced the scattered clouds. At the indicated door, she knocked. No one answered.

The narrow street was empty except for herself and a bony cur gnawing at something dead in the gutter six doors away. Zala inserted her knife in the gap between the door and frame, lifted the latch, and slipped inside.

The room beyond was dark and uninhabited. When her eyes had adjusted, she crept through the room toward the rear of the house. An open window framed a swatch of green and brought the scent of flowers to her nostrils. Remembering the fellow had been called a gardener, Zala slipped warily out the back door. What she saw stopped her in her tracks.

In the small area behind the house, where most folk would have a chicken coop, pig pen, or privy, there was indeed a garden, and no mere kitchen plot for herbs or root vegetables. A verdant carpet of jade-colored grass covered what soil was not already filled with flowers. And such flowers! Sunflowers taller than Zala herself with heads so heavy they had to be supported by strips of ribbon tacked to the lath wall behind; roses, with blooms large as soup bowls and the color of ox blood, filled the air with their dense perfume. Creamy white lilies were beginning to close for the day. Cornflowers, yellow daisies, irises in bold purple and pale gold, violets, and marigolds stood in serried ranks like perfect soldiers. Most remarkable of all was a stand of enormous dandelions, with puffy white heads as big as Zala's own.

In the center of this magnificent display grew an apple tree, its branches still covered in white blossoms. Fat bumblebees buzzed through the branches, and narrowly avoided collisions with a profusion of butterflies in nearly every color of the rainbow.

Zala's astonished trance was abruptly shattered by a scraping sound. It came from only a few steps away, from behind a screen of trumpet lilies, their white blooms spotted with red, like blood on snow. Although she circled around the screen with customary stealth, the figure kneeling on its other side knew she was present, though his back was to her.

"You needn't skulk there. Come forward," he muttered, continuing to dig the point of a small trowel into the black earth around the lilies.

She advanced, but halted when he turned to look up at her. Her shock was mirrored on his face, and both of them recoiled.

The gardener was a Silvanesti. That fact itself was startling enough, here so far from the elf homeland. But what truly took her aback was his appearance.

Never in her life had Zala beheld such a homely member of the ancient and elegant race of Silvanesti elves. His long hair was a dull dusty gray, tied at the nape of his neck by a scrap of ribbon. Eyes the pale blue of Quenesti Pah's crystal staff might have been arresting, if they hadn't been set so close together. Add a long, thin nose, and pale skin covered by too many splotchy brown freckles, and she fully understood the sobriquet he'd been given: he was an unsightly gardener indeed!

For his part, the strange elf recovered quickly from his surprise and said, "So, you've come to kill me."

"What? Why should you think that?" Zala stammered.

"You have the tread of a hunter, but you're a female half-breed. Such a combination speaks of desperation, so I take you for an assassin."

Zala folded her arms and put her nose in the air. "I am a tracker, not a murderer. Who are you, that you expect assassins in your own garden?"

"You don't know me?"

Zala shook her head. He stood, brushing dirt from his Ergothian-style trousers, and said, "I am Janissiron Tylocostathan, formerly general of the armies of the city of Tarsis. Among humans, I am called Tylocost."

"You're the one called 'Tolandruth's captive?' "

"I am. I was defeated in battle and taken prisoner by Lord Tolandruth."

Time weighed heavily on Zala. Abandoning discretion, she asked, "Where might I find Lord Tolandruth?"

Tylocost smiled, revealing an uneven set of teeth.

"So that's why you've come. I'm sorry. I don't know where he is."

He stooped to retrieve his trowel. When he straightened, Tylocost found himself staring down Zala's blade. The length of polished iron drew nothing more than a shrug from the former general.

"I still don't know."

"I think you do. Silvanesti never forget an injury, and this Tolandruth did you a grave one when he humbled you by defeat. You know where he is."

He reached out a long arm and plucked a white rose from its trellis. "You have a fair face for a half-breed," he said, smiling. The smile vanished as Zala pushed the point of her blade through his cloth jerkin.

"I didn't come here to kill you, General, but that doesn't mean I won't hurt you to find out what I must know!"

He stepped back. "I believe you, my dear."

"I'm not your 'dear,' " she snapped. "My name is Zala."

Pigeons flew low over the rooftop. Tylocost glanced up.

"Day is done," he murmured. "Come inside. We'll talk."

She followed cautiously, mindful of treachery. For a Silvanesti and a general, this Tylocost was certainly an odd one. He didn't seem proud or martial. He seemed—well, very like a gardener.

Tylocost blew on the cinders in the hearth grate until they glowed. With these he lighted a thick, stubby candle. He took a wooden mug from a shelf, filled it with water from a bucket, and placed his white rose in it. He set this on the table. Pouring more water into a tin pan on the table, he carefully washed his hands and face. Zala bit her lip and waited, determined not to betray her impatience. In the course of his ablutions, Tylocost stripped off jerkin and trousers, until he was standing in only a loincloth. Unclothed, he was even more unsightly. The brown spots on his face continued over his body.

Seeming unconscious of his appearance (or at peace with it), the elf donned a light linen robe and fixed a gilded band around his forehead. He seated himself at the table and gestured for her to take a chair. She did so, and asked again for Tolandruth's whereabouts.

"Time is running out, General—for you and this town,"

she added. "The nomads may attack any day now."

"Within three days, I estimate. And I doubt the town will survive. The garrison was withdrawn by Lord Bessian after bakali destroyed Lord Hojan's hordes. Fewer than eight hundred warriors remain. The townspeople have taken up arms, but they won't delay the nomads for very long."

"However," he added, "I'm not worried, because you're going to get me out of here." His upraised hand cut off her protests. "That's my price, dear. I'll lead you to Lord Tolandruth, if you take me out of Juramona and get me away from the human savages beyond the walls."

With a disgusted snort, Zala stood. She pulled her hood over her head again and turned to go. He waited until her hand was on the door latch before he spoke.

"Empress Valaran does not brook failure, I'm told."

She froze. "How do you know my patron?"

"Logic, dear, logic and reason. Someone very powerful wants to find Lord Tolandruth." Tylocost laid a bony finger alongside his nose. "Ackal V would never send for him, not for any reason. His hatred of my captor is well known. Who then would go to such lengths? The Empress of Ergoth, of course—Tolandruth's lover."

Zala blinked in astonishment, but would not be sidetracked. "Who the empress loves or hates is not my concern. My task is to find Tolandruth and return him to Daltigoth as soon as possible."

"Or else—what?"

In the dim little room, redolent of the flowers in the fantastic garden, Zala felt her world shrink, like a noose drawing tight around her neck. She clenched her teeth. Despicable, homely, Silvanesti. What choice did she have?

"I'll bring you out of Juramona, if you guide me to Tolandruth," she said. "In seven days or less."

"Why the hurry? Do you think to fetch him back here to save Juramona?"

Zala shrugged, but did not share her thoughts. How could a stranger understand that it was not merely her honor on the line, but her aged human father's life as well? The empress knew where he lived. If Zala failed to carry out her mission, she knew her father would pay the ultimate price. And he was far too old and weak for Zala to consider spiriting him away from his home in Caergoth.

The unsightly elf rose and took a heavy glass decanter from the shelf. He poured two libations from it and offered one cup to Zala.

"Nectar," he said. "My only remaining contact with the homeland."

Zala drank. She resolved to slay this smirking Silvanesti if he caused her any more than the promised delay. As she lowered her glass and beheld his misshapen features again, she realized he knew exactly what she was thinking.

❧ ❧ ❧ ❧ ❧

Egrin lingered in the Dom-shu village, hoping to convince Tol to change his mind. Since Tol spent his days chopping wood and many of his nights roving the forest, Egrin saw him only rarely. His heart seemed closed to his friend's urgings.

Life in the village had resumed a normal rhythm. Egrin glimpsed the chief one day as Voyarunta held court. Though his hair was as white as ever, the old fellow sat straight and moved easily, radiating health and strength. Miya had explained that the Repetition of Births ritual involved every male warrior in the tribe giving up a small part of his vigor to renew the chief.

Kiya, too, was often away, on her father's business. Egrin's time was spent mainly with Miya and Eli. One afternoon, Egrin noticed the boy playing in the shadows at the far end of the hut. Something in his hand glittered in the feeble light.

Egrin rose from his spot by the hearth. His knees cracked like dry kindling, and something caught in his lower back, sending a sharp pain through his hip. His Silvanesti heritage gave him a longer lifespan than a human, but it did not guarantee health or vigor for one who'd spent so many years in battle. Too bad there was no Repetition of Births for aging warriors.

Eli shoved the shiny object out of sight as Egrin approached. When Egrin asked what he was playing with, the boy quickly said, "Nothing!"

Egrin sat and smiled at him kindly. "Your nothing gleams like metal. May I see?"

A small leather box was reluctantly produced. Egrin raised the lid, expecting to find a knife. The object within was indeed metal, but circular, like a bracelet. It rested on a scrap of black cloth.

"Don't tell Ma I was playing with it," Eli whispered. "Please?"

So, it was a trinket of Miya's. Egrin was about to close the box when something about the object's design caught his eye. He took it out to examine it more closely.

This was no bracelet. The circlet was made of three strands of metal—gold, silver, and a reddish one, maybe copper—woven together in an intricate fashion. The braid was as thick as Egrin's finger, its ends joined by a polished spherical bead of the red metal. The bead was delicately engraved with whorls and lines, every line inlaid with gold. Strangest of all, the center of the metal ring was completely filled with a flat disk of polished black crystal.

Eli denied knowing its purpose, adding, "It belongs to Uncle Tol. I'm not supposed to touch it."

The odd circlet was surprisingly lightweight, and the center crystal was just clear enough to allow light to pass through. Egrin turned toward the fire and peered at it through the crystal—

The object was suddenly snatched from his hand. Miya stood over him, eyes wide and cheeks crimson with anger.

"Where did you get this?" she demanded.

He would not have implicated the boy, but Miya divined the truth before Egrin could answer. "Eli! What have I told you? You're not to touch your uncle's things!"

Eli ducked behind the old marshal. His mother didn't strike him often, but when she did, it was memorable.

Egrin tried to placate her, but Miya would have none of it.

"This was hidden," she said, glaring at her son. "You

couldn't have found it unless you were looking for it!"

Rising, keeping himself between the two, Egrin said, "The boy shouldn't have disobeyed you, Miya, but you have the trinket now. No harm was done."

The formidable Dom-shu woman relaxed a little and he added, "What is it, by the way? I've never seen anything like it."

"It belongs to Husband. It's very old, very precious. No one's supposed to know of it."

Ah, Egrin thought, now he understood. The circlet must have been a gift from Valaran. The treasuries of the imperial palace were extensive, and all sorts of precious things were kept there, torn from their rightful owners by campaigns dating back to the days of Ackal Ergot himself. It made sense Valaran would have given Tol something to remember her by—as if he could ever forget her.

When romance bloomed between Tol and Valaran, Egrin had known nothing about it. Only later, after Tol's exile, did the rumors reach his ears. Even so, Miya's reaction seemed out of place. She and Kiya had always had a sisterly relationship with their ostensible husband. The sisters had known of Tol's love for Valaran almost since it began, and no hearts had been broken by it.

As Miya returned the circlet to the leather box Egrin noticed her fingers were trembling. She ordered them both outside, not wanting them to know the box's new hiding place.

Twilight had come. The fine spring day was ending. Wind stirred the trees, sending a flurry of blossoms over the Dom-shu settlement. The scene was so peaceful and pleasant that Egrin had to force himself to remember the terrible devastation going on a hundred leagues west.

Eli thanked him for acting as peacemaker. "Ma gets kind of wild when the stone turns up."

Cocking an eyebrow, Egrin said, "Then perhaps you shouldn't meddle with it."

Eli grinned. "She's just afraid Uncle Tol will find out she's still got it. He told her to get rid of it after we came here."

The situation made little sense to Egrin, but then he hadn't been in love in—how long had it been? Nearly fifty years? A great span to be alone, by any reckoning.

"Will your uncle be home tonight?" he asked.

"Nah. He took a bow and possibles bag this morning, so he'll be huntin' all night."

Kiya came striding across the village square, looking weary. She'd carried her father's words to the chief of the Karad-shu and returned, a long journey, all in one day.

"Egrin. Boy," she greeted them. She put a fist under Eli's chin and lifted it. He responded by punching her on the arm.

Miya called for Eli and he went inside. Kiya asked, "Have you convinced Husband yet?"

The old marshal shook his head, frustration in every syllable as he replied, "If he cares nothing for the empire, you'd think he'd fight for Valaran! Her life is as much at risk as anyone's!"

"I think he's worked so hard for so long to stop hurting, now he hardly feels anything."

Egrin fought back a wave of pity. There was nothing he could do to ease Tol's pain, yet there was much Tol could do to ease the empire's suffering, to help every man, woman, and child in Ergoth. Egrin had to break through the wall Tol had erected, stone by stone, around his heart.

"He must go! Everything depends on him!" he said, driving a fist into his palm.

Kiya regarded him in silence for a long moment, then said, "When you see him next, speak of her, not the empire. It's Valaran owns his heart, not the land of Ergoth."

She went inside, leaving Egrin alone in the deepening dusk.

❦ ❦ ❦ ❦ ❦

Running hard up the leafy hillside, Tol pulled an arrow from the quiver on his back. This would be his last chance to take the deer. Light was failing and his quarry was outpacing him. He saw a flicker of white tail as it fled through the trees, each bound covering three paces. He drew the bowstring to his ear and let fly. With a thrum, the arrow sped through the intervening foliage. Panting, Tol waited for the tell-tale sound of the broadhead striking.

He never heard it. In truth he heard nothing at all, not even the rhythmic thud of the deer's small hooves. Complete silence had engulfed the woods. Puzzled, Tol moved slowly through the stillness. His footfalls sounded muffled and far away. He nocked another arrow, his last. A good hunter never returned home with an empty quiver. Kiya, fine archer that she was, would have much to say about his sad performance.

The quiet was unsettling. Creatures of the forest became silent in the presence of great danger. Tol's approach was not enough to cause such alarm. Something else had disturbed them.

He approached the hilltop with care. This place was known to him. On the other side of the hill was a wide, shallow ravine, filled with closely growing alder and beech saplings.

As he crested the hill, there was an intense flash of light. Heat seared his face and his bare left arm when he threw it up to shield his eyes. Hair sizzled away on the back of his exposed arm. For an instant he wondered if lightning had struck at his feet, but he felt no pain, and the brilliant light did not fade. Gradually, his eyes adjusted. Lowering his arm, Tol beheld a marvel.

The ravine at his feet had been transformed. In the midst of the slender saplings was a great orb of light, whiter than the sun. It hovered a few steps off the ground, its radiance hot, but not unbearable.

Tol took cover behind a nearby tree. Instinctively, his right hand went to a spot just below the waist of his trews. This was where, for decades, he'd kept the Irda nullstone, sewn into a secret pocket in his smallclothes. However, he no longer carried the artifact. Not trusting himself to destroy it, he'd asked Miya to do it for him when they arrived in the Great Green.

Now, staring at the bizarre orb of light that pulsed, like some enormous heart, at the bottom of the ravine, he wished he'd kept the artifact. His dealings with the rogue wizard Mandes had given him a healthy distrust of magic, whatever its purpose. It had had no part in his life in the forest. Still, it seemed to have found him again, even here.

*Tol... Tol...*

Someone was calling his name, a faint, barely discernible sound. He raised the bow, his final arrow nocked, and prepared to draw the bowstring back.

*Tol, where are you? Come to me!*

Strange. The voice sounded female. In fact, it sounded like—but couldn't be. It couldn't be her.

*Tol, it's Valaran. I need you. Come to me!*

He nearly dropped the arrow. It *was* her voice!

"Valaran," he whispered. Then, more loudly: "Valaran!"

He hadn't spoken her name aloud in years. Once his injuries healed, he hadn't allowed himself even to think of her. Such thoughts were pointless, bringing only pain.

"Val! I hear you! Where are you?" He stepped out from behind the tree. The bark on the other side was beginning to smolder. Leaves scattered on the forest floor had turned brown, edges curling.

*Do you hear me, Tol? A messenger will come for you. Hurry to me!*

Tol called to her several more times, but it seemed that Valaran could speak to him, but not hear him. When the orb began to dwindle in size, Tol threw down his bow and raced down the slope toward the fading light. He had to let her know he had heard her message!

Shouting her name, slipping and sliding in the loose leaves, he lost control near the bottom of the slope and blundered forward. One of his outstretched hands penetrated the very center of the shrinking globe. He half-expected to be burned, but instead the orb exploded in a noiseless flash, lifting him off his feet and tossing him into the scorched saplings.

By the time he'd shaken off the impact and recovered his sight, he beheld a very different apparition. The pulsating orb of light was gone. In its place was a city.

Small as a child's toy, the city lay dead center in the ravine, bathed in bright sunlight. The walls and towers were no higher than Tol's knee, as though he viewed a real town across a great distance. The apparition was so perfect and life-like, Tol recognized the place immediately. It was Juramona.

Smoke billowed from various buildings, and flames topped the old wooden walls. The High House, residence of the Marshal of the Eastern Hundred, was engulfed in fire. Swarms of men on horseback galloped through the smoke and chaos. The south gate was breached, as was the east. Sabers rose and fell. Tiny figures on foot fell like scythed grain. Juramona was being sacked.

Gradually Tol heard the noises. Softly at first, and garbled, they soon sorted themselves into distinct sounds—the crackle of flames, hoofbeats, the clash of arms, and above it all, the wailing cries of the dying. A thousand swords struck down a thousand victims—men, women, and children. The smell of blood filled the air, an odor as thick as the smoke.

A new sound arose, slowly growing louder. At first he couldn't credit it, it was so utterly out of place. Soon it drowned out all the other noises and there was no mistaking it: laughter.

A single male voice was laughing at the carnage. As surely as Tol knew his own name, he recognized that laugh. It was Nazramin, who now ruled Ergoth as Emperor Ackal V.

The laughter swelled in power and volume until it beat at his ears, pounding in his head like a relentless sea. Eyes squinting against the agony, Tol fell to his knees.

Was this the same kind of strange, waking dream that had tormented him on his journey to slay Mandes? If so, then Tol could make it stop. He could wake himself from it.

Lifting a hand high, he slammed his palm down on a sharp stone.

The burning town and killing laughter vanished. Tol was lying on his back, staring up at the stars through gently waving tree branches. Over the ringing in his ears, normal night sounds—tree frogs, crickets, birds—made themselves heard once more.

Tol sat up. Blood stained his right hand, and his bow lay in the leaves a short distance away. The bowstring had burnt in two. As he moved, the leaves around him disintegrated into ashes.

The vision was gone. The ravine was populated by nothing more than the closely growing trees, their spring foliage dark in the filtered moonlight. The taste of the experience lingered strongly: Valaran's piteous call, the wails of the dying in Juramona, and the emperor's malevolent laughter.

He wrapped his torn hand with a strip of leather, and started back to the village. On the way he thought about what he'd seen. Valaran must be searching for him, which meant something had changed in Daltigoth. Why now, after six years, would she reach out to Tol? Were the twin invasions by bakali and nomads reason enough for her to risk the emperor's wrath, should she be discovered?

The second vision was equally troubling. How could a town as large and as well-defended as Juramona fall to nomad tribesmen? Had Val sent him the second vision as well? It made no sense that he would be shown something that had already happened, something he could do nothing about. He must have been given a glimpse of the future—a future he might yet be able to change.

In spite of his rapid pace, midnight had come before Tol reached home. With a shout, he roused the inhabitants of the sod hut. Kiya and Egrin sprang awake with bare blades in their hands. Eli sat up, blinking in confusion, black hair wildly awry. Miya, sleeping next to him, only shifted slightly.

Tol briefly described his second vision in the forest. The first, of Valaran calling to him, he kept to himself.

Kiya was disposed to think it was a trick, but Egrin wasn't so sure. The changes in the town's defenses that Tol had described had been added only after Tol's exile, by Egrin himself. Although not compelling proof, Egrin felt this was significant evidence the vision was a true one.

Whether trickery or truth, Tol had made up his mind already. If there was a chance he could prevent the town's destruction, he had to try.

"I leave for Juramona. Tomorrow," he announced.

Kiya felt he was acting hastily, but knew there was no

point trying to dissuade him. Eli jabbered excitedly about horses and swords, journeys and battles. Egrin, still trying to absorb the news, asked Tol what he planned to do when he got to Juramona.

"What I can."

From anyone else, this would have sounded pathetic. From Tol of Juramona, it amounted to a sacred vow.

# Chapter 4
## Footsteps of Fire

The great plaza before the imperial palace in Daltigoth was ablaze, lit not by looters' fires but by massed torches. Six hundred imperial guards, standing shoulder to shoulder, ringed the plaza. The light of their blazing torches cast a brilliant, wavering glow on the high stone walls surrounding the Inner City, and gave their polished armor a coppery sheen.

Within the perimeter of straight-backed guardsmen a smaller contingent of armed men stood more casually. Lean and unkempt, with gimlet eyes and hard, scarred faces, each man wore a wolf pelt on his back, the beast's head perched atop the crown of his brass helmet. These were the Emperor's Wolves, Ackal V's private guard.

The emperor was seated in an ornately carved and gilded chair. Various officials were arranged behind him—Lord Breyhard, general in command of the Riders of the Great Horde; court functionaries; and important city leaders, such as guildmasters, merchants, and priests. To the emperor's right stood the empress, holding the hand of a small, black-haired boy. A misty green veil covered her face. Custom had long decreed that no man could be alone with the empress. Ackal V had added to the stricture: in male company, the empress must be veiled.

All eyes were on the figure who occupied the space between emperor and the Wolves. Out of the entire multitude, only the emperor was smiling at the sight.

Oropash, chief of the White Robe wizards in Daltigoth, lay flat on his back, wrists and ankles chained to heavy stone balls. A thick wooden platform, about the size and shape of a common door, rested on the wizard's chest. The platform was covered with lead ingots, and the Wolves stood ready to add more. Oropash's face and bald pate were flushed deep red, his breathing dreadfully labored. The platform and ingots formed a terrible weight.

"Tell me, White Robe, what traffic had you with the lizards?" Ackal V asked loudly.

"None, sire! None!" Oropash wheezed.

"Then, how do you account for their success?"

The wizard made several abortive attempts to reply, finally gasping, "I am not a military man!"

"No. You're not." Ackal V gestured to the Wolves. "Another half hundredweight."

Five more ingots were placed on the platform. The additional burden wrung a high-pitched groan from the wizard. Valaran looked away, and her son buried his face in her robe.

"I require you to see this," Ackal V said sternly. Valaran's shrouded head turned back. The boy didn't move.

"Prince Dalar, too." When she did nothing, he added, "Turn him, or I shall."

Valaran knelt and spoke softly to the boy. Only five years old, the Crown Prince of Ergoth was obviously his father's son. He had the high forehead and rather sharp features of the Ackal line, but his mother's influence could be seen in the green of his eyes and the dimple that appeared at the corner of his mouth when he grinned.

Dalar whimpered, and shook his head at his mother. She placed a gentle finger under his chin, whispering, "Do as you're told. Your father commands it."

This close, Dalar could see through her veil, could see the loving expression only he was privileged to know. For everyone else—especially for the emperor, his father—her face was always set in a cold, hard mask, her green eyes as unyielding as the peridot ring Dalar wore on his little finger.

Taking a deep breath, the boy turned his head. The old

wizard no longer struggled for air. His eyes were open, unblinking, and his tongue protruded from between his teeth. Now Dalar found he could not look away.

Ackal V stood abruptly. Many in the crowd behind him drew back quickly, but his glare was directed at the crown prince.

"I arranged this lesson for your benefit," the emperor said, as though the old wizard's death was a lecture on history or swordsmanship. "Do you think I question high mages every day? He died too quickly, and the lesson was wasted."

Without turning, Ackal V pointed to a scribe seated on the ground by his chair and intoned, "Crown Prince Dalar will have nothing but bread and water for the next three days."

Valaran drew breath to speak. Still not moving his eyes from the shivering boy, the emperor added, "If the empress protests, she'll have the same for a fortnight!"

She had borne worse, but Valaran would not give him the satisfaction of punishing her in public. Taking Prince Dalar by the hand, she left.

"Tathman!"

"Yes, Majesty!" The captain of the Wolves stepped forward. Tathman, son of Tashken, was a tall, rawboned hulk. Lank brown hair was gathered in a single braid reaching well past his shoulders. Narrow brows cut a straight slash over dark eyes. The eye sockets of the wolf pelt Tathman wore held polished garnets, a sign of his patron's favor that only added to the captain's frightening appearance.

"Have the traitor's carcass removed. Hang it from the outer wall, head down."

"The whole body, sire? Not just the head?"

"That is your order, Captain."

The Wolves began clearing away the weights. A delegation of White and Red Robe wizards approached the emperor cautiously. They had chosen a middle-aged White Robe named Winath to speak for them.

"Gracious Majesty," Winath said. "Permit us to honor our late chief with a proper burial."

"Oropash was a traitor," was the cold reply. "Like his colleague, Helbin."

Winath bowed. "It is true Helbin has disappeared from the city, Mighty Emperor, but poor Oropash had nothing to do with that. Oropash was no traitor."

The Wolves ceased their labors, their eyes fixing on the wizard. Behind Winath, her colleagues froze. They too stared at Winath's slight figure, but for a different reason. A glance at the Wolves would be taken as a challenge.

Ackal V replied with deliberate emphasis. "Under Oropash's leadership, you failed, not once or twice, but three times to keep the bakali host from entering the heartland of the empire. Is that not so?"

The female White Robe inclined her iron-gray head. "It is, Great One."

"Oropash was a weakling, a fool, and incompetent. That makes him a traitor, too."

Silence descended in the plaza as Winath considered Ackal V's words carefully.

"If Your Majesty judges so, it is so," she finally replied, and it seemed that all present, save the Wolves and their liege, breathed a collective sigh of relief.

The emperor delayed dismissing the wizards until they had witnessed one final humiliation. A rope was tied around one of Oropash's ankles, and two Wolves dragged him away. The knot of mages tried to show no reaction. Many failed.

Ackal turned his attention back to Winath. "You're the traitor's successor, are you not?" he said.

She nodded. She had been Oropash's second, and until the White Robes convened and elected a new leader, she had command of the order.

"I want new and different spells," said the emperor. "The bakali have reached the bend of the Dalti River, barely twenty leagues from here. They are not to cross it. Do whatever is needed to stop them."

"Is that not a task for the Great Horde, Majesty?"

Winath's boldness earned her one of Ackal V's unnerving smiles.

"The army is being re-formed. You keep those lizards east of the river, or I'll begin to question your loyalty, too."

From the palace emerged a group of Wolves, manhandling

some prisoners. The captives, eleven in all, had cloth sacks over their heads. Unable to see, their hands bound behind their backs, the prisoners stumbled awkwardly down the palace steps. The Wolves yanked them roughly to a halt at the bottom.

"Wait a moment longer," Ackal said to Winath, his tone almost pleasant. "I have another lesson to give."

Drawing his saber, he swept away from the closely clustered wizards. The emperor's weapon was no flimsy ceremonial blade, but a standard cavalry saber, deeply curved and well oiled. Only the ornate golden hilt and egg-sized ruby in the pommel distinguished it from an ordinary sword.

"Down, you worthless dogs!" Ackal bellowed, and the Wolves kicked the prisoners' legs out from under them. The hooded men fell hard to the ancient mosaic pavement. At the emperor's command, the hoods were removed.

Shocked exclamations, hastily muffled, rippled across the imperial plaza. The men kneeling before the emperor were well-known warlords. Their long hair and beards had been crudely shorn.

"By the law of my illustrious predecessor, Ackal Dermount, I sentence you all to death," the emperor said. "You abandoned your men and your honor on the field of battle. For that, your heads will dry on the city wall!"

In the center of the line of captives was Lord Relfas, face bruised, beardless jaw looking naked and pale in the torchlight. He tried to straighten his back, struggling against the harsh grips of the Wolves who held his shoulders.

"Majesty!" he cried. "The fault is mine! I commanded the army. Kill me, but spare the others! They fought well! They did not dishonor the empire!"

Ackal V sneered. "You lost. That's dishonor enough." Smiling, he added, "Still, since you accept the fault of failure, I shall give you this dispensation: you will be the one who dies last."

The Wolves guffawed at their master's clever joke. What he called a favor was of course the worst of punishments. Lord Relfas must watch his subordinates executed, one by one, before the mercy of death blotted out his horror for good.

Relfas's face went ashen. Two Wolves yanked him to his feet and dragged him to one side.

No specially trained executioner was called. No broad headsman's blade was used to cleanly behead the captives. The Wolves simply drew their swords and slashed the ten warlords to pieces. When they were done, Ackal V turned and beheaded Relfas with a single sidelong blow. The Wolves raised a cheer for his keen eye and steady hand.

Ackal V returned to the group of wizards. "Remember what I said. Impede the bakali—now."

He wiped his blade with a hood that had once covered a captive's head. Relfas's blood ran down the back of the emperor's hand.

Dismissed at last, Winath led her colleagues across the great plaza and through the line of torch-bearing guardsmen. As they entered the grove that surrounded the Tower of High Sorcery, one of the Red Robes would have spoken, but Winath's upraised hand silenced her.

With the setting of the white moon, the great tower's usual brilliant halo had dimmed and the lofty structure glowed only softly, like foxfire in the forest. Alabaster walls appeared seamless and translucent by starlight. Small minarets sprouted from its sides at regular intervals all along its height. Their crystal peaks gave off a faintly pinkish light.

Winath always allowed herself at least a brief moment to drink in the sight of the tower. It never failed to steady her. For her predecessor, the unfortunate Oropash, the tower had been a hiding place. He hated every moment he was outside its enclosing safety. Winath did not share that feeling. There was too much she wanted to accomplish, goals that could be attained only through the concerted efforts of herself and her colleagues. For her, then, the Tower of High Sorcery was the rational center of her being, an unchanging certainty amidst the maelstrom of the uncertain world.

Enclosing the tower on three sides was the wizards' college. Each of its four floors was faced by a colonnade. Although the columned walkways were deserted just now, lights burned in several of the building's many windows. Few were the nights that found no lights burning in the wizards' college, and sleep had become even more rare since the invading bakali had pushed closer to the capital.

The wizards quickly traversed the white marble courtyard surrounding the tower. The instant they crossed the threshold of the tower's only entrance, silence could be maintained no longer.

"Beast!" exclaimed a Red Robe. "He murdered Oropash!"

The deaths of the dishonored warlords meant little to her, but Oropash had been one of their own. Other Red Robes echoed her sentiments.

"Remember where you are!" Winath snapped. All knew she referred not to the sanctity of their surroundings, but to the prevalence of imperial spies. The emperor could have eyes and ears even in their ranks, and any number of spies might be hiding behind the alabaster columns of the two levels of galleries overhead.

"We should all have left with Helbin," another Red Robe despaired.

"No!"

Winath stamped her sandaled foot. The movement made little noise in the vast, circular chamber, yet the tower quivered from foundation to pinnacle. Already the power that had been Oropash's was beginning to flow within her.

"Helbin betrayed us all!" she said, her voice ringing off the chamber's domed ceiling. "For three hundred years we slaved to establish this sanctuary in the heart of the empire. In my lifetime I have seen a living tower rise where nothing but a dream once stood. I will not endanger the gains we have made by running afoul of the emperor!"

"He's a madman!"

This came from one of her own order, but Winath folded her arms and directed her words to the entire assembly. "Read your chronicles. Many cruel tyrants have worn the crown of Ackal Ergot. We have survived them, and we will survive this one—if we keep our heads!"

Her unfortunate phrasing reminded them of poor Oropash, being hung in disgrace from the Inner City wall. On that somber note they dispersed to their private chambers.

Winath climbed the stairs to her former master's rooms,

which opened onto the second level of galleries overlooking the main chamber. His quarters still smelled of berry jam, for which Oropash had had a well-known weakness. She uttered an illumination spell. Every lamp ignited at once.

On the table in his study were several manuscripts, a brass censer, and a shard of pottery covered with figures scrawled in Oropash's distinctive hand. Winath studied the scrolls. They were notes on tele-clairvoyance—it appeared this had been Oropash's last conjuration. He had summoned an image of the future, but not for himself. Winath frowned. To whom had he sent it? And why?

She took the pottery shard back to her own room, on the opposite side of the tower. The writing was a cipher of Oropash's own devising. Knowing him well, it took her only one mark to discern who he had gifted with a glimpse of the future. The name surprised her.

Winath rubbed away the letters with a piece of cloth. If anyone in the emperor's pay saw that name, the life of every White Robe in Daltigoth would be forfeit.

❦ ❦ ❦ ❦ ❦

"Down! Down!"

Zala grabbed Tylocost by the hem of his tunic and dragged him to the ground. A band of mounted nomads galloped past, brandishing firebrands and screaming. Although the stars and moons were shrouded by clouds, Zala feared discovery. The blazing town cast a great deal of illumination.

Juramona was in flames. Mounted nomads filled the streets, battling the few townspeople still trying to fight. Zala and Tylocost lay next to a gutted tavern, in the cover provided by a jumble of broken wheelbarrows and crockery.

"We waited too long," she murmured.

"The actions of savages are notoriously difficult to predict," Tylocost answered. His pedantic tone was at odds with his disheveled appearance. Free of its confining band, his hair hung loose about his shoulders, and soot stained his face and clothing.

"I heard that some townsmen thought they could save

their own lives and property by arranging for Juramona to fall without a fight. They opened the south gate for the nomads." Zala shook her head. "I hope they were among the first to die!"

"Humans. They're never so foolish as when they think they're being clever."

The last of the mounted nomads passed. In the lull, Zala and the elf sprang to their feet and ran for the open gate. Away from the dying town. Away from the flames and screaming.

Tylocost might be ill-favored in some ways, but he was by no means awkward physically. He easily outpaced his companion during the dash across the open ground beyond the city gate. He reached a line of cedars and pushed through, promptly colliding with a fiercely painted nomad.

Elf and man both were shocked at the unexpected encounter. While they gaped at each other—for no more than a few heartbeats—Zala sprinted by, ran the man through, and kept going. Tylocost stepped over the falling body and raced after her.

Near a dry creekbed, they found horses tethered to a stand of saplings. Zala dropped to the ground. With commendable silence, her companion fell into place beside her. She glanced his way and almost cried out. Tylocost's face and chest were covered in blood. She quickly realized the gore had come from the nomad she'd slain, but the elf resembled a ghastly specter, come back from the dead.

Composing herself, Zala turned her attention back to the tethered horses. Their owners were arguing over the division of the booty they'd taken from the town. Zala could see the men's bare, suntanned legs on the other side of their horses.

"Mocto killed the Ergoth warrior. Let him have the first choosing!" said one loud voice.

"Warrior? Ha! An old man with a soup pot on his head!"

"But I did kill him," said a third voice, presumably Mocto.

"Well, I killed the woman and boy who carried the goods in a rolled-up rug," said a fourth voice. "I should get first choosing!"

Disparaging remarks were made about parentage. Punches were thrown, and one nomad fell to the ground. More curses filled the night air.

Zala gathered herself, holding her knife so its blade lay flat against her forearm. Soundlessly, she slipped between two of the tethered horses. The biggest nomad, the one who claimed to have slain a woman and boy to steal their goods, received the point of her long knife in his kidney. He dropped to his knees, his face a mask of astonishment. He died thinking one of his comrades had murdered him.

The other three spotted the intruder in their midst and lunged for the weapons they'd left sheathed on their saddles. Zala got one fellow in the ribs. He backhanded her, sending her reeling away, then fell to his knees, lung punctured, unable to breathe.

A third nomad drew his own knife. He and the half-elf traded cuts, but her fighting style confused him. Zala feinted an overhand stab, which the nomad tried to block with both hands. Pivoting backward on one heel, she drove her blade into his chest.

The last nomad had taken to his heels, running back toward Juramona and his comrades. Tylocost retrieved a bow lying next to the nomads' swag, nocked an arrow, and let it fly. The fellow tumbled head over feet and did not get up.

It was a skillful shot, and Zala congratulated Tylocost on his prowess.

"I was a warrior of House Protector. I am proficient with all arms, no matter how coarsely rendered," he said, dropping the bow.

Nettled by his arrogant tone—after all, she had dispatched three of the savages—she swung herself gracefully into the saddle of a painted horse without touching the stirrup and asked sarcastically, "Can you ride?"

In answer, Tylocost vaulted over the rump of the nearest animal, using his hands to boost himself over the leather pillion and into the saddle. He leaned down and loosened the reins. With a quick glance at the stars, he pulled his mount's head around and cantered off, south by east.

Zala thumped heels into her mount's flanks and followed,

wrapped in a thoughtful silence. Her peculiar companion was proving to be rather useful.

Being mounted proved a camouflage for the two travelers. Several times they passed sizable bands of nomads in the dark, yet none challenged them. They were taken for fellow plainsmen, or perhaps it was the blood-spattered visage of the elf that forestalled questions. Tylocost certainly looked as though he'd come from a frightful battle.

They rode long into the night with Tylocost in the lead, following a trail only he could see. Other than studying the stars periodically, he did not take his eyes off the tall grass before him.

A few marks before dawn they halted by a small creek that wound around the foot of a bramble-covered knoll. While their mounts drank, Tylocost splashed water on his gory face.

Zala watched his ablutions in silence for a moment then said, "You're not the overbred, high-toned fellow you pretend to be."

"Well, I certainly am overbred. How else did I acquire this misshapen face? I'm high-toned, too, if I understand your meaning." He looped wet hair behind ears that stood out like jug handles. "What I am not is a weakling, or a fool."

"No? Then why did you stay in Juramona all these years, even after Lord Tolandruth was exiled? You could have left any time."

"And gone where? I'm an outcast in my homeland. Besides, I gave my word of honor to Lord Tolandruth when he paroled me. After my defeat at Three Rose Creek, I could have been executed or imprisoned. Tolandruth preserved me from that. In return, I swore to remain where he sent me and not take up arms again. It was a matter of honor." Clean but dripping, he sat back on his heels and looked up at her. "Though you're a half-breed and a female, I think you know what honor is."

Ignoring the gibes, Zala gave a slight nod. Completing her mission for the empress was not only a matter of earning her pay, or protecting her father from the empress's anger should she fail, it also was a matter of honor for Zala. She had given her word to the empress. She would not break that vow.

A search through their saddlebags produced provisions enough that they wouldn't starve any time soon. Zala offered Tylocost venison sausage and a roll of pounded vegetables and seeds called "viga," nomad trail food. He accepted the latter. Sitting in the sand by the small creek they ate their rough meal. Zala asked where they were headed.

"The Great Green. That's where Tolandruth is."

She chewed a mouthful of spicy, smoky deer meat. "How do you know?"

"Reason, dear." He drank water from his cupped hand. "That pair of giants he called wives are members of the Domshu tribe. Exiled from imperial territory, where else would he go but to his wives' people?"

His reasoning was impeccable, but now that they were away from Juramona and the rampaging nomad hordes, Zala wondered how much she could trust him. Was this slippery Silvanesti taking her to Tolandruth, or merely leading her on a wild goose chase?

"You must trust me, dear," he said, deducing her thoughts with irritating accuracy. "You've kept your part of our bargain, now I shall keep mine."

"The Great Green is vast. What makes you so sure we can find him?"

False dawn was brightening the eastern sky. Tylocost had finished the viga. He dipped his hands in the creek and shook them dry. "Think of Lord Tolandruth as a mountain peak," the elf said. "He stands above most men, and such a landmark can be seen from far off."

He smiled, and for the first time Zala did not shudder at his looks.

❦ ❦ ❦ ❦ ❦

From its usual temple-like calm, the house of Voyarunta's daughters had taken on all the frenetic activity of market day in Daltigoth. Every possession had been turned out, piled in twin heaps outside the door. Miya and Eli dragged items to the door while Tol and Kiya sorted them into "take" and "leave" piles.

The morning had begun on a contentious note. Kiya said she would accompany Tol to Juramona, but Miya declined, using Eli as her excuse. The boy protested; he wanted to see "Jury Moona" for himself.

"Are you going to abandon Husband now?" Kiya demanded. "And me? After all we've been through together?"

Miya returned her sister's glare. "I'm not abandoning anybody. You're the ones leaving!"

"Where Tol goes, I go. And so should you."

They argued through breakfast, through Eli's bath, and through the first stages of sorting their belongings for the trip. Finally, Tol intervened.

"Eli stays. War is no place for children—and he needs his mother."

Eli complained and Kiya argued, raising Miya's ire and pulling her into the fray. Tol's shout finally put an end to the discussion. He rarely asserted himself directly over his boisterous family, but when he did they obeyed resentfully.

The sisters and Eli returned to packing. Baskets and blankets were flung, clothes trampled, and gear deliberately mislaid. If the rift between Miya and Kiya hadn't been so serious, Egrin would have laughed.

He was heartily glad his friend had chosen to return to Ergoth. Once there, Egrin was certain Tol would realize the rightness of joining the fight against the bakali and the nomads.

"Blanket!" shouted Miya, flinging a brown horsehair cloth at Tol. It hit him on the back of the head, enveloping him in its dusty folds.

"We have blankets!" Kiya retorted. She was shouting, too, of course.

"It's for the horse!"

"What horse?"

Miya, flushed from her exertions, paused in the open doorway. "You don't intend to walk all the way to Daltigoth, do you?"

"I've done it before!"

Tol dragged the blanket off his back. "We're not going to Daltigoth," he said, waving away the clouds of dust. "And if we buy horses, we'll buy blankets for them, too."

"Then give it back!"

Kiya snatched the heavy cloth and flung it at Miya. The latter stood aside and let it go winging into the hut's interior. From within came Eli's howl of protest. The boy stomped out and threw the blanket at Miya's feet.

"How do you stand it?" Egrin asked, his mouth close to Tol's ear.

Tol smiled. "You get used to it. If they didn't shout at each other every day, I'd think I'd gone deaf."

By midday Tol had worked the "take" pile down to three bundles of manageable size, one for each of them to carry. The chosen equipment was spare indeed—a water bottle each, a bedroll, dried and smoked rations for the road.

Egrin asked about weapons, and Tol went inside. He stood on a block of firewood and reached up into the rafters, half-way between the chimney vent and eaves. Visibly alarmed, Miya asked what he was doing.

"Fetching Number Six." This was the remarkable steel saber he'd been given by a dwarf merchant, after Tol's party saved the dwarves from bandits in the Harrow Sky hill country.

Miya hurried over. "I'll get it for you!"

Before she reached him, the tip of Tol's buckskin-wrapped bundle snagged on something further down the rafter. A small leather box fell to the dirt floor.

Miya tried to pick up the box, but Tol's hand closed over it first. He opened the box. For the first time in six years he beheld the nullstone, the ancient Irda artifact that possessed the ability to absorb any magic directed at the one who possessed it. After gazing at it for a silent moment, he tugged a small leather bag from under his sash belt. After dumping out its contents—four silver coins—Tol put the nullstone in and tucked the bag inside his pack.

Miya's eyes were screwed shut, her body braced to receive his fury, but it never came. Instead, he patted her cheek. Her eyes flew open in shock. At that moment Egrin and Kiya entered.

"What's this?" Kiya sputtered.

"Just thanking Miya for keeping my weapons safe and sound," he said, winking. Miya's face was bright red. "You know me, I don't always take proper care of these things."

He handed the leather-wrapped sword to Egrin. The old marshal had seen the box overturned on the floor and recognized it as the one Eli had been playing with. He said nothing, only freed the saber from the oily buckskin. The iron hilt was frosted with tiny flecks of rust, which oil and sand would soon remove. Number Six's blade still had the slight bend it had acquired in a battle with Mandes's mercenaries, six and a half years ago.

Egrin presented the hilt to his friend. "Your sword, Lord Tolandruth."

Tol took Number Six. "Thank you, Lord Egrin," he said wryly.

By midafternoon the trio was nearly ready to depart. Egrin was alone in the sod hut with the Dom-shu sisters, as Tol said his farewells to Eli outside. Once more, Egrin found himself the unwitting cause of an argument between members of Tol's family.

The old warrior was nearly ready to join Tol outside, when he noticed Kiya holding a piece of jewelry. Crouched by her pack, she was wrapping a beaded headband in soft leather before packing it. The headband was very fine: multicolored beads worked in an intricate pattern, with a fringe of tiny, carved ivory animals on its lower edge. Its ties were as long as Egrin's forearm, and were decorated with more carved beads and ivory animals. When he commented on its beauty, Kiya's reaction—and Miya's—took him by surprise.

"Jewelry?" Miya exclaimed, hurrying over to investigate. "Sister owns no jewelry, except—"

"Shut up!" Kiya snapped.

Miya demanded, "Why are you taking your burial beads?"

Although Egrin didn't know the particulars, the term "burial beads" certainly had a gloomy ring to it. However, Kiya brushed aside Miya's question, reminding her that they were going off to fight, after all.

"Besides," the elder Dom-shu added, directing a glare

first at Miya and then Egrin, "it is my concern and no one else's."

Egrin nodded quickly, embarrassed to have intruded on such a private matter. Miya gave her sister glare for glare, but said nothing more.

Outside, they found Tol kneeling by Eli. The boy was trying not to cry but he was failing. When his mother appeared, he hurried to her and held her hand tightly.

Chief Voyarunta and his senior warriors had come to see the travelers off. The crow's feet had vanished from the chief's eyes. His hair was now yellow streaked with white. Yellow stubble sprouting from his chin.

"Son of My Life, it pains me to see you go," Voyarunta declared. He embraced Tol Dom-shu fashion, clapping a hand on the Ergothian's broad back.

Tol nodded. "I thank you, Father of My Life. Your kindness has been boundless." He waited, prepared to receive whatever wisdom the forester chief felt appropriate, but Voyarunta's next words caught him by surprise.

Dark blue eyes agleam with ancient ferocity, the chief said, "Take back what is yours, Son of My Life. You are a warrior of warriors, a bear among dogs. Do not let a few curs steal your glory. Your land was made by the sword—by the sword it can be saved, and you with it."

Egrin wanted to shout agreement, but solemn silence seemed more suitable to the moment. Tol's thoughts were unreadable. He stood back from the chief and saluted him, open handed.

Voyarunta embraced Kiya, too, adding an affectionate chuck on the chin.

"No wise words for me, Father?"

"What can I tell one wiser and braver than me?"

The praise was so unexpected that Kiya stared openmouthed at him. Grinning, he added, "The gods walk at this man's heels. Stay by him, and some of their favor may fall upon you, too."

Without further ado, Voyarunta departed.

Eli fled into the hut, unable to watch his aunt and uncle leave, and only Miya remained to watch the three shoulder their packs and walk away. Tol waved good-bye to her, as he had many times since coming to the forest. Always before he'd been going hunting or fishing, or just roaming the woodland. Now he was traveling much farther, heading deliberately into harm's way.

Miya waved back. In her other hand, she held the empty leather box.

Chapter 5
# Much Sought After

Like a stone falling into a quiet pool, the conquest of Juramona sent ripples of fear and excitement across the empire and beyond. Fear filled the hearts of ordinary Ergothians.

The nomad army was an army in only the loosest sense of the word. The disparate tribes were held together by a common desire for victory against the empire that had taken lands across which nomads once had roamed freely—that, and a desire for plunder. Their heady success induced many nomads to dream of taking the greater cities of the south and west, such as Caergoth and Thorngoth. The imperial army, hammered by the bakali at the bend of the Solvin River, was nowhere to be found in the Eastern Hundred.

Spring gave way to summer's heat. The vast open country of the Eastern and Mountain hundreds baked under the remorseless sun. Towering fortresses of cloud, sculpted white against the steamy blue sky, sailed overhead but yielded no rain. The dry season was upon the land, the time of dust and fire.

Tol and his two friends emerged from the Great Green into the midday glare of the sun. They stepped out of the trees and into the great open field known to the Dom-shu as the Lake of Flowers, and to the Ergothians as—

"Zivilyn's Carpet," Egrin exclaimed, surprised to find himself back where he'd first entered the forest. "Did you bring us here on purpose?"

"I just followed my nose," said Tol, shrugging.

Kiya, swabbing her face with a piece of homespun, had a different view. "The gods led you here," she said firmly. "It's a good omen!"

The sunlit meadow was dense with a fog of pollen and the perfume of a thousand wildflowers. The air was thick as well with flying things—honey bees, bumblebees, butterflies of every hue, and tiny, ruby-throated needlebirds.

Kiya unslung her bow. Without the cover of the trees they were vulnerable, and she had no intention of being surprised.

A morning glory caught Tol's eye. Its purple petals were streaked with white. A tapestry hanging near the library in the imperial palace depicted that same flower. In a flash of memory, Tol saw Valaran passing before it, her head down as she perused an academic tome.

Shaking off the image, and the memory of her voice calling to him in his vision, Tol set out across the meadow at a trot. Egrin and Kiya jogged to catch up, neither seeing any reason for such hurry.

Tol increased his pace until he was running flat out. Sweat poured off him. It stung his eyes and pooled where his sword-belt gathered his jerkin close to his skin. Without warning, he stumbled, his feet tangling in a bed of thick vines. He fell hard onto hands and knees, and his pack went flying. Sweat from his face dripped onto purple blossoms crushed beneath his fingers. More morning glories.

Now Valaran's face appeared before him. She asked, "Are you coming? Tol, I need you!"

Her desperate plea echoed her earlier words to him, the vision he'd had while hunting in the forest. He stood and a wave of dizziness washed over him, setting the sky to spinning. Before him, a path appeared in the dense carpet of wildflowers. The plants weren't trampled. They simply parted of their own volition, leaving a clear trail three steps wide.

Kiya and Egrin reached him.

"Are you all right?" Egrin asked.

"You're talking gibberish," added Kiya, handing him his pack.

# Paul B. Thompson and Tonya C. Cook

As soon as Tol took the pack from her, the strange dizziness vanished and the heaving sky calmed. The trail through the foliage melted away.

Tol shoved his bundle back into Kiya's hands. The weird dizziness resumed, and the path across Zivilyn's Carpet appeared again, the plants swaying gently apart.

Strange magic was once again at work. The nullstone was in his pack, and while he carried it he couldn't see the trail. When the nullstone's influence was removed, the trail was revealed.

Senses still reeling, Tol tried to explain what was happening. Both Egrin and Kiya were concerned, but Tol insisted, "It's her. She calls me!"

Unsteadily, he set off, leading them along a trail only he could see. Valaran did not appear to him again. Kiya and Egrin followed warily, she with arrow nocked and he with sword drawn.

The path continued for a league or more, and the flowers of Zivilyn's Carpet gave way to the waist-high grass of the plains. Except for the stiff, dry grass, the land looked much as it did around Juramona—low, rolling hills separated by the flat floodplains of ancient, long-dry rivers. The few trees were small and widely spaced. Good terrain for horsemen; bad for fighters on foot.

When the path dwindled to a mere shadow in the tall grass, Tol slowly came to a stop. The dizzy sensation of magic had faded, but in the distance, the same direction in which the trail had been leading, he saw a thin column of smoke rising.

His companions saw it as well. By its color, they knew it came from a wood fire, and not smoldering grass. Why burn a campfire by day, and in such warm weather? The smoke was bound to draw attention for leagues in all directions. Although his friends advised against it, Tol led them toward the distant plume.

After a time, a shift in the wind brought more than the smell of woodsmoke to them. It also brought the sound of voices. Tol drew his saber, but kept going. The phantom trail had pointed directly at the smoke plume and he was determined to find out why.

He sent Egrin out in a wide circle to the left, and Kiya to the right. He approached straight on. His tan buckskins blended well with the waving grass. Using the stealth he'd learned during his years in the forest, he crept up on the unseen speakers. One voice (he couldn't tell whether male or female) was doing most of the talking. Wood clattered on wood, and a fire crackled and popped loudly.

Tol halted abruptly, cursing himself for a fool. There was only one voice ahead—a stalking horse, one of the oldest ruses in the world! The fire and the speaker could be bait to lure the unwary.

A rustling behind him brought Tol whirling around. Not giving his unseen opponent time to attack first, he ran forward. Just as he neared a screen of tall bushes, a sword-wielding figure exploded from cover.

Smaller than Tol, and covered by a hooded cape, the figure parried Number Six's savage cuts. The figure gave ground, skillfully using the available cover to his own advantage and dodging out of reach.                                        •

Tol leveled his saber at the fellow and demanded, "Who are you? Ergoth? Or nomad?"

The figure lifted a hand and pushed back his tan hood. Tol realized "he" was a "she," and a half-elf to boot. Dark eyes regarded Tol warily.

"Who are you?" she asked.

"A cautious man. My comrades are in your camp. We mean you no harm. Lower your sword, if you're not an enemy."

Slowly, she did so, and Tol likewise dropped his point. He gestured at her to precede him. She moved past, wary as a cat.

They arrived at the campfire, built next to a mossy log, to find Egrin and Kiya already conversing with a person seated on the fallen tree. Egrin's sword was sheathed, and the Domshu woman had set aside her bow. Their ease relaxed Tol. Kiya's instinct for danger was far keener than his own.

Egrin hailed him. The mention of Tol's name seemed to surprise the half-elf woman, and she regarded him through narrowed eyes.

"Husband!" Kiya said. "Look who we've found! The ugly elf!"

It was indeed Tylocost, sitting on the old log, feeding the small, smoky fire from a bundle of twigs at his feet. He inclined his head in greeting.

The half-elf circled them, keeping clear of Tol, but staring at him quite markedly.

"What ails her?" Kiya asked.

"You mean, besides being a half-breed female hireling?" The Silvanesti poked his fire absently. "Just now, she's astonished. Her name's Zala, by the way. I'm sure she didn't bother to introduce herself."

Tol gave Tylocost a severe look. "By leaving Juramona, you've broken your parole," he said.

"Regrettable, my lord, but I could hardly await your leave to depart Juramona when Juramona is no more."

He described the sad state of the town's defenders, and their subsequent betrayal and slaughter by the nomads. Shaken by the news, Tol and Egrin sat down heavily on the log by Tylocost.

"Between forty and fifty *thousand*, you say?" Egrin repeated hoarsely.

The number was staggering. Every tribe from the eastern savanna must have taken part in the attack. Tol considered Juramona his home, having been brought there as a boy by Egrin, but the news of its destruction was even harder on the elder warrior. Although Ackal V had removed him from his post as marshal, Egrin had continued to live in the town. He had many friends there, warriors and common folk alike.

"Do any imperial soldiers stand between them and Hylo?" Tol asked. Tylocost shrugged. He had no way of knowing.

While the three males sat in silence, Kiya sized up Zala. She was a head shorter than the forester woman, the gracile build of an elf melded with the muscles of a human. Her manner was tense, and her eyes never still. Probably a good hunter, Kiya thought.

"What's your story?" Kiya asked amiably. "You're not this old gnome's mate, I hope."

"Astarin save me! I'd sooner marry a donkey."

"Such refined taste you have," Tylocost shot back.

Ignoring the gibe, Zala addressed Tol. "Lord Tolandruth, I was sent to find you," she said.

Egrin and Kiya exchanged a worried look. Ackal V's hatred of their friend was well known. Had the emperor, even after all this time, sent an assassin after Tol?

Zala untied a thong around her neck, bringing forth a small leather pouch. From the pouch, she took a golden ring. "I was told this would draw you to me." With a pointed glare at Tylocost, she said, "How else should our paths cross on so wide a plain?"

She offered him the ring, adding, "A certain high lady said you would recognize this trinket."

Tol's pack, with the nullstone inside, lay on the ground a short distance away. When Tol took the ring, the magical effect was immediate and overwhelming.

Valaran stood before him. She was clad in flowing scarlet, the empress's crown resting lightly on her pale brow. Her chestnut hair fell in a luxuriant cascade to her waist, longer than Tol remembered. Not only could he see her but, most disturbingly, he could smell her honeyed perfume. "Tol," Val said, "I need you! Come to me!"

The others watched his suddenly anxious face, not seeing the vision.

He returned the ring to the half-elf, and the vision vanished.

"How did you come by that?" he asked quietly.

"I had it from the hand of the empress herself," she said, putting the ring away again.

The ring was one Tol himself had given to Valaran years before. He explained to his companions what he had seen. But he had trouble crediting the half-elf's story.

"Empress Valaran lives in seclusion in the heart of the imperial palace," he said. "She has no way to hire trackers or send messages beyond the walls of the Inner City. The emperor would not allow it."

The huntress's dark eyes narrowed. "I do not lie. The empress hired me to find you, to bring you to her. She had a spell of finding placed on the ring, to help me locate you. She seemed worried the magic wouldn't work on you, but it did."

It was this last that convinced Tol. Valaran was one of the few to whom he'd confided the secret of the nullstone's existence. She would know that, should he still have the Irda artifact, a spell of finding (or indeed any spell) would have no effect on him.

At Egrin's request, Tylocost explained how he'd met Zala, and told of their departure from Juramona three days earlier. Tol realized that his initial vision of the burning town had occurred four nights before; he had indeed been given a glimpse of the future, but not early enough to allow him to stop Juramona's destruction. His journey had only begun, and already it had failed.

He rose and moved away a short distance, wanting to think while the others continued talking. Without conscious effort, his hand naturally came to rest on the hilt of his sheathed sword.

He'd come this far, but now what? Zala's explanation of her mission seemed honest enough, but it did not answer the question of why Valaran needed him, why now she had chosen to reach out to him. And the vision of Juramona's future—had that been Val's doing as well? It seemed curious that she could tell him what was happening in other places, far away from her life in the palace.

Shaking his head to clear his mind, Tol vowed that whoever was behind his summoning, he would not play the predictable, lovesick swain any longer. He would do no one's bidding save his own.

In spite of its destruction, Juramona was still his goal. Any Ergothian warriors in the Eastern Hundred would naturally gravitate to the provincial capital, even should it be in smoldering ruins, to regroup under new leadership. They would expect a warlord from Daltigoth to come, to relay the emperor's commands. Tol's arrival would be unexpected, but if it was his destiny to leave the forest and save his homeland, there was no better place to begin the task than where he himself had begun.

Egrin agreed with his reasoning.

Their lack of horses was a hindrance. Horses would allow them to travel faster and reach those parts of the Eastern

Hundred as yet untouched by the nomads—the great estates of the landed hordes to the north and east. These retired warriors and their armed retainers would be powerful allies.

Tylocost commented that he and Zala had had horses, but had lost them. He seemed to blame Zala for this. She flatly blamed him.

"In any event, my lord," Tylocost said, stroking his beardless chin, "in Juramona you might collect two, maybe three thousand men of very mixed fighting ability. What can you do with so few against so many barbarian tribesmen?"

"He defeated you with three hundred," Kiya pointed out. The elf's ears reddened, and Zala grinned at his discomfiture.

Tol's gaze turned northwest, where Juramona lay. "I'm not going after the nomads. Not yet. Juramona's lost, but it is only one town. What's important is to save the Eastern Hundred. To do that, we'll need to send messengers to Hylo."

Kiya's eyes widened. Zala scoffed. None of his companions could see any reason to involve the light-fingered kender of Hylo, but Tol was adamant.

He requested Tylocost's aid. "I can make use of you," he told the elf. "But I would never compel an unwilling captive. If you wish, you may walk back to Silvanost. I give you leave."

Tylocost had been toying with a twig. Studying the slender stick, he said, "Flaxwood. A native of the north country, beyond the Khalkist Mountains. It's very out of place here." He tossed the twig on the fire. "If it can grow here, why not I? I haven't commanded troops in a long time, but if I can be of assistance, I'm willing."

"Your allegiance is easily gained," said Kiya.

"Plainsmen are the enemies of my blood, woman. And if we can hammer them here, the deed will resound in the halls of the Speaker of the Stars. Such a victory may open other doors for me—doors that have long been closed."

They prepared to depart. Tol asked Tylocost why he'd built a fire, on such a hot day.

"Zala insisted. She awoke this morning, clutching that ring and raving about the need for a fire."

"You might have drawn every savage for a dozen leagues," said Egrin.

"I don't think so," the elf said. "The land betwixt here and Juramona is largely deserted. The nomads are busy plundering farms and villages further west."

They set out. Tol found himself at the rear of the party, next to Kiya. "Are you certain you can trust the half-elf?" she murmured. "She could be lying."

Tol looked ahead at Tylocost and Egrin. The former marshal of Ergoth and the former general of Tarsis were rehashing the tactics of some old battle, each animatedly defending his point.

"We travel with old friends and old foes, so why not liars?" Tol said.

❦    ❦    ❦    ❦    ❦

Bells tolled across Daltigoth. The city held its breath as the tidings spread street by street, through each quarter.

"Victory! Victory!" the heralds cried. "Lord Breyhard has crossed the Dalti at Eagle's Ford and smashed the invader! Victory! Victory!"

Valaran stood on the roof of the imperial palace and listened to the joyous celebrations that spread through the streets. No such relief eased the knot of worry in her stomach. She'd read the general's dispatches to her husband. With one hundred and eighteen thousand warriors at his command, all Breyhard had done was force a crossing against light bakali resistance. Ackal V had ordered the bells rung and the news proclaimed in the streets as a great victory.

Valaran returned to a small bench sitting in the lee of two life-sized statues of Emperor Pakin III, the father of the current emperor. The statues were poor likenesses and had been mutilated by drunken Wolves, hence their exile to this rooftop corner. Valaran had been pleased to find them, however. This aerie offered her at least the illusion of freedom, with no walls pressing in, and the great statues acting as shields against the ever-present wind. Besides, old Pakin III had always been kind to her.

Kneeling, Valaran unrolled a detailed map of the Dalti bend. She noted the positions of Breyhard's hordes and the locations presumably now occupied by the bakali. The general had a small hook in the enemy's flesh, but the question was, could he exploit it?

She pushed the scroll open further, revealing Caergoth and the Eastern Hundred. Valaran touched a fingertip to the town of Juramona. It seemed a ridiculous gamble now, sending a lone tracker to find a single man somewhere in the hinterlands beyond the empire. She had tossed a pebble in the ocean, hoping to hit a whale. Still, the gamble had to be taken.

The current celebrations notwithstanding, Daltigoth was awash in fear and doubt. There were daily executions of food hoarders, street thieves, and those who made treasonous utterings against the emperor. Ordinary folk were hanged. Well-born victims of the emperor's justice lost their heads. The spikes atop the Inner City wall were never empty. Courtiers, warlords, and mages rose to prominence by the sudden death of their predecessors, only to fall themselves when they failed to give satisfaction. Valaran wondered who would ruin Daltigoth first, the emperor or the invaders.

One of her attendants—she never bothered to learn their names—appeared at the cupola door and called for her. The woman's expression showed her dismay at finding the Empress of Ergoth sitting on a dirty stone bench, her wine-colored silk gown creased and soiled.

Valaran knew the woman would bleat on and on until she acknowledged her, so she let the large map spool shut and asked the woman what she wanted.

"Gracious Majesty, the emperor has sent for you!"

Valaran rose and tucked the scroll under her arm. "Where is he?"

"His private quarters, Majesty."

*Gods, give me strength.* The emperor in his private rooms might want anything, from her opinion on a banquet menu to his conjugal rights. Ackal V wasn't especially fond of her company. As a husband he was little more demanding than his brother, her first husband, Ackal IV. Ackal IV had been

## Paul B. Thompson and Tonya C. Cook

of a scholarly bent, and frequently preoccupied with various projects. This emperor's pleasure sprang more from terrorizing his people than making love to his wives.

Three more attendants were waiting below. They curtsied, their bowing heads topped by fashionable starched headdresses. Rising, they swept away in a crackle of heavy cloth, clearing the hall ahead of her. By law, no male could come within ten steps of the empress unless the emperor was present. Male servants and courtiers were expected to disappear when her attendants materialized, as they heralded her approach. As a result, Valaran's excursions through the heart of the palace were attended by crashing crockery and slamming doors as various males rushed out of her path.

Ackal V's private quarters were in the palace's lower floors. The suite formerly had been occupied by Emperor Ergothas II, whose interest in architecture had led him to design an airy living space devoid of interior walls. A double line of columns bisected the room. In Ergothas II's day, hanging tapestries divided the vast chamber into smaller private spaces. Ackal V had ordered the tapestries removed and the large windows bricked up. He slept in a great bed in the very center of the suite and, save for a few pieces of furniture, the rest of the hall was empty. The emperor's favorite hounds ran free in the space, and his Wolves often staged rowdy revels in the side passages.

The Wolf standing guard at the suite's door was a favorite of Ackal V, who had dubbed him "my Argon," after the god of vengeance. The fellow was a giant, well over two paces tall. He bore a tattoo of a horned deer on his cheek skull and wore an especially large and smelly wolf pelt that was silvery gray in color. Like all the Wolves, he was unwashed, unkempt, and willing to do anything his patron requested without hesitation. Wolves were the only males not required to retreat at the empress's approach.

As Argon opened the doors, she glided past without acknowledging his existence in the slightest.

The chamber reeked of smoke and spilled wine and dogs. It was also stiflingly hot. The emperor's peculiar susceptibility to cold seemed to increase every month. Any room he

78

occupied for more than a few moments had to have a roaring fire, even in summer.

The twin rows of columns stretched ahead of her. Each was decorated with a gilded sconce holding a flaming torch. The floor between the columns was covered by a golden carpet. Valaran's slippered feet made no sound on the woven pile. In the shadows on each side of the lighted path shapes stirred. Some were hounds. Others were not. She did not look at any of them.

As Valaran drew near the heart of the chamber, the warmth increased. A fire blazed in an open hearth and a bell-shaped copper flue drew in the smoke and sparks, carrying them off to the roof. Straight-backed chairs were arrayed before the fire, but Ackal V was sitting on his high bed, scrolls lying on his lap and piled around him.

"Your Majesty sent for me?" Valaran halted at the foot of the bed, hands folded at her waist.

"Yes, some time past," he said, not looking up from the scroll he was perusing. After allowing some moments of silence to pass, he lowered the document and asked, "Where were you?"

"On the roof, sire. Listening to victory bells."

His lip curled at her sarcasm. Although a captive wife, Valaran used her considerable wit to annoy her husband. It was a delicate dance, their marriage. The emperor left much of the mundane, day-to-day work of running the household to his wife, freeing his own time for personal amusements. In return, he tolerated a certain small amount of insolence from her. Not a week went by that he didn't remind her he could kill her—or worse—any time he chose.

"The only victory Breyhard gained was not getting his men slaughtered crossing the river," Ackal said. "He has elements of twelve hordes on the east bank, with more crossing all the time."

Valaran said nothing. The last time she had remarked on military matters in the emperor's presence, he'd slapped her hard enough to bruise her jaw.

"You've read many books," he went on. "What do you know of the bakali? What are their weaknesses? What moves them? Why are they here?"

"Those are complex questions, sire—"

"Use small words."

His tone told her she was treading on thin ice. She drew a deep breath, choosing her words with care. "No one knows their motives, sire. In ancient times, they marched and fought at the command of the Dragonqueen herself."

"Do you think she commands them now?"

"I doubt it, Majesty. No mortal can know the will of a god, of course, but the bakali invaders don't seem bent on taking over the empire. They fight in a very unusual way. They annihilate all in their path, but don't spread their attack in any organized fashion. They destroy what they choose to destroy, but a league or so beyond their marching column, no harm has been done."

He thumped a thickly coiled scroll with one hand. "This fellow claims the bakali were the first thinking creatures in the world."

"That would be Rathmore, the dwarf historian. His reasoning is suspect—"

Ackal V swept aside half a dozen scrolls, sending them cascading to the floor. Valaran winced at his abuse of priceless manuscripts.

He held up a newer tome. "In your *History of the Silvanesti*, you say the bakali were exterminated at the end of the Second Dragon War." A heartbeat's pause, then he shouted, "So why are we troubled with them now?"

Valaran frowned in thought, pressing her fingertips together at her lips. "All the lizard-folk were slain at the Battle of Time, sire, when the four Mages opened the earth to swallow the dragons and their army. Evidently, some bakali—not part of the force thus destroyed—survived. It is reported our foes arrived on the north coast by ship, like the ones slain in Hylo twenty years ago by Lord T—" Valaran bit off her words, just as Ackal threw her a sharp look. "The earlier expedition may have been a reconnaissance. That it was destroyed may have spared us a direct invasion." Without speaking his name, she gave Tol credit for saving the empire, for a time.

Ackal V tossed back the bedclothes and swung his feet

A Hero's Justice

to the floor. He wore only a breechnap. Sinewy and pale-skinned, his body was covered with the same rusty red hair as his head. He flung on a quilted red velvet robe and tied the sash with a yank.

Valaran continued, "It was the dream of the Dragonqueen to conquer the world, Majesty. We know her forces were defeated here, but no one can say they didn't triumph else-where. There are lands beyond the sea—"

"Yes, yes," he snapped, turning his robe's fur collar up around his ears. "And they had to pick *my* reign to return. Thank Corij no dragons have come with them!"

He shoved an ornate dagger through his sash and poured a cup of hot mulled wine from a pot on the hearth. After drain-ing the goblet, he said, "Consult with the chief of the White Robes—what's her name? Winath. I need magical means to confound the bakali. Breyhard has courage, but his tactics are lackluster. What I need is a general with wits and luck enough to best these damned lizard-men!"

Catching her eye, he read the thought flashing through her mind. He covered the distance between them in three strides and seized her wrist. He pushed his face so close that his wine-scented breath burned her eyes.

"Does a day go by that you don't think of him?" he hissed.

She stared right back at him. "No, Your Majesty."

He trailed the fingers of his free hand down her throat. She bore his touch in stoic silence, eyes fixed on the fire behind him.

After what seemed an age, a smile curved his lips. What his touch could not do, the smile did; Valaran shivered.

"I wonder," he said. "Does he dream of you as he squats in a squalid little hut somewhere? Or do he and his giantesses have children by now?"

Valaran did not move.

Abruptly, he released her arm and stepped back, telling her to get out. He turned back to the pot of mulled wine.

Relief coursed through Valaran, but she showed no emo-tion as she walked out of the suffocating heat, her husband shouting at his suffering servants to bring more wine.

81

Valaran did not return to her rooms to change, even though her gown was drenched in sweat. Flanked by her attendants, she hurried up the central stairs to the imperial library. Her approach cleared the library of the scribes working there. The men had to abandon their work and withdraw immediately, leaving styluses soaking in inkpots and unfinished scrolls lying beneath their corner weights. Valaran sent away her attendants, then locked the doors. At last, she was alone in her favorite room in the world.

Today, the library's scholarly peace did not soothe her. Filled with fury, she smote a marble tabletop several times with her fist and used language as crude as any sailor. When her anger had cooled, she straightened her disordered hair and clothing, then busied herself among the shelves.

The item she sought was the *Ergothinia*, a collection of the sayings of Ackal Ergot, founder of the empire. Once required reading for all members of the royal house, the huge tome had fallen out of favor since the days of the usurper, Pakin Zan. Now it was relegated to a high shelf at the rear of the library. The long cedar chest in which it was kept was covered by a thick layer of dust.

Valaran opened the chest. The four parchment rolls inside were dark with age. One by one she removed them and carefully set them aside. Dipping her hand in once more, she drew out a small, flat box. It was made entirely of mirrored glass, a rare material produced by the Silvanesti which yielded uncannily clear images, unlike the brass or tin mirrors made in Ergoth.

Valaran raised the box's hinged lid. The interior held another mirror set horizontally. She drew a lamp nearer and looked down at the mirror's smooth surface.

A man's face appeared. He had short, carefully groomed, sand-colored hair, and his chin was beardless. He wore the loose crimson raiment of a Red Robe wizard.

"Master Helbin," Valaran whispered. "Can you hear me?"

"Yes, Majesty," the image replied, its lips moving naturally to form each word.

"The army has crossed the Dalti to attack the bakali."

The image nodded. "The gods go with them. Elsewhere, there are evil tidings. Juramona has fallen to the nomads."

The words chilled her heart. "Any word of the huntress Zala?"

"She was there, but escaped. I keep watch on her, as you commanded, Majesty."

The sound of footsteps in the corridor outside the library set Valaran's pulse racing. "I must go," she whispered. "Keep safe the gift of Mandes!"

"It is an evil thing, Your Majesty, crafted by an evil man—"

"Yet it may be our salvation, wizard! Yours, mine, and Ergoth's! Guard it well!"

Valaran closed the lid and returned the mirrored box to the cedar chest. Covering it with the dusty scrolls of the *Ergothinia*, she knew her secret was well guarded by the forgotten words of a savage old conqueror.

Chapter 6
# Raising the Standard

From a league away, Juramona was a heap of ashes. Ribbons of smoke rose from debris that had once been houses, halls, and places of commerce. As Tol's party of five approached, still on foot (no horses having been found to speed their journey), frightened survivors fled. Kiya tried calling out reassurances, but no one listened.

Closer, the town's charred ruins revealed worse sights. The smoldering piles contained not only burnt wood, shattered crockery, and twisted metal, but broken skulls and blackened bones. Not a dwelling was left standing.

Atop the motte, the highest point in town, stood the remains of the High House, the marshal's home. Tol led his group up this hill. The going was slow and treacherous, as the way was impeded by heaps of charred timbers and broken masonry. The air shimmered with heat still rising from the ruins. They were forced to tear apart some obstacles and clamber over others. A slab of bricks gave way under Egrin, and only Kiya's quick hands saved him from a nasty fall.

As they ascended, Tylocost held back from the labor. However, sharp words from Tol caused the elf to fall in beside Zala and help pull down a soot-stained length of wall that barred their way.

The marshal's dwelling had been reduced by fire to a great pile of blackened wreckage. Several chimneys still stood, silent sentinels above rubble too chaotic to cross. Backs aching, all of them stained head to toe with ash, Tol and his companions turned to look out over the gutted town.

Egrin's face was pale beneath its smears of soot, and he fought to control his feelings. At his side, Kiya laid an unusually gentle hand on his shoulder. The forester woman did not share the same deep connection to Juramona, but it had been the site of her first home with Tol and Miya.

Zala dropped wearily onto a cracked slab of slate, once part of the hall floor in the High House. Tylocost tried to clean his hands in a small puddle of muddy water. Giving up, he sat down to rest near the half-elf.

Tol rooted in the debris until he found a long wooden pole, reasonably intact. From his bedroll he withdrew a large piece of scarlet cloth, the mantle he'd once worn as an imperial general.

None of the others could fathom his purpose, so they watched in exhausted silence as Tol tied the corners of his mantle to the pole and furled it tight. He shouldered it and entered the precarious jumble that had been the High House. Burned timbers snapped under his feet, and gouts of ash flew up every time something gave way. As he broke through the outer crust of cinders, fresh plumes of smoke poured out. When one pile shifted, throwing him dangerously off-balance, Egrin shouted a warning, but Tol kept going.

"For a lord and general, this Tolandruth seems careless," Zala remarked. She'd tied a length of cloth around her head to hold her sweaty hair out of her eyes.

Tylocost shaded his close-set eyes from the morning sun. "Spoken like a hireling," he said. "I believe he means to send a message."

That was indeed Tol's plan. He planted the pole on the highest point in the ruins. The breeze caught his mantle, setting its red folds to flapping. With a cape from the empire that had dishonored him, Tol had created a flag of Ergothian crimson. Anyone passing within sight of Juramona would know the empire still held sway.

When Tol was back with his comrades again, Kiya warned, "Your flag may draw a swarm of nomads."

## Paul B. Thompson and Tonya C. Cook

He shrugged. "If so, all they'll find are a few humble peasants, who know nothing about warriors or flags."

The trip back down to level ground was accomplished more quickly since they'd already cleared a path. When they arrived, they found a small group gathered to greet them. Eight Juramonans—three men, four women, and a small child—covered in soot and ashes, hailed them. All but one sported crude bandages on their heads or limbs.

The sight of Tol drew a shriek from one of the women. "It's him!" she shouted. "It's Lord Tolandruth! Praise Mishas, it's Lord Tolandruth!"

One of the men, a middle-aged fellow with saber cuts on his shoulders, flung himself at Tol's feet.

"My lord!" he gasped. "We prayed, and you have come!"

Tol raised the injured man to his feet. "Far too late, my friend."

The woman who'd recognized him pushed forward. "It matters little, my lord! You're here. Now the savages will learn what retribution truly means!" Her lust for revenge was reflected on the faces of the other survivors.

Tol and his comrades shared what food and water they had with the destitute townsfolk. The lone uninjured man, a young fellow with sharp features and darting eyes, sidled up to Zala.

"Water's for horses. Care for wine?" he whispered.

"Where are you going to get wine in these ruins?" she demanded, keeping her voice low, too.

He laid a finger aside his nose and assumed a knowing expression. "Things below ground survived. May I show you?"

She accepted his offer. Leering, he took her hand and led her away. Kiya saw them going and would have spoken, but Zala warned her off with a brief shake of her head and a lift of her dark brows. The Dom-shu woman shrugged and said nothing.

The sharp fellow's name was Artan. With many blandishments about her beauty and wit, and hints at the concealed riches of Juramona, he led Zala through the ruins. After several twists and turns (designed mainly to confuse her,

86

she decided), they passed a makeshift corral containing three horses. Zala planted her feet, yanking him to a halt, and asked about the animals.

"They belonged to nomads who lost their way in the ruins." He drew a finger across his throat. "They won't be claiming them."

Next thing he knew, Zala's sword point was at his chin. He sputtered and demanded an explanation.

Zala's smile was deceptively sweet. "We're going back to the others. I'm sure Lord Tolandruth will want to thank you for your patriotic donation of horses to his cause."

Artan found himself marched back to the others. He went sprawling when Zala kicked his feet out from under him. Sheathing her sword, she explained what she'd found.

While Artan was forced to lead Tylocost, Kiya, and Zala to his cache of food, Tol and Egrin went to fetch the horses.

Typical plains ponies, the three animals had short legs, thick bodies, and could run all day without tiring. Egrin pronounced them sound.

"We were due for a piece of luck," Tol said, stroking one horse's shaggy brown flank.

Soon they heard Kiya's shrill whistle. Their comrades were returning, laden with casks of wine. Artan bore a pair of smoked hams. The others carried packets of dried beef, small kegs of flour, and baskets of dried fruit. As much as the discovery of the horses, the sight of the food lifted Tol's heart. Food was a vital ingredient in his plan. Townsmen and farm folk would be wandering the countryside, searching for victuals. He meant to draw them to the ruined town by feeding them, then enlist them to defend the empire.

Now they were all together again, Tol revealed the plan he'd been formulating.

"It's plain that we cannot rely on the emperor to save the eastern provinces. We must save ourselves, but we need fighting men, warriors."

Kiya noted they were a little short on such just now, and Tol said, "That's why you and Egrin are going to go and find some."

Egrin knew the rural warlords of the Eastern Hundred

well. He had served with them on many campaigns under emperors Pakin II, Pakin III, and Ackal IV. All had sworn fealty to him when he was installed as marshal of the province. He would take one horse and ride east, visiting the large estates and smaller holdings, rallying the gentry. These landed hordes so mistrusted by Emperor Ackal V would form the backbone of Tol's new army.

Another of the ponies was to be Kiya's. Despite her protestations, she was heading to Hylo.

Egrin was still not convinced the kender would be of any use. Tol reminded him and Kiya of how few choices they had.

"You might be surprised what kender can do."

Unpleasant thoughts of the havoc kender could wreak continued to bedevil Egrin, but he didn't argue the point further. Instead, he asked, "Will you be all right here, alone?"

Tol smiled a little. "Not so alone. Tylocost's loyalty is guaranteed by his oath."

"And the huntress?"

"I've nothing to fear from her. She's charged with delivering me alive to Daltigoth."

During the journey to Juramona, Zala had tried to convince Tol to go directly to Daltigoth. He assured her it was his ultimate destination, but he had no intention of walking alone into Ackal's capital city. He would explain no further, and she'd finally stopped hounding him, but neither man believed she'd given up.

"I don't trust either one of them," Egrin said quietly. "The elf lives and breathes stratagems, and the huntress is young and desperate."

"We're all desperate," Tol countered. "Be of stout heart, son of Raemel! I'll harness these two hounds, and they'll do good service."

❦ ❦ ❦ ❦ ❦

They established a simple camp just outside the burned walls, but didn't bother setting up defenses. They were too few to defend the camp if nomads attacked, so Tol felt the best defense was helplessness. He doubted the nomad host would bother a few survivors trying to eke out a spare existence in the ruins of Juramona.

The crimson flag Tol had planted did its work. People began to gather in the camp. Scores of Juramonans emerged from the ruins, certain the great Lord Tolandruth could protect them from any menace. Lean-tos and shanties sprang up, constructed from whatever could be salvaged. Despite the seemingly total devastation, much useful material was collected by the careful gleaners. Many cellars had survived intact, as Artan proved, and yielded up a bounty of food and drink.

Tol wanted Egrin and Kiya to depart the next day, at sunrise. The former marshal had readily accepted his mission, to rally the landed hordes, but Kiya was still not happy with hers.

"Kender troops?" she exclaimed. "Husband, you can't be serious!"

"It does seem a contradiction in terms," Tylocost put in dryly.

"Any arm that can wield a sword is welcome," Tol said, looking at each of them. "If Hylo hasn't yet felt the wrath of the nomads or bakali, it will. Remind King Lucklyn or Queen Casberry of that."

Lucklyn and Casberry, married co-rulers, were never in Hylo City at the same time. While one remained at home, ruling, the other went off wandering, in the way of kender. Tol hoped Kiya would find Casberry in residence. He'd dealt with the queen before, when he and three hundred hand-picked warriors had sought out and slain the monster XimXim. Casberry was a cunning old pirate, but the kender queen knew where her best interests lay—just the sort of ally Tol needed now.

For the first time, Kiya openly regretted Miya's absence. The younger Dom-shu sister, a haggler of fearsome reputation, would have been fully equal to bargaining with the doughty Queen Casberry.

Once she'd spoken Miya's name, Kiya fell silent. The sisters had never before been separated for so long. Although the stoic Kiya would never admit it, Tol knew she missed Miya terribly.

After Kiya finally agreed to go to Hylo, Tol went to make a tour of the growing camp, alone. He wanted to gauge the mood of the survivors. An entourage would only draw unwanted attention. As a concession to Kiya's concern, he promised not to go beyond the outermost ring of shelters.

Duty and love had called Tol out of the Great Green, inspired by the strange visions he'd had in the forest, but as he walked among the exhausted, frightened people squatting by campfires, he felt a surge of anger. Witnessing the brutal hand of war laid upon the land and people he knew filled him with righteous outrage. He knew who was to blame—not the nomads, nor even the mysterious bakali. The true author of this misery was the Emperor of Ergoth.

In Tol's view, Ackal V had betrayed his people by appointing incompetent warlords to command the empire's hordes. The emperor demanded personal obedience from his hirelings; martial skill was secondary. This valuing of loyalty over skill could bring about the downfall of the empire.

As he passed among wounded women and children, Tol recalled that he had been favored by the gods never to fight in a losing battle. He'd seen warriors maimed and killed, but had never known the harsh hand of war on his own people. This destruction was a strange new experience. Seeing the people's suffering brought home to him that it was not only defeated soldiers who paid the price for losing, but the soldiers' families, and the village, farm, or town each warrior claimed as home.

Shame burned through him. To have lived forty years and only realize this now!

In spite of his own fury at the emperor's failures, Tol found no corresponding resentment among the encamped Juramonans. Stunned resignation seemed to be the prevailing mood, followed by a thirst for revenge. Most disturbing were the scavengers, like Artan, who saw in the empire's troubles an opportunity to enrich themselves. Artan himself had managed to slip away after his cache was confiscated. Stern measures might be needed to keep his kind in line.

As Tol passed by two families huddled around a blazing fire, an old man reached out and gripped his hand. Aged eyes looked up at Tol with desperate hope. Touched, Tol patted the oldster's gnarled hand and bade him and the others good night.

❦ ❦ ❦ ❦ ❦

Everyone was bedded down when he returned—everyone save the huntress. She sat, fawn-colored cape draped around her shoulders, facing the dying fire. Tol knew that the age of a half-elf was notoriously hard to judge, but in this light, Zala looked almost like a child.

"Trouble sleeping?" he asked.

Zala kept her eyes on the flickering flames. "I'm wondering when we'll get to Daltigoth."

"So am I." He sat down next to her. Half-joking, he said, "Worried about collecting your fee?"

She lifted the leather pouch from around her neck and poured its contents into one hand. In addition to Valaran's ring, Tol saw that a small gold locket lay in her palm.

"Here are the reasons I worry," she said. "Your empress and my father."

The locket was a plain golden disk, about the size and thickness of an imperial crown coin. Tol pried it open with a fingernail. Within was a small circle of parchment, carefully cut to fit the depression in the locket. Painted on the parchment in skillful detail was a portrait of a gray-haired human with pale eyes and a pointed chin.

Tol could see the resemblance between father and daughter, around chin and nose. He closed the locket, and Zala took it back, clenching her hand around it.

"If I don't produce you in a timely fashion, the empress will have my father killed." Tol scoffed at this notion, but Zala hissed, "She told me so to my face!"

"Zala, we are all taking risks. And if we fail, it's not only our own lives that are lost"—he gestured at the people sleeping around them—"but the lives of those who love us, those who depend upon us."

"It's a terrible land that lives by such ways!"

Tol waited until she had returned the locket and Valaran's ring to the leather pouch around her neck, then he said, "Gods willing, I will get to Daltigoth, but the route may be long and the way dire, and I need your blade, Zala. If I guarantee your father's life, will you stand with me?"

"How can you make such an offer? Caergoth is far away, and ruled by a cruel governor!"

"I'm Lord Tolandruth. I have ways." He smiled disarmingly. "Give me your sword, and I will do everything in my power to preserve your father's life."

She rested her chin on her updrawn knees, considering. Could this human be trusted? No one she'd met seemed to be neutral about Lord Tolandruth. Love him, hate him, fear him—everyone had definite ideas. She knew a bit of his history, knew he was the son of a farmer, the sort that Riders of the Great Horde usually trampled on their way to battle. Yet he had become their master, a general of armies and warlord of the Great Horde. Even Tylocost—haughty, infuriating Tylocost—had vowed to follow this peasant warrior.

*Kaoth.* That's what the elves called it. Fate. One was either its victim or its master. Although she'd known him only a short time, Zala had no doubt which of those applied to Tolandruth.

She made up her mind. Rising gracefully to her feet, she looked down at him.

"Safeguard my father, and I'll stand by you until this business is done." Dark eyes bored into his. "You have my word."

He gave his solemn promise. She would not take his hand, but nodded once and turned away to find her bedroll.

# Chapter 7
## Crucible

Forty horsemen galloped up to the summit of a low hill, the highest point for leagues. Dawn was not long past, and pallid strips of fog still clung to the low places. At the riders' backs, the silver stream of the Dalti River gleamed. Golden sunlight fell about the horsemen, promising heat later in the day.

Lord Breyhard removed his helmet, already sweating. His slightly paunchy frame and prematurely graying hair made him look older than his thirty years. Standing in the stirrups, he craned his neck in as wide an arc as his armor would permit.

"Where are the damned lizards?" he growled.

Fifty hordes were poised behind him on the rich flatlands of the Dalti's floodplain, ready to sweep forward at his command. Three days ago they'd crossed the river after a brisk fight. Since then, no sign of the bakali army had been found. Another fifty-eight thousand warriors waited on the opposite shore. They were to cross the river and take the enemy in the flank—once the enemy was discovered.

"Send word to General Crumont," Breyhard ordered his nearest aide. Crumont commanded the fifty-eight hordes on the other shore. "Tell him to head south to Traveler's Cove, and begin his crossing at once. He will establish a bridgehead and remain there until I summon him."

The aide saluted with his dagger and put spurs to his horse. Another warrior moved forward to take his place. Breyhard addressed him.

"Vintox, lead the Red Hawk and Solin Star hordes on a sweep of the countryside north and east of here. The enemy must be there. Find them."

Breyhard had reasoned, not poorly, that the bakali would withdraw to rougher, more wooded ground. If imperial horsemen could catch the slower-moving enemy foot soldiers in the open, the bakali would find themselves at a disadvantage. He was certain the bakali had retreated to the pine hills northeast of the river bottoms.

Vintox departed, and another warrior guided his horse forward to his general's side, but Breyhard looked around. He wanted someone else.

"Where's Casselron? Where's the wizard?"

A man in late middle age, his blond hair pulled back in a rough queue, rode slowly through the press of burly warriors. Casselron the White Robe, looking saddle-sore and wan, hoarsely hailed his commander.

"Find the enemy," Breyhard snapped.

The wizard rubbed his chin. Spending so much time in the saddle did not allow him to keep to his usual standards of grooming. He grimaced at the feel of his unshaven face, and at the situation in which he found himself. A wearer of the esteemed White Robe should not be traveling in the company of such ignorant warriors, required to perform spells like a market fair entertainer, but this was his mistress Winath's notion of how to please the emperor.

Casselron pulled his attention back to the matter at hand.

"As you command, my lord, but—" Breyhard's eyes narrowed, and Casselron made his voice as deferential as possible. "General, I remind you that divination has consistently failed to locate the bakali since their entry into Ergothian territory."

Like most Riders, Breyhard had a distrust of magic and those who wielded it, no matter which creed they followed. "So, your skills are inferior to the lizard-men's," he scoffed. "I've said it all along."

Casselron flushed but wouldn't be baited into an argument. It would be pointless. He promised to do his utmost and departed. Like its rider, his horse was unaccustomed to the rugged life of a warrior. At a shambling trot, the animal carried the wizard a few paces away to open ground.

At home, in the Tower of High Sorcery, Casselron would have employed a full invocation before a polished pan of sacred oil, calling upon Manthus, Corij, and Draco Paladin to reveal the enemy to his eyes. Here, on a damp hilltop leagues from any city, he was forced to improvise.

He turned his back on the troop of anxious, yet arrogant warriors surrounding Lord Breyhard. From a leather sheath on his saddle, he drew his staff. The wooden stave was some two paces in length, topped by a golden dragon's claw. The claw gripped an opaque white disk slightly larger than Casselron's palm. Lips moving silently, Casselron gazed into the white disk.

His vision pierced the milky surface. Distance melted away and flowed past his probing gaze. Leagues flashed by—north, east, and south. He saw farms, emptied and abandoned, roads clogged with overturned carts, fields devoid of activity. Unlike the rampaging nomads, the bakali didn't slaughter and loot indiscriminately, but their advance across Ergoth had driven common folk from hearth and home into the walled cities, where they waited for the emperor's hordes to subdue the invaders, making it safe for them to return home again.

But Casselron saw no lizard-men. The farther he looked, the fewer signs he saw of the bakali's passage. They must be close.

Something touched the wizard's consciousness as he roamed over field and farm. It was a fleeting sensation, as though a shadow had crossed the sunlight of his vision.

Casselron was one of the best scryers in Daltigoth—he'd been chosen to accompany Lord Breyhard for that reason— and this delicate contact alerted him at once. The bakali were provided with magic of their own! It cloaked their movements and befuddled every attempt by Ergothian mages to use their powers against the invaders. Such protection did not require an army of powerful sorcerers. One dedicated practitioner, if skillful enough, could block all prying eyes.

This was Casselron's theory, at any rate: a single adept

mage was assisting the bakali. The mage could be a rogue wizard with an axe to grind against the empire, like Mandes, or a forester shaman of unusual skill, a heathen priest, even a Silvanesti. The gods alone knew what mischief elves were capable of.

Abruptly, Casselron found himself face to face and mind to mind with the other. The confrontation happened so suddenly it had to be a deliberate revelation.

"You!" Casselron cried, utterly astonished. Gray eyes, curly, sand-colored hair—he knew this face!

A sharp blow to his chest ended Casselron's vision. He looked down. An arrow protruded from his chest. That wasn't right—

Lord Breyhard saw the White Robe topple slowly from his saddle. Breyhard fumed. Weakling! The fool had fainted before providing any useful information!

A hail of arrows showed Breyhard he was wrong. Horses reared as missiles struck home. Warriors fell to the ground, arrows in faces or shoulders. Someone shouted, "Ambush! Ambush!"

As the shafts fell around him, Breyhard called for his own bowmen. "Get those spawn of snakes!" he roared.

A contingent of Seascapers from the far west rode forward, short bows ready. The arrows had come from a copse of trees atop a nearby low hill. The gray-green bakali were hard to spot among the leafy branches, but a few Seascaper arrows found their targets. With shrill cries, injured lizard-men plummeted from their perches.

"If any of those live, I want them!" Breyhard ordered.

Warriors around him drew sabers and spurred forward to sweep up the fallen. They hadn't ridden ten steps before noise erupted behind them. From the hilltop, Breyhard could see a melee breaking out on the floodplain. Fully armed bakali had sprung up out of nowhere among the idle troops.

The general bellowed, "Cornet, sound formation!"

The boy put his brass horn to his lips. An arrow in the back knocked him forward over his saddle, but the young Ergothian bravely managed to sound the horn, relaying his commander's order, before he succumbed.

The bakali had buried themselves in the soft black loam of the river bottoms. Apparently, they could go without air for an amazing length of time. So utterly still had they lain, the Ergothians had rode right over them, ignorant of the danger beneath their feet.

More lizard-men were appearing every moment. Brawny, scaly, stained with dirt, they uttered high-pitched screeches as they raised high their axes and swords. They cut at the legs of the Ergothians' horses, and when the riders were thrown down, three or four lizard-men would fall upon them and hack them to bits. Blood and soil mixed to make a dark and fearful clay.

The Ergothians tried to sort themselves into the usual fighting formation, but the enemy was among them, all around them, shrieking, slashing. Breyhard could not rally his confused, frantic men. He allowed himself another moment to curse the vile beasts he faced, then drew his saber.

It was not the sort of battle the Ergothians were accustomed to. There were no lines, no maneuvering, no great, sweeping charges. Fifty thousand Ergothians, more or less stationary on horseback, had been surprised by at least an equal number of bakali. A vast, formless brawl ensued as both sides fought to the death. Swords clashed, spears thrust, blood flowed. Men and horses screamed as they perished, and bakali keened their strange, shrill cries. Unhorsed soldiers, filthy from the same black earth that had hidden the bakali, continued to fight on foot. In the awful confusion, sometimes man fought man and lizard slew lizard. It was every warrior for himself.

Gradually, Ergothians gathered on the strand, pushed to the edge of the river by the great mass of lizard-men. Rafts and boats, used by Breyhard's army to cross the Dalti earlier, had been tethered to the rickety piers of Eagle's Ford. Masses of camp followers and other noncombatants attached to the army had been crowding aboard the boats. Such was their terror and confusion, nearly three-quarters of them still remained, fighting frantically to board the vessels.

Breyhard, bleeding from five wounds, sent word that the remaining watercraft were to be cut loose. His lieutenants

# Paul B. Thompson and Tonya C. Cook

blanched at the order, but the general was insistent that there
be no retreat. Breyhard had realized that if the bakali defeated
his men and captured their boats, they would be able to cross
the Dalti in strength today—and the only other imperial force
with a hope of stopping them, General Crumont's, was busy
crossing the river to the south, as Breyhard had ordered. The
whole of western Ergoth would find itself wide open to the
invaders.

The boats, freed of their moorings, slowly spun away,
heading downstream. Empty boats collided with those carrying terrified camp followers, most of which were barely
half full.

Breyhard turned his bloody, mud-stained face back to the
battle.

"Let's kill some lizards," he said to his lieutenants, manag-
ing a savage grin. "I never could stand the smell of them!"

He urged his wounded war-horse into the fray. Shoulder to
shoulder, his retinue followed their commander.

❦ ❦ ❦ ❦ ❦

Valaran closed the mirror-box. The battle was over. The
leather case beside her yielded a sheet of foolscap, which
she lay on the reading table before her. She dipped a stylus
in ink, then, choosing her words with great care, put pen
to paper:

*Your Majesty,* she wrote. *Lord Breyhard is lost, with half his
army. Many bakali have likewise been slain. The Dalti crossings
are unguarded.*

She stopped there, offering only the bare facts, not advice.

After sanding the short note, she folded it and sealed the
edges with wax. One strike on a small gong summoned a
waiting servant. She was an elderly woman, whose crimson
livery hung loosely on her gaunt frame.

Valaran commanded her to take the note to the emperor,
warning her to pass it to one of his minions and not to give
it to him herself.

"Do you understand?" Valaran asked.

Blue eyes, yellowing with age, regarded the empress

98

without any change of expression. The old woman nodded. She had served in the palace for decades and did indeed understand. Whoever gave this note to the emperor risked a beating—if not death.

Alone again, Valaran unrolled a map of central Ergoth. Eagle's Ford was slightly less than twenty leagues from the capital. If General Crumont extricated himself quickly, his fifty-eight hordes would suffice to defend the city, but he would not have enough men to attack the bakali. The initiative would pass to the invaders.

Grim but satisfied, she allowed the map to curl shut.

"Grasp every circumstance, make use of friend and foe alike," she whispered. The little-known saying of her ancestor Pakin Zan had become the maxim by which she lived her life.

Valaran's desire to be rid of her cruel husband had increased tenfold with the birth of her son. Dalar had arrived a full year after Tol was exiled, but Ackal V had made the first few months of her pregnancy hellish, until he was absolutely convinced the child she carried was his own.

Valaran loved her son, though she'd never craved children as some women did, but Dalar also provided her with the means to attain the end she wanted. As a woman, she could never gain the support of the warlords for herself, but they *would* support her son, the rightful heir to the throne.

The arrival of the bakali had been a gift from the gods. She had resolved to use lizard-men, nomad barbarians, and any other opportunity that presented itself to discredit her husband and display his utter unfitness to rule. By grasping every circumstance, making use of friend and foe alike, she would be rid of Ackal V. Dalar would become emperor, and Valaran empress-regent.

🦉 🦉 🦉 🦉 🦉

Egrin and Kiya departed on their missions. The Dom-shu woman was not happy leaving Tol with "one and half elves," as she put it. Tol did not share her fears. Zala lived by her word, the same as Tol. She would stand by the pact they had made. As for Tylocost, Tol's command over him was based in part on his old victory, and in part on the Silvanesti's own notion of honor.

"Trust their honor?" Kiya had said sarcastically, when he explained. "Not too much to ask!"

She rode off north, and Egrin headed east. Tol asked Corij to watch over both of his friends.

The makeshift camp outside the still-smoking rubble of Juramona grew and grew. Five days after Tol's arrival, it held a thousand people, mostly former residents of the town. By the time the sun set on his eighth day there, almost four thousand had gathered. Fully half of this total were able-bodied men—farmers, craftsmen, shopkeepers, and the like.

One night, standing by a leaping bonfire, Tol addressed them. "Men of Ergoth! I stand here as one of you—landless, destitute, an exile in my own country. I have come back to fight the enemies who burned your homes and laid waste to your lands. If you will have me, I shall lead you."

A few shouts of support rose from the crowd, but the response was hardly enthusiastic. One fellow cried, "We're not warriors!"

"Anyone who takes up a sword or spear can fight! I was not born to arms, but I learned the art, and I can instruct you. Will you not fight to expel the invaders? Will you not take back your own country?"

This time the answering cries were more definite. Tol asked if anyone had fighting experience. Ten-score out of two thousand came forward. Most were former foot guards in the service of Marshal Baroth, Egrin's replacement as Marshal of the Eastern Hundred. Baroth, a young crony of the emperor's, had left Juramona to ride with Relfas's army and had never been seen again. When the nomads attacked, the foot guards had defended the High House, but couldn't hold out against the spreading flames from the burning city. The men had drifted back to the shattered town when they heard an imperial banner was raised. Tol was deeply glad to have them. His new army would require captains.

One man stepped forward. Completely bald, between thirty and forty years of age, he had the carriage of one who'd once borne arms. He said his name was Wilfik, and he'd been a foot soldier of the Juramona garrison.

"How can we fight the nomads?" he asked loudly. "We've no horses, and even if we did, we're not Riders."

"Soldiers on foot can stand up to horsemen," Tol said. "I'll show you how."

A rag-clad townsman with burns on his hands and face said, "What if we don't want to fight?"

"No one will abuse you for choosing not to fight. But mark this: any man who takes up arms for his country will never be anyone's servant again. If we take back this land—" He grinned. "*When* we take back this land, it will be ours, and no one will be able to wrest it from us again!"

His meaning was clear. Since the warlords had failed to protect the Eastern Hundred, they would have no claim over it once the nomads were expelled. It was a revolutionary notion, and sent a thrill through the assembly. No more raiding nomads—and no haughty imperial overlords either!

"Juramona for all!" someone shouted, and "Free land! Free men!" cried another. More of the group joined in, and soon these shouts echoed through the makeshift camp.

After the assembly broke up, Tol talked with the men who'd claimed to have soldiering experience. He named each man a captain in the new corps, and chose Wilfik to command them. The bald former foot soldier seemed steady and sturdy, his no-nonsense manner just right for leading others.

Everyone knew Kiya and Egrin had ridden off to find help. Wilfik asked what support they might expect. Tol's reply was blunt.

"I expect none. So should you."

Dismay colored every face. Tol planted fists on hips and said, "Have no illusions, men! The imperial hordes have always fought to win battles, not to survive them. We won't make that mistake. In a fight for our lives, we will outlast our foes. Nomads fight for glory and plunder; if they don't get it fairly quick, I doubt they'll stay around for a long war. It's whose men are left standing that matters!" He clapped the nearest man on the shoulder. "If help arrives, we'll rejoice! But don't count on it."

The men dispersed, leaving Tol with only one companion. Tylocost squatted nearby, in the shadows beyond the fading bonfire, idly toying with a stout stick. It was a most undignified posture for a former Silvanesti general. In the uncertain light, with his ungainly features, the elf resembled an enormous insect.

"So, General, what did you think of my address?" Tol asked him.

"I think we shall all end in nameless graves soon."

Tol's lips twitched with amusement. The Silvanesti's pessimism was curiously refreshing. "I've faced worse odds, you know."

Tylocost rose to his feet in one smooth motion. Such graceful movements reminded Tol his charge was no ordinary fellow. Whatever his looks and high-handed manner suggested, Tylocost was a mature Silvanesti elf, with all the intelligence and subtlety that implied.

"It's not the nomads I fear, nor even the bakali," Tylocost said. "You just declared war on the empire, and that, my fortunate foe, is a losing proposition."

Tol grinned widely. "Perhaps. Can I count on your support?"

"To the death."

"Good. I intend to give you a command of your own."

For once the elf had no quick comeback. He stared at his conqueror, then recovered his accustomed poise.

Inclining his head graciously, he said, "Thank you, my lord. I will do my best."

*And someone will suffer for it,* Tol thought. He hoped it would be the enemy, and not himself.

As Tol retired to his lean-to, Tylocost went for a walk along the fringes of the camp. Hands clasped behind his back, eyes on the trampled grass in front of him, his thoughts were far away.

He'd circumnavigated a quarter of the sprawling camp when he suddenly stopped and pointed the stick he still carried toward the outer darkness.

"Half-breed, why do you shadow me?"

Zala emerged from the night. "You heard me?" she said, impressed.

"You're only half-stealthy."

She grimaced. "You never speak to me without flinging mud on my ancestry!"

"The mud is already there. Answer my question."

Biting back the retort that sprang to her lips, Zala settled on simple truth: "You're a goodly distance from your bedroll. You might be thinking of running away, to betray us to the nomads."

His eyes widened. "Twenty years I've lived as Lord Tolandruth's paroled prisoner. I could have escaped any time I wanted, but I pledged to honor my surrender until he released me, and I shall."

"Silvanesti have no allegiance but to their own kind!" she snapped.

The silence held for a moment, then Tylocost shrugged and tucked the stick under his arm like a cane, turning away and resuming his walk. She fell in step beside him, and they proceeded in silence for a while, circling the sleeping camp from south to north. Cookfires dying to dull embers dotted the scene. Dark mounds of sleeping humans, covered in salvaged blankets, lay in irregular ranks on the dewy ground. Everywhere was the smell of smoke, sweat, and desperation. Zala's pity for the survivors was obvious. If Tylocost felt anything, he did not show it.

"What do you know of my homeland?" he asked, his low voice just audible over the sound of their footsteps.

"Very little," she admitted. "My mother was Silvanesti, but she never returned home after she married my father."

"Foreigners cannot imagine the glory of the Speaker's realm. Silvanesti worship, above all things, beauty. They have, by art and artifice, made Silvanost the single most beautiful place in all the world." Zala had heard the same from those few fortunate enough to have seen the capital of the elves. "Imagine how I was regarded in such a place."

Her footsteps faltered only slightly before she recovered. Zala could indeed imagine. The unsightly gardener must have stood out like a boil on the face of a beautiful girl.

"My paternal ancestors were noble in the extreme. They stood at the right hand of Silvanos himself. My grandfather

103

slew a dragon—the black dragon Tasak'labak'kanak, in the First Dragon War. He rode his war griffin Skyraker up to the monster's very jaws and drove a silver spear through its eye and into its brain. My father, if he still lives, is high counsel to the Speaker of the Stars."

"You don't know whether your father lives?" she asked, and he shook his head. She thought of her own father, the frail, kindly scholar whose life depended on her success. When he died, wherever she was, she would know it.

Tylocost continued. "One day, as the great Silvanos held court in the Tower of the Stars, a comely lady caught my father's eye. Her name was Iyajaida, an exotic word meaning 'moth-wing.' No one knew her. It was said she'd come from the northland. In spite of her unknown lineage, my father pursued and won her, besting several other rivals. Not long after, I was born."

Tylocost abruptly stopped walking. For an instant Zala thought he'd seen a danger, nomads lurking in the night perhaps, but he only stared straight ahead and said, "The day I was born my mother vanished, never to be seen in Silvanost again. People said she took one look at me and fled in shame."

In spite of his even tone, Zala knew he was baring soul-deep wounds to her. As diplomatically as she could, she asked him why he was telling her these things.

"Because you will understand," he replied. "Comely though you are, you're a half-breed, and despised by elves and most humans, too. I am a full-blood Silvanesti from a fine and noble line, yet all my life I've been persecuted for my ugliness. The first time I ever felt wanted was when the Tarsans hired me to lead their army. But the first person who ever showed me true respect was that damned peasant, Tolandruth."

Males were very strange, Zala decided. Tolandruth, so imposing with his muscles, piercing eyes, and great victories, seemed an overgrown boy, burning with notions of justice and honor. This elf, more arrogant than a cartload of emperors but one of the shrewdest people Zala had ever met, was consumed with loneliness and shame. She began to understand the empress's devotion to Tol, and Tol's trust in his former foe.

When Zala returned to the here and now, Tylocost had slipped away. The stick he'd carried stood where he'd been, its end thrust into the sod.

# Chapter 8
## Rolling the Bones

D ust rose in choking clouds around the Juramona camp, churned up by the feet of hundreds of men. The dust of the Eastern Hundred was infamous, a fine, floury, yellow soil that coated everything once the anchoring grass was stripped away.

The members of Tol's new army bore weapons salvaged from the town—spears, halberds, or in many cases, merely sharpened wooden stakes—as they practiced moving in unison and deploying to attack or defend. He organized them into squads of ten, with five squads making up a company. Ten per company would have been better, but he didn't have the manpower. Twenty days after his arrival at Juramona, his effective force comprised a scant thousand men under arms, a single horde of raw infantry. At least that many more had slipped away or begged off joining Tol's tiny army. He let them go. A man unwilling to fight was no asset anyway.

At Tol's side stood Wilfik, the former High House guard he'd appointed as chief of his company captains. Less than a handspan taller than Tol himself, Wilfik had proven a capable drillmaster. Perhaps to counter his bald pate, he sported the thickest, blackest beard and brows Tol had ever seen. The eyes beneath those redoubtable brows were an unusual color—pale gray. The combination of light gray eyes and beetling brows gave him an especially fearsome aspect when he was angry.

He was angry now.

Shouting curses, Wilfik stormed over to a company that

had maneuvered clumsily. He grabbed the captain of the wayward group and spun him around.

"Left!" Wilfik roared directly into the fellow's face. "You purblind donkey! I said 'counter-march *left*'!"

After shoving the fellow back into line, Wilfik rejoined Tol.

Spitting a mouthful of dust, the bald soldier said, "Lambs to the slaughter! Dull-witted, thick-headed lambs to the slaughter, that's what this lot will be when we meet the nomads again!"

"They're willing enough," Tol responded mildly. "What they need is confidence."

The troops, dubbed the Juramona Militia since they were volunteers instead of levies, were drilling on the plain south of the camp. Further west, Tylocost and a work gang were preparing surprises for any nomad attackers.

Tol had offered the Silvanesti command of half the militia, but Tylocost declined. Although a warrior from birth, he knew the training of raw troops was not his strong suit. A better use of his time, he tactfully suggested, would be building field fortifications. For three days now those not fit to fight had labored for the elf, hauling timbers, brick, and other debris from the ruined town to the open plain. Mounds of masonry rose, interlinked by fences of heavy timber.

Tol bent to uncover the water bucket at his feet, but the wooden lid was whisked off by another hand. Zala's.

The huntress rarely left his side, having appointed herself his personal guard in order to fulfill the pledge she'd made: to bring Tol to the empress and thereby collect her payment. The half-elf was a capable tracker, and certainly knew the sharp end of a blade from the dull, but Tol wondered how she would stand up to open battle. She'd never tasted the terror and mayhem of war.

He sipped from the gourd dipper, then offered it to Wilfik. Wilfik poured the contents over his sweating head. As Tol refilled the dipper, Wilfik drew his attention to the southeast, where dust was rising from the plain. They had no men training or working in that direction.

Tol dropped the gourd into the bucket. "Have the men fall in."

Paul B. Thompson and Tonya C. Cook

Once the companies had assembled, their marching feet stilled, the hot breeze soon cleared away the dust they'd churned up. All eyes watched the rising cloud; it was moving from southeast to east, toward the morning sun.

"A scouting party?" Zala asked hopefully.

"I make it five hundred horse, at least."

Tol's comment erased the hopeful expression from Zala's face and she grimaced. Not a scouting party—more likely, an entire nomad tribe on the move.

A runner was dispatched to warn Tylocost. The militia and its leaders headed back to camp at a quick march.

The dust column was moving fast, circling wide to the east at a distance of two leagues or less. There was a dry stream bed along that line, Wilfik remarked. The horsemen were probably using it for concealment. The rising dust had given them away.

Reaction to the ominous portent was quick back at the camp. The returning militia found no one except those too old or sick to work for Tylocost. The rest had abandoned their tents and lean-tos, seeking the imagined protection of the Juramona ruins.

Tol deployed his raw troops in company blocks of one hundred men. He spread sixty hand picked men, all young, in a skirmish line a hundred paces in front of his foot soldiers.

Although he had a horse, Tol chose to lead on foot. Zala, white-faced with worry, stuck to him like dew on a leaf.

The dust column died away. The horsemen had stopped.

Tylocost appeared, striding through the trampled grass. His floppy gardener's hat shaded his face, and he gripped not a sword or spear but his long walking stick.

"Poor sports, these nomads, coming up on our undefended side," he said. "Still, what else can you expect from barbarian—"

"Shut up," Tol said. To Zala's amusement, the elf obeyed.

A covey of partridges flew up from the tall grass a long bowshot away. Tol drew Number Six.

"Skirmish line, kneel." He didn't shout. A calm, even voice was needed to steady his men. All went down on one knee, including Tylocost and Zala.

108

"Present arms."

His skirmishers, armed with salvaged pikes, extended their weapons, sweaty hands gripping the fire-blackened poles too tightly. Tol suddenly wished Kiya was at his side. Her unfailingly accurate bow and unflappable calm would have been a welcome addition to this pitiful force.

A distorted wail rose from the plain. It began as a single voice, then others joined in.

Several of the men closest to Tol began to shift nervously. The unease spread outward, along the skirmish line.

"Tylocost, did I ever tell you how I acquired this dwarf steel blade?" Tol said conversationally.

Never taking his eyes off the horizon, the elf replied, "No, my lord, you never did."

"It was in the Harrow Sky hill country, after the surrender of Tarsis."

As Tol continued to speak, his voice carrying, the general nervousness visibly lessened, but he didn't get to finish his story. From where the partridges had flown now rose a swarm of nomads. Tol knew this trick. Short-legged nomad ponies had been trained to crawl on their bellies while their riders crawled alongside. When they were close enough to charge, man mounted horse and both sprang up.

The abrupt appearance of the enemy, seemingly from nowhere, drew gasps from the defenders. More than one of the skirmishers showed signs of panicking.

"Stand fast!" Tol barked, raising his voice now. "Run now and they'll kill us all! Remember: we must stand together!"

The enemy came on, screaming. Again, Tol called for his men to stand fast, but his mind was busy reckoning the numbers. Only eighty or ninety were approaching. The others lurked out of sight.

The nomads covered the ground quickly. They made straight for Tol's line, confident they could ride down the few, widely spaced foot soldiers. The upraised pikes should have given them pause, but they had beaten Ergothians before, and in greater numbers than this. Howling and waving their swords, the nomads kept coming.

"Aim for the riders not their animals," Tol said.

109

The first wave of horsemen ran themselves straight onto the skirmishers' pikes. A score of nomads and their horses fell. The impact drove the Ergothians back, and many lost their pikes as the impaled riders fell.

"Fall back to me!" Tol ordered. Terrified, the skirmishers formed a knot around him, and Tol told them, "Don't just stand there! If you've lost your pike, draw your sword!"

There was no more time for orders as the second wave of nomads broke over them. Tol warded off a blow from one rider, ducked a second, then delivered a sideways slash that emptied the saddle of a third attacker. When the nomad hit the ground, Tol planted a foot on his chest and stabbed him through the throat.

Something snagged his leather jerkin. He turned to find a nomad swinging a saber at him. Zala dashed by Tol, her sword pointed, and ran the attacker through the ribs. Tol acknowledged her help with a quick wave, then faced new enemies.

More from self-preservation than training, the skirmishers formed a tight circle to fend off the horsemen, who continued to gallop around them, yelling and taking opportunistic cuts at the Ergothians. Bowmen could have picked off the nomads at their leisure, but what few archers there were Tol had sent to guard Tylocost's work party.

A bold rider, full of battle-lust, plunged straight into the ring of desperate foot soldiers. Tol's newly minted warriors cringed before his mount's flailing hooves, but Tylocost stepped up and thrust his blunt stick at the man's face. The attack caught the nomad squarely on the chin, and he flew backward off his horse. Neck broken, he was dead by the time he hit the ground.

The fight went on until, as at some silent signal, the nomads suddenly withdrew. Tol sent his skirmishers back to Wilfik's line. A third of their number remained behind, dead in the torn-up, bloody grass.

Wilfik, good soldier that he was, had not broken ranks to rescue Tol's company. He held the Juramona Militia in line as the retreating skirmishers filtered back among them.

"Brisk set-to," he observed, pale eyes fixed on his men.

"They're aggressive all right," Tol agreed. He was covered in sweat and blood, the latter not his. Zala, her sword gripped in both hands, stared with wide eyes at the plain. She, too, was spattered with the blood of others. Tylocost pushed her blade down gently.

"Draw a breath," he advised. "You're safe for the moment."

A moment was all they had before the full complement of nomads came charging out of the dry creek. About five hundred of them this time, Tol noted, taking grim satisfaction at the accuracy of his earlier estimate. There were men and women both, all furious at their initial repulse.

"Companies, present!"

The Ergothians held a numerical advantage. They were nine hundred eighty-eight strong, although only a fraction were experienced warriors. At Tol's order, they presented their spears and a thorny hedge blossomed in the front of each block of one hundred men.

"Stand fast!"

To the experienced eyes of Tol, Tylocost, and several others, it was obvious they faced members of several nomad tribes. Some of the oncoming riders were covered head to toe in buckskin, others fought bare-chested. Hair was long, either braided or loose, or heads were shaved, then painted or covered by leather skullcaps. Their favored weapon was the saber, much like those wielded by the Imperial hordes, although some carried the short bow or light, throwing spear. Fully a third of the attackers were female—as formidable in battle as their male comrades. Like the Dom-shu, some of the nomad tribes made little distinction between male and female warriors; it was skill that mattered, not gender.

Tol sheathed Number Six and took up a pike. Zala stood on his left, trembling. On his right, Tylocost leaned casually on his staff.

"One charge is all we'll get," the elf said.

Wilfik looked back over his shoulder. "Eh? How do you know?"

"I've been fighting human nomads since long before you were born," Tylocost replied. "They're fierce, but they don't have the determination to stand and fight it out with steadfast troops. If we don't give way, they'll give up."

"Ten gold pieces says you're wrong!" Wilfik said, eyes glinting beneath his fearsome brows.

The Silvanesti nodded. "Accepted."

The enemy was closer now, their screeching cries audible over the pounding of their horses' hooves.

It was too much for one company of the militia. The Seventh, to the right of Tol's position and some forty paces away, threw down their pikes, turned tail, and ran. Wilfik bellowed curses to no avail.

Half the nomads veered, heading toward that gap in the formation. Immediately, Tol ordered the three leftmost companies to advance as they swung right. The two companies on the far right, isolated by the desertion of their comrades, were given leave to fall back, but in a slow and orderly fashion.

With the lines seemingly giving way before them, even more horsemen concentrated on the gap yawning ahead. The nomads had no formation, no discipline. None of them noticed the troops on the left moving out and arcing around them. None of them noticed that the ground over which they galloped sloped gradually upward, slowing their charge.

Tol ordered the two retreating companies to halt. Their lines were ragged, and they could barely hear him over the din, but they stopped. In the next moment, they were engulfed by rampaging horsemen.

The rest of the nomad column hit Tol's position. For an endless time, there was nothing in the world but screams, rearing horses, and the clash of arms, but slowly, very slowly, the hundred-man companies began to push the horsemen back. The block of Ergothians with Tol maneuvered to strike the nomads from behind. On the far left wing, the last company jogged through the dust to close in.

At last the nomads realized their peril. Those at the rear of the melee warned their fellows: they were surrounded by solid phalanxes. The nomads tried to break away, but engaged on two sides, they could not. Finally, the center of the mass of horsemen slashed their way through and galloped away.

It was a heady sight for the militia. Their enemy was in flight. Two militia companies opened ranks and gave chase, cheering in triumph. Tol shouted himself hoarse calling them back, but they either didn't hear or wouldn't heed him. As he feared, the retreating nomads abruptly wheeled their ponies and attacked, hacking down scores of the running Ergothians. The heedless militiamen, scattered and isolated from their fellows, were easy prey.

The surviving soldiers came streaming back to Tol. He ordered two companies who'd held formation to move forward and fend off the pursuers. With their foe regrouping, the nomads abandoned the fight and rode for the western horizon.

The battle was done. In moments, the breathless chaos of combat had given way to abrupt calm. Agonized voices groaned for water. Dust hung in a red haze over the field.

The victorious foot soldiers started back toward camp, desperate for drink and attention to their injuries. Tol, Wilfik, and the other officers went quickly among the staggering ranks, shouting anew.

"Back in line! No one dismissed you! Get back in line! This retreat could be a feint!"

Cuffed and shoved by their furious officers, the men gradually returned to formation. Tol stalked up and down the line, glaring at his troops.

"What have I told you, day in and day out, since this began? Stay together! The only way men on foot can fight and win against horsemen is if they stay together!" He wove his fingers together and shook his hands at them, bellowing, "*Together*!"

He pointed down the hill to where many of the militia had fallen. "Do you see them? They were so pleased by their little victory, they broke formation and chased the enemy. Now they're dead! Those are your comrades, your brothers, lying lifeless in the dirt! That will happen to all of you if you dare part ranks in the presence of the enemy again!"

Silence fell over the battlefield. Tol kept them there, standing shoulder to shoulder under the midday sun, while he hammered home the lesson. What must they always do? he would roar. Stay together, a few voices croaked in reply. Again, he shouted the question, and again, until every voice joined in the reply.

# Paul B. Thompson and Tonya C. Cook

Tol knew their throats were parched from thirst. So was his. He knew their hands were blistered, arms and backs aching from the unaccustomed exercise. And more, he knew their heads reeled from all they'd been through. Still, they had to learn this lesson. Their lives depended on it.

He dispatched Wilfik and the Second Company to recover the dead and wounded, Juramonan and nomad alike. Much useful information might be gathered from the enemy, whether living or dead. He then ordered the First Company to fall out. The men in question looked at each other dazedly for moment, then shuffled out of line and back to camp.

Once the First had departed, Tol heard a low sound behind him and realized Zala was still on the battlefield. She sat in the grass, holding her head in her hands. She looked up at him, her eyes red-rimmed.

"Horrible," she whispered.

Tylocost was some thirty yards south, standing among those who'd fallen in the first clash. Leaving the three remaining companies still standing at attention, Tol walked through the dead men and horses until he reached the elf general.

"Some are alive," Tylocost said, indicating wounded nomads moaning among the dead. "They can be questioned."

The Third Company carried the injured nomads to the village and kept them under guard. As the enemy wounded were pulled from beneath their fallen horses, Tylocost reminded Tol of another problem that must be dealt with: the Seventh Company's desertion.

"I know," Tol said tiredly. " But I can't afford to make examples of one hundred men."

"You need not hang them all. One in ten should be sufficient."

Cruel as it sounded, Tylocost's suggestion was quite lenient by Ergothian standards. In the Imperial Army, one man in three would have been beheaded for desertion in the face of the enemy. But the Juramonans weren't true soldiers, Tol pointed out, not yet. They could hardly be expected to act like professionals when many had touched a pike for the first time only days ago. Still, discipline must be served, lest the example of the panicked company spread to the rest. Those

114

who'd run away had to be punished, not for their good, but for their fellows who'd stood firm.

Wilfik arrived and offered his commander a skin of water.

"No sign of the savages," he said, grinning. Two of his teeth had been broken out years before, giving him a gap-toothed smile. Slanting a look at the Silvanesti, he added, "I owe you ten gold pieces, elf!"

Tol passed the skin to Tylocost. "How many dead?" he asked Wilfik.

"Forty-two of our men, and sixty-six wounded to varying degrees. I count thirty-five nomads dead." Wilfik's black-bearded grin faded. "We also have fourteen prisoners."

"Keep them under tight guard. I'll want to interrogate them."

Tol started back to the waiting army, but Wilfik caught his arm.

"Some of the prisoners are known to us, my lord. They looted Juramona, murdered many. Our men want to see them pay for that!"

"They're prisoners of war," Tol replied firmly. "I order them spared. They can give us valuable information about the larger bands of nomads."

Tylocost fell in step beside Tol. Together they crossed the field toward the three companies still standing at attention.

"The deserters, my lord?" Tylocost said relentlessly. "One in ten?"

Tol halted. "Very well. See to it. One in ten—but no more, understand?"

With a nod, the elf departed. Tol studied his retreating back. Was that a smile on Tylocost's face as he turned away?

Forty of the militia had collapsed from heat and fatigue while they'd waited for Tol's return. They had to be carried by their comrades when Tol at last ordered the men back to camp. Ragged cheers greeted the victors. The aged, the young, and the infirm were buoyed by the sight of the fearsome nomads fleeing from their former victims. Tol's name was chanted, but once he started shouting orders, the survivors of Juramona fell to, bringing food, water, and medicine to their defenders.

The captives were taken to a ruined stone house in Juramona. Fourteen rangy nomads—five women and nine men—sat disconsolately as glaring militiamen stood guard on the low walls surrounding them. Most of the nomads had minor wounds.

"Who is chief among you?" Tol called out.

Fourteen pairs of sullen eyes gazed at him, but no one answered. Tol repeated his question more sternly, and a blond youth with sword cuts on both shoulders spoke.

"Our chief is Tokasin," he said. "He will hear of this outrage, and his wrath will be terrible!"

Tol laughed. "Every nomad in Ergoth will hear about this day. That's for certain! Your days of terror are coming to an end!"

A black-haired woman with blue tattoos on her cheeks asked, "Who are you, grasslander? You're not one of these sheep."

He told them. From their nervous shifting, they obviously recognized his name.

Although he asked several times where their chief was, they would say no more. He ordered they be given food and water, but no treatment for their wounds until they decided to talk. The sergeant of the guard he warned to be alert for any who might show a change of heart.

Feeling bolstered, Tol returned to camp. On the way he saw soldiers routing out Seventh Company deserters who were hiding in the town's ruins. The militia men had no qualms about arresting their former comrades. Their own lives had been put at risk when the Seventh ran away, and they were none too gentle about catching the cowards who had endangered them. Near the ruins of the town wall, a gang of workmen was knocking together salvaged timbers in an open area. As he passed this gallows, Tol's fragile confidence gave way to gloom.

Zala, freshly scrubbed, was waiting for him at his shelter. She had bandages, a jar of ointment, and a basin of clean water. She ordered him to take off his jerkin and let her inspect any damage. Amused by her imperious tone, he did so, and she commenced scrubbing his back.

"Ow! What is that, sharkskin?" he complained.

"Quiet!" She resumed scrubbing at the dirt and blood with the coarse bit of wet cloth. "Some warrior! Can't take a little cleaning!" She resumed with a vengeance.

The washing revealed that Tol hadn't so much as a scratch. Zala muttered something about luck, and he smiled. Kiya was always saying he was the luckiest dolt the gods ever made.

Despite the roughness of her ministrations, Tol found his eyelids growing heavy. He hadn't tasted battle in six years, and no amount of wood-chopping in the Great Green could substitute for the adrenaline rush of open combat. Exhaustion claimed him. His chin dropped to his chest.

Zala stepped back and regarded him in amazement. He was snoring! The great ox was asleep!

Tol shifted position, easing himself onto his side without ever waking. Zala watched him, a frown on her face. What she'd been through today would trouble her own sleep for many nights to come.

❦ ❦ ❦ ❦ ❦

Ackal V let the empty cup fall to the flagstone floor. It was solid gold, cast in the reign of Ackal Dermount, but without wine in it, it was just so much cold metal. He reached for a full cup, this one of translucent crystal etched with the Ackal arms.

His private chambers were alive with revelry. Smoke from the roaring fire mixed with the smells of incense, sweat, and spilled wine. The emperor had decided to forget his troubles with a little celebration. Breyhard had failed, and his army was lost. Crumont had managed to return across the Dalti River and fall back to the Ackal Path, ready to defend the capital from a bakali assault. It had never come. The lizard-men disappeared once more into the rich farm country northwest of the city. The Great Horde was searching for them.

The only ones invited to this party were the Emperor's Wolves and a few special guests, including Breyhard's kin. His two wives were chained to pillars, with his three children cowering at their feet. Breyhard's brother had been arrested as well, but the Wolves had been careless and allowed him to fall on a concealed knife, cheating the emperor's vengeance.

Filthy, unkempt Wolves lurched around the captives, bellowing insults and drenching them with wine or cider. In the shadows beyond the firelight, Ackal's hounds were savaging something: a beef joint from the cooking spit, or one of the servants—the emperor couldn't tell which.

Ackal V got up from his couch, brushing aside a sodden courtesan. With the exaggerated dignity of the intoxicated, he smoothed his wrinkled crimson robe and tightened its sash. Without being called, Tathman appeared silently at his master's elbow.

"I've neglected my guests," the emperor said. "Come."

Two Wolves had passed out while berating the dead warlord's wives. Ackal roused them with kicks. Once they crawled away, he addressed the chained women.

"You know why you are here, don't you?"

The elder wife, a plump, dark-eyed brunette, nodded curtly. The younger, red haired and half Breyhard's age, only sobbed and hung slack against her bonds.

"I have decided to be merciful and spare your lives," he said, weaving slightly as he tried to stand straight. "You will be consigned to slavery in Windgard." This was the capital of the Last Hundred, the province at the extreme western end of Ergoth, south of the Seascapes and west of Thorngoth. "The marshal there will be your master, and will do with you as he sees fit."

The elder wife pleaded, "Majesty, send me away, but please don't punish the children. They can serve the empire well when they grow up, but as slaves, their lives will mean nothing!"

"The law is clear. A general who loses his army loses his life and family."

The younger wife, red-eyed behind her ginger hair, cried, "Not me! Don't send me away, sire! I married Breyhard only half a year ago—I thought he was to be a great warlord!"

He lifted her chin. "You married him for his position? Not love?"

"Yes!"

He let go her chin and glanced back at Tathman. "Have her head put on the wall."

The woman screamed, but Ackal roared at her, "I'll not have my warriors wedded to greedy, ambitious wenches!"

Tathman signaled to two reasonably sober Wolves. They took the younger wife away. As she shrieked and begged for her life, Ackal V calmly returned to the pillar holding the elder wife.

"Lady, I'm going to set you free," he said. "You asked for your children's freedom, not your own. You're the kind of woman the empire's warriors need. Take your children home and raise them to be better Riders than their father."

Moving carefully but quickly, the elder wife gathered up her children. They disappeared into the darkness between the double line of columns.

Tathman was gnawing his long lip, staring after the departed group. "Speak," Ackal told him.

"You're too generous, Majesty," the chief Wolf said in his vast, deep voice.

"Maybe. I've had a great deal to drink."

He cast about for another full cup. Tathman took a goblet from a tray borne by a jumpy servant and handed it to the emperor. Ackal drained it.

"Still," he said, "by sparing one, I'll make loyal subjects of the rest."

Tathman bowed his head. "The emperor is wise."

What Ackal V did not know—or forgot in his drunken state—was that Breyhard's elder wife was Kannya Zan, cousin of the late Pakin Pretender, and no friend of the Ackal line. Delaying in the capital only long enough to pack a few essentials, she and her children made for the port of Thorngoth. On the way south, Kannya told the story of her humiliation to every Pakin relative she encountered, and there were many.

Chapter 9
# Cast a Giant Shadow

T he day after the repulse of the nomads, Tol awoke wooden and groggy. He'd grown too accustomed to the relative comfort of his Dom-shu hut. His bedroll seemed to grow harder with every night. He was getting too old to be sleeping on the ground.

After stretching the stiffness from his limbs, he left the lean-to. A grim sight greeted his bleary eyes. Tylocost's gallows had been filled overnight. The Seventh Company deserters hung there, dark against the brightening sky.

Strong emotions filled Tol: anger, that men should have to die like this, but forgiving cowardice in war only bred more cowards. Then came sadness, at this reminder of the frailty of life.

His melancholy musings suddenly were replaced by puzzlement. The Seventh Company comprised one hundred men; he'd told Tylocost to punish only one in ten, so there should be ten men on the gallows. Yet, more than twice that number of bodies dangled from the improvised gibbets. Those at the far end wore buckskins.

Furious, Tol shouted for Tylocost and Wilfik.

The first person to respond was Zala. In response to his demand for an explanation, she said, "Your Silvanesti did as you ordered. Then they hanged the nomad prisoners."

She could not tell him who had ordered the execution of the prisoners. So, Tol strapped on Number Six and strode into the awakening camp. He shouted again for his lieutenants. Tylocost appeared.

"You bellowed, my lord?" the elf said politely.

"Who gave the order to execute the nomads?"

"Wilfik. It was a popular decision."

"Why didn't you stop them?"

Tylocost pushed back his floppy gardener's hat. "I am Silvanesti, and still your captive. I have no authority over these people, save what you grant me."

Tol could barely speak, he was so angry. "They were prisoners of war under my protection! And they could have told us much about the nomad armies!" Lives and opportunity both had been wasted, lost at the end of a knotted rope.

Wilfik arrived at last. His explanation was simple. "The savages weren't going to tell us anything else, my lord," he said flatly. "After what they did to Juramona, hanging was too good for them."

Tol's fist connected with Wilfik's broad jaw, and the warrior went down. All around them, heads turned. Even more turned when their warlord's powerful voice reverberated over the camp.

"Get out of this camp, Wilfik! Get out of my sight! If I see you again after midday, I'll string you up beside those men!"

Wilfik looked up at his commander in stunned confusion. He opened his mouth to protest, but the fury in Tol's posture left no doubt he was utterly serious. With as much dignity as he could muster, Wilfik stood, straightened his brigandine, and walked away.

Tol began to berate Tylocost again, saying the elf should have awakened him before letting the prisoners be hanged.

The Silvanesti shrugged one shoulder gracefully. "As a rule, my lord, I try not to interfere when humans are killing each other, but if you wish it, I shall hereafter."

This bland indifference to the injustice swaying in the wind only infuriated Tol anew. He considered banishing Tylocost, too, but a sliver of reason intruded itself. That might be exactly what the elf was hoping for. Perhaps he was regretting his decision to fight alongside his captor, but his oath of surrender bound him until Tol freed him. And Tol wasn't yet ready to lose the former general's expertise.

Instead, Tol ordered Tylocost to have the dead cut down and decently buried. The elf departed, and Tol was alone with Zala.

"In war horror begets horror," he said.

Tol's loathing of executing helpless prisoners had been learned at a tender age, when he was forced to watch the Pakin rebel Vakka Zan beheaded in the town square of Juramona. Egrin had been required to do the deed, honor-bound to obey the marshal of Juramona, Lord Odovar.

There was nothing more he could do for the dead, so Tol turned his attention to the soldiers who'd guarded the captives. Once they were brought to him, he asked whether the prisoners had said anything useful to them.

One fellow scratched his head with a meaty hand. "Some of 'em talked bold," he allowed. "Said as how their chief, Tokasin, would come back an' kill us all."

The captives had mentioned two other chiefs—Mattohoc and Ulur—but it was on Tokasin they pinned their hopes. He was chief of the Firepath tribe, which they called the boldest and hardest-riding folk on the plains.

Tol, like most Ergothians, saw the nomads as a faceless mass of mounted foes, cruel, with quicksilver tempers. Learning the names of their chiefs was worthwhile information.

The guards contributed one other piece of information gleaned from the nomad captives. The prisoners claimed to be scouting for a much larger band. Their comrades who had survived yesterday's battle would return to the main force and that, they boasted, would be the end of Juramona's pitiful defenders.

Tol drilled the militia all day. He didn't share what he learned from the guards, but word got around. There was no more trouble with shirkers. The twin specters of nomad blades and the deserter's noose had resolved all qualms. It was fight or die.

The trick, as Tylocost dryly noted, was to make certain the militia fought, and the nomads died.

♥ ♥ ♥ ♥ ♥

Two nights later, Tol went to inspect Tylocost's work west of camp. The wind was up, sweeping across the long grass. Zala, his omnipresent escort, carried a torch that flared wildly with every gust.

Tylocost had erected a large number of obstacles to screen the vulnerable western approaches. What appeared as random piles of loose masonry and fire-blackened timbers hid a grim purpose. Riders would have to slow their mounts to navigate the narrow passages. When they did, they would be perfect targets for archers and pikemen concealed behind the mounds.

As he drew nearer and details of Tylocost's defenses became clear, Tol's brisk pace slowed.

The elf had left an open lane through the center of the field. The enemy would be funneled into this lane. The thigh-high plains grass gave way to loose dirt. A length of rope was buried just under the surface. Some distance further along, Tol could see another patch of disturbed soil. The seemingly clear lane was filled with traps.

"That elf is tricky as a kender," Tol muttered. Trained Ergothian warriors would never fall for such an obvious ploy, but the reckless, unsophisticated plainsmen just might.

Zala interrupted his admiration of Tylocost's deadly ingenuity. "My lord, do you hear that?"

Tol started to shake his head—all he could hear was wind moaning around the piles of debris—then came a lull, the gusty breeze died, and he heard it. Zala's keen ears had discerned a faint rumbling. Not like thunder, rolling through heavy clouds, this was more like the steady, distant roar of a waterfall. Tol knew that sound.

"Run!" he shouted, and they legged it for camp.

Zala's torch expired, snuffed by the wind of their passage, and she threw it aside without pausing. She covered the ground rapidly, with Tol only a few steps behind.

As soon as the camp came into view, he raised the alarm. Sentries took up the warning, beating an improvised gong—a battered brass tray from a Juramona tavern. Men and women came stumbling out of their shelters, grappling with helmets, bits of armor, and weapons. Tylocost, moving with all the speed and agility ascribed to his race, dodged the clumsy humans and hurried to Tol.

"Horsemen," Tol panted. "Massed horsemen coming from the west!"

Tylocost rounded up his makeshift troops and led them out to his crazy-quilt fortifications. The able-bodied men had joined Tol's foot companies, so following the elf was a motley band of boys, women, and old men. It was a lot to ask, that these folk should bear the brunt of the nomads' first assault, but the survival of every soul at Juramona depended on their steadfastness.

It was two marks before midnight, and the night sky was streaked with clouds. Moving fast across the field of stars, the clouds were stained pink by the light of Luin, no more than a crescent of scarlet and hanging low on the horizon. Solin, the white moon, had already set. Tol hated night battles. Facing horsemen with green militia was difficult enough, but the dark gave an even greater advantage to veteran fighters.

He arranged his militia outside the dark, frightened camp in an arrowhead formation. Foremost was the reconstituted Seventh Company, led by Tol himself, with two of his steadiest companies behind them, and the rest echeloned behind. At Tol's order, any who fled the coming battle were to be cut down in their tracks. The soldiers clutched their pikes, looking sleepy and frightened at the same time.

To the west, Tylocost doffed his gardener's hat and tied a strip of white cloth around his forehead, to make it easier for his people to pick him out in the dark. He climbed atop the highest of the brick mounds to search the deep darkness for signs of the enemy. He could certainly hear them. Even the dull-eared humans couldn't miss the low, constant thud of so many hooves.

In the open lane, he had arrayed a few troops as bait. Should the nomads prove reluctant to charge into his trap, the presence of those pitifully equipped foot soldiers should entice them.

Shards of brick skittered down the side of the mound on

which Tylocost stood, shaken loose by the growing vibration of the enemy's approach. The Silvanesti's vision, far keener than a human's, detected movement upon the plain. Bits of brass horse tack glimmered, as did hundreds of bare iron blades. It was only the advance guard. From the sound of it, thousands more nomads were behind the outriders.

Tylocost had done his best with the defenses, but inwardly he doubted that few if any of his people would survive the night. For the first time in his long life, he admitted the possibility of his own death, acknowledged he might never again look on the crystal spires of Silvanost, never walk among his own graceful, civilized people. Ugly, despised Janissiron Tylocostathan would die before his time, alone, surrounded by crass, bloodthirsty humans. Astarin and all the gods would weep!

The first wave of nomads cantered toward him. None seemed to take particular notice of Tylocost's defenses, which looked very like the rest of the ruined town. The riders now were only paces from the stakes the elf had driven into the turf to mark maximum effective arrow range.

He removed the white cloth from his head and raised it high. "When I give the signal, loose all!" he called down to his troops. "Mark your targets well, but don't dawdle! There are plenty for all!"

The first line of horsemen rode over the wooden stakes. Tylocost brought the white cloth down sharply. His archers let fly.

A rain of arrows in the dark is an unnerving thing. The nomads couldn't hear the snap of bowstrings, or the thrum of the approaching missiles, over the noise of their horses. They glimpsed the hardwood shafts falling through the air only an instant before the arrows struck.

Riders toppled from their horses. The vanguard hesitated, then spied the bait troops huddled in the open lane between the obstacles. With much shouting, the enraged nomads charged.

Tylocost descended from his perch and stood beside his tiny band. Most were visibly trembling, but all remained where they were, gazes shifting between their unlikely leader and the oncoming horsemen.

"Remember what I taught you," he called over the swelling noise. "At my command, fall back!"

Archers in the front ranks continued to sting the nomads, and marksmen atop the mounds also took their toll. A few plainsmen shot back, concentrating on the bowmen they could see silhouetted against the stars. One by one the Ergothians were picked off.

"Steady," Tylocost said. "At my order, not before."

When the nomads were just twenty paces away—close enough to see the flaring nostrils and gnashing teeth of their hard-charging ponies—Tylocost gave the command, and the small block of townsfolk broke apart. They streamed back down the dirt path, still clutching their weapons.

Ten paces along, the elf general halted and gestured with his bared sword. Eight Juramonans dropped to their knees and took hold of the buried ropes. Tylocost raised his sword, and the Ergothians hauled on the lines. Sixteen sharpened stakes rose up, hinged at the base, which was buried in the dirt.

There was no time for the leading edge of nomads to avoid the trap. They piled up on the stakes, and the press of horsemen behind them added to the carnage. Men and horses screamed.

"Withdraw!" Tylocost ordered. The Ergothians let go the ropes and followed as he backed slowly away.

Their charge disrupted, the nomads milled about in confusion. Finally, twenty riders worked their way around the first obstacle, and came on. Tylocost's people uncovered a second set of ropes. The nomads reined up.

After raising the second hedge of stakes and tying the ropes to anchors already driven into the ground, the Ergothians withdrew further, and raised a third line of sharp pilings. Their part of the battle done, Tylocost's troops filtered back through the waiting militia and returned to camp.

Donning his floppy hat once more, Tylocost joined the militia.

"Not much of a helmet," Tol remarked.

"So far I'm having good luck with this hat. I'll keep it."

Their respite was brief. Horsemen had picked their way

through the garden of traps and obstacles the elf had created, but arrived at the camp to find Tol's troops drawn up to meet them. With veteran soldiers, Tol would have attacked the disorganized riders, but he didn't dare break ranks to advance with his newly minted militia. Much of their courage came from solidarity with their fellows.

The nomads threw spears and showered arrows on the motionless blocks of Ergothians. Now it was the defenders' turn to fall prey to death arriving out of the darkness. They raised their shields high, but not everyone had a shield, and the arrows slowly pared their ranks.

Tol held his men steady, knowing that, as bad as it was, the bombardment was another ploy to make the Ergothians break formation.

Zala, standing behind him, said, "Can't we do something to stop the arrows?"

He watched shafts pepper the turf at his feet. "Send word to the leftmost companies," he said. "At my order, they will advance into a solid line with us." Zala hurried to deliver his message.

Tol's blood was up. The nomads wanted to make things hot for them—he'd teach them what war was really about!

With much shuffling and clanking, the companies on Tol's left moved forward. Immediately, the hail of arrows faltered as the enemy horsemen crowded forward. Pikes leveled, the militia halted in place.

"All front ranks will kneel," Tol said. His order was repeated by his officers throughout the companies. The first line of Ergothians went down on one knee.

He drew Number Six. "There will be no retreat. When a soldier falls, the man behind him will step up and take his place in line."

Tylocost drew a slim, straight blade and stood beside Tol, darkness cloaking his homely features.

"Juramona!"

Tol's battle cry boomed out over the anxious Ergothian line. Raggedly, they echoed the shout. He repeated it, and this time the response was stronger.

The nomads hit the end of the line, trying to outflank the

leftmost company. Tol's men faced about, forming a square bristling with pikes. The horsemen couldn't reach them with their shorter swords. After a sharp struggle, the riders broke off.

This continued for a seemingly endless space of time—nomads surging against one spot, only to be repelled by Ergothian pikes.

"This isn't like them," Tylocost panted, gesturing with his sword at the withdrawn enemy. "Usually, it's one hard charge, then they quit!"

Tol agreed. Since their first attack on Tylocost's defenses, the plainsmen had been fighting the Ergothians persistently for many marks, probing here and there. Although they broke off when things got too hot, they didn't ride away, but came back at a different point.

Drenched in blood and sweat, the Ergothians battled on, leaning on their pikes to rest whenever the enemy gave them breathing space. Perhaps this was the nomads' new strategy—to wear them down—but surely they and their animals must be exhausted, too.

Clouds in the eastern sky showed the first pink tinge of the coming dawn. Tol's little army was drawn up on a slight rise below the ruins of Juramona, the western plain spread out before them. The first sliver of sun peered over the horizon at their backs, its light sending their shadows out ahead of them, banishing the last of the long night.

On beholding what the new sun illuminated, Tylocost exhaled slowly, face blank with disbelief.

"Astarin have mercy," he breathed.

From north to south, as far as the eye could see, the western plain was covered with horsemen. The prisoners' boasts had been true—the main body of nomads had returned when word of their advance party's trouble reached them. The defenders of ruined Juramona, whittled by battle to barely eight hundred, faced thousands upon thousands of fresh, ferocious enemies.

The banquet hall of the imperial palace in Daltigoth was an enormous room one hundred paces long and forty-four wide, paved in black granite and walled with the finest North Coast gray marble. The vaulted ceiling rose to a height of two stories. A single massive table filled the center of the hall. It seated six hundred, and more guests could be accommodated at temporary tables erected alongside. For an imperial banquet, massive bronze ovens were wheeled in to keep hot the tremendous quantities of food necessary to serve so many.

The hall was so large it had its own weather. On damp days, mist formed in the high crevices of the ceiling, and dew collected on the cold stone floor. The worst heat of summer never penetrated the thick stone walls. If the great ovens weren't present, roaring with contained fire, the chamber could be downright chilly.

Most found the banquet hall unpleasant unless it teemed with diners, but Empress Valaran relished it. In the vast open space, she could tell she was not being spied upon. Her every whisper in the palace was heard, frequently by the wrong ears. In the echoing emptiness of the banquet hall, she almost felt free.

Clad in a white dressing gown quilted with red thread, the Empress sat at the head of the long table. Her son, Crown Prince Dalar, sat on her right. The only other occupant of the hall was a single female servant, standing a few steps away by a wheeled sideboard.

Dalar slurped loudly at his soup. The empress rapped her pewter spoon once on the rim of her golden bowl. Chastened, the five-year-old prince swallowed his next mouthful more decorously.

Twenty rooms and three floors away, the Consorts' Circle was celebrating the birthday of Princess Consort Landea, the emperor's fourth wife. A well-fleshed, vain chatterbox with a fondness for sweetmeats, Landea followed her husband's example: the news of Lord Breyhard's defeat did not interfere with her merrymaking. Her suite rang with shrill laughter, as sweet wine and honeyed confections were consumed in staggering quantities. The festivities would go on all night. Never mind that Breyhard's army lay dead along the Dalti shore. Never mind the city seethed with discontent, riots, and murder. Not even the execution of Breyhard's young wife dampened the spirits of Landea and her idiot friends.

A clang of metal on metal echoed lightly in the hall, pulling Valaran out of her dark thoughts. Dalar had tapped his spoon on the rim of his soup bowl and was looking up at her with a glint in his green eyes.

"Mama," he said, "you're fidgeting."

Valaran realized she'd been drumming her fingers on the tabletop, just the sort of restless behavior for which she always chided her son. The look on his face was so endearing she couldn't help but smile, but she thanked him quite seriously.

The boy returned his attention to his soup, pleased at having caught her. His mother never fidgeted. She could sit unmoving through even the longest, most boring speeches and ceremonies.

Her own dinner had congealed by this time, but Valaran didn't notice. She continued eating mechanically, her thoughts once more on the terrible situation in the city.

Since word of the debacle at Eagle's Ford, Ackal V had been on a rampage. Enraged beyond the point of reason, he ordered the families of the leading warlords in Breyhard's hordes punished. Labeled as weaklings unfit to serve the empire, the warlords' adult sons were beheaded. Their wives, sisters, and daughters were condemned to slavery on imperial estates far from the city. Any councilors or courtiers known to have favored Breyhard were likewise punished. The headsmen had been at it for days—another reason Valaran supped in the banquet hall. Here she was spared the sickening sound of the executioner's axe.

The doors at the far end of the hall burst open. Two Wolves entered, one announcing, "His Majesty, the Emperor of Ergoth!"

Valaran touched her lips with a snowy napkin, and stood. The servant stepped forward to shift the heavy chair for the young prince, and Dalar hopped down.

Ackal V stormed in. These days he was perpetually furious. No richly bedecked councilors or warlords in glittering panoply dogged his heels. He was surrounded, as always, by his brutal, loyal Wolves. A black bearskin cape of prodigious weight was draped over his shoulders, and he had taken to wearing gloves, even indoors, but never could seem to keep warm.

"Lady, why are you here?" he rasped. Out of breath from his continuous tirades, he was disheveled, red hair and beard untrimmed and wildly awry.

Valaran replied calmly, "For dinner, Your Majesty."

"I can see that! Why aren't you with the Consorts' Circle? Your absence is an insult to Landea!"

Valaran bowed her head. "I wished to dine with our son, sire. My heart is too heavy with recent events to pass an evening in idle pleasure."

Ackal V plucked a morsel of bread from his son's plate and chewed it rapidly. "You always have a glib excuse, don't you?" She said nothing, as he glared at her. "Someday I'll have your head, lady."

"Your Majesty has my head any time he desires it," she said, gazing steadily at him.

The Wolves, lounging casually around their master, exchanged startled looks. Few dared to speak thusly to the wrathful emperor, but Ackal V reacted with dark amusement.

"By the gods, you're the only man in the whole palace, besides me!"

The emperor's mercurial mood had turned remarkably affable. Perhaps it was all the bloodletting in the plaza. Dispatching underlings always cheered Ackal V.

Dalar had been edging slowly toward his mother since the emperor's arrival. He stood now half-concealed by her dressing gown, pulling nervously at a red thread hanging from its silky surface.

Ackal V approached his son's chair. The servant moved quickly to pull it back but was forestalled by a glaring Wolf. The emperor seated himself. His lip curled as he regarded the meal before him.

"What is this filth you're feeding the boy? Carrots? Milk soup? A man needs meat!" He sniffed the pewter cup. "Fruit juice? He should be drinking beer!"

"He's only a child."

"I'll make a man of him," Ackal said, and bawled for a libation.

The servant filled a tall goblet with beer. The emperor drained it. The servant refilled it, and Ackal ordered Valaran to sit. Dalar stood by her chair, on the side farthest from his father.

"Have some beer, boy." When Dalar didn't move, Ackal V grabbed the boy by the back of the neck and shoved a brimming cup to his lips. Dalar swallowed once, then coughed convulsively. Disgusted, his father took the drink away.

A snicker came from one of the Wolves. The emperor looked to the giant he called "my Argon," and snarled, "No one laughs at my son and lives!"

From beneath the silvery wolf pelt he wore, the giant drew a dagger in a lightning-swift motion and plunged it into his hapless comrade. The fellow dropped to the black granite floor and lay still.

Valaran was so proud of her son. Although Dalar's hand clenched convulsively around hers, the boy made no sound at all.

Ackal finished the last of his son's meal, drained the goblet of beer again, and jumped to his feet. Valaran stood as well.

"I've ordered the raising of a hundred new hordes from the western provinces," he said. "They will form at Thorngoth under Lord Tremond. Our ships will carry them across the bay to the far shore and land behind the lizard-men. That will put paid to the beasts!"

Lord Tremond was one of the few warlords remaining from the reign of Pakin III. He was an honorable man, and had been a redoubtable warrior, but as governor of Thorngoth and Marshal of the Bay Hundred he hadn't taken the field in ten years. New hordes would take time to gather and train. An aging commander in charge of green troops could have little hope of success against the wily bakali. The emperor was doing nothing less than sending thousands more to certain death.

"Do you intend to defeat the bakali by drowning them in blood?" Valaran asked, voice rising.

"If necessary." He smiled. "Whatever succeeds is right—isn't that what your ancestor Pakin Zan always said?"

"Pakin Zan was a cunning warlord, not a butcher!"

Ackal V kicked over his chair, face white with sudden fury. "Take care, lady!" he shouted, spittle flying from his lips. "You are useful, but do not task me! No life is sacrosanct in my realm—displease me, and yours will be forfeit!"

She'd heard similar threats so many times before, they no longer held any terror for her. She knew she could be killed at any time, but when the emperor was stomping about, shouting, she wasn't much concerned. Only when he was still and quiet did she become frightened. Quiet meant Ackal V was thinking, and the thoughts of such a vicious, pitiless man were terrifying indeed.

Her silence pleased him. Thinking her cowed, Ackal V drew back, his color returning to a more normal hue.

"It's always a delight to see you, lady. You never fail to stir my blood."

He turned and walked away, followed by Argon. Just as the tension binding Valaran's shoulders began to ease, Ackal V reached the far end of the great table and turned back to her.

"You will come to my chambers later tonight. One of my men will come for you."

She acknowledged his command, and Ackal V swept out. Argon slammed the banquet hall doors closed behind them.

Valaran sank into her chair, her knees suddenly weak, an icy chill gripping her heart. She hardly noticed when Dalar climbed onto her lap. His frightened trembling forced her to put aside her own fears and focus on her son. He was small for his age, too small, like a seedling struggling for sunlight at the base of an overgrown oak. She held him close, stroking his smooth black hair and murmuring words of comfort.

Her glance fell on the gleaming utensils beside her plate. The knife's silver blade was delicately engraved, its edge keen enough to slice tough parchment.

Not yet, she told herself. Soon perhaps, but not yet. Endure, Valaran. Endure, for him.

Chapter 10
# Fortress without Walls

he dawn lit up a plain teeming with nomad horse-men—the very tribes that had destroyed Juramona, a walled town defended by a professional garrison.

Tol, keenly aware of his own tiny, amateur force, ordered his companies to form for a quick march back to camp. The kneeling men rose wearily to their feet. The nomads kept a wary eye on the Juramonans as they moved away.

Tol was watching the nomads just as carefully. "All companies will retire in line," he said. "Keep your faces to the enemy!"

The Ergothians withdrew slowly. The nearest nomads followed, maintaining the distance between the two groups. When the rear of the militia reached the edge of their camp, the noncombatants gathered behind them. Civilians and soldiers alike backed through camp, trampling their own tents.

Zala found herself next to Tylocost. "Where are we going?" she asked.

"Hylo Bay?" he suggested.

The rear ranks reached the ashes of Juramona. When the front ranks, those closest to the enemy, were treading on ashes, Tol called a halt. With the ruined town at their backs, they could not be outflanked; no riders would dare try to enter the tangle of broken walls and burned timbers.

To their credit, the Ergothians stood ready, pikes leveled. The noncombatants, clutching their pitiful belongings, huddled behind them, some sobbing, others tight-lipped. Fear, the morning's heat, and the ash churned up by their passage had soldiers and survivors panting. Tol called for water. The bleating of a ram's horn sent him up onto a pile of scorched masonry for a better view.

A small group of riders left the main body of nomads galloping forward. Some wore brightly burnished helmets, no doubt taken from slain imperial officers. One fellow rode ahead of the rest and blew again on a curved ram's horn.

"Sounds like they want to parley," Tol reported, coming down from his perch. "Tylocost, stay here. If there's treachery, command falls to you."

"How nice." The Silvanesti continued to wipe the grime from his sweaty face.

Tol shouldered through his exhausted, doomed men, with Zala following.

"You should stay here," he told her.

"I know," she replied, not slackening her pace.

The small group of nomad riders had formed themselves into a semicircle. Three helmeted figures sat in the center—the three chiefs, Tol surmised: Tokasin, Mattohoc, and Ulur. Once Tol and Zala drew near, the two ends of the curved line swept forward, closing the circle.

The nomads were lean and sun-browned, dressed mostly in leather, with bits of captured armor here and there. Some had the fair hair and long jaws of high plainsmen, others the burnished bronze complexions and tightly curled hair of the northern seafarers. Unlike the forest tribes, who decorated themselves with feathers, bones, and seashells, the plains nomads favored metal adornments. They traded extensively with Hylo, Ergoth, and Silvanost, obtaining silver and golden trinkets from their settled neighbors. Tol observed quite a lot of jade. The only source of the mineral he knew was in dwarf territory; the plainsmen must be dealing with Thoradin, too. All the nomads in the group were male.

The youngest of the three chiefs was a rough but striking rogue with a shoulder-sweeping mane of red hair and a thick mustache. Despite the warmth of the morning, he wore a fine, heavy mantle of fox fur, whose color matched his hair perfectly. On his right was an older, thick-bodied man, with a bull neck, dark skin, and a lumpy, shaven head. The third chief was older still, but lean and tough as whipcord. His iron gray hair was twisted into numerous long braids, his beard divided into three plaits, held tight by jade beads woven into them.

Although he could hear Zala's rapid breathing behind him, Tol felt surprisingly calm. This was his element, matching wits against dangerous foes. The despair that had gripped him on beholding the vast nomad host vanished. Time to show these barbarians who they were dealing with.

Zala noticed the change in his attitude. Tol's back had straightened, his expression hardened, and a new spring was now his step. She couldn't fathom it. In her head, a single word pounded over and over: run. Only by sheer force of will did she keep her eyes fixed on the waiting chiefs and fight the urge to bolt and not stop running till the walls of home surrounded her again.

Tol murmured, without looking at her, "Calm yourself. We're not lost yet."

He strode forward, halting only when they were within arm's reach of the red-haired chief's horse; its roan color matched its rider's furs and hair. Raising a hand, he greeted the three chiefs Dom-shu fashion.

"You have come to speak. Speak."

The red-haired chief leaned forward on his horse's neck and grinned unpleasantly. He'd cut quite a dashing figure until then. The image was spoiled by a mouthful of crooked yellow teeth.

"I wanted to see who'd put spines in these dirt-foots," he said. "Must be you, Ergoth."

"I command here."

"You've put up a good fight," said the oldest of the three chiefs, tugging on one of the three plaits of his beard. "For this, we're willing to let you and your people leave this place. It is ours now."

Zala's gasp was audible only to Tol. He said, "We are where we must be. It is you who must go."

Red Hair laughed. "Who are you, Ergoth?"

Tol gave his name and the dark-skinned chief, heretofore silent, exclaimed, "I heard Tolandruth was dead, slain by the treacherous slavemaster he called emperor!"

The chiefs exchanged glances. Braided Beard said, "Since you have given us your name, I will speak ours. I am Ulur, chief of the Tall Grass Riders." He indicated his burly colleague. "This is Mattohoc, chief of the Sand Treaders."

The dark-skinned nomad grunted in acknowledgment. Red Hair spoke for himself, saying, "I am Tokasin, chosen chief of the Firepath people, and leader of this warband."

Warband he called it. There must be ten thousand nomads at his back, a greater concentration of plainsmen than had ever been known.

"My itch has been scratched," Tokasin announced to no one in particular. "Tolandruth or not, put down your arms and depart, or we'll trample you into the ashes of your city!"

"It is you who must depart, Tokasin," Tol said coolly. "I have come back from exile to drive every marauder from the empire. Return to your lands in the east and I will not punish you further." He gestured with his chin at the ruined town behind him. "Many injustices have been inflicted on your people in the past by the empire. I will count the sack of Juramona against that tally, but here your cruelties must end. Go home!"

Ulur and Tokasin laughed at Tol's bold demand. Mattohoc did not. He regarded the Ergothian thoughtfully.

Tokasin ended the parley with a ringing boast: "I will build a tower of skulls here, and yours will sit at the top, Ergoth!"

The three chiefs wheeled their horses in tight circles. They and the rest of their party began to ride back to their waiting warriors. The two heralds blew their horns, ending the truce.

Tol started back to his people, with Zala pointedly guarding his back. She never took her eyes off the nomads.

"Are we going to die?" Zala muttered.

"Certainly," he replied. "But only the gods know when."

The Ergothian pikemen parted ranks, allowing Tol and Zala to pass.

Tylocost hailed them. "Welcome back, my lord. Did they surrender?"

Tol repeated the gist of the discussion, with Zala adding Tokasin's remark about building a tower of skulls. The tired militiamen stirred anxiously, like a herd of elk scenting a panther.

Frowning, Tol loudly declared, "Our fate is in our hands, not theirs! They're not sure of victory, else they would not have bothered to parley. Companies, stand to!" The Juramonans took up their pikes.

Tol went to the rear of the formation and spoke to the unarmed refugees huddled in the ruins. With the enemy host before them, all must play a part in the coming battle. He told any who could stand and bear a weapon to do so.

No one argued. The old and infirm, the sick, and the injured—all shuffled into place, adding some three hundred bodies to the lines. When the stock of salvaged pikes ran out, Tol armed them with axes, billhooks, scythes, and any other long-handled weapon or tool that could be found.

Tol walked down the line with Tylocost and Zala behind him, speaking not only to the new recruits, but to all his people.

"Keep your eyes forward. Pay no heed to what's behind you. All that matters is the enemy before you. No one is to break ranks without orders. The surest way to kill yourself and the rest of us is to open our lines, so keep your heads. Don't fence with the enemy. Keep your points to them, and let them exhaust themselves trying to break through our wall of spears."

He told Tylocost to take the right, the north, where the ground was higher, the ruins steeper.

The Silvanesti's pale eyes narrowed. Abandoning his usual flippant tone he snapped, "You need not give me the easier position to defend!"

"That is my order."

"Well, at least keep the half-breed with you. She'll only get in my way."

Zala glared at him. She'd never intended to leave Tol's side, and all of them knew it.

Saluting with his sword, Tylocost said, "Here's to luck, my lord. I trust the gods have granted you an everlasting supply."

The relative calm was shattered by the screeching cries that heralded a nomad attack. The plainsmen were coming now and at a gallop. A ripple of nervous fear passed through the Ergothian ranks, but Tol and his officers speedily moved to quash it.

The dead-on charge puzzled Tol. It would have been much easier for the nomads to stand off and rain arrows upon the Ergothians. Instead, Tokasin was gambling on a quick, crushing victory, using a hammer when a needle would do.

The morning sun bathed the nomads in golden light. They were charging directly into its glare. This seemed to cause them little difficulty, but five paces from the Juramonan spearpoints they wrenched their horses hard around. It was obvious the militia would not simply break and run in terror, and the riders had no intention of impaling their animals.

Just to provoke them, Tol ordered a single company—his Seventh, the deserters—forward just far enough to drive the riders back. Some slower nomads were plowed down by the phalanx of pikes, but most danced out of reach. When other nomads poured in to attack the exposed sides of Tol's company, he swiftly withdrew his men again.

A deadly rhythm ensued. The nomads charged, stopped, and the Ergothians sallied out to drive them back. The strange dance went on all morning, a tense, exhausting business, where the slightest misstep could mean disaster. The sun mounted higher in the sky, and the defenders of Juramona prayed Corij would send a scorching day. The militia had access to the town's wells; children brought water to those fighting. The plainsmen had only the water they carried, and this was soon gone.

The god was pleased to answer their prayers. The heat increased; the yellow dust of the Eastern Hundred choked every throat, coated man and horse alike. The Ergothians drank deep and hung on.

Two hundred dismounted nomad archers gathered well out of pike range and began loosing volleys of arrows at the closely packed militia. Their shields went up, along with makeshift covers of scavenged planks, canvas, and wicker. The standoff continued.

Zala wiped gritty sweat from her forehead with an equally gritty hand and drew Tol's attention to Tylocost. The elf sat atop a broken column in full view of the enemy, legs crossed and floppy hat tied securely under his chin.

She pronounced him a fool, but Tol, shaking his head, said, "He is one the finest generals of this age."

"You beat him."

"I was fortunate. Even the gods can be undone by an un-expected turn of fate."

Horns blasted to the right and left. A solid wall of horsemen, brandishing swords, rumbled past the archers and started up the hill toward the center of the Ergothian line. As they had done this many times before (though never with so many riders), no one was overly concerned. The militiamen—once craftsmen, traders, and merchants, now increasingly seasoned as fighters—braced for the onslaught.

Ten paces away, the massive column picked up speed.

"They're charging home!" Tol said, looking left and right along his lines. "Dig in! Stand firm!" He drew Number Six.

Three paces was as close as the nomads could approach and still have room to turn their ponies aside. That limit was reached—and still they came on. A spontaneous shout went up from the Ergothians, a third of whom were kneeling with their pikes butted against the ground.

"Juramona!" cried a thousand hoarse voices.

The nomads hit the Seventh and the companies on each side, the Third and the Eighth. Sheer weight of numbers bowled the Ergothians down. Many were trampled. An equal number of nomads and their horses were shredded by the hedge of spearpoints.

The Ergothian line was eight ranks deep. In moments the riders had bludgeoned halfway through. The clang of iron, the screams of the dying and their killers rose to a deafening roar. A nomad herald raised a horn to his lips and blew, but not a note could be heard over the unimaginable din.

A flash of color caught Tol's eye. Red-haired Tokasin was

flank to flank with his men, driving them forward.

Tol pushed through his tightly packed men, heading for the nomad chief. More than once he fended off attacks, cut at enemy riders, and felt the whiff of a blade through his hair, but he was making progress toward his goal. Then, a horse's hindquarters swung around and caught him full in the chest. Down he went.

Unshod hooves kicked at his ribs and back. He scrambled to his feet, only to find himself directly in the path of a sword-wielding horseman about to cleave his head in two. Suddenly, a Juramonan thrust a fire-blackened spearhead into the no-mad's neck. Tol was astonished to see his savior was Wilfik. All this time he must have been hiding, in the ruins.

The dishonored guardsmen said nothing. Neither did Tol. Battle drew them apart again.

Tol continued to fight his way through the press toward Tokasin. When a riderless pony came across his path, he swung onto its back and bawled a challenge. Whooping with joy, Tokasin spurred his red horse at Tol.

The two horses collided hard enough to loosen both men's teeth. Tol thrust overhand with Number Six. The chief leaned out of reach and aimed straight at his opponent's eyes. Tol parried, noting the nomad chief wielded an Ergothian cavalry saber.

Tol urged his borrowed pony forward. Seizing the collar of Tokasin's fox mantle, he drove his hilt into Tokasin's jaw. The chief's head snapped back, but he kept his seat. Tol hit him again just as their horses stumbled apart. Nose streaming blood, Tokasin fell sideways off his horse.

There was no opportunity for Tol to push his advantage. A heavy blow fell across his shoulders. Instantly his arms went numb, an icy chill racing to the tips of his fingers. He knew he was falling—the dust-veiled sun wheeled past his gaze—but he didn't even feel himself hit the ground.

All sound ceased. Horses towered over him, pirouetting in the dance of battle. Blades and spears continued to fall. Yet he could hear nothing. He thought this must be what it was like to die.

You never see the blade that kills you, Egrin used to say.

That homily was meant to reassure nervous new *shilder*. Now Tol knew it was true.

He became aware of a shadowy figure standing over him. He thought it was Tokasin, come to finish him off, but soon realized the figure was in fact defending him from any who drew too near. Vision blurred by the stunning blow and the roiling dust, he couldn't make out his protector's identity.

Tol struggled to rise, cursing his awkwardness. The figure looked down at him, and he caught a glimpse of a bushy black beard and formidable brows over pale eyes.

Wilfik.

A set of hooves suddenly came plummeting toward Tol's head, and he had to roll swiftly aside. Continuing the motion, he retrieved Number Six from the dirt and sprang to his feet. When he got himself upright, Wilfik was gone.

Tol was a good nine paces from his own line. The nomads had broken his half of the militia in two, driving the right portion northward, back to Tylocost's position. Pride swelled in Tol as he saw the remaining Ergothians withdrawing in good order to the stump of a tower that had once graced the wall of Juramona.

Coated with dust, Tol was indistinguishable from the mounted foes around him. This fact saved his life. The nomads took him for a fallen comrade, as no other Ergothian had dared break their line. He wended his way through the milling horsemen, felling only a sole nomad who tried to stop him.

When he reached the broken tower, the militia regarded him in breathless wonder. They thought he'd been killed.

Tol nodded tiredly. "I thought so, too. Where's Wilfik? I have him to thank for my rescue."

The soldiers regarded him blankly. Tol said the disgraced soldier had fended off nomads until he could get back to his feet.

The captain of the Eighth Company shook his head. "It couldn't have been Wilfik, my lord. I saw him slain before you were unhorsed. A nomad blade took his head from his shoulders."

If the captain was certain of what he'd seen, no less certain was Tol. Apparently, even after death, Wilfik had been determined to redeem himself.

A furious blast of rams' horns ended the discussion. Plainsmen wheeled their ponies about and flowed back down the hill. The slope before the broken tower was heaped with the slain and wounded from both sides. Injured horses fought to stand. Men cried out for water, or mercy.

One of the pikemen near Tol cried, "Mishas spare us!"

He pointed. The nomads were re-forming, plainly preparing to charge again. The brave defenders of Juramona could not withstand another assault.

Before panic could take hold, another blast of horns sounded, this time from the far right of the nomad host. A sizable body of horsemen faced about and rode off to the west. The remaining nomads milled about in confusion, an emotion mirrored on the faces of their foes.

Tol shaded his eyes from the late afternoon sun, trying to see what was afoot. At the same time, he warned his people to stand fast.

Yet another fanfare sounded on the left, from east of the ruins. A roar went up in the distance, which was quickly drowned out by the thundering sound of horses approaching at the gallop.

A battered pikeman sank to his knees, blood draining from his face. "We're dead!" he moaned. "More nomads have come!"

The leather-clad host before Tol's position wavered, then spontaneously broke apart. Half the riders turned their steeds east and galloped away. The rest scattered to the winds.

The horns sounded again, closer, and a great rush of relief surged through Tol's veins. He lifted Number Six high, shouting, "Those are *brass* trumpets! Ergothians! Riders of the Great Horde!"

Arrayed in the famous wedge formation created by Ackal Ergot himself, four hordes of imperial cavalry passed through the confused ranks of the nomads like a knife into a sack of grain. The remaining plainsmen resisted briefly, then they too scattered.

The armored wedge drove straight across the field. Any

plainsmen in its way were ruthlessly sabered. Before the sun touched the western horizon, no living enemy remained.

From their last-ditch position at the base of the shattered tower, the weary militia knew they'd been given back their lives. Without orders, the men sank to the ground. A few were asleep as soon as their heads touched the burned turf.

A score of Riders peeled off from the main horde and cantered toward Tol. The first face he saw was Egrin's. A broad grin split Tol's face. The grin became wide-eyed surprise when he spotted Egrin's companions. Riding beside the former marshal of Juramona was a gray-haired warrior in an old-fashioned pot helmet. All the Riders wore armor twenty years out of fashion, and bore the standard of the Plains Panthers horde.

Egrin reined up and dismounted. Tol limped to him and they clasped arms.

"Never have I been so glad to see your face!" Tol declared.

"And I yours, my lord," Egrin replied warmly.

Tol asked how they'd found him, and Egrin gave a rare grin. "All the raiders in the Eastern Hundred had gathered here," he said. "Why else would they return to a despoiled town but to kill Lord Tolandruth?"

The gray-haired warrior riding beside Egrin was a big, clean-shaven fellow mounted on a fine gray gelding. The Rider had a familiar, misshapen nose.

"Lord Pagas!" Tol said, saluting the commander of the Plains Panthers, with whom he had campaigned long ago in the Great Green. "You looked like Corij himself, coming to our rescue!"

Pagas looked pleased by the praise but made no reply. A warrior of long service and steadfast courage, he had a high, nasal voice, the result of his misshapen nose. Although the injury had been honorably received in battle against centaurs, Pagas found his childish voice a severe embarrassment, and spoke little.

The Plains Panthers was one of the landed hordes, not part of the regular imperial army. All were former Riders of the Great Horde, who now lived and worked on country estates.

In time of crisis, an emperor could summon the landed hordes to his service. Ackal V had never called the Panthers, nor any other landed horde, to war. Unlike his full-time warriors, Ackal couldn't bully the gentry, nor chop off their heads if they displeased him.

"He's losing the war," Pagas said, referring to the emperor. Word had spread about the defeats inflicted by the bakali. The debacle at Eagle's Ford was only the latest in a series of blunders.

The lizard-men were now across the Dalti, Egrin related. Whether they would attack Daltigoth was still an open question. Thus far, they had not directly assaulted any walled city, as they lacked siege equipment. But west and south of the capital lay the richest land in the empire, the very heart of Ergoth. The region's farms and herds fed the entire country. What was more, the sea route to the Gulf lay that way, too. If the bakali ravaged it, or worse, simply occupied it, the empire would be done. The cities would starve. Ergoth would shrivel.

Tylocost's half of the Juramona militia marched over, providing Lord Pagas and his retinue with the shocking sight of a Silvanesti in command of Ergothians. Tol asked Egrin if he'd received word of Kiya, but the old warrior had not seen the Dom-shu woman since she'd departed for Hylo.

Pagas ordered his men to pursue the defeated nomads. Another landed horde, the Firebrands, marched half a day behind the Panthers. When they arrived, the Firebrands would occupy the site of Juramona and await new orders.

Once these dispositions had been made, Pagas dismounted. He drew his warrior's dagger and held it aloft in salute.

"My lord," he piped, reddening at the sound of his voice, "I pledge my honor and loyalty to you! Command us, and we shall follow you, even into the Abyss!"

It was a stirring pledge, but Tol heard none of it. Leaning against Egrin's war-horse, he'd passed out cold.

Chapter 11
# Small Assistance

How could the same journey take twice as long on the return trip? This question was much on Kiya's mind as she finally reached the fringes of the Eastern Hundred, on her way back to Tol.

She had arrived in Hylo City after a difficult three-day journey. At one point, surrounded by nomads, she had her pony galloping flat-out through a forest of ferns. The jeering plainsmen took her for an Ergothian, fleeing for her life. Kiya would never forget the looks on their faces when she pulled out her saber, unintentionally concealed by her rough woolen cloak. She relieved one nomad of his right arm and sent him flying from his horse. The barbarian on her left reached for his sword, and received Kiya's point in the throat.

The remaining nomads fell back, regrouped, and came on again, cursing instead of laughing. She wove through the trees, dodging arrows. She hoped her pursuers would get careless and tangle with a sapling, but the nomads were born to the saddle and maneuvered skillfully around every tree.

She finally escaped them by resorting to a deed so outrageous it paralyzed her enemies with astonishment. She found herself on a bluff overlooking the Old Port Water, the stream that flowed north into the kender town of the same name. She was trapped, with a twenty-pace drop to the water before her and jeering nomads close behind. Her pursuers pulled up and approached at a trot.

Kiya was out of ideas—save one. Whipping her cloak over her pony's head, so he wouldn't shy, she thumped her heels hard into his flanks. He bolted forward. His hooves thumped a handful of times on the turf, then horse and woman sailed into space, turning a slow somersault on their way down to the slow-flowing water.

She knew the river was deep near the town of Old Port. Seagoing ships often sheltered there when storms raked Hylo Bay. The question in Kiya's mind during her breathless plummet was, was she downstream far enough for the deep water? If not, her life would soon be over.

The pony hit the green water half a heartbeat ahead of the Dom-shu woman. A tall fountain of spray shot skyward. Kiya landed feet first, and the impact numbed her legs all the way to her hips. Down she plunged, deeper and deeper. Deep enough—now, back to the surface!

Kiya swam to the north shore. The pony was there already, thrashing its way up the mudflat. The nomads on the bluff finally overcame their shock and sent some arrows flickering toward her, but these landed in the water far behind.

The remainder of her journey to Hylo City was not only dull but frustrating. The kender capital lay northwest, she knew, but the few kender she encountered as she made her way through the countryside either shunned her, or gave conflicting directions. That was only the beginning of her frustrations with the kender.

An entire day had been required to persuade Queen Casberry to lend aid. The kender queen looked exactly as Kiya remembered her from their last meeting more than a decade and a half before. Tiny, even by the standards of her race, Casberry's face was seamed by a thousand fine lines, like an apple left too long in the sun. Her hair was snowy white, pulled back in a tight bun, but her brilliant green eyes were lively as a child's. Kiya couldn't even begin to guess her age.

Casberry explained (at length) that she held Lord Tolandruth in high esteem for vanquishing the monster XimXim and for clearing her country of Tarsan mercenaries. Because of this high regard, she would join the fight against the nomads for a mere one hundred gold pieces per day.

Paul B. Thompson and Tonya C. Cook

Lacking her sister's patience and skill at haggling, Kiya simply agreed and insisted they depart the next morning. The matriarch waved aside this ridiculous deadline. The Royal Loyal Militia must be given time to assemble.

Casberry made no proclamations, sent forth no heralds, yet in two days' time a large number of kender gathered in the square before the royal residence (a dilapidated three-story house no one could call a palace). To Kiya's jaundiced eye, the Royal Loyal Militia resembled a market day mob more than a military force. Their uniforms comprised matching green leggings and scale shirts; the remainder of their attire followed no pattern at all. Most of the kender were armed with short swords, but Kiya saw some carrying bows and a few bearing swords obviously sized for beings at least twice their height. Still, they were what Tol wanted, and Kiya vowed she would deliver them, come what may.

Now, three days into the return journey, they had at last reached the Eastern Hundred. The slowness of the return had nothing to do with the nomads—they had encountered none thus far—and everything to do with Queen Casberry and the Army of Hylo.

In addition to the Royal Loyal Militia, the queen was accompanied by her Household Guard, a band even more unlikely than the Royal Loyals. The Householders, some two hundred strong, were foreigners, hired blades of dubious distinction, whose ranks included humans, kender from outside Hylo, a dwarf healer who prescribed potatoes for every injury or ailment, and a centaur standard bearer whose stench was so strong he was made to march at the rear, defeating the purpose of giving him the banner of Hylo in the first place, although no one would dream of hurting his feelings by asking him to relinquish it, Casberry said. The Householders were armed with whatever they fancied: spears, axes, swords, even garden rakes. When Kiya saw a group shouldering push brooms, she protested.

"They're outlanders, too poor to pay for weapons," Casberry explained. In fact, she'd been throwing dice with the foreign kender and had won all their money. They'd pawned their arms to eat.

"Don't you pay them?" Kiya asked, growing tired of endless kender peculiarities.

"I pay them to march and fight. If they don't march or fight, they don't get paid. Next payday's not till New Moon Day, though."

The Household Guard marched directly behind the queen. After them came the Royal Loyal Militia, whose exact number Kiya had given up trying to calculate. Kender soldiers left when the mood struck and rejoined the column later, coming and going whenever they pleased. Kiya estimated there were between four and five hundred of these erratic kender.

Even more than the lackadaisical habits of the kender or the innumerable chests of flamboyant attire Casberry insisted on carting along, it was the Royal Conveyance that kept their progress to a crawl.

The Royal Conveyance, the only way Queen Casberry would travel, was a sedan chair borne on the shoulders of two identically brawny humans she called Front and Back. One was dark-skinned and wore a gold headband. The other was fair-haired and sported a bull tattoo on his chest. Kiya wasn't sure which was which. Perhaps it depended upon who was leading and who was following. The sedan chair itself was made of oak and cedar, ornately carved, inlaid with gold, and very heavy.

With Kiya in the lead—and leading kender was like herding squirrels—the Army of Hylo had wound its way through the hills and forests of the kender realm and into the Eastern Hundred. Once within the empire, they saw ample signs the nomad raiders had passed by but encountered no resistance. One battle-shocked Ergothian farmer, picking through the remains of his home, spied the Household Guard and fled, screaming. Kiya knew exactly how he felt.

Scouting ahead, the Dom-shu woman paused by a wide stream. Her pony lowered its head to drink. Sunshine sparkled off the flowing water as it rippled over well-worn boulders. The opposite bank was dotted with trees. Although not the friendly giants of her home, the slender poplars and oaks still allowed Kiya to imagine herself back in the Great Green where life made sense, with the cool green of trees above her and the softness of moss and fallen leaves beneath her bare feet.

From her mounted vantage, she spotted the telltale yellow soil of the Eastern Hundred, exposed several paces downstream. She urged her horse in that direction and found a wide trail trampled into the green turf. Horsemen had been through here. Many horsemen, and not long ago.

There was a matching trail on the other side of the creek. The riders had come from the east. As no organized bodies of imperial troops occupied the region, the horsemen must have been nomads. Kiya had to warn Casberry their enemies were near.

Then a remarkable thing happened. The sky was a clear blue, dotted with only a few small, puffy white clouds, but a thunderclap of considerable strength suddenly rolled over the woodland. The sound was strong enough to frighten a flock of birds into taking wing and cause Kiya's pony to shy.

At the spot where Kiya had watered her horse were four of Casberry's Householders. A human and a kender were filling waterskins. Another kender stood waist-deep in the stream searching (he said) for gold; a second human was staring nervously at the sky. All had heard the thunderclap.

Kiya sent the nervous human jogging off to warn the queen of nomads in the area. She sent the other Householders back to the column. All went except the gold prospector. That kender, his large ears protruding like window shutters, turned his head slowly from side to side.

"I hear horses," he announced.

Kiya drew her sword. Before she could ask where the sound was coming from, a gust of wind rushed through the trees, causing her horse to shy again, and three riders burst from the trees on the western bank.

The three were nomads, dressed in buckskins and woven twig armor. They were bent low over their mounts' necks, horses galloping hard. Two swung wide and rode around the sword-wielding Dom-shu woman without even pausing.

Startled by this tactic, Kiya concentrated on the remaining fellow. His horse reared when she slashed at him. She missed the man but cut his reins, and he toppled backward into the water. In the blink of an eye, his horse was gone, galloping after the other two.

Jumping from her horse, Kiya pressed her saber to the fallen nomad's throat.

He threw up his hands and cried, "Save me!" With a terrified glance not at his conqueror, but at the shore from whence he'd come, he added, "We were attacked by fell magic!"

She dragged the gibbering man back to her companions, put him in the care of two kender from the Household Guard, then told the queen what had happened.

Casberry, clad in a brilliant, pink-and-gold striped shirt, squinted down at the prisoner from the extra height afforded her by the Royal Conveyance. In response to her high-pitched, imperious demand, the nomad told his tale.

The nomad and his comrades from the Skyhorse tribe had been foraging when they came upon a stone blockhouse by the Juramona road. These blockhouses, dotting the roads at regular intervals, were meant to serve as havens for imperial couriers. The Skyhorse men knew such couriers carried fine weapons and gold. The door was bolted from the inside, so they surrounded the blockhouse and yelled at its occupants to surrender. No one answered.

Undeterred, the nomads were gathering kindling so they could burn the wooden door when a clap of thunder sounded from the clear sky. The four of their number nearest the door were knocked flat by the blast. The others tried to come to their aid, but the windfall kindling they'd been collecting suddenly leaped into the air and hurled itself at them. When stones loosened themselves from the ground and joined the barrage, the nomads fled.

"Your Majesty, we should investigate," Kiya said. "Someone important may be inside this blockhouse." Only the rich or the noble could afford to have a mage in such a place.

Casberry tapped a long, bony finger against her yellow teeth. The map of fine lines on her wizened face lifted. "Might be a reward in it," she mused. "I'll go myself. Pick up your feet, Front and Back!"

The nomad captive was left to six Hyloans, who wrestled the prisoner to the ground. He flailed his arms and legs, but several kender sat on him as others tore off his clothes. Howling curses, the nomad promised terrible retribution for any violence done to him. The kender ignored him. When he was stripped to the skin and pinned to the ground on his back, a pot of red paint was produced, along with several brushes. The kender proceeded to paint the man red from head to toe.

When they were done, they released him. He rolled quickly to his feet.

"Is that it?" He laughed nervously. "Is that all?"

Kiya suppressed a shudder. "It's enough. Look."

The nomad peered at his reflection in the creek. The red paint, together with his pale blond hair, made him look like some insane wraith. Splashing water on himself, he quickly discovered the paint would not come off. He scrubbed himself with handfuls of sand, but the result was same.

This was the punishment known in Hylo as the "Judgment of the True Skin," usually inflicted on kender who refused to leave home and wander as royal law prescribed. The paint was said to be permanent, but knowing how the little people exaggerated, Kiya reckoned it would probably wear off in a few days or weeks. Still, it was not an experience she cared to have. Anyone the nomad encountered would flee in horror at the sight of him, if they didn't slay him as a monster first.

The man had begun to draw blood with his vigorous scrubbing, and he continued to scream at them all. Kiya pointed her sword at him and told him to go. To emphasize her words, the kender began tossing mud from the creekbank at the painted man.

"You're crazy!" the nomad shrieked, backing away. "All of you—you're crazy!"

"Crazy as kender," Kiya agreed.

Defeated, humiliated, he scrambled up the opposite shore and crashed away through the underbrush. They could measure the naked man's progress by the curses that echoed through the trees every time he encountered a thorny obstacle.

Casberry's army meanwhile straggled onward through

the woods. The slender trees finally thinned, revealing the imperial road from Caergoth to Hylo, called by many the Plucked Path. It had been built by ogre slaves, who literally tore trees out of the ground with their hands. Not a paved road like the Ackal Path, its surface was dirt, layered with crushed seashells brought all the way from the Gulf of Ergoth.

Before her mount broke through the trees onto the road, the Dom-shu woman heard loud voices ahead. She tapped heels to her pony's sides, wondering what new insanity she was about to experience.

Casberry's bearers stood in the center of the road. The kender queen was leaning forward in her chair, shaking a finger at a gray granite blockhouse and demanding its occupant come out. Around her chair gathered the humans and kender of her Household Guard. Royal Loyals lolled in the greenery on either side of the path.

The blockhouse was a massive structure, two stories high, with a flat roof and arrow slits for windows. The only entrance faced the road and was a squat door of dark oak, strapped with bronze plates. A scattering of broken kindling, and the tracks left by nomad horses supported the story told them by the painted man.

Kiya rode closer to the door and hallooed loudly. A faint stirring sounded from within.

"Are you Ergothian?" she called. "Don't be afraid! We go to join the army of Lord Tolandruth, camped at Juramona!"

More sounds of movement within, but no response. Kiya dismounted. The door was inset within the large blocks. She glanced at the motley bunch at her back and added, "This is the army of Queen Casberry, of Hylo. They've come as allies of the empire."

*Go away!*

Flinching, Kiya backed up a step. The whispery, insistent voice seemed to come from right beside her.

*Depart now. Go at once!*

The command had the opposite effect on the stubborn Dom-shu. She hammered on the bronze door plates with her sword pommel and demanded that whoever was inside come out. Each blow boomed hollowly. The papery voice did not speak again.

Casberry appeared at Kiya's side. So quietly did she move the Dom-shu had no notion of her presence until, drawing back her arm for another blow, she smacked the queen on the top of the head.

Kiya apologized. "I'm afraid it would take a battering ram to get this door open!"

The queen planted bony fists on her hips and took in the door and surrounding structure with a narrow-eyed glare. "I'll get us in," she announced. Turning, she shouted, "Bonny Waterwide! You and Rufus, come here."

Two kender emerged from the soft ferns. Bonny Waterwide was rather tall (for a kender), wearing a leather vest and trousers and sporting blue-black hair gathered into a long topknot. Rufus had short, spiky red hair framing a pale face. He was spinning a toy top on the palm of his hand.

"First one of you to get in there gets a gold piece," the queen said.

"Three gold pieces," countered Bonny promptly.

"Two gold pieces."

"Two gold pieces, and I get to ride in your chair for a day."

The queen made a face, but agreed.

Bonny grinned, showing long, yellow teeth. "Done!"

Their haggling complete, Rufus quickly began his assault on the blockhouse. Inserting his fingers and bare toes into various arrow slits, he managed to climb the sloping wall to the roof. He lifted the cap off the chimney and climbed down into the flue.

"Good job!" Kiya said.

Hardly had the words left her mouth when a loud yell reverberated from the chimney. Thinking poor Rufus was being gutted, Kiya started for the bolted door, but Casberry's tiny hand closed around her wrist.

"Wait," the queen said.

A gout of soot erupted from the chimney. Simultaneously, a loud boom sounded and a red-haired projectile shot skyward. Rufus hit the top of a larch tree, then descended, flopping from branch to branch, finally landing in a cloud of soot on the wildflowers beside the road. After an instant of surprised silence, nearby kender cheered. A Royal Loyal rolled Rufus over and announced he still breathed, but was out cold.

A tapping, pinging sound brought attention back to the blockhouse. Bonny Waterwide had been busy gathering shell fragments from the road and now was tossing these, one at a time, at the structure. Several pieces flew through the arrow slits.

Keeping up the odd bombardment, she stealthily approached the door. She drew a metal object from her scabbard, not a thin sword but a slender iron rod.

In between tossing her seashell fragments, Bonny measured off a section of the rod, then bent it, with some difficulty, over her knee. She spaced off a longer length and bent the rod again at a different angle.

Kiya queried the queen with a glance. Casberry merely looked wise.

Bonny tossed all her remaining shells up the side of the blockhouse. They cascaded down, bouncing and clicking off the close-fitting stone blocks. Before the sound died, she had slipped the rod under the door and twisted it upwards. She stepped down hard on the upraised end of the rod. There was a distinct clank as the door was lifted up slightly, and then Bonny pushed the portal inward.

With a whoop, Kiya rushed forward, sword out. Much of the Household Guard followed.

A wall of wind erupted from the dark interior, sweeping Bonny off her feet. The larger, heavier Kiya leaned into the blast. With great effort, she dragged her feet forward until she could grasp the doorjamb. A lone figure stood inside the blockhouse. The only illumination came from the arrow slits, striping the interior with narrow lanes of dark and light.

The gusting wind suddenly eased, and curious kender scrambled past Kiya. The wind died completely when two knelt on all fours behind the stranger while others bowled him over. Like a pack of puppies, the kender swarmed over the fallen man. Kiya's sword was at his throat in the next moment.

"Peace, peace! I am not your enemy!" he cried.

Kiya seized him by the front of his robe and shoved him outside into the sunlight.

With much injured dignity, he swept shell fragments and dirt from his red silk robe. He was a tall fellow, and thin, with tightly curled sand-colored hair and a short beard. Every finger bore an ornate, jeweled ring.

"There's no need for violence," the Red Robe said. "I told you, I'm not your enemy!"

"That's for us to decide. Who are you?" asked Kiya.

He refused to say. Several kender hands began reaching for his rings, and he drew back, closing his fists tightly. "Each and every ring is warded! Touch them, and there will be dire consequences!"

Now he had his audience's undivided attention. The kender demanded they be allowed to see "dire consequences" immediately. Only Kiya's threats silenced them long enough for her to continue her questioning. The wizard still would not tell her anything about himself or his purpose, but kept insisting he was not their enemy.

He began fingering the large opal ring on his left forefinger. The kender perked up, obviously hoping for a dire consequence, but Kiya laid the flat of her sword tip on his wrist.

"Stop what you're doing, or I'll chop off your hands."

Her calmly delivered threat shook him, but he hissed, "You have no idea who you're meddling with, barbarian!"

"No, I don't. So tell me your name."

Heavy silence ensued. Surrounded by armed, insatiably curious kender and a forester woman with a thirsty blade, and with bands of hostile nomads in the vicinity, the Red Robe made his decision.

"I am Helbin, chosen chief of the Red Robes of Daltigoth. You mentioned Lord Tolandruth; you may take me to him."

Kiya recognized his name. "You're not one of Husband's enemies," she said, sheathing her sword. "What are you doing so far from the city?"

"I cannot divulge my purpose, except to Lord Tolandruth himself."

Kiya shrugged, secure in the knowledge that Tol would know how to handle the mage.

After Helbin gathered his possessions and was put under guard, the army prepared to move on. Several kender lifted the still-groggy, soot-covered Rufus onto a horse. Casberry returned to her sedan chair. Immediately an argument erupted between the queen and Bonny Waterwide. Bonny claimed her payment of a day's ride in the Royal Conveyance. The queen reminded her no particular day had been specified.

"So you'll just have to wait," Casberry finished with a satisfied smile.

When they were finally underway, Kiya ruminated on the fact that half a dozen nomads had failed to draw the wizard from his hiding place, but a single kender had succeeded. Maybe Tol's idea to recruit Casberry and her army wasn't as ridiculous as it seemed. But what was Helbin doing in these parts? Whether or not he was a respectable member of the Red Robe order, Kiya distrusted anyone from Daltigoth. In her opinion, people from the capital were either Ackal V's lackeys or his collaborators.

She would keep an eye on Helbin. At the first hint of treachery, she would act. There would be no humiliating red paint for the Red Robe. If he played her false, he would die.

Chapter 12
# A Fatal Slip

The bakali were across the Dalti.

The news flashed through the streets and squares of Daltigoth. No one knew who first delivered the awful tidings, but within a day, everyone in the capital had heard them. Prices of food, wine, cloth, leather, and other commodities tripled in a single day. A family's carefully horded savings evaporated before their eyes. For the common folk of Daltigoth, there was only one recourse: they rioted.

Hundreds of people spilled out into the streets and market squares, smashing sellers' stands and assaulting merchants. The city guards were quickly overwhelmed. In the Canal District, warehouses were broken open and looted. This encouraged hundreds more to take to the streets and make their way to the waterfront to join the plundering.

Ackal V, wrapped in furs despite the summer heat, listened stone-faced as anxious representatives of the merchants' guilds recited the growing chronicle of lawlessness. When they finished, silence descended on the audience hall. The interval lengthened, grew awkward, and the guildmasters and merchants nervously shuffled their feet.

"Summon the city garrison, Your Majesty!" urged the chief of the goldsmiths. "Give the rioters a taste of imperial iron!"

Still, Ackal V said nothing. He seemed lost in a dream, eyes staring into the distance. Valaran, seated at his side, prompted him almost inaudibly. Her veil, white this time, allowed her to do this without attracting the notice of the assembled commoners. Ackal V glanced at her and smiled. The empress drew in a breath. The closest ranks of petitioners recoiled from the deceptively benign expression on Ackal V's face. They knew only too well that when the emperor smiled, blood would flow.

"The garrison is arrayed to protect the Inner City," he said. "There it will remain."

The merchants and guildmasters dared not protest. Valaran did so on their behalf, albeit most tactfully, her voice low.

"Sire, please reconsider. The safety of the city depends on order being kept."

"Oh, I shall put Daltigoth in order." He raised his voice. "Tathman! Captain Tathman, where are you?"

The Wolf stepped forward and bowed stiffly.

"Captain, you and the Wolves will stop the rioting," Ackal V said simply.

Equally simple was the reply: "As you wish, Majesty."

Tathman's sepulchral voice always made the hair on Valaran's neck rise. The assembled guildmasters were stricken. The thought of the Emperor's Wolves set loose on the city stunned and terrified all.

The emperor said, "You want order, don't you? You want an end to the looting, don't you? My Wolves will pacify the city in one day—maybe less."

They had come to beg for protection, so the merchants and tradesmen could hardly protest, yet all knew the Wolves were capable of any atrocity. Recruited from the poorest, most distant provinces of the empire, they owed nothing to Daltigoth and everything to their patron.

Ackal V stood abruptly. In a body the guildmasters shrank back from him.

"You see? You have only to ask, and your emperor responds!" He folded his arms and glowered down at the cowering men. His words laced with irony, he added, "I know you're anxious to return to your shops. Go, and spread the word that peace will soon return to the city—peace guaranteed by the Emperor's Wolves."

They managed to depart without actually trampling each other, but no one could mistake their desire to be elsewhere.

Ackal nodded to Tathman. The captain and the other Wolves followed the guildmasters and merchants out.

The next order of business was the emperor's council with his warlords. Lackeys struggled forward with a carpet-sized map of the land east of Eagle's Ford. They unrolled it at the emperor's feet, and the leaders of the Great Horde lined up along the map's edges. The warlords saluted Ackal V, but there was a notable lack of fervor in their greeting.

Consternation gripped Valaran as she realized she didn't recognize a single face among them. The warlords from her first husband's reign were gone—slain by bakali or nomads, or executed by their own emperor for failing to win victories. Only two commanders of experience remained, Lord Tremond and Lord Regobart. Tremond governed the city of Thorngoth, on the south coast. He and his hordes guarded the mouth of the Thorn River, doorway to the heartland of the empire. Regobart commanded the garrison at Six Dunes, the imperial fortress near Tarsis. The empire's long-time enemy had been quiet so far, but Ackal V did not dare withdraw Regobart's hordes, for fear the Tarsans would join against the empire.

Most of the new warlords were quite young. There were a few graybeards, men loyal to the Ackal line who'd been recalled from home and hearth to serve in this time of crisis. But not one of them had ever commanded more than a handful of hordes, much less an army.

"The enemy is across the Dalti," Ackal V said, his matter-of-fact tone at odds with the frightening news. "Their strength and purpose are unknown. Where and how do we destroy them, my lords?"

One of the graybeards, Andruth by name, stepped forward. "Your Majesty, we have twenty hordes concentrated at Verdant Isle." He bent stiffly and placed a fist-sized onyx token on the map at a spot some five leagues from the capital. "Twelve more are coming down from the Northern Hundred under Lord Ducarrel, and eight are mustered at Bengoth. Lord Crumont's army has fallen back to the Ackal Path to defend the capital." Andruth set more tokens down at those spots.

"A line two hundred leagues long and only ninety-eight hordes to defend it?"

Andruth scrubbed his iron-colored beard and exchanged a look with several of his older comrades.

The emperor knew the meaning of that look. "I will not call up the landed hordes! Fat landowners and their sheepherder minions! I might as well cast the crown of my ancestors into the gutter and be done with it!"

"Majesty, the landed hordes are loyal to the empire."

Valaran admired the old general's nerve. His well-chosen words were a veiled reproof—loyal to Ergoth did not necessarily mean loyal to Ackal V.

"In the reigns of my uncle and father, of unfortunate name"—the emperor meant Pakin II and III—"landed hordes fought against the dynasty and for the line of the usurpers."

Many provincial hordes had indeed aligned themselves with the Pakin Pretender. That was ancient history to everyone but Ackal V.

Andruth nodded, "Few warriors from those days remain, Majesty. There are over one hundred and fifty landed hordes available. They need only be summoned to service."

Ackal kicked over the onyx marker signifying the troops at Verdant Isle. "Mention those traitors again and I'll have your tongue out!" he snarled. Andruth firmed his lips and said no more.

"Send couriers to the Seascapes and the Southwest Hundred," Ackal V said, resuming his seat. "Muster every imperial horde in both provinces and march them"—he looked at the map—"to Gaer."

This was a small town in the fertile, forested triangle between the Thorn and Dalti rivers, southwest of the city. Scribes took down the emperor's order, and couriers were dispatched immediately.

The warlords took turns describing the progress of the bakali through the open country northeast of the capital. Following their usual pattern, the lizard-men moved in a tight column, driving out every human they encountered.

Thousands of refugees were streaming south, to Daltigoth, seeking protection. So far the enemy was moving more west than south, toward the hill country between the capital and Ropunt Forest. There would seem to be nothing there to entice them—no cities, not even many farms. The council listened to learned sages from the College of Wizards speculate on the bakali's goals, but in the end, no one could say with confidence what the lizard-men would do.

A courier arrived, and hurried to whisper in Andruth's ear. The old warrior said, "Your Majesty, there is news from the east—a messenger from the governor of Caergoth!"

The messenger came forward. Although exhausted and still covered by the dust of his journey, he saluted his emperor smartly.

"Wornoth, by Your Majesty's grace Governor of Caergoth and Marshal of the Plains Hundred, sends you greetings," the messenger declaimed.

He then described rather grim conditions in Caergoth. The city was strongly held by eleven hordes, but food was in short supply as marauding nomads had cut off incoming supplies.

The emperor appeared bored by another litany of trouble, but the courier's final piece of news pierced his disinterest.

"There is good news Your Majesty! We have word of a victory over the plainsmen!" Surprise rippled through the council. "Lord Wornoth has it on good authority that the raiding tribes of Chief Tokasin were defeated near the razed town of Juramona."

The name of Tol's hometown made Valaran's pulse quicken.

"Who has done this? What general? What hordes?" Ackal V queried sharply.

The courier flushed. "Nothing more is known, Your Majesty. Foragers from Caergoth caught some nomads fleeing south. Lord Wornoth had them questioned. Under torture the savages admitted that their chief, Tokasin, had led some four or five thousand plainsmen to Juramona to destroy a band of Ergothians. Instead, he was himself destroyed!"

"Andruth, what imperial troops remain in the vicinity?" the emperor asked.

The old general, lately come to his post, plainly didn't know. "They could be remnants of Lord Bessian's men."

The courier shook his head. "Forgive me, Majesty, great lords, but the nomads said the Ergothians were not Riders of the Great Horde. They fought on foot."

Astonishment gusted through the audience hall. Valaran found her husband glaring at her. His thoughts were plainly the same as hers, only far less kindly intended.

"Where's Winath?" Ackal shouted. "Send the Mistress of the White Robes forward!"

Steady old Winath slipped through the press of armored warlords. She looked small among such company, but carried herself with great poise.

"Old woman," Ackal said, "scry for me what's happening at Juramona. Put all your sages to work on this. Nothing else is important right now."

"Yes, Majesty." After a brief pause, she added, "We've not had much success scrying the distant provinces, sire. An unknown power obscures every scene, like a wall of fog."

The emperor's eyes were hard. "Your failures interest me not at all, White Robe. Find out what I want to know, or give way to someone who can."

Winath understood him perfectly. If she did not succeed, she would face the same gruesome death as her predecessor, Oropash.

As the wizard departed, Valaran, claiming fatigue, excused herself. She exited slowly and with all decorum, but outside the audience hall, she dismissed her escorts and hurried up a small, hidden staircase that led to the rear of the imperial library.

A male scribe working within uttered a startled squeak as he beheld the empress's entrance. He fled as the law required, and the other scribes likewise abandoned the library. As the main doors banged shut behind them, she knew she need not fear interruption.

She flipped her veil back over her head. Heart hammering, hands shaking, she took down the cedarwood chest that held the *Ergothinia* and quickly freed the magic mirror from its hiding place. She lifted its lid, but only her own wide, shadowed eyes stared back at her from the mirror's perfect surface.

"Where are you, wizard?" she hissed. "I must speak with you!"

She continued her attempts to contact him until the lamp's oil was exhausted and the smoky yellow flame went out. Helbin never appeared. Valaran slammed the mirror box shut, all but cracking the precious glass with the force of her frustration.

Where was Helbin? He was supposed to remain at Tuva's Blockhouse on the Plucked Path, keeping watch on the advancing bakali, while waiting for Lord Tolandruth to appear from the east. Valaran had no doubt the victory at Juramona was Tol's doing. Only he could lead foot soldiers successfully against swarms of horsemen. But where in Chaos's name was Helbin?

Valaran took a deep breath, mastering her emotions. She had to maintain her poise, or Ackal V would know his suspicions were correct. He would know Tol was back in the empire. There could be any number of innocent reasons for Helbin's silence. He might be involved in an incantation, or perhaps he'd left the blockhouse for a short time and not taken his mirror.

Or perhaps he'd been detected! The wizards in the Tower of High Sorcery had not gained their places by being foolish. Winath's people might have found Helbin and neutralized his activities. He might even have fallen victim to random brigands or nomads.

She returned the mirror box to the cedar case, and the case to its place on the shelf. Her fears were pointless. Whether Helbin was lost, she certainly was not. She had many resources, her design would go forward. As long as there was breath in her body, she would not give up.

And what of Zala? The half-breed had had plenty of time to find Tol, and perhaps she had succeeded. Valaran could easily imagine Tol, upon learning of his hometown's fall, rushing there to rally the survivors in the province. It would be a logical step, and an honorable one, just like him. It also would explain both Zala's tardiness and the unexpected victory over Tokasin's rampaging tribesmen.

For the first time in weeks, Valaran smiled. Even now Tol might be on his way to her.

She seated herself at a nearby table. Taking a fresh page of vellum and a sharp quill from the small store on the table, she unfastened the pendant from around her neck.

The pendant was a rose, wrought in silver, three finger-widths wide. Hollow, it was actually a tiny flask. Such trinkets were nothing out of the ordinary—two other intricately worked pendants had been made for the empress, to hold the scents she preferred. Valaran had chosen the innocuous silver rose to hold not perfume but a special ink. She'd learned of this unique fluid while reading the private memoirs of the Empress Yetai, chief consort of Emperor Ackal III.

She opened the tiny concealed cap and dipped a nib in the ink. On touching the page, the colorless ink turned pale lavender. Valaran wrote swiftly. As the ink dried, it faded from sight, and would become visible again only when the letter was held in steam containing certain herbs. Empress Yetai had used the vanishing ink to communicate with her lover, Lord Gonz Hellmann, as they plotted the murder of her husband.

Valaran preferred not to dwell upon the final fate of Yetai: betrayed by her lover to save his own life, the long-ago empress had been found guilty of treason and executed by her husband.

The note was addressed to her chief agent in the city. *The plan is progressing,* she wrote. *The Wolves are coming, but do not fear. Proceed as you have been doing. Our reward comes soon.*

Even with the concealment of Yetai's ink, she kept her words vague. After adding some coded details about money and arms, she turned the parchment over and wrote on the other side, in normal ink, an innocent order for writing supplies for the imperial library. The order would be delivered to the Scriveners' Hall today, where her minion would pass it along to its true recipient, who knew how to uncover the secret message.

Valaran tucked the sealed missive into the sleeve of her

gown. In the corridor outside the library she encountered the chief White Robe, Winath.

The wizard greeted her. "Seeking a palimpsest?" Valaran asked.

"No, Majesty, I seek you."

Valaran offered her chilliest royal smile—lips firmly together, eyes half-closed—as she looked down at the older woman. "Yes?"

At the wizard's suggestion they moved away from the library entrance. Once they turned the corner into a narrow side passage, Valaran heard the pack of impatient scribes scurrying back into the library.

Satisfied they were alone, Winath said, "Majesty, I have recently come across some writings of my predecessor, Yoralyn. I think they offer insight into the current crisis."

Valaran could think of numerous crises facing them just now, but she merely waited for the White Robe to continue.

"The inability of our scryers to observe the doings of the bakali has always smacked of interference, Majesty. Now I am sure of it."

Alarmed but outwardly composed, Valaran prompted her with a nod.

Winath lowered her voice even further. "Has Your Majesty ever heard of a nullstone?" Valaran said she had not. "It's an artifact, made by the ancient Irda race, for protection against magic," Winath explained. "It works, so the old books say, like a sponge, absorbing all ethereal power it encounters."

Although an interesting fact to Valaran the scholar, Valaran the empress could see no point to this conversation about a legendary artifact. She allowed her impatience to show.

Winath added quickly, "Majesty, according to Yoralyn's papers, Lord Tolandruth possessed just such an artifact!"

Not even Valaran's great self-possession could withstand that revelation. Astonishment bloomed on her face. The old woman's words explained so much that Valaran instantly believed her claim.

Years ago, Tol and Val had enjoyed trysts in the garden of the wizards' college, despite the barrier spells that protected it. As long as Valaran was with Tol, she could pass through the spells without hindrance. She'd asked him about his ability, but he would say only that knowing the secret would endanger her. He'd also survived every murder attempt by the rogue wizard Mandes, when others fell like autumn leaves around him. People said Lord Tolandruth possessed the gods' own luck. Perhaps it was not luck, but the ancient knowledge of the Irda that protected him!

"Majesty," Winath said loudly, interrupting Valaran's thoughts. "I feel it must be the nullstone that obstructs our efforts to spy upon the bakali. I'm sorry."

"Sorry?" Valaran did not understand the old wizard's apology.

"Sorry to be the one who tells you that Lord Tolandruth must be collaborating with the enemy."

The statement was so absurdly wrong Valaran almost laughed. Poor Winath. Although a notable scholar, she had never really been groomed for leadership. When it came to politics, she was out of her depth.

"Majesty, Lord Tolandruth must have turned against the empire out of hatred for his humiliation and exile."

Valaran's slow nod hid her racing thoughts. A chilling realization suddenly came to her. Maintaining her regal mask, she said, "Have you told anyone else about this, Winath?"

"No, Majesty. Yoralyn's manuscripts are protected by grievous wards. Only the chief of the order has the power to read them." A dark shadow passed over the wizard's lined face. "Oropash must have known—may he rest in the arms of Draco Paladine."

"You have not approached the emperor?"

Winath looked distinctly uncomfortable. "Such a powerful artifact should not fall into the wrong hands," she replied carefully.

The empress agreed, and Winath relaxed. "Majesty," she asked, "what should be done about this?"

Valaran linked her arm in the old woman's. The wizard was startled by the intimate gesture. As Valaran began to walk, the White Robe accompanied her.

"That is indeed the question: what is to be done with this

knowledge?" Valaran murmured. After a thoughtful pause, she asked, "You've had no success piercing the veil surrounding the bakali?"

Winath admitted they had not. Even attempts to scry ahead and behind the field of obscurity, thereby detecting the direction of the enemy, had yielded contradictory and unhelpful results.

The two women mounted the winding stairs leading to the servants' quarters. It was midafternoon, and the warren of rooms was empty.

"Is it possible, Winath, that the veil over the bakali is a simple ward, well cast by a powerful magician?"

"It's possible, Majesty, but there aren't many who could work so deep and long-lasting a spell."

"Could you?"

Winath shook her head, looking somewhat regretful. "My specialty is language and conjuration. I was never strong with wards. Yoralyn was a powerful wardmaster, as was Helbin."

The White Robe glanced at the empress, but she did not seem especially disturbed by mention of the Red Robe, branded a traitor and coward by the emperor.

A whiff of smoke came to them. They were passing a window slit in the circular stairwell. Valaran glanced out and saw plumes of gray smoke rising from various parts of the city.

"Helbin, you say?" she murmured. "He disappeared, yes?"

"Yes, Majesty. Before the bakali reached Caergoth, he stole out of the city and fled. The Red Robes searched for a time, but Helbin is clever. If he doesn't want to be found, he won't be."

Winath stopped abruptly. "By all the gods! Helbin! Majesty, do you think he—?"

"Why not? You said he was skilled at warding."

"But why would Helbin aid the bakali?"

The empress did not reply. They had reached the top of the spiraling stair, a turret on the roof of the palace. Still linked arm in arm with the White Robe, Valaran said, "Come, let me show you something."

They went out onto the narrow balcony that encircled the turret. The balcony was protected by a low parapet. From here, the vast panorama of the imperial capital spread out beneath them. Four distinct columns of smoke rose from the sprawling collection of buildings, and the wind brought the sound of harsh voices, the clatter of arms, and the screams of the angry and anguished.

"The city is reeling," Valaran said sadly, "like the empire. What has taken two centuries to create could be lost in our lifetime, Winath, unless we are prepared to fight for it."

"Of course, Majesty." Winath gripped the empress's arm with both hands.

Valaran's voice hardened. "The emperor is more than a cruel tyrant. He is mad. Not like my late husband, the unfortunate Ackal IV. He lost his wits completely. No, Ackal V knows exactly what he is doing, and he chooses the path that most gratifies his lusts. Do you understand?"

"No, I'm sorry. Majesty, let's go back inside, please."

"I have suffered many outrages, to my person and my lineage. When the bakali appeared on our border, I took them for a sign from the gods. They would be my instrument for removing Ackal V from the throne of Ergoth."

The wizard's face was ashen, and not from fear of the height.

Valaran added, "It was I who sent Helbin out of Daltigoth. And Helbin, not Lord Tolandruth, raised the veil over the bakali."

Her eyes were distant, clouded by emotions Winath couldn't read. "To save a dying man, it is often necessary to administer very strong medicine, unpleasant though the remedy may be. When the Great Horde is defeated, and the emperor's authority exhausted, he will be overthrown."

"That's treason!"

The strange distance vanished, and Valaran looked down into Winath's shocked face.

"No," the empress said firmly. "Patriotic necessity."

Valaran caught the wizard's wrists in her hands and pushed her backward to the low parapet. Disbelief showed on Winath's face for only a heartbeat, then horror suffused her expression. She fought the younger woman, but was borne inexorably to the edge. They struggled briefly, Winath's eyes tearing from wind and terror, Valaran grimly determined. All the hate for Ackal V that she'd stored over the years seemed to flow outward through her hands. A final shove, and Winath toppled. White robe fluttering like a moth's wing, the wizard vanished into the canyon of lower rooftops. Her thin scream was barely audible above the wind.

Valaran was trembling so violently, she had to clutch the parapet to keep herself from falling. She'd had no choice. It had to be done. Winath knew too much. A guileless old woman, she would never have kept Valaran's secrets, not with the emperor's spies swarming about.

Shouts echoed from the open stairwell. Valaran turned away from the drop as servants and guards burst out onto the balcony. Seeing the empress, they halted, astonished.

"Your Majesty!" sputtered a guard, lowering his gaze quickly from her unveiled face. "What happened?"

"Winath of the White Robes has killed herself." She had no need to counterfeit the tremor in her voice. "Unable to find the bakali army, she confessed her fear of the emperor's punishment and leaped. I could not stop her."

Still exclaiming in shock, the male guards and servants departed immediately, leaving the women with the empress. A plump, motherly washerwoman looked over the edge, then regarded Valaran with pity.

"How terrible, Majesty! What does this mean?"

Valaran let out a pent-up breath. She lowered the white veil over her face. A part of her mind noted with pride that her hand did not shak. She was Empress of Ergoth. She was equal to the task she had set herself.

"It means," she said calmly, "the White Robes must choose a new chief."

# C h a p t e r   1 3
## Pursuit

With a blast of horns, a wall of armed horsemen emerged from the screen of trees. They raised sabers, shouted a war cry, and attacked the slow-moving column.

This time, it was not buckskin-clad nomads sweeping down upon hapless farmers and traders, but Ergothians falling like a thunderbolt upon an assemblage of ox-drawn carts and nomad riders dozing in their saddles. This time, it was the nomads who were caught completely by surprise.

Nomad women and children dropped their scanty baggage and scattered. What few warriors there were turned to face the Ergothians, lashing their ponies forward.

The fight was over in moments. The plainsmen were overwhelmed, and their terrified families were rounded up. Horses and weapons were stripped away. Children cried and babies howled. Ringed by stern-faced riders, the nomads huddled together, expecting no mercy.

In the days following the relief of Juramona, the fortunes of the nomads had taken a severe reverse. With the rapidly growing camp at Juramona as their base, the Firebrand Horde, arriving just behind Lord Pagas's Panthers, set out to strike the nomads wherever they could be found. Faced with such relentless pursuit, the tribes dispersed like drops of water on a hot griddle.

Pagas, Egrin, and Tol rode forward, watching as the latest

# Paul B. Thompson and Tonya C. Cook

crowd of frightened survivors was searched. Traditionally, prisoners taken by the Great Horde were sold as slaves in the nearest city, after the most infamous among them faced summary execution. By Tol's order, notorious killers were arrested, stolen booty reclaimed, and the chastised nomads were then driven out of the empire. Not only did he consider slavery evil, but if word got out they were enslaving captives, Tol knew the remaining raiders would fight all the harder. He wanted the nomads to flee, not fight.

Tol spied a familiar face in the clumps of women and old people. He ordered the man brought forward. Riders wove through the crowd, converging on the man, and driving him out to face Lord Tolandruth.

"Chief Mattohoc?"

The dark-skinned chief of the Sand Treader tribe glared up at his captor. Shame and fury stiffened his hulking frame as he acknowledged his name. He had obviously fought hard: shoulders and arms were striped by sword cuts, a deep gash laid open his forehead, and his left thigh was tightly wrapped with bloodstained bandages.

Tol asked him where the rest of his tribe was. Mattohoc's reply was an impossibly obscene suggestion. An irate Ergothian kicked him between the shoulders, and the chief fell forward to his hands and knees.

"Enough!" Tol barked. "We do not abuse prisoners!"

Tol had a waterskin brought to the badly wounded chief. As Mattohoc drank noisily, Tol called for a healer to tend him.

"Heal him?" Pagas was so astonished, he broke his usual reticence. "By rights we should separate him from his head!"

"That may happen. But for now, Mattohoc is a captured chief, and he will be treated with respect." Mattohoc's expression showed no gratitude, only impotent fury.

Later, as the Ergothian commanders dined under a canvas fly pitched on the summit of a nearby knoll, Mattohoc was brought before Tol.

Landed hordes, eager to take back their country from the invaders and to serve the famous Lord Tolandruth, were still arriving from the south and east. From their vantage point, the commanders could see a seemingly endless stream of newcomers riding to their camp. As Mattohoc approached, limping, Tol waved him to a stool. The chief's wounds had been dressed, but his face was gray and he grunted as he sat. Cider, bread, and a joint of meat were placed before him. He regarded the repast with disdain.

"You won't make me talk by showing me kindness," he sneered.

"No one's asked you to talk. Eat or not, as you please," Tol replied, then bade Egrin continue his report.

The old warrior was marking tallies on a scrap of parchment. "With the arrival of the Silver Star Horde, our strength is now thirty thousand," he said. "Plus two thousand, six hundred twelve foot soldiers."

"We need more. I want fifty thousand men under arms by the time we reach Caergoth." Tol poured himself another draught of cider and looked a question at Egrin. At his nod, Tol refilled his cup as well.

Across the folding table, Lord Argonnel said, "Why so many, my lord? Surely this campaign is winding down?"

A brown-bearded fellow of middle years, Argonnel commanded the Iron Scythe Horde, made up of gentry from the extreme northeast corner of the empire.

"This campaign has just started," Tol replied. "Once the nomads are defeated, there will be other enemies to fight."

The warlords made cheerfully belligerent noises. Lord Tolandruth planned to take on the lizard-men, too? So be it!

Lord Trudo, of the Oaken Shield Horde, raised another issue. "My lord, why did you leave command of the militia to that—to that elf?"

The question was not unexpected. After Tokasin's defeat, Tol had gone with Egrin and Pagas in pursuit of the shattered nomads, leaving Tylocost in command of the Juramona Militia. The Juramonans, impressed by the Silvanesti's skill and cool demeanor during the battle, accepted him without qualm. Veteran members of the landed hordes were not so open-minded. To lessen the conflict with the hordes (who regarded elves and infantry as equally suspicious), Tol had ordered Tylocost to bring the militia cross-country to a planned rendezvous. Tol's hordes and Tylocost's infantry would meet by the bluff where the eastern and western sources of the Caer came together to form the mighty river. It was at this spot, known as the Great Confluence, that Tol had found the Irda nullstone decades earlier.

Tol plucked a grape from a bowl. "Tylocost is a great general," he said. He popped the grape in his mouth. "I trust him."

"But he's Silvanesti!" Argonnel protested.

"So he is." Tol turned to their captive. "Chief Mattohoc, would you let a former enemy ride in your warband?"

Mattohoc, eating awkwardly with his uninjured left hand, grunted an affirmative.

"Why?" Tol asked.

The chief swallowed and said, "Men fight for many reasons. Loot, glory, or a lust for battle. If I find an enemy who fights for other reasons, that man can stand beside me as easily as face me."

"What other reasons?" asked Egrin.

"Honor, foremost."

This drew a laugh from the warlords. All save Egrin and Tol scoffed at the notion of honor among such savages as the nomad tribes.

Tol asked, "Would you fight for me, Chief?"

Astonishment robbed the warlords of speech, and even Egrin was taken aback. The edges of the canvas roof flapped in the hot summer breeze, and a mockingbird's complicated song sounded loud in the silence.

"No," Mattohoc finally said. He wiped sweat from his shaven head. "My father was Krato, chief before me. When I was a stripling, he took the pay of the Tarsans and led our warriors in their service. They entered the land of the kender, on the way to join the army of Tylocost. By night they were ambushed and slaughtered. The commander of the grasslanders that so treacherously slew my father and kinsmen was Prince Nazramin, who you now call emperor!"

"The Battle of the Boulder Field!" Egrin exclaimed, remembering. "Nazramin's warriors killed everyone, even those who surrendered!"

Mattohoc nodded. His father's headless corpse had been found on the field of battle and brought home to his native range. Since then, Mattohoc had dreamed of the day he would avenge himself on the Ergothians.

"Every man in my tribe can tell a like story. You grasslanders take our land, kill our people, or make them slaves. I would rather cut off my own hands than lift a sword for you!"

Mattohoc did not accept Tol's explanation that Ackal V, formerly Prince Nazramin, was his enemy, too.

"You fight to save him!" the nomad spat.

"We fight to save our country," Egrin countered.

Mattohoc would not be persuaded. He clung obstinately to his hatred of all Ergothians. Reluctantly, Tol had him taken away. Even without his weapons and chiefly garb, he was still a redoubtable figure. He and Tol stared at each other for a long moment before he limped away, head held high.

Argonnel said, "He's a forceful leader and a danger to the empire, my lord. If you set him free, he'll organize his people again and attack!"

It was no more than the truth. Tol had hoped to make Mattohoc his ally, as he had Makaralonga and Tylocost. When he'd first met the doughty chief at the parley with Tokasin, he'd sensed in the Sand Treader a strong sense of honor. Unfortunately, Mattohoc had an even greater thirst for vengeance.

"He must be dealt with," Egrin said. "In the name of peace and safety."

Tol did not want to give the order. But as Egrin made to rise from the table, he knew he could not allow his old mentor to shoulder the responsibility that was, by rights, his.

"Mattohoc cannot be allowed to trouble the empire again," he said quietly. "The order for his execution is given."

Egrin saluted silently and took his leave. One by one the other warlords departed, until Tol sat alone. He got up from the table and left the shade of the tent. Closing his eyes, he lifted his face to the harsh sun.

🦇 🦇 🦇 🦇 🦇

A winding column of foot soldiers trailed back through the trees. They were an odd mixture: one-time farmers and town merchants, former guards and volunteers who'd never held a spear before the last time Solin's face was new. Each man had his own reason for joining Lord Tolandruth's cause. Some loved their homeland. Others wanted revenge against the hated invaders. More than a few, having lost their livelihoods to the war, saw a chance for loot. With Lord Tolandruth in charge, each had confidence in achieving his goal.

Leading the ragtag column were Zala and Tylocost. The half-elf still worried that Tol, without her to personally watch out for him, would get himself killed, in which case there would be nothing to protect Zala or her aged father from the empress's wrath. Her fears had been temporarily forgotten, as she was forced to listen to Tylocost's endless chatter.

By the gods, the elf could talk! History, politics, warfare, food, and gardening were his favorite subjects. After five days' marching, Zala felt she knew enough to go into business as a gardener herself. At least he'd stopped calling her "half-breed," although "girl" wasn't much better.

They'd encountered armed nomads several times since leaving Juramona for the southward trek to the Caer River. At first, the warbands had attacked, seeing only a motley band of Ergothians on foot. However, finding themselves faced with Tol's tactics and Tylocost's generalship, the plainsmen quickly gave up the attacks as bad business. Horsemen now rode away as the marching men approached, and the sight of fleeing riders never failed to raise a cheer from the foot-sore soldiery.

Their only serious contest came five days into the journey. Tylocost had kept them tramping forward after sunset that day, though they usually made camp at dusk. Stars began to dot the indigo sky and still they marched. Tylocost was certain the enemy was near, and that a fight was brewing.

Zala was startled by his calm certainty, but did not doubt him. Word was passed back through the ranks, and the marching men quieted. Helmets were donned, spears gripped a little tighter.

They were northeast of the Caer confluence, an area known locally as Riverine. It was hilly country, devoid of settlements and dotted with small, ancient woods. Several of these woodlands contained crumbling ruins, so worn by time as to be completely unidentifiable. Trees far older than even the long-lived Tylocost rose among the stones, endlessly, patiently, prying apart sandstone blocks the size of small huts. Although ruins of one kind or another dotted the land between Hylo and the Gulf of Ergoth, Riverine was particularly rich in obscure relics.

As whippoorwills began calling from the shadowed trees, Tylocost stopped, one hand upraised. The column clattered to a halt. The Silvanesti climbed a pinnacle of ancient masonry, looked around briefly, then descended. He ordered six companies to circle right, around the hill before them. The men moved out, advancing carefully through the trees.

Zala hadn't liked fighting in the dark at Juramona, and she liked it even less here, stumbling through an unknown wood. "This is crazy," she muttered. "Fighting a battle in the dark—it's crazy."

Tylocost drew his sword and leaned against the ancient stones. "Happens all the time," he assured her. "In the First Dragon War my ancestor, Amberace Tylocostathan, won a signal victory by attacking a dragon host on a moonless night."

Zala knew little, and cared less, about ancient history. "You mean, an army of dragons?"

"No, ignorant girl. The great dragons of that age sometimes had followers, men, and even elves, who fought their own kind in return for treasure."

A messenger came crashing through the trees. "My lord!" he gasped. "A large camp! Nomads! On the other side of the hill!"

"I thought so." Tylocost snapped upright. "Form a column of half-companies. Swordsmen to the front. We'll have to get in close to see who we're fighting."

The foot soldiers sorted themselves as commanded. No sooner had they done so than a pack of mounted nomads came galloping over the hill. They were few, and probably wouldn't have attacked if they'd realized how numerous were the Ergothians.

Shouting, they charged. The leading Ergothians, fifty men in each half-company, moved sideways out of the path of the horsemen while the rear companies lowered pikes and made ready to take the shock of the charge. Tylocost climbed atop the ruins for a better vantage. The position also exposed him to the enemy.

Appalled by his careless courage, Zala climbed up beside him.

"Guarding me now?" he said mildly.

"Somebody should," she grumbled.

There followed a short, sharp clash in the night-veiled woods. Small-scale skirmishes were common as soldiers and nomads fought among the trees. The contest swayed back and forth until the din of fighting behind them spooked the nomads. In threes and fours, they quit and rode back over the hill.

The six companies Tylocost had sent to circle the hill had taken the enemy in the flank.

"Forward, forward! We've got them now!" the elf cried.

The balance of his column stormed over the hill. A very large camp filled the dark ravine below. To the right, the flanking companies were briskly engaged with nomads, also on foot. A large herd of horses milled about, neighing nervously.

The Ergothians reached a low stockade that impeded their progress. They tried to force their way through the rough-hewn rail fence, hacking at the barrier with swords, or tearing at it with bare hands. Nomad archers stood their ground, felling man after man.

Dead and wounded were piling up when a section of stockade finally collapsed. With a roar the Ergothians flooded through the gap, overwhelming the horseless nomads. Beset on two sides, the plainsmen abandoned the fight. Many leaped onto horses, cut their tethers, and galloped away bareback.

The remaining nomads threw down their arms. Tylocost had to restrain his fevered troops from killing their surrendered foes in revenge for the outrages they'd perpetrated. Tylocost felt the professional's distaste for partisan warfare. Battles were much easier to control when the forces involved were true-born warriors, not armed peasants who lost control of their emotions.

Fortunately, cooler heads—old guardsmen from Juramona—prevailed, and helped him herd the captives into a corner of the stockade. Order was restored, and torches lit.

The nomad camp was unusual. Plainsmen didn't usually bother erecting a stockade. The reason for it soon became clear. Not only were there several hundred horses in the gully, but also heaps of valuables liberated from Ergothian strongholds. The horses weren't plains ponies either, but long-legged Ergothian breeds. Judging by their brands, most had been captured from Lord Bessian's shattered army.

Tylocost pulled off a weathered tarp covering a head-high pile of goods. A hodgepodge of kegs, crates, and baskets was revealed, each filled with plunder. They held gold coins, silver plate, loose gems, jewelry, bolts of brocade and silk, fine swords, and ritual objects stolen from Juramona's razed temples. Other piles contained armor, weapons, and the war standards of the defeated hordes. There were enough sabers to equip eight or nine hordes.

Zala asked the elf why he looked so grim. She found the treasure an exhilarating sight.

"What do you suppose will happen when the men find out what they've captured?" he said. "What's to stop them from seizing this loot for themselves?"

"You will. Remind them who they are and what they're fighting for. Their pride will stop them."

He appraised her anew. "For an unschooled woods-runner, you have insight."

The double-edged compliment drew a snort from the half-elf.

Omitting only the troops that were needed to guard the nomad prisoners, Tylocost assembled his army. All eyes widened as the men beheld the piles of looted treasure the elf had left uncovered.

"Here are the stolen treasures of your country!" Tylocost

179

shouted, his voice ringing through the nomad camp. "The gods have seen fit to reverse the tide of war and return it to you. Now we have a grave duty. We must secure this hoard for Lord Tolandruth until the rightful owners can be found."

A rumble of talk sounded from the assembled men. One called out, "Can't we make use of just a little of it, General? I got a homemade spear and brass pot for my head. There's real blades and armor there!"

Tylocost looked thoughtful, as though the notion had not occurred to him. "That does sound fair," he allowed. "I'll appoint a quartermaster to distribute the arms appropriately."

There were nods and grins all around.

Tylocost added, "The rest of this booty shall be sacred. No one is to touch it, on pain of death."

The men nodded. Theft by a soldier in the field was punishable by hanging, and every man present remembered the fate of the deserters at Juramona.

Guards were posted to watch over the valuables. Tylocost called for volunteers with riding experience. These men were mounted on captured Ergothian horses and ordered to find Lord Tolandruth's army and report what they'd captured. Heavy wagons would be required to move the weighty treasure, and until they arrived Tylocost and his troop would remain to safeguard it.

Daybreak arrived, cloudy and warm. The ravine seemed airless, cut off by the hills from the usual summer breezes. Face red with heat, Tylocost soaked a kerchief in water and knotted it around his neck.

"Hey, gorgeous, whatcha doin'?"

The unfamiliar, high-pitched voice brought Tylocost whirling around in surprise. He saw a kender perched atop a pile of treasure. The little fellow was idly twirling the elf's floppy hat. No one had seen him arrive, much less climb up the mound of booty, so his appearance prompted much consternation and drawing of swords.

"Who in Chaos are you?" Tylocost demanded. "And give me my hat!"

"Curly Windseed. Fine. It's too big for me anyway!" the kender replied rather confusingly. His brown hair was clipped short and a fringe of straight bangs fell into his light blue eyes.

He sent the hat spinning through the air to its rightful owner. Tylocost caught it deftly and ordered him off the treasure pile.

"This is the property of the Ergoth Empire," the Silvanesti added.

"So this is Ergoth? Good!" the kender pronounced, leaping nimbly to the ground. "You know, gorgeous, you could use a new hat. For a fee, I could find you a really good one."

Before Tylocost could deliver a scathing reply, he heard himself hailed. A soldier was running toward him through the piles of stolen goods.

"Strangers are in camp!" the soldier cried. "Kender!"

Tylocost muttered, "Of course. There's never just one aphid on the roses."

"Friends of yours?" Zala asked Curly Windseed.

"Sure. Well, some of them. I don't much like Duck; he cheats at games. And Rambletoe snores like a donkey. Downy's okay—Downy Redfoot, that is. She—"

Tylocost gave a frustrated snarl and stalked away to order his troops to assemble. Zala was fascinated. A few minutes with a kender had shattered the Silvanesti's impeccably cool demeanor.

Soon, ten kender had gathered around Curly Windseed. Tylocost pegged them as wanderers, poking their noses where they weren't wanted, and ordered them sent on their way.

Zala wondered at their attire. All the kender were armed with short swords and dressed in scale shirts and matching green leggings.

"Why are you dressed alike?" she asked Curly.

Idly poking through a crate of stolen goods, he said, "Because we're scouts."

"For the Queen's Own Royal Loyal Militia," another kender put in.

Zala whirled on Tylocost, exclaiming, "These are the allies Lord Tolandruth sent for!"

The elf sneered in disbelief, but Curly confirmed that they had indeed been led here by their queen, Casberry of

Hylo, and a towering, blonde human woman whose name he couldn't remember.

"Kiya!"

Curly shook his head at Zala. "No, that's not it." He and his comrades began arguing amongst themselves over the giant's proper name.

Tylocost put a hand to his forehead. "Lord Tolandruth must be mad, sending for these pests."

Zala reminded him how easily the kender had penetrated the stockaded camp, with the Ergothians awake and vigilant. If Lord Tolandruth could harness the natural abilities of the kender, it could only help their cause, she said.

Another runner arrived, bringing additional news: more kender were coming, following a strange wooden fetish borne on the shoulders of two brawny humans. The fetish was attended by a Red Robe wizard.

This was incredible, even for kender. Tylocost and Zala hurried through the nomad camp. At the north end, by a broken-down section of the stockade, they found the kender—and Kiya.

The Dom-shu looked sunburned and weary. Beside her was a man of middle years, wearing a dusty, faded crimson robe. His hands were bound in front of him, with Kiya holding a rope attached to his bonds. Behind them stretched a long, straggling column comprising a couple hundred armed humans and a substantial sprinkling of kender. The procession was indeed headed by two brawny, sweat-slicked men bearing on their shoulders an elaborate sedan chair of cedar and gold. A tiny figure sat in the chair. As the runner had said, the figure appeared to be carved from dark hardwood, weathered by long exposure to sun, wind, and rain. It was draped in shiny purple cloth.

Kiya hailed Tylocost. "By the gods, I never thought I'd be glad to see your face again!" she said.

"And you smell as delightfully as I remember," the elf retorted. "What is this menagerie, woman?"

"What Husband requested. This is the army of Hylo—and may Corij have mercy on us all!"

She jerked the rope and brought her prisoner forward.

"This fellow claims to be Helbin, chief of the Red Robe wizards in Daltigoth, but will say no more about his business. He's certainly a wizard all right, so watch him."

"I demand to be taken to Lord Tolandruth," Helbin said irritably.

Ignoring the wizard for now, Tylocost asked Kiya, "What is that peculiar fetish at the head of your army? It's hideous!"

Kiya looked blank. "Fetish?" The truth dawned on her, and she threw back her head and laughed. "Come. I'll introduce you!"

When they drew nearer, they could hear a faint rasping coming from the figure.

"It's alive!" Zala exclaimed.

"Very." Kiya rapped a fist against the chair rail. "Your Majesty! You have visitors!"

The wizened doll opened one eye. "Hmm? Is it noon already?"

"May I present Queen Casberry of Hylo," Kiya said. "Your Majesty, this is the famous general from Silvanost, Janissiron Tylocostathan, known as Tylocost."

Casberry leaned forward, staring hard at the elf. "Whew!" she exclaimed. "How did you survive such a beating? What a face they left you with!"

Her bluntness made Zala blink. The elf replied genially, "Bold words indeed from a carved totem." He bowed in the best courtly Silvanesti fashion. "Your Majesty is a tribute to her embalmer." It was clear these two were not going to get along.

Kiya explained they had gone first to Juramona, but learned Tol had moved on. They had been following the track of Tylocost's column, knowing it would lead them to Tol eventually.

Queen Casberry wanted breakfast. The little group made their way to the center of the former nomad camp, where Tylocost's men had kindled a cookfire. Kiya, still leading the sullen Helbin, asked Zala about Tol. The half-elf reported she hadn't seen him for some days now.

"That must have been quite a fight at Juramona," Kiya said.

Zala's memory echoed with screams, and the remembered

scent of blood caused her to shudder. To her surprise, the stoical Dom-shu woman gave her back a consoling pat.

"Things happen around Husband. They always have." Rubbing her hands together, Kiya added, "I'm starving! How about you, wizard?"

The three of them joined the others at the cookfire, where the Ergothians were dishing up boiled bacon and bean porridge left behind by the defeated nomads.

After breakfast, the balance of the day was spent repairing the stockade and sorting through the arms they'd discovered. Once the presence of treasure was discovered by Casberry and her troops, the number of kender in camp began to decline rapidly. The treasure piles also underwent a reduction. Despite Tylocost's alert guards, the gemstones and trinkets weren't safe, and entire kegs vanished. By sundown, the Royal Loyal Militia was down to half its original strength.

Gathered again at the cookfire for supper, Kiya demanded that Casberry stop her people from stealing.

"Kender don't steal," Casberry said quite seriously. "That's a great lie spread about my people wherever they go."

"Can't imagine why," Tylocost said dryly.

In addition to a purple silk gown and a short leather vest dyed brilliant scarlet, the queen now wore a golden circlet. It was the first badge of office Kiya had seen her wear, and she wondered which pile of Ergothian loot had yielded the delicate crown.

While the others debated the reputation of kender, Zala slipped away. She wandered through the covered piles of booty, with no particular goal in mind, and came upon Helbin. Kiya had picketed him, very like a horse, away from the campfire, so the mysterious wizard couldn't overhear their plans for the coming days. Two spearmen had been left to guard him, but they stood at a wary distance. The wizard sat on an overturned keg, his hands bound, seemingly lost in gloomy thoughts.

Noticing her, Helbin rose. Zala mumbled an apology for disturbing him and backed away.

"Please, don't go. You're not unknown to me. You're called Zala, yes?" She kept going, and he called desperately, "We have something in common. Release me and I'll tell you what it is."

She laughed. "That ruse is older than both of us!"

Zala was about to vanish around a pile of loot when Helbin blurted, "You and I owe allegiance to the same master! Or, I should say, the same mistress? The Lady of the Books."

She hesitated. Pressing his advantage, the wizard said, "I know you are Zala Half-Elven. It was I who searched the hunting fraternity for a skilled female tracker and found your name. I recommended you to her in the first place."

"What was my charge?"

"To find Lord Tolandruth and bring him back to Daltigoth."

That was not good enough, and Zala told him so. That information was common knowledge now, among the Juramona Militia.

"I also know your human father is held hostage to your success. He's a prisoner in Caergoth."

The mention of her father sent anger flooding through Zala. She drew her sword. The wizard recoiled as she put the sword tip under his chin and demanded to know what he was up to.

"We're on the same side!" Helbin insisted. "Set me free! I cannot work bound up like this. Dire things may happen if I am not free!"

"If you're such a high sorcerer, why don't you hex the cords from your hands?"

Helbin grimaced. "I am not a sorcerer. I am a wizard of the Red Robes." Such distinctions obviously mattered little to her, so he added, "I need to move my hands in order to perform conjurations—"

She dropped the point of her sword to his chest. "Is my father safe?" she asked, voice husky with fear.

"He lives. He's held by the governor of Caergoth, Lord Wornoth."

"What is your purpose here? Speak true, or I'll cut your throat!"

"Our lady has sworn me to silence. I may speak only to Lord Tolandruth!"

He seemed genuinely distressed, but that meant nothing. City folk were like that, Zala knew. They lied as easily as they breathed.

"If you kill me, all we have fought for will be lost!" Helbin announced.

"And what exactly are 'we' fighting for?"

Zala flinched hard at the unexpected voice behind her. Her sword point pierced Helbin's silk robe, and he yelped.

Tol had just emerged from behind a pile of treasure. Arrayed behind him were Kiya, Tylocost, Queen Casberry, and a sextet of warriors.

"So, Master Helbin," Tol said. "It's been a long time, hasn't it?"

# Chapter 14
## Debts Repaid

An eerie silence had enveloped Daltigoth. Born of terror, it was a palpable presence, like an evil spirit unknowingly summoned from the Abyss. Streets were empty, market squares abandoned, and wind tumbled rubbish over the cobbles where commerce once reigned. Ground level windows were either boarded up or broken out, empty black holes hinting at tragedies within.

Ackal's Wolves had run rampant through the city for four days. The rioting, which had plagued the capital off and on since the beginning of the bakali invasion, ceased completely. So had all trade. From the Quarry District to the canal quay, Daltigoth was quiet—as a corpse is quiet.

Backed by imperial authority, Captain Tathman had proclaimed a curfew. Anyone found outdoors between sundown and sunrise faced swift, certain death. No one was immune—neither lords nor ladies, wizards, priests, artisans, or laborers. Ackal V's thugs moved in a body from district to district, sounding their terrifying wolf calls. These strange instruments, made from cow horn and brass, gave a perfect lupine imitation, the last sound many ears in Daltigoth heard.

Thieves, malcontents, spies, and petty intriguers who continued to ply their trades were slain. So, too, were innocents slaughtered. Workers caught unawares, and folk whose only crime was to be drunk enough to think they could negotiate the back alleys with impunity, paid for their folly. The curfew also gave the Wolves a legal excuse to dispose of their personal enemies. Most were dragged out of their homes, declared in violation of the curfew once on the street, and summarily executed.

The number of deaths was so large a wagon service had to be hastily organized to remove the bodies, to prevent the outbreak of disease. Prisoners from the city jail were conscripted to dig a mass grave. Each morning the wagons rolled to the green fields outside Daltigoth's vast walls and deposited their cargo in the hard earth.

The City Guards, the usual keepers of the peace, had achieved nothing more than a stalemate after a half a year battling the rioters. When the Wolves began their pacification of the unruly streets, some Guards joined them. The rest returned to their barracks and closed their shutters.

With the city growing more tomb-like each day, the emperor became increasingly buoyant. He'd ordered Tathman to keep detailed lists of the "criminals" executed, and he pored over these lists at breakfast and dinner. When he spotted the name of some old enemy, the emperor drank a toast to the victim's demise, then added a gold coin to the cup as reward for Tathman.

One evening, Ackal V held a macabre banquet in the great plaza. He was the only guest. He sat at the head of the great banquet table dining on venison and squab, while facing him was rank upon rank of empty chairs, arranged in lines as precise as a military parade. Each chair represented a resident of Daltigoth slain by the Wolves. The emperor ate and drank well into the night, served by silent, expressionless lackeys. Now and then one would bring a new chair to the rear of the formation.

Empress Valaran lost contact with her chief agent in the city on the second day of the curfew. She sent him another message written in Yetai's secret ink. The courier also disappeared.

In the late afternoon, a few days after her husband's bizarre banquet, Valaran ascended to a high palace corridor to look out on the city's now-quiescent streets. She avoided her old sanctuary. The palace roof reminded her too strongly of

Winath's death. She contented herself with the view of the city's southwest quarter offered by this high, long corridor, which connected the imperial suite to the Consorts' Chambers. From here she could see much of the New City and the Canal District.

Six days had passed since her last communication with Helbin. During that time she'd brought the magic mirror to her own bedchamber, hiding it in plain sight on the high table that held her toiletries. There it seemed nothing more than an exotic Silvanesti trinket, and she could make multiple attempts during the day to contact the wizard, without arousing suspicion by too frequent trips to the library. She had no success; the mirror showed nothing but her own face.

Columns of smoke no longer obscured the city rooftops. The swell of angry voices, once as regular as the ocean tide, likewise was stilled.

Couriers brought war news. The bakali had crossed the Dalti River without boats by resorting to a remarkable tactic. Working night and day, they created a low, short wall of stones about twenty paces out from the eastern shore. They filled this backwater with all manner of rubbish—whole trees, rubble from human homesteads. The result was a huge floating weir of debris. It dammed the Dalti sufficiently to lower the water level behind the obstruction enough for the lizard-men to cross to the far shore. Once loose on the west bank, they swarmed through the rich farmlands northeast of Daltigoth, driving out everyone in their path. They tore down houses and barns, dragging the broken timbers and masonry along with them.

Halfway between the Dalti and North Thorn rivers the bakali host halted and began building an enormous fortified camp. The flat alluvial plain seemed an odd choice for a stronghold; it offered no heights on which to build. Undaunted, the lizard-men erected a huge earthen mound, bolstered by stolen timber and brick, and commenced digging a deep ditch around it. Other parties of bakali carved channels in the black soil back to the Dalti River. When they completed the channels, they could flood the low-lying land around the earthen mound, and create a wide, deep moat.

Faced with these developments, Ackal V scrapped his earlier plans and ordered all the empire's remaining hordes to muster for battle. The Great Horde came together at the village of Verryne, on the east bank of the Thorn River, fifteen leagues from the capital. Only a few cavalry bands remained between Daltigoth and the bakali host, scouting and watching the enemy. This left the city open to attack, but the emperor wasn't worried. The walls of Daltigoth were formidable, the city could be supplied indefinitely via the imperial canal.

Although the bakali seemed the greater danger, strange reports from the east disturbed Ackal V more. They gave Valaran a secret thrill of hope. Rumor had it new Ergothian forces were gathering on the plains north of Caergoth. The nomads had been smashed, and someone was driving the plainsmen back to their home range beyond the Thel Mountains. In her heart, Valaran knew who must be leading these Ergothians. So did Ackal V.

From her vantage point, Valaran watched as the disk of the sun touched the hills west of Daltigoth. Sunset had once been the signal for public houses and wine shops in the Canal District to spring to life. No more. Not with the Wolves' and their brutal curfew.

Valaran visited a public house in the Canal District once, many years ago. For the first and only time in her life, she had ventured into the city of her birth and mixed with common folk in The Bargeman's Rest. Tol had escorted her there. A fight had broken out, and the public house had burned, and Tol had kissed her for the first time. She could still remember that kiss: The awkward press of lips, the stubble of beard on his chin, the taste of . . .

Feminine laughter broke the spell of Valaran's memories. The Consorts' Circle was coming. The fashionably pale, uniformly foolish faces of Ackal's other wives and the women of the court regarded the empress without interest. As custom demanded, each dropped a quick curtsey as she passed in a hiss of silk. None addressed Valaran, and soon she was alone again in the high corridor.

❦ ❦ ❦ ❦ ❦

Word of Tylocost's coup reached Tol, causing excitement among the landed hordes. A cache of treasure would be a welcome addition to their war chest, which, as Egrin wryly pointed out, previously had comprised whatever coins they happened to have on them.

Tol left Egrin and the bulk of the army to continue harrying the nomads from the country and rode swiftly to meet up with Tylocost. With him, he took Riders from Lord Trudo's Oaken Shield Horde and Argonnel's Iron Scythe Horde, some one thousand men on the swiftest horses. Trudo and Argonnel came as well.

Arriving at Tylocost's camp, Tol was cheered even more to discover Kiya there.

Kiya took him by the shoulders and shook him. "Husband! Are you getting enough sleep?"

"Only in the saddle," he joked.

After this characteristically brief reunion, Kiya led him to Tylocost.

The elf's rough tally of the treasure cache—even with all the kender "borrowings"—was impressive. Unwilling to burden their ponies with too much heavy loot, the nomads had made the airless ravine the repository for nearly all the wealth stolen from the eastern provinces.

Tol went to pay his respects to the queen of Hylo. Casberry's first words brought a smile to his face.

"Don't forget your loyal allies, my lord, when it comes time to divide up all that lovely gold!"

They grinned at each other. The queen's face was partially obscured by a jewel-encrusted tiara made to sit upon a brow much larger than hers.

Kiya took Tol aside and told him how they had found Helbin. It was her considered opinion the Red Robe was spying for the emperor. Tol acknowledged this was possible. Unlike his high-minded, White Robe colleagues, Yoralyn and Oropash, Helbin had always struck Tol as an opportunist.

Kiya, Tol, and an escort of warriors then went to where Kiya had left the wizard. They arrived just in time to discover

Zala standing before the wizard with her sword at his throat. She told them the Red Robe claimed to be on their side, to be working for the same patron as she.

"That remains to be seen," Tol replied. "Master Helbin, you'll be judged by how you behave, so no tricks."

With great dignity, Helbin nodded once. Tol cut his tether and bade the wizard follow him. They returned to the campfire. Casberry was sitting in her sedan chair, which rested on the ground. Front and Back lay nearby, snoring softly.

In spite of Helbin's tacit cooperation, Tol left the wizard's wrists bound. Two guards stood behind him. Folding his beringed hands in his lap, Helbin settled himself on the ground across the campfire from Tol.

"Speak, wizard," Tol said at last. "Why are you so far from your tower?"

Helbin met Tol's eyes squarely. "I cannot talk freely before so many, my lord. There's no telling to whom all these ears belong."

"Hang him and be done with it," Tylocost commented.

Judging by the expressions around the fire, most agreed with this suggestion. Either offended or frightened, Helbin remained silent.

"So you claim to work for Zala's patron . . ." Tol said. Like the half-elf, he avoided using Valaran's name openly. In truth, there were too many ears listening. "Can you prove this?"

The Red Robe thrust out his bearded chin. "My word is beyond question!"

"Not with me."

Tol drew his steel saber and held it up, studying the striations of the forged edge, marked with age and faint traces of rust. It was a brilliantly crafted blade. In a conversational tone, he remarked, "The last wizard I had dealings with ending by losing his head. You knew him, I believe?"

Helbin blanched. Mandes the Mist-Maker, Tol's mortal enemy, had been a Red Robe wizard, before the lure of darker magic turned him into a rogue. "My baggage contains documents from the person in question," Helbin said tersely.

The wizard's belongings were brought to Tol. As he opened the appropriate satchel, Helbin's anxiety was plain.

Tol held up the empress's charge, read it silently, and passed it around.

*Be it known,* the parchment stated, *The bearer is acting for the good of the Empire. By My Command,* (signed) *VALARAN, Empress.*

Valaran's seal, an owl clutching a scroll in either claw, was genuine, but Tylocost, for one, was not impressed.

"He could be an imperial rat-catcher. Or he might have stolen the document," the elf said, drawing a look of outrage from the Red Robe.

The remainder of the wizard's books and papers yielded nothing of particular interest. He'd kept a log of his travels and had copious notes regarding magical processes, such as warding off scryers, confounding pursuers, and cloaking a location from sight—all perfectly reasonable since Helbin's specialty was seeing far and not being seen. Then the searchers came upon a small brass-bound box just over two handspans long, one wide, and one deep. Its seamless sides betrayed no lid.

"Don't touch that!" Helbin snapped at the warriors handling the box. He refused to say what it was, so Tol ordered his men to break it open.

The wizard tried to stand, but the soldiers behind him pressed him down again. "My lord, please!" he begged.

"I will have this open, Helbin," Tol said flatly, lifting Number Six.

Brass and wood, however cunningly joined, could not withstand a stroke of steel, and Helbin gave in rather than see the box broken. "As you wish, my lord, but I should like to reveal its contents only to you!"

Though Kiya protested, Tol agreed. He and the wizard left the others by the campfire. Kiya tried to follow, but Tol ordered her to remain.

Wizard and warrior went to the center of the nomad camp. Shielded by piles of stolen goods higher than their own heads, they stopped.

As Helbin complained about his treatment and the general lack of respect shown to him, Tol examined the box. It was weighty for its size. There was no obvious clasp or latch. If the box was sealed by magical means, the nullstone Tol wore in a concealed pocket should have dispersed the spell by now. He shook it hard, but heard nothing rattle inside.

"My lord, I beg you," Helbin urged. "Do not open this box. I give you my word it is not dangerous to you. But opening it—" The wizard shuddered. "The effect could be incalculable!"

Sweat had beaded Helbin's sunburned brow and trickled into his close-cropped beard. Tol was beginning to wonder about the possible danger. Still, he had to know what was in this box.

With Tol's wary gaze upon him, and muttering all the while about dire consequences, Helbin opened the box. On the middle finger of his left hand he wore a large amethyst ring. He tapped the round purple jewel on the box four times. One edge of the brass rim popped up.

Tol waved him back and lifted the hinged door. The box was lined with soft black felt. Nestled inside was a dully gleaming object, a statuette wrought in gray lead.

The small figurine hardly seemed worth all the trouble. Tol noticed tiny screw clamps attached to its head. His puzzlement showed, and Helbin, averting his eyes from the figurine, whispered, "Look at its features."

Tol bent closer, then straightened abruptly, nearly dropping the statue in shock.

"Nazramin!"

Helbin nodded miserably. "The image you hold was made by the late sorcerer Mandes. These"—he flicked a finger toward the screw clamps—"are intended to destroy the emperor's mind, slowly and painfully."

Tol was far less shocked than Helbin by the statue and its purpose. It surprised him not at all to discover that the devious, traitorous Mandes had been hexing his own patron. Then Helbin's last words suddenly sparked a revelation.

"This is how Nazramin destroyed his brother!" he exclaimed.

Image magic was the lowest, vilest form of sorcery, a practice of scrubby shamans or mercenary sorcerers. It shamed a proud wizard like Helbin to possess such a monstrous object.

Seeing it again loosed the floodgates of Helbin's memory, and the story of how it had come to him poured out.

After Mandes's death, one of the wizard's servants had delivered certain scrolls and the figurine to Empress Valaran. The scrolls described how Prince Nazramin had employed Mandes to ruin the mind and body of his brother, Ackal IV, through black magic. The prince did not know, of course, that Mandes had made a second image, of Nazramin himself. The new emperor's natural cruelty had been magnified tenfold by Mandes's sorcery.

Tol stared at the figurine. The cunningly crafted metal face bore the perfect impression of the emperor's outthrust chin, high forehead, arrogant eyes, and his perpetual sneer beneath an upswept mustache.

Helbin begged Tol to put the statuette back in its box. Instead, Tol asked, "If I damaged this thing, would the same hurt be inflicted on Ackal V?"

"Not literally. With sympathetic magic, parallel harm occurs," Helbin said. The two screw clamps, he explained, were simply a representation of the power summoned to damage the emperor's mind.

Why had Mandes sent this awful object to Valaran after his death? Tol wondered. Not for atonement. The rogue wizard had never felt a moment's remorse in his life. No, Tol realized this was Mandes's final act of malice. Valaran, loathing Ackal V herself and inviolate within the imperial precinct, was the perfect choice to inherit the figurine and fulfill Mandes's plan for revenge.

He asked Helbin why Valaran had sent the statuette out of the city.

"Her Majesty enlisted me in her plan to save the empire," Helbin said slowly. "I was glad to oblige. The bakali were pouring across the border. What everyone else saw as a disaster, Empress Valaran saw as the possible salvation of Ergoth. She ordered me to travel the countryside, using my skills to obscure the movements of the bakali host from my colleagues in the Tower of High Sorcery. Without advance knowledge of the enemy's movements, the incompetent generals of the Great Horde stood no chance of defeating the invaders."

The explanation took Tol's breath away. "That's treason!"

Helbin stiffened. "Strong medicine for an ailing patient, my lord. The emperor's corruption and brutality will surely destroy the empire. Empress Valaran lacks powerful allies at court. She reasoned, quite sensibly, that a major military defeat would stir the provincial warlords to rise up against the emperor, inspiring the cowed warlords in Daltigoth to follow suit."

Tol swore under his breath. Scheming wench! In her grand design, who did Valaran see leading the landed hordes to the rescue? That simple, dutiful soldier, Tol of Juramona, of course! He couldn't decide whether her grandiose machinations filled him with pride, or fear.

"You still haven't answered the question—why send the image out of the city with you? Why not use it to destroy Ackal V, as the Mist-Maker used one to kill the emperor's brother?"

Helbin said distastefully, "My lord, Empress Valaran is a woman of high purpose and great courage. She would not stain her soul by stooping to Mandes's methods. She reasoned that if conditions in the palace deteriorated too rapidly, her life, and that of her son, Crown Prince Dalar, would be in danger. Her Majesty placed the statue in my keeping to ensure it remained hidden."

That was face-saving nonsense. Ridding herself of the figure removed the temptation to kill her husband outright. His death, at this time, would be inopportune. Valaran was of noble blood, but not royal, and she would have no support to rule herself. Claimants to the imperial throne would spring up like toadstools after a summer rain. The result would be chaos on an unimaginably bloody scale.

That's where Tol came in. Returned to Daltigoth, he and his army could maintain order while the warlords deposed or executed the crazed Ackal V. The crown prince could be enthroned, with Valaran overtly or covertly the power behind the throne, backed by Tol's hordes. It was a brilliant plan, devious and twisted, worthy of a lifelong resident of the imperial palace.

Helbin was still talking, but Tol had stopped listening. He

grasped the clamp encircling the statuette's temples, and the wizard yelped. Helbin might loathe the statuette and all it stood for, but it had been placed in his charge by the empress herself.

Ignoring his protestations, Tol removed the two clamps. Deep dents remained on both of the statuette's temples and on its forehead.

"This is not how Ergoth will be saved," Tol said. He waved Number Six, torchlight flashing off its polished steel blade. "*This* is the instrument of our deliverance! Nothing else!"

He hunted up a piece of cloth from a nearby pile of loot, wrapped it around the evil image, and tied the whole thing to his back, where his mantle concealed it. After filling the small brass-bound box with coins and jewels from a nearby pile of treasure, he led a sorely complaining Helbin back to the campfire.

Queen Casberry and Tylocost were trading stories about the stupidity of humans. Kiya hailed Tol in relief.

"You arrive just in time, Husband. These two are talking us all to death!"

Tol dropped the box on the ground. Rubies and golden coins spilled out.

"That's all there was," he said, meeting their eyes. "Release Master Helbin from his bonds."

Kiya wasn't certain this was wise, but Tol said the wizard was joining their company. He directed a pointed look at Helbin, adding, "His freedom and continued good health are entirely in his own hands."

Tol sent for horde commanders Trudo and Argonnel. The treasure confiscated from the nomads would be invaluable in sustaining their fight and must be safeguarded against any attempts by plainsmen (or others) to abscond with it. Tol wanted the treasure promptly moved, all of it.

White-haired Trudo, eldest of the commanders of the landed hordes, stroked his beard thoughtfully. "Where are we to take it?" he asked.

"To the only place strong enough to hold it: Caergoth."

His words provoked ominous silence. Trudo and the younger Argonnel exchanged worried looks. Zala, not understanding the swift change of mood, whispered to Tylocost, "What's the matter?"

He murmured, "Caergoth's governor is one of the emperor's most notorious toadies. Lord Tolandruth is proscribed. In Caergoth he can be arrested, even executed."

After an instant's surprised silence, Zala laughed. The bright sound earned scowls from the assembled warlords. Queen Casberry demanded to know the joke.

Zala grinned at the somber faces. "Lord Tolandruth should fear going to Caergoth?" she said, disbelieving. "I think you've got it all backwards. It's Caergoth that should fear Lord Tolandruth!"

Casberry cackled, and Tylocost muttered about wisdom from the mouths of children.

❦ ❦ ❦ ❦ ❦

Valaran awoke with a start. An instant later, the noise came again: a loud knock at her door and the sounds of movement in the antechamber.

"Come," she said, sitting up.

The door swung inward. Framed in the dark opening was a disheveled servant bearing a lamp. "Your Majesty," she said, "the emperor is calling for you!"

Valaran frowned. "Now?"

"Yes, Majesty. Most urgently."

Dismissing the servant, Valaran slid out of bed. A silk robe of brown and gold brocaded with crimson metallic thread lay across the foot of her bed. She drew it on and donned matching slippers. Her long chestnut hair was braided for bed, so she merely tucked a few errant strands behind her ears before fitting a copper-colored veil over her head and face.

The servant who'd awakened her had withdrawn beyond the tall white doors that marked the entrance to the empress's suite. There she waited, flanked by sleepy ladies-in-waiting with no more idea what was happening than Valaran. With the women surrounding the empress, the entourage journeyed through the maze of palace corridors.

The doors to the emperor's rooms stood wide open.

Surprisingly, the opening was flanked by two ordinary soldiers, members of the Household Guard. Ackal V had relied on his Wolves so long Valaran scarcely saw regular Householders anymore. One of the soldiers escorted the empress and her ladies within.

Even from a distance, Valaran could feel the absence of the stifling heat Ackal usually maintained in his chambers. The cavernous hypostyle hall was rapidly cooling to normal. She walked a little faster.

The fire had been allowed to die out in the enormous fireplace. The emperor, wearing nothing but a soldier's white loincloth, stood before it. He was drinking wine straight from a tall silver urn. Piled on the floor around him and on his bed were the furs, gloves, and heavy clothing he usually wore. The lamplight showed how emaciated he'd become. His ribs were easily visible, and the knobs of his collar bone stuck out like doorknobs at the base of his hollow throat.

Paralyzed by the sight of their nearly naked sovereign, the empress's escort fell back in disarray. At Valaran's command, the warrior escorted them out and she found herself alone with her husband.

"Lady, what day is it?"

Taken aback, Valaran regarded the emperor in silent confusion. He repeated the question, and she stammered, "Day four of the Quarter Moon of Luin, Your Majesty. Year Seven of your reign."

"I did not ask the year!" His temper was unchanged, at least.

He picked up his discarded trews and used them to wipe sweat from his face and chest. "I feel as though I've come out of a fever. It was hot as dragon's breath in here!" he exclaimed, drinking again from the urn.

Valaran's thoughts were racing. A symptom of Ackal V's madness, as far back as when Mandes was still alive, was an extreme sensitivity to cold. Obviously something was amiss. Had his madness veered onto another course?

"Helbin," said Ackal V, lowering the pitcher of wine.

Thank the gods she wore a veil. Hearing that name made Valaran's face flame with alarm. Her hands, tucked into her sleeves, gripped her forearms tightly. "Who, sire?" she stammered.

"The Red Robe. You know who I mean. I want Helbin found and arrested."

Was he toying with her? She cleared her throat and asked, "For what charge, Your Majesty?"

"Treason. This business of our seers not being able to observe the bakali—they must have some magical aid." He waved a hand. "Any idiot could see it. Helbin disappears, then our search for the invaders is stymied. And the Red Robe's expertise?" The emperor grinned, showing long teeth. "Protective wards and veils of obscurity! He's aiding the lizards the same way that Mandes did decades ago. I want him dragged back here in chains. Then we'll find out what the bakali are doing."

He swept the debris of clothing and furs from his wide bed and climbed into it, dismissing her.

Cautiously, she asked, "You Majesty, why do you give me this order? Such matters are not usually my responsibility."

"I can't find Tathman at the moment. He must be in the city somewhere."

Yes, somewhere in the city killing people. "I will convey your wishes to the warlords, sire."

"Ignorant, worthless fools, the lot of them," he muttered, closing his eyes to sleep. "I shall take personal command of the Great Horde. It all falls to me. I will wipe the bakali from the face of Krynn!"

When she was safely out of his sight, in the darkness of the far end of the hall, Valaran was seized with a violent shaking. Mandes's spell was broken! There could be no doubt. The emperor had recovered his wits. As cruel and unfeeling as ever, his reason was returning—and that made him even more dangerous.

She must relay his order for Helbin's capture. Ackal V would know if she disregarded his command. But that wouldn't stop her from trying to warn the Red Robe that his part in her plot was now known. He must not be captured. If he should be made to divulge what he knew—contemplating that disaster made Valaran's heart shrink to a small, frantic knot.

She fought her rising panic, bracing herself against a column. If the blood of the Ackals ran strong in her husband, the blood of their rivals, the Pakins, flowed with equal strength in her. The Ackals had always been savages; the Pakins ruled by their wits. Cold, at times harsh, to be sure, the Pakins were the intelligent strain in the dynasty. She must call upon that acumen now to save herself and, even more importantly, to save her son. She had to out-think the emperor.

Let Ackal V lead his army into battle. Maybe the bakali would accomplish for her what Mandes, Helbin, and even Lord Tolandruth thus far had not.

# Chapter 15

# A Clash of Worlds

acking the time to procure wagons, Tol decided to transport the nomads' plunder by horse. The loot was distributed among the herd of captured animals, with especially bulky items loaded onto travois. Strung out in single file, the caravan was quite long. Tylocost's foot soldiers trudged close alongside the column, while Riders patrolled at a distance. Two thousand men made a formidable escort for the treasure train, but it was a long way to Caergoth.

"Tempting target," observed Queen Casberry, swaying along in her sedan chair.

"For whom?" asked Tylocost, walking at her side. He considered the kender more of a danger to the treasure than any nomads.

She ignored him and spoke to Tol, who rode on her other side. "It's a good thing you have us here, my lord."

"I am grateful for Your Majesty's help," Tol replied gravely.

"Grateful. Mmm, yes. About that—your lofty wife made certain promises to us, certain offers. I'd like to take this matter up with you now, my lord."

Tylocost snorted. Kiya was on the far side of the column, leading the Juramona Militia, and could hardly speak for herself.

"Beware, my lord!" Tylocost warned. "Tiny fingers are reaching for your purse!"

"Tiny fingers soon will be reaching for your eyes, elf!" Casberry snapped.

Tol suppressed a smile. "Speak your mind, Majesty."

She launched into a long, rambling address about how long she had lived, how many places she'd visited, and what a good friend to the empire Hylo had always been. She made it sound as though Ergoth and Hylo had been allies and equals for decades, although it was her husband, King Lucklyn the First, who had signed treaties that reduced Hylo to Ergoth's vassal.

"When the monster XimXim infested our country, the empire sent you to defeat him," she said. "We won't dwell on the many years it to took for Ergoth to aid us in our battle against the dreadful creature."

"Yes, don't dwell."

She gritted her teeth at Tylocost's interruption, but continued, "It's only fitting that now, when the empire faces its most harrowing moment, Hylo returns the favor. However—"

"Here it comes!"

Casberry lashed out with her fly whisk, made from the severed tail of a donkey. Tylocost ducked the blow.

Annoyed, the queen declared with unkenderlike brevity, "We were promised one gold piece per day, per blade!"

Tylocost exclaimed, "That's double the going rate for mercenaries! And for what? Them?" He waved a hand at the Royal Loyals, most of whom were dragging their scabbards just to see the patterns of dust that arose.

"A generous offer," Tol remarked. A good portion of the kender army's wages, he knew, were kicked back to Casberry. That was simply how business was done in Hylo. "Is Your Majesty not satisfied with it?"

Casberry stared. "You mean, you'll pay?"

"If Kiya proposed it and you accepted, I must hold to the agreement."

She sank back against her cushions, beaming. "You're a prince, Lord Tolandruth. A true prince among humans!" Tylocost sighed, and shook his head.

A dusty rider was galloping toward them. He held aloft a leather cylinder. A message. Tol reined up, and the order to halt was passed down the line. The kender dropped where they were and broke out their skins. Cider and homebrew flowed freely.

Kiya rode over to see what had prompted the stop, and Zala arrived from the trailing ranks. She, too, was mounted on a nomad pony, as was Helbin, trotting close on her heels. Tol had set Zala the task of minding the wizard.

Helbin's standing was still somewhat murky. Tol had demanded the wizard remove the shield that hid the bakali from the scrutiny of the Daltigoth wizards. Helbin objected, citing the empress's orders. Tol had then refused to unchain his wrists and placed the Red Robe under Zala's care. A few days scourged by fetters ought to convince the soft, city-bred Helbin to do as Tol required.

The messenger saluted and handed over the leather cylinder. "Compliments of Lord Egrin," he said.

Inside the cylinder was a spool of parchment. The message was brief. Tol passed it to Tylocost, then summarized its contents for the others.

"The hordes with Egrin and Pagas have been skirmishing with a large formation of nomads, riding east. Egrin asks if I will move up and join the attack."

"The nomads are fleeing; let them go," said Zala.

Tylocost handed the scroll to Kiya. "Hammer them, my lord," he said. "The harder the better, for the sake of future peace."

Kiya agreed. "I know plainsmen, Husband. If you let them ride out unmolested, they'll convince themselves they were never defeated. Eventually, they'll be raiding the empire's borders again."

"My lord, I'd be happy to safeguard the treasure," Queen Casberry piped.

"The fox guarding the henhouse," cracked Tylocost.

They began to trade insults, but Tol didn't hear them. He'd taken the dispatch back from Kiya. Its last line bothered him.

*According to prisoners from the Firepath tribe,* Egrin had written, *it is likely their chief, Tokasin, rides with the host ahead of us.* So Tokasin, the red-haired nomad who'd led the attack on Juramona, was still alive.

"Tylocost," Tol said, interrupting the bickering. "See the caravan safely to Caergoth. I will ride ahead to the rendezvous point at the confluence, gather the hordes there, and go after the nomads."

Casberry's kender were all on foot and couldn't keep up with Riders anyway, so Tol agreed she should remain behind and "guard the treasure" as well. There was no question Kiya would accompany Tol, but when Zala offered to do likewise, he demurred, telling her to stay with Tylocost, the kinder, and the wizard.

"Besides, you have business in Caergoth, don't you?"

He had written a pardon for Zala's human father, held captive in the city. It held no legal standing, but should be sufficient to get the old man released if used in conjunction with the empress's ring and seal, which Zala still carried.

The huntress was plainly torn. Although eager to free her father, she didn't like letting Tol out of her sight. If he got himself killed, she would lose the huge bounty owed her by Empress Valaran, and she and her father would likely be targets of the empress's wrath. However, her father was aged and alone. Lord Tolandruth was neither. She agreed to continue south with Helbin and the elf to Caergoth.

"Don't worry, girl," Kiya said. "I'll watch out for Husband."

The Dom-shu woman understood the half-elf's quandary. She disliked being parted from Tol, too. Miya had never felt the same way about him, and teased the tough, stoical Kiya for her "motherly concern." Kiya thumped her sister soundly, but couldn't explain her feelings. Perhaps they sprang from Tol's lack of concern about his own safety. Although he'd lived four decades, he still seemed like a younger brother, one a bit too naive for the dangerous company he kept.

Knowing it was risky, Tol left only a demi-horde of Riders to protect Tylocost's foot soldiers and the treasure caravan. Of greater concern to Tol than brigands was imperial intervention. Caergoth housed a large garrison, reinforced by remnants of the armies defeated by the nomads. If Governor Wornoth took it on himself to seize the treasure on behalf of the emperor, there would be little Tylocost could do. The war chest of Tol's burgeoning campaign would be lost.

Still, Tokasin's band had committed many outrages in the eastern provinces, of which the burning of Juramona was only one. Tylocost was right. To preserve future peace, the tribesmen must be punished as severely as possible.

With just over two hordes, Tol and Kiya rode away from the slow-moving caravan. They arrived at the rendezvous point before midday and found eight landed hordes mustered near the confluence of the east and west branches of the Caer River. Tol proclaimed this the new Army of the East. He and ten thousand Riders headed off to join Egrin's pursuit of the fleeing nomads.

Ten hordes take up a great deal of territory. The landed hordes, former imperial warriors, knew how to sort themselves into formation. From wing to wing, Tol's force covered almost three leagues.

By noon the next day, the Ergothians began to see signs of what lay ahead. Dust rose over rolling hills and woodlands, marking the movements of large bodies of horsemen ahead of them. Scouts were sent out to locate friends and foes. Word came back from the southern wing of Tol's army: armed men, several hundred strong, were riding toward them.

"Nomads?" asked Tol. The sun was high, the air humid; a breeze stirring through the pines around them offered little relief.

"No, my lord. They're in armor," said the scout. "They wear yellow capes and golden breastplates, and bear white plumes on their helmets."

Tol frowned. Why did that sound familiar?

"Probably pirates," Kiya said absently.

Tol pivoted his horse in a tight circle. "What?"

"Is your hearing failing, Husband? Men your age often start to lose their prowess in one way or another—"

He shouted for his horde commanders. Yellow capes were the mark of Tarsan soldiers. Tarsan marines, not pirates, wore brass breastplates and plumed helmets.

The news caused the warlords to swear roundly. If Tarsis had broken the peace treaty so hard won by Tolandruth and Lord Regobart, the empire was in worse danger than ever.

Tol halted his army and swung it south, to face the

unknown band of Tarsans. Scouts estimated their strength at a few hundred, but they could be the advance guard of a much larger force.

All ten hordes formed the famous scythe formation long favored by Ergothian commanders. The warriors sorted themselves into a great crescent, with the horns of the scythe facing the enemy. If their foes rode straight in, they faced encirclement. If they tried to attack either end, the rest of the hordes could strike them. The silent mass of horsemen rode forward at a fast walk. No sense tiring their animals on so hot a day before a possible battle.

Scouts ranged wider and deeper, to get behind the unknown cavalry. They sent back confirmation. No larger force was in sight. The Tarsans, if Tarsans they were, had only this small band.

When the oncoming force was reported to be only half a league distant, Tol brought his army to a halt. The dust they'd churned up rolled forward over their sweating bodies. They faced an open field. On its far side rose a low hill, its base sprinkled by tall poplars.

They were on familiar ground: the Eastern Hundred. Tol had been born not ten leagues from this spot. The civil war between the Ackals and Pakins had raged back and forth through this province for six years. Later flare-ups, like the raids that had first brought Tol into contact with Marshal Odovar, had not died out completely until Tol was in his teens. Thinly populated and devoid of large cities, the Eastern Hundred was a crossroads for armies moving east and west, traveling to and from the heartland of the empire.

Over their own enforced silence, the Ergothians heard the clatter of metal-clad men and horses on the move. The high, tinny notes of a fife lilted above the noise. Tol drew his sword. Ten thousand warriors followed suit.

"No one is to move until I say," Tol commanded. "Not one blade!"

At the far side of the field, a wedge of horsemen, mounted on light-colored animals, emerged slowly from the poplar trees. Their brass cuirasses and plumed helmets threw off painfully bright reflections from the high sun; their yellow mantles were stained with grime. The lead riders bore standards of white and gold, but instead of leaping dolphins, symbol of the Tarsan marines, the banners were decorated with golden balance scales.

Tol inhaled sharply, hardly crediting his eyes. It had been many years since he'd seen that symbol on the livery worn by guards of the House of Lux—the guild of goldsmith and gem merchants in Tarsis.

"Everyone, stand fast," he said, easing his horse forward out of line. Kiya followed him. He opened his mouth to tell her to remain, and she said flatly, "I'm not everyone. I'm your wife."

The two of them advanced slowly. The Tarsans stopped, and the fifer ceased his tune. The foremost horseman held up a hand in greeting.

"Hail, Ergoth!"

Tol reined up, resting his hands across the pommel of his saddle. Empty hands were a gesture of peace, but Number Six's grip was close, just in case.

"Hail to you, Tarsis," he replied. "Who are you, and what brings you to imperial land?"

The rider removed the heavy polished helmet. She was a young woman, with yellow hair cut boyishly short. In each earlobe she wore several tiny gold rings. Her face was familiar; in memory, Tol heard a girl's high voice saying, *"Most call me Val."*

"Valderra."

She smiled briefly. "My lord flatters me by remembering."

Valderra was the personal herald of Hanira, Syndic of Tarsis. Years ago, she had led Tol to the Golden House for his meeting with Hanira after the fall of the city.

She added, "You see before you the Free Company of the Golden House. We are here at the bidding of my mistress."

At Valderra's nod, the fifer played a lively trill. In response, a trio of riders emerged from the poplar woods at the rear of the Tarsan troop. Although Tol could hardly believe it, Syndic Hanira was one of the three. Flanking her were two bodyguards. She headed directly to Tol and bestowed a radiant smile on her conqueror.

"My Lord Tolandruth," she said. "It has been a long time."

She was dressed in gray leather. Her night-black hair was pulled forward over one shoulder, in a single, loose braid. A gray leather hat with narrow brim shaded her face. Some seven years had passed since Tol had last seen her, but Hanira looked exactly as he remembered—elegant, sophisticated, and beautiful—even here in the sunbaked hills of the Eastern Hundred.

Kiya cleared her throat, and Tol straightened in the saddle, recollecting his somewhat scattered thoughts.

"Why are you here, Syndic?" he asked tersely. "And with armed troops? This violates the treaty between Tarsis and Ergoth."

Hanira lost her pleasant smile, and her tone grew cool. "Syndic I am, but you could spare a kind word to greet a friend."

"Are you a friend?" asked Kiya bluntly.

"I am. No treaty has been broken, my lord. This is not Tarsis before you now, only the House of Lux."

Hanira's guild had hired three hundred twenty veteran mercenaries and equipped them with surplus Tarsan arms. Hanira herself assumed command, although the day-to-day running of the Free Company was left to a professional warrior, Captain Tindyll Anovenax, son of Tol's former foe Admiral Anovenax. Captain Anovenax rode one of the other horses, but stayed silent behind Hanira.

"We come to offer our help in your time of need," the syndic said. "My men are at your disposal, my lord."

Three hundred well-trained mercenaries were a modest but welcome addition to his army. Yet Tol was astonished that Hanira should have paid the cost herself, through the wealthy guild she controlled. Even more amazing, she had accompanied her troops into the field.

Kiya, ever distrustful, asked, "What's it going to cost us?"

"Nothing. Everything. In politics, as in trade, personal relationships matter most. I am here—*we* are here—to preserve our longstanding friendship with Lord Tolandruth."

The Free Company had left Tarsis before the fall of Juramona, sailing west to the Gulf of Ergoth and disembarking at the mouth of the Caer River. They had traveled east to avoid the imperial hordes and bakali hovering around Daltigoth. Hanira had intended to reach Juramona, Tol's hometown, before the new phase of Solin, but captured nomads had told of the town's destruction and the plainsmen's subsequent defeat at the hands of a new Ergothian army.

"I knew it must be you," she said simply. "We followed the trail of panicked tribesmen, and here you are."

Tol maneuvered his horse closer to hers, and extended a hand. "Then accept my apology—and my welcome to Ergoth, Syndic."

Bypassing the hand, she grasped his forearm warrior fashion. Clever Hanira had turned the simple gesture of friendship into a declaration of equality.

She called her captain forward. With his dark hair and olive skin, young Tindyll Anovenax seemed at first glance little like his choleric father, but his face, like the admiral's, bore the lines carved by wind and sun. He also proved to have the voice of one accustomed to bellowing orders at sea.

Captain Anovenax agreed to follow Tol's command—it was his syndic's will, after all. He agreed, too, with Tol's reasons for ordering him and his men to the rear of the Ergothian formation. More than a few warlords would attack on sight should they spot Tarsans leading a charge.

The Tarsan troopers and their small caravan of supply wagons took their place in the rearguard. Hanira, Valderra, and one of the syndic's bodyguards remained with Tol. The guard's high cheekbones, long jaw, and somber expression gave him the look of an ascetic priest. Hanira introduced him as Fenj, the finest swordsman in Tarsis. Fenj's complete disinterest in conversation wasn't mere stoicism. His tongue had been cut out when he was captured by pirates as a boy.

The Army of the East and their new allies continued the eastward journey to join up with Egrin's hordes. Before nightfall, the dark edge of the Great Green was visible on the eastern horizon. Small groups of plains folk, mounted and on foot, could be seen hurrying northward, parallel to the forest edge.

Tol dispatched Lord Trudo to bring back prisoners for questioning. In the gathering dusk, three companies of Trudo's horde galloped out to seize a band of nomads fleeing on foot. Mounted plainsmen turned back to defend their comrades, and a sharp conflict ensued. Numbers prevailed, however, and soon the Ergothians were herding a line of ragged, frightened captives back to Tol.

Looking down at them from horseback, he asked about their tribe, wanting to know if any were from Tokasin's Firepath tribe. No one answered. Trudo offered to behead a few, to encourage the rest to talk. Tol ignored him.

"We've not much time!" he told them. "Where is Tokasin? Speak, and you all will be spared!"

A woman clutching a small child spat, "Liar! We know you'll kill us once you find out what you want to know!"

He couldn't blame her for thinking so. Any other warlord would do just that.

"My word as Lord Tolandruth, you will not be harmed."

The woman turned away in stubborn silence, but an older nomad, his gray beard spattered with blood, shouted, "Many here are Firepathers! They're trying to reach their chief at the Isle of Elms!"

This was a large grove of elm trees, a half-league from the Great Green. The closely growing trees, sited atop a slight rise, would make an excellent defense against imperial horsemen.

Shoving broke out among the prisoners as Firepathers vented their anger against the old fellow for speaking, but other tribesmen, young and old, defended him. The alliance between tribes obviously was wearing thin. Ergothians moved in to quell the disturbance.

"Why didn't the savages just run for the forest?" Hanira said, gesturing at the Great Green in the distance.

Kiya said tartly, "These 'savages' are no more at home in the greenwood than you are, Syndic. They're plainsmen, riders. The people of the forest would treat them as invaders!"

As he had vowed, Tol released the captives once they'd

been disarmed. Some of his horde commanders protested, but he had no intention of burdening his army with prisoners. The freed nomads scattered rapidly as the ten thousand Ergothians veered north toward the Isle of Elms. Sunset was nearly upon them, but Tol would not delay. He was certain Chief Tokasin was the true leader of the nomad invasion. Mattohoc and the other chiefs, however great their hatred of the empire, were not charismatic enough to forge their disparate tribes into a single army. Tokasin had done that.

They rode through the night. Darkness made it impossible to hold formation. By daybreak Tol's ten hordes were strung out over four leagues.

When the sun rose, its light revealed the Isle of Elms ahead. Towering trees, on a low hill, were isolated from the primeval growth of the Great Green by a half-league of rolling field. Morning light also picked out the iron blades and helmets of the hordes under Egrin's command. Their numbers had not been sufficient to surround the Isle. The arrival of Tol's hordes would remedy that situation.

The trumpeters sounded assembly. Tol needed to bring his straggling hordes together, and quickly. Egrin's men were engaged. If Tokasin was smart as well as fierce, this would be no more than a rear guard, a small force left to hold off Egrin's hordes while Tokasin and the main body slipped away.

At Hanira's suggestion, Tol sent her Free Company on a wide sweep around the Isle of Elms, to prevent such an escape. The Tarsans, on fresher mounts than the hard-riding Ergothians, could move fast. Captain Anovenax vowed that not a single nomad would get through, then his disciplined company galloped away.

Valderra begged the syndic for permission to go with them. This request obviously surprised Hanira. Her herald was no soldier.

"I can fight," the young woman insisted. She drew the slim saber from her gilded scabbard. "Let me go, mistress. I will do you honor!"

The syndic hesitated, then gave her leave to go. Valderra twisted her horse's head around, and Hanira added, "But mind you come back, Val! It's very hard to get good heralds these days!"

Smiling under her heavy helmet, Valderra galloped after her comrades.

"Your herald shows a warrior's pride," Kiya commented.

Hanira sighed. "She and Tindyll hope to wed. She doesn't want to be parted from him, even in battle."

Half the morning had gone before Tol's scattered force had regrouped into fighting formation. Nerves and the day's heat conspired to drench them all in sweat by the time he gave the order to advance.

Ranks of horsemen trotted through the trampled, brown grass. Any sounds of the fighting ahead were lost in the thunder of their own horses' hooves. Veteran of many battles, Tol felt the old tightness in his throat, the hot tension forming in the pit of his stomach. Battle was never routine. It remained a hard, bloody business to which no sane person ever grew accustomed.

At his command, horns blared from the leading hordes. Answering blasts came from Egrin's men. Arrows were flying, and riders surged back and forth along the edge of the elm grove. Some nomads had taken up positions among a tangle of windfall trees.

A messenger rode up and saluted.

"Lord Egrin requests Lord Tolandruth lead his men into the gap between the Isle of Elms and the Great Green, to cut off any escape attempt by the enemy," he panted. This was the very route Anovenax's Tarsans had taken.

"Tell Lord Egrin we will deploy as he suggests," Tol replied. He added a warning about the Tarsans' presence. It wouldn't do for Egrin's men to attack their new allies.

Horns blared commands right and left. The Ergothians drew their sabers, resting the dull edge against their ironclad shoulders. Surveying the lofty elms, Tol regretted sending Tylocost and the Juramona Militia on to Caergoth. Riders would never be able to get at the nomads hidden among the lofty trees, but the militia might.

Denser clouds of dust rose in front of them. Captain Anovenax's force was already engaged. It wouldn't do to let hired Tarsans have all the glory.

"Forward, at the canter!" Tol ordered.

He glanced once at Hanira. She was keeping pace, with Fenj a few steps ahead of her. He carried an oversized shield to defend her, if need be. It was astonishing that anyone as rich and powerful as a syndic of Tarsis would risk her life in someone else's battle, but Hanira was no ordinary woman. Even so, Tol knew she wasn't motivated by loyalty or love. She expected to profit from her deeds in some way.

The Free Company, a streak of brass amidst the gray and brown mass of nomads, was fighting furiously against a far larger band of plainsmen. Tol ordered the pace increased to a gallop, and with a roar his Ergothians charged forward. They were echeloned to the right to cut off any attempt by the nomads to reach the Great Green.

The last few paces before the clash, all sounds seemed to still. There was only the drum beat in Tol's head, the sound of his own heart. Although loud, it was steady, not racing. He held Number Six high, point out. He might have been bellowing, but at that moment he could hear nothing.

—and then he collided with a nomad, horse to horse, blade to blade. His opponent wielded a captured Ergothian saber, and they traded several cuts until Tol shifted around and brought his saber down hard on the nomad's wrist. Steel hissed through the man's buckskins, and beyond. His hand, still gripping its stolen sword, fell and was lost amid the churning horses.

Tol slashed at the next nearest foe, a plainsman with a straight sword and leather-covered buckler. The nomad attacked, his point scoring a bloody line along Tol's jaw, before Tol drove Number Six through the man's small shield and into his chest. The fellow slid off his horse, eyes wide in astonishment.

The weight of Tol's hordes washed over the enemy like high tide over a lonely rock. Pinched between the Tarsans and the Ergothians, the nomads were pushed back, half their number driven toward the Isle of Elms and the other half to the distant Great Green. Still they did not break, for these were Tokasin's Firepath warriors, considered by all to be the fiercest fighters among the nomadic plainsmen. Their buck-skin shirts bore a design, worked in red beads, of a stylized thunderbolt. Red beads likewise decorated their long hair, in imitation of their chief's fiery hair.

The melee separated Hanira and Fenj from Tol, but Kiya remained by him, protecting his back. She took a hard knock from the hilt of a nomad sword and reeled in the saddle, blood welling in her mouth. Dazed, she found herself staring up at the summer sky. It was filled with towering clouds, sculpted white shapes against the hazy blue. As she grappled with her reins and fought to stay atop her tough plains pony, she was amazed to see the clouds changing shape. The white columns flowed into definite forms: separate individuals standing shoulder to shoulder and gazing down onto the battlefield with cloud-white eyes. The image was so clear Kiya froze, head thrown back, staring up.

The clang of blade meeting blade in front of her face shocked her out of her stupor. Tol had leaned over and fended off an attack by a black-bearded nomad.

"Kiya!" Tol roared. "Kiya, are you hurt?"

She shook her head and squeezed her eyelids shut so tightly her vision was blurred when she opened them again, but the cloud-people remained, staring implacably down on the enormous field of battle. This was no time to mention such a thing. The black-bearded plainsman was aiming another cut at her, so she brought up her sword and slashed him from neck to waist.

"I'm all right!" she shouted, pushing Tol away.

The nomads who had been cut off on the Great Green side of the meadow were annihilated. The remainder rode hard for the Isle of Elms. Whooping with victory, the Ergothians spurred after them, but when they neared the trees the pursuers faced a new attack.

Nomads on foot—women, children, and wounded warriors—concealed within the safety of the elms launched arrows, as well as deadly accurate stones from slings. Too many Ergothian saddles were emptied before Tol could make his jubilant men withdraw. The hordes moved out of range and mustered on the plain in full view of the shattered, exhausted nomads hiding in the trees.

A call sounded from the high-pitched Tarsan trumpets. Not knowing what the signal meant, Tol ordered his men to hold their places while he went to see what the Tarsans wanted.

The mercenaries were drawn up in a hollow square when Tol reached them. Captain Anovenax and several others knelt in the center of the square. The Tarsans parted ranks to allow Tol and Kiya to ride in.

"A brisk fight!" Tol declared. "Well done, Captain!"

At that moment, Hanira's bodyguard Fenj stepped aside and Tol realized the focus of the kneeling group was a supine figure: Valderra. Her gilded breastplate was pierced through and stained red, her young face waxen in the harsh sunshine. Helmetless, her short golden hair was sweat-slicked and filthy. Captain Anovenax gently closed her staring eyes, his expression eloquent. He wept silently, but without shame.

Tol murmured, "I'm sorry, Syndic. What happened?"

"Too many foes, too little skill." Hanira looked up, and her face seemed to have aged a decade.

A whirlwind of dust announced the arrival of a quartet of Ergothians. The lead Rider brought Egrin's greetings, and the news that Tol was needed for a council of battle.

Tol acknowledged the message, and finally noticed Kiya. Her chin was stained with dried blood from a lower lip cut and growing puffy. More blood sprinkled her buckskin shirt. She was looking up at the sky dazedly.

He asked if she was well, and she assured him she was. Still concerned, Tol told her to remain here. Surprisingly, she agreed without argument.

Once Tol had ridden away to join the war council, Kiya glanced again at the sky, but the clouds were only clouds now. The images she had seen during the battle were gone.

When she looked down again, Kiya saw Hanira and her bodyguard had gone. Captain Anovenax had covered Valderra with his own golden mantle and was still kneeling beside her, holding her hand. His unembarrassed emotion surprised her. Ergothian warlords prided themselves on their hardened feelings, as did Dom-shu warriors. Apparently,

Tarsans did not. Dismounting, she led her pony over to the grieving man.

"I sorrow for your loss," she said. "The syndic has departed?"

"She had to take her leave." Tindyll's voice was hoarse, freighted with terrible sadness. "Her sorrow is very great."

Kiya had never much liked Hanira. She muttered, "Off to hire a new herald, I suppose."

The captain gave her a dark-eyed glare. "You don't understand," he said, choking. "Valderra was not merely her herald. She was Hanira's daughter."

# C h a p t e r   1 6
## Walls of Stone

en thousand mounted warriors crowded the square before the imperial palace, completely covering the mosaic of Ackal Ergot's victories that decorated its vast surface. They were arrayed in two huge blocks, separated by a narrow avenue. Drawn from the city's garrison, they represented a quarter of Daltigoth's defenders. Their scarlet mantles were like a sea of blood; their polished iron helmets gleamed. Lining the steps and stone plinths on either side of the palace doors were a thousand drummers, pounding in unison. The thunderous booming reverberated off the walls of the Inner City and shook the palace down to its foundation. High above the scene, watching from a turret window, Valaran could feel the drumming through the soles of her slippers, feel it in her very bones.

It might have been a stirring sight, glorious and terrible, but Valaran knew only a growing, suffocating sense of desperation. Two days had passed since the emperor's sudden recovery of mental clarity. His energy in that time had been breathtaking. Man by man, he had culled the garrison of its best warriors, made battle plans with his warlords—the ones he hadn't banished or executed—and ordered a huge amount of food and arms from the imperial stores. He also reversed a lax trend in his household and forbade his family to set foot outside their private quarters.

Yet another custom dating back to Ackal Ergot's day—the

confining of the empress, consorts, and their children—had begun as a means to protect the imperial family, and preserve the purity of the dynasty's bloodline. But Ackal V invoked the Purity Sanction to prevent Valaran from intriguing behind his back. She couldn't be certain exactly what he knew about her plotting, and the uncertainty was maddening. As with all his enemies, he used her doubt to keep her off balance.

Now he passed two calm evenings with his wives and children, playing the role of good husband and stern father. Valaran found his insincere serenity more unbearable than his casual cruelty, for it left her in an agony of suspense, never knowing when his mood might shift and he would order some new outrage. He took Crown Prince Dalar on his lap while continuing a conversation with his other children, and Valaran's blood ran cold. Seeing her son in his hands was like watching the boy menaced by a deadly serpent. The question wasn't *if* Dalar would get hurt, but when.

At the end of last night's family dinner, Ackal V had risen from the table at last—his appetite had been prodigious since the breaking of Mandes's spell—and called for Tathman. The Wolf captain arrived and stood by his master, a silent, hulking menace. Then Ackal addressed his family.

"I leave tomorrow to destroy the invaders," he announced. "But you need not fear. In my absence, both the Purity Sanction and my Wolves will ensure your safety. I could not face the enemy without knowing all I hold is safe."

Valaran fumed silently. Not only was he imprisoning her in the palace, he was setting his killers to watch over her. Tathman's men would not dare lay hands on her, but her every action would be reported to the emperor.

Ackal took up a golden goblet filled with nectar. He drank it slowly, as though savoring the liquid's delicate flavor. He was up to something, keeping them together like this. Valaran could see in his eyes it was the continuing suspense he savored, not the drink. Finally, he let the other boot drop.

"Crown Prince Dalar will accompany me."

"Sire, no!" Valaran was on her feet before she was even aware of having moved.

His false smile vanished. "The boy goes where I say he

goes! He will see his first campaign, and what better place for that than with his father?"

Valaran could barely remember the rest of that horrible evening. Ackal's decision was unprecedented, his motives hardly paternal. Dalar, so small, so fragile, was to be a hostage to her good behavior. More than ever she thought the emperor must have learned of her seditious activities. Since recovering his wits, he had been closeted with advisors, spymasters, and unsavory practitioners of magic. Had he divined the cause of his own madness—the same evil he'd visited on his own brother, Ackal IV?

There was no better news from the College of Wizards. Helbin's successor as chief of the Red Robes, the wizard Eremin, reported they had at last broken through the veil that so long shrouded events in the east. They had seen imperial forces driving the nomads from the empire.

Eremin did not know the horde names, and so described the standards they'd seen. As Ackal V identified each one—the Plains Panthers, the Firebrands, the Corij Rangers, the Black Viper Horde—he grew more angry. All were landed hordes, the provincial gentlemen he loathed and had refused to call to duty.

Eremin was astonished by the emperor's furious reaction to what he believed would be welcome news. With nomads raging throughout the Eastern and Riverland hundreds, surely it was better that the local hordes raise themselves, rather than allow savages to rampage unchecked.

The Red Robe could not tell his liege who led the landed hordes. The visions had not been that precise. He promised to work hard to improve them, but it was plain Ackal V already knew who was responsible for the uprising.

All this Valaran remembered as she watched the warriors in the plaza await the arrival of their supreme commander. Beset with doubts and fears, she held on to Tol as her lifeline. His love for her and his hatred of Ackal V were the greatest assets she had left.

In her mind she saw him, not as he'd been when they parted, beaten and lying in the back of a creaking cart, but as he had been when they first met, a vibrant young warrior, newly come to Daltigoth for the dedication of the Tower of High Sorcery. It wasn't his broad shoulders or rough-hewn looks that had ignited her love, but his open mind and good heart. Too good, really. Born far from the fount of power, the peasant's son was ill equipped to match wits with Prince Nazramin. Time and bitter exile should have cured Tol of his naïveté, but she hoped the goodness remained.

Valaran's thoughts were interrupted by the concerted roar from ten thousand throats, which silenced the pounding drums. The emperor had appeared.

Ackal V wore armor enameled in crimson and inlaid with gold. His head was bare, displaying thick red hair untouched by gray. The roaring cheer continued, grew even louder, and Valaran winced against the painful volume. Tyrant though he was, Ackal V was revered by the many Riders of the Great Horde. The emperor descended the palace steps to his waiting troops, revealing the tiny figure who followed behind him. Valaran caught her breath.

Dalar, dressed in a breastplate and helmet made just for him, moved hesitantly. The roar of the fighting men frightened him. Valaran's hands ached to snatch her child back, for his sake and hers. All she could do was grip the ledge of the window before her, until the stone cut her palms.

Ackal's horse waited at the foot of the palace steps. Sirrion, named for the god of passion and fire, stood sixteen hands. He was one of the special royal breed whose hide was a striking shade of ruby red. His mane and tail were a darker oxblood, and his broad, black hooves had been polished until they gleamed. Only those of imperial blood could ride horses of the Ackal Breed.

The senior warlord of the Warblade Horde stood by Sirrion, a position of great honor. Bending forward, the warlord cupped his hands. The emperor placed a booted foot in them and swung onto the magnificent horse. Another soldier hoisted young Dalar onto the pillion behind him. Alarmed at finding himself so high off the ground, the little boy clutched his father's back.

Ackal V drew his saber. The chanting of the warriors ceased. The abrupt silence left Valaran's ears ringing.

"Forward, Ergoth!" commanded Ackal.

The ten thousand horsemen took quite some time to funnel out of the Inner City gate, but Valaran remained at the window until all were gone.

Where in Chaos's name was Helbin? She had to know what was happening in the east. More importantly, where was Tol?

🦉 🦉 🦉 🦉 🦉

The nomads clung stubbornly to their green bulwark, fending off sortie after sortie by the Ergothians. By this time the hordes had encircled the Isle of Elms completely, but every attempt to storm the forest stronghold, on foot or horse, was bloodily repulsed.

Night fell. A steer was roasted. Over beef and beer, the Ergothian commanders debated what to do next. There were two camps: those who wanted to attack again immediately, and those who thought it better to besiege the nomads and starve them out.

Egrin, to Tol's surprise, was in the attack faction. Usually a cautious tactician, Egrin was not given to fire-eating. When he counseled immediate attack, Tol wanted to know why.

Firelight played on Egrin's features. His half-elven heritage, carefully concealed from all but Tol, had kept him a vigorous warrior some three decades after their first meeting. In spite of their closeness, Tol knew almost nothing of Egrin's life before that time. The former marshal was as taciturn as a Dom-shu.

"We don't know what resources the nomads may have," Egrin said, "but Lord Argonnel says there's a spring in the grove, so they do have water." Argonnel nodded. He owned large tracts of this land and knew it well.

Egrin went on. "Our men can't sustain themselves unless we move and forage. If we besiege the nomads, we may end up being hungrier and thirstier than they are." He spat into the fire. "Worse, while we delay here, the treasure caravan is making its way to Caergoth. I, for one, do not want to leave the caravan too long in the hands of a renegade elf and hundreds of kender."

The other warlords agreed. Tol turned to Hanira, seated on his left and asked her opinion. She'd been silent through the entire council, eating little but imbibing quite a lot.

Face rosy from wine, she said flatly, "They're savages. They should be slain to the last man."

"If that means attack, then I agree," said Kiya, on Tol's right.

Tol also agreed. However, they needed a practical means for forcing their way into the Isle of Elms. They had no way of knowing how many nomads were there. Best guess was five or six thousand, but not all were fighters. Nomads traveled with their entire tribe, so a goodly number hidden in the elms would be old folks, children, and the wounded of earlier battles. Trapped as they were, the nomads could be expected to resist to the bitter end.

They wrangled, as old soldiers will, over the best way to assault the Isle. Simultaneous attack on multiple points was best, said some. Others were positive that quiet infiltration under cover of darkness would bring victory. Disguise a small group as nomads and send them in to confuse the defenders.

As they argued, Hanira left. Lord Mittigorn, returning from a trip beyond the circle of firelight, saw her heading in the direction of her pavilion in the Free Company's camp.

"Just as well," said Trudo. "Women and foreigners have no place at a council of war." Kiya glared, but the callous old Rider did not apologize.

Egrin's plan of infiltration was close to winning the day—fifty warriors would dress as nomads and sneak into the woods—when Pagas lifted his head suddenly.

"Something burns," he announced, sniffing the wind.

The scent was stronger and greener than the dying campfire before them, which had been laid with dry wood. A freshening breeze brought more smoke. Mittigorn cried out and pointed to the distant Isle of Elms. The formerly dark wall of trees stood out starkly against a dull red sky.

Fire. The night wind was driving flames toward the trees.

Tol took off at a dead run, Kiya at his heels. The warlords followed.

The source of the fire was soon discovered. Tarsans in brass breastplates were jogging through the waist-high grass, setting the scrub alight with torches. Tol grabbed one and spun him around, demanding an explanation.

The Tarsan stammered, "I'm following my mistress's orders, my lord!"

Cursing the syndic, Tol ordered the man to smother his torch, then he and Kiya hurried through the smoldering grass, putting a stop to the efforts of the other Tarsans. Each told the same story: the fire had been ordered by Syndic Hanira.

Before long they came upon the woman herself. She stood in a patch of burned grass, a blazing torch in each hand. Her dark purple gown was black with ash. Her hair was unbound, and long black tendrils blew wildly around her face. She was singing a Tarsan lullaby at the top of her lungs.

He shouted her name and she turned to him. Her eyes, usually a warm honey color, were like dark holes in her ashen face. Tears had made tracks in the soot on her cheeks.

"Let them burn!" she screamed. "Murdering savages! Let them all burn!"

Tol feared she would get her wish. The fire, fanned by the night wind, had become unstoppable. It devoured the dry grass and caressed the dark trunks of the ancient elms. The nomads did not wait for the fire to engulf the wood. On horseback and afoot they fled the forest, racing for the faraway shelter of the Great Green.

Egrin, Trudo, and the other warlords ordered the Riders to horse. Argonnel's men met the mounted enemy and drove them back. The nomads surged out again, striking Mittigorn's Black Viper Horde.

Kiya rode up, bringing Tol's horse. "Come, Husband. The battle is joined."

As Tol mounted, Hanira dropped her spent torches and held out her hands toward the fire, as if warming herself. Kiya shuddered.

"She looks like Azalla herself!"

Azalla, the Fire Lady, was the Dom-shu goddess of revenge and evil, said to be the child of Argon and the Dragonqueen. Nomads had dared kill Hanira's daughter, and the mistress of the Golden House would not be denied vengeance. Had it happened in Tarsis, she would've hired assassins to exact her revenge. Here, on the plains of Ergoth, she took matters into her own hands.

Kiya and Tol galloped off to join Pagas's horde. So desperately did the nomads fight, they came within a heartbeat of breaking the Ergothian line before the Plains Panthers arrived to reinforce Mittigorn.

The fight was fierce, but brief. When the last nomad warrior was unhorsed, those remaining on foot finally ended their resistance. Tol halted the slaughter. He left Egrin to oversee the sorting of the prisoners, and to look for Tokasin among the captured, then he himself went to search for the chief among the fallen.

The Isle of Elms was fully ablaze now, lighting the scene with a garish orange glow. Kiya, riding with Tol through the battle site, watched as the roiling smoke rose skyward, obscuring the stars. The gray columns came together to form figures like those she'd seen before: giant human shapes standing shoulder to shoulder and looking down on her and everyone else. They resembled the stone statues she'd seen in Daltigoth, inert yet watchful. She wondered if the smoke-figures were gods.

"Eh? Gods?" asked Tol, his attention on the bodies sprawled on the ground.

"Nothing," she said quickly, as she realized she'd spoken her thoughts aloud. "It's nothing."

They found Tokasin. He lay dead amidst a circle of warriors who had died trying to defend him. When Tol turned him over, they realized the chief had taken his own life at the end, by falling on his sword. Tokasin knew the fate of enemy commanders captured by Ergoth.

Day came, and the woods still burned. Elms, many hundreds of years old, flamed like giant candles and eventually toppled over, sending up gouts of smoke and glowing embers. The heat from the hard, heavy wood was intense, keeping everyone well back. The animals in the grove had long since fled—birds, deer, rabbits, even a wild boar or two had dashed out while the Ergothians sorted out their victory.

Tol sat on the blackened turf back to back with Kiya. She was asleep. He drank from a wineskin while Lord Trudo reported.

"One thousand, twenty mounted enemy warriors dead," recited the commander of the Oaken Shield Horde, consulting the strip of bark on which the computations had been scratched. "Of the nomads on foot, six hundred ninety-seven were killed. One thousand, two hundred sixteen are our prisoners."

Altogether, not quite three thousand had been in the woods, fewer than Tol had estimated. He asked Trudo about their own losses.

"Four hundred nine killed and five hundred forty-one wounded to a greater or lesser degree." Trudo stroked his white beard complacently. "Not so bad, my lord."

Tol took the bark tally from him, moving with care so as not to disturb Kiya's rest. He wished he could sleep, but knew his next task could not be put off any longer.

"Bring the syndic to me."

Hanira and her bodyguard Fenj arrived. They were accompanied by Egrin.

"My lord," the old marshal said, "I have come to speak on the syndic's behalf."

Hanira, red-eyed, soot-stained, and haggard, said coldly, "I don't need your help."

Undeterred, Egrin directed his words to Tol. "I know you're angry, my lord, but Syndic Hanira's actions, harsh though they were, resolved a pressing problem. We were debating how best to come to grips with the enemy, and she supplied the way."

"She meant to kill them all."

"Pity I didn't succeed." Hanira brushed lank tendrils of hair from her face.

Tol, mindful of her loss, kept his voice calm. "I did not ask you to come and fight," he said. "You joined of your own accord. You agreed to accept my authority and obey my orders. Your actions last night were treacherous, vindictive, and insubordinate. The fact that you resolved the matter in our favor does not excuse you!"

From behind him, Kiya said sleepily, "Send her home."

Since she was awake, Tol stood and handed Kiya the wine-skin. "No. The syndic will stay."

"You think to punish me like some errant servant?" Hanira sneered.

"I don't intend to punish you." Not in the way she was thinking, at any rate. Tol locked gazes with her. "You joined this campaign, Syndic, and I expect you to see it through. But if you ever disobey my orders, or take such a deed upon yourself again, I'll clap you in irons!"

Silent Fenj tensed, ready to interpose himself between his mistress and Tol, but Hanira suddenly laughed.

"By Shinare, I believe you! There's not a Tarsan general or admiral who'd dare, but you would!"

Their exchange seemed to restore a measure of Hanira's poise. She straightened, and her manner underwent a subtle shift. Although still dirty and disheveled, she seemed more like the woman Tol remembered.

"I will send Tindyll to you for our orders," she said briskly. "Are we bound next for Daltigoth?"

The abrupt change surprised Tol, but he answered her readily enough. "We have one stop to make first," he said.

"We have business in Caergoth," Kiya put in. "A treasure to reclaim."

❦ ❦ ❦ ❦ ❦

At that moment, Tylocost beheld the pale walls of Caergoth. The southward march of the treasure caravan had been without undue incident. The vigilance of the Juramona Militia and Tylocost's active cavalry escort discouraged any from approaching too closely.

The ranks of the Royal Loyal Militia dwindled as the city drew near. No one ever actually saw a kender leave, but a handful vanished each day. The weird desertions were not confined to the kender; the Household Guard evaporated as well. Some days the only sign of Casberry's personal guard was the dwarf doctor and centaur standard bearer, who could always be located by his uncommon stench. By the time the towers of Caergoth came into view, the kender queen led barely a hundred followers, most of whom were hired humans. She wasn't distressed. In fact, she acted as if nothing untoward had happened. For his part, Tylocost was happy to have fewer kender to deal with.

They approached the empire's second largest city with caution, using the line of hills northwest of the city to hide their line of march. Studying the walls from a hilltop just over a quarter-league away, Tylocost found it strange they had encountered no Riders from the city's garrison. With bakali and nomad invaders about, warriors should be patrolling the countryside.

With his more than human vision, Tylocost could see the city gates were shut, save for one, the Dermount Gate on the north side. It was guarded by several hundred troops. A thin stream of people came and went through the portal.

The elf's plan was to wait for Tol, keeping out of sight until his arrival. Like any good general, though, he craved information, and wished he could know what was happening in the city.

He made this comment in Zala's hearing. With a shrug, she said, "I could find out if you like. I could enter the city."

Since her father was a resident of Caergoth, Zala had a glean—a brass token that identified her and allowed her to pass in and out of the city. Given the threat hanging over Caergoth, her glean might no longer be honored. She was willing to try. She could find out whatever Tylocost wanted to know, and look for her father at the same time.

She put aside her weapons, save for a belt knife, and commended Helbin to Tylocost's care. The wizard had been distracted. He'd spent much of the day toying with a small glass mirror, fitted in a hinged wooden box. It appeared to be an activity that caused him great frustration.

"You watch yourself, girl," Tylocost told her.

Zala felt strangely pleased by his concern. The Silvanesti was arrogant and opinionated, but there was something about him that made her want to please him. If he weren't so hard to look at—

She ruthlessly suppressed that thought. No good could come of such feelings.

Leaving the hidden caravan behind, she started down the hill toward the city. As she descended the slope, she picked up speed, until she was jogging rapidly. She'd been too long in the company of soldiers, refugees, and captives. The exhilaration of being on her own flooded through her. For a moment she allowed herself to think of freeing her father and running away with him, away from unsightly, vexing elves, notions of honor, warlords, and kender. If she ran without stopping, beyond the empire, to the end of the world, perhaps she would find peace.

By the time she reached the queue of people waiting to pass through the Dermount Gate, she'd put away such extraneous thoughts. Instead, she concentrated on appearing to be nothing more than a young woman bent on visiting her aged parent.

All those entering Caergoth were searched. Soldiers carried out this process with rapid, rough thoroughness. Packs were opened, their contents dumped on the ground; pushcarts were upended, babies' swaddling was groped. Faced with bared swords, no one protested.

The officer in charge of the gate guards examined Zala's glean and pronounced it outdated.

"What's your business in Caergoth."

"I'm visiting my father. I haven't seen him in a while."

Her mixed heritage gave rise to ribald comments from the soldiers. The harassed officer growled at them to shut up. He daubed the glean with a spot of white paint.

"This means you have twenty-four hours. If you're caught in the city after that, you'll be thrown in prison as a suspected spy."

She nodded curtly, moving on.

The city beyond the thick wall had changed since her last visit. Caergoth had always been an orderly city, with wide, clean streets and well-scrubbed stone buildings. No longer. Now the lanes were crowded with people, wagons, horses, and livestock. Half the population of the province seemed to be trying to squeeze within the walls. It was obvious they did not know that Lord Tolandruth and the landed hordes had driven out the raiding nomads.

## Paul B. Thompson and Tonya C. Cook

Her father lived on the top floor of a rooming house in the scribes' district. His two rooms were small, but cheap, clean, and except on festival days, quiet. He wouldn't be home—the empress had had him taken to the citadel—but Zala headed there first anyway. If possible, she wanted to wash and change clothes before going to the governor's palace. Tiring of the lewd and ugly comments from passers-by, she untucked her hair from behind her ears so it would hide their shape.

The trip through the clogged streets to the scribes' quarter took an age. Market squares, once lined with neat, widely spaced rows of stalls and pushcarts, were now crammed with tents and squalid with the offal of thousands of squatters. Pickpockets and cutpurses worked the mobs. After fending off a fourth attempt to steal her purse, Zala grew so annoyed she broke the pickpocket's wrist and left him howling on the pavement.

The last square between her and the scribes' district was the city's largest, Luin's Field. Bounded on three sides by Caergoth's major temples, it was a sacred space used for religious ceremonies and imperial parades. It was always kept spotlessly clean, with not even the smallest bit of litter allowed.

When Zala beheld Luin's Field, however, shock froze her in place. The square had been turned into an army camp. Warriors were quartered along its sides, and its center was taken up by huge cages, row upon row of stout wooden posts joined together by iron strapping. The cages were filled with people. Some, clad in buckskins, were plainly nomads, but others looked to be city folk or peasants. At least a thousand captives were being held in Caergoth's most sacred square.

An Ergothian soldier, trying to get by her, asked sarcastically, "Something ailing you, girl?"

Instantly, Zala assumed a slightly hunched posture and looked at him with wide eyes. Stammering, she asked, "Who are those people, sir? Why are they here?"

As she'd guessed from his voice, the soldier was an older man. Her shy, deferential manner caused his tone and expression to soften. She imagined that he had daughters of his own at home.

"We need every room in the citadel to house the garrison,"

he said. "Lord Wornoth emptied the citadel dungeon and put the scum here."

After admonishing her to "get herself on home," the soldier moved away, and Zala approached the cages. In the general confusion, she was able to get within a few paces. She walked slowly along, looking anxiously for her father among the wretched captives.

"Has anyone seen Kaeph the scrivener?" she asked as she walked. "An old man with white hair and a bald spot on his crown? Anyone know Kaeph the scrivener?"

For a long stretch all she heard were negatives. Finally, one of the prisoners, a coarse-looking woman with a city accent, answered in the affirmative. Zala stepped closer to her cage.

"I seen him," the woman repeated. "He's in with the condemned—the cages around the corner, facing the Temple of Corij."

Zala thanked her. The woman thrust a hand through the bars, snatching at Zala's sleeve. "A favor for a favor! Tell Mextro I'm here! Mextro, the innkeeper at the Golden Galley! My name—!"

Her plea was cut off as a soldier thrust the butt end of a spear through the bars and struck her in the belly. The woman fell back. Under the guard's unfriendly glare, Zala moved on.

As befit a warrior nation, the Temple of Corij was the largest and most splendid in Caergoth. Built of white marble, it was floored in red granite, to honor all the warriors' blood spilled for the empire. The temple rose in a series of sloping terraces, making a step-sided pyramid. At the pinnacle, in a small columned portico, an ever-burning flame was tended by the warrior-priests of Corij.

The cage facing the temple was isolated from the other enclosures. Warriors on horseback circled it. Friends and family of those within hovered outside the perimeter of guards, looking for loved ones among the many prisoners.

Zala called her father's name, but could hardly make herself heard over the cries of the others around her. "Kaeph the scrivener! Where is Kaeph the scrivener?" she shouted.

"He may be dead already."

The words had come from a woman prisoner sitting close to the bars a few paces further along. Zala walked quickly toward her. The woman was very tall, even sitting down. Her hair, cut to chin length like Zala's own, was brown, and she wore the embroidered deerskins of a forest woman. Her accent was urbane, also like Zala's.

"Why do you say that?" Zala demanded.

"Many have been beheaded—the latest batch was three days ago. Go to the citadel, you can see the heads."

"Do you know Kaeph the scrivener?"

The woman shook her head. "I don't know anyone but the Dom-shu I came with."

Zala recognized that name. Lord Tolandruth's constant companion, the female warrior who called him "Husband," was a Dom-shu. Perhaps she could persuade this sullen giantess to help her if they proved to have a mutual acquaintance.

"I know a woman of your tribe," she said. "Her name is Kiya. Very tall, like you, but with blonde hair."

The Dom-shu's weary gloom vanished instantly. "Father! Come here!" she shouted, bolting to her feet. Her head touched the bars roofing the cage.

A tribesman joined her. His yellow hair and beard were streaked with white, but he moved smoothly through the shuffling prisoners.

At the female prisoner's request, Zala repeated what she'd said.

The elder's face glowed with relief. "She lives! She is free! What of the Son of My Life?"

The Dom-shu woman leaned close to the bars and murmured, "Does Kiya travel with a man, brown hair, brown eyes, a short beard, and nearly as broad in the shoulders as he is tall?"

"Yes. Lord Tol—"

"Keep that name between your teeth," the Dom-shu woman snapped, then grinned widely. "The gods still love him, and his friends, too, I pray! Girl, I am Miya, sister of Kiya, and wife of that man you know!"

# C h a p t e r 17
## Good for Nothing

All that remained of the Isle of Elms was a few score tree trunks, upright but limbless and charred black. They stood, stark and lonely, across a great scar of burned land. Upwind from the smoldering remains, the Army of the East was arrayed on the plain in parade formation. The time had come to deal with the captive nomads.

As with the nomads captured after the battle of Juramona, infamous malefactors, those who had committed specific outrages against the people of Juramona and other towns, were identified and culled from the prisoners. These thirty or so nomads received summary justice. The rest of the defeated were stripped of horses, weapons, and armor and turned loose.

From horseback, Tol regarded the sullen crowd of captives before him. His expression was grim.

"I give you mercy this once," he said. "If any of you enters the empire under arms again, you will receive no quarter. Now go home!"

Riding away at Tol's side, Egrin asked, "How do you know they'll leave?"

"The land for leagues around has been stripped bare. They must go home to hunt and fish, or starve."

Egrin cast a glance back over his shoulder. As predicted, the mass of defeated plainsmen was moving off to the east, a gray-brown body hugging the scorched plain.

Zala returned to Tylocost in a fever of excitement. She had found her father, alive but ill, in the same cage that held the Dom-shu. Once she told them who he was, the Dom-shu prisoners agreed to look out for him, and she swore on her life to return with help. They told her to hurry. The governor was fond of staging random executions, to intimidate the restless refugees sheltering in his city. There was no telling how much time the Dom-shu or Zala's father had.

There were eleven Dom-shu in the cage: Miya, her father, and the small retinue of warriors who had accompanied them. Miya introduced her father as Voyarunta, a name she seemed to find amusing. As Zala did not speak their language, she missed the joke. The Dom-shu had been captured by a company of imperial horsemen, riding south from a losing encounter with Tokasin's nomads. To Ergothian eyes, a barbarian was a barbarian; they made no distinction between forest-dwelling Dom-shu and plains-dwelling Firepath. When Miya pointed out she was Lord Tolandruth's wife and the Dom-shu were at peace with the empire, all she got for her temerity was a boot between her shoulders. She and her people had been languishing in Caergoth's cages for eight days.

"This is what I get for chasing that fool husband of mine," Miya grumbled to Zala.

"You insisted on going," said her father. "All was calm in the village until you decided to leave the Great Green and search for your sister and husband."

"You did not have to come along!"

The forester chief folded his brawny arms. "Am I to let my last daughter go wandering across the grassland without a strong blade at her side? What kind of father would do such a thing?"

"I didn't need you following me! You only slowed me down!"

"You'd be in a nameless grave by now if I hadn't come."

Father and daughter were still arguing when Zala stole away. Despite the threat of random beheadings and the days they'd spent in the fetid, uncomfortable cage, the foresters were in good spirits. Their faith in Lord Tolandruth was unshakable. .

Zala's father, on the other hand, was in very poor health. A cough had settled in his chest, and he'd grown pale and haggard. He could not remain much longer in the open, at the mercy of the sun's heat and the night's damp, living in filthy conditions with meager food and water.

Tylocost received her fervent outpouring of news with his usual aplomb. He evinced more interest in the conditions inside Caergoth than the condition of the prisoners. Zala paced up and down before the Silvanesti and Queen Casberry as she described what she'd seen: the crush of refugees, the nearly impassable streets, the patrolling soldiers.

"How many soldiers?" he asked.

She shrugged, and he made an offhanded remark about ignorant girls who couldn't count beyond their own fingers and toes.

Zala backhanded him. She lashed out so quickly Tylocost was caught completely by surprise. Her hand connected solidly with his cheek, rocking his head back and leaving a livid impression of her long, tapering fingers. Militiamen around them snickered and Casberry applauded.

"My father's life is in peril, elf! Save your insults for later!" Zala spat.

Tylocost made no move, just stood, hands at his side, staring at the shaking huntress. His face was bright red. Finally, he cleared his throat.

"What would you have us do?" he said, his voice low. "We don't have sufficient strength to attack the open gate, much less storm the city. And the treasure must be guarded. Lord Tolandruth will be here soon—"

"I'll free them," Casberry said matter-of-factly.

The kender queen stood up in her chair. She straightened her orange shirt and buckskin trousers, tugged at the bottom of her leather vest—this one dyed sky blue—and stepped out onto the ground.

"I'll free the prisoners."

Tylocost, his acid tongue temporarily muted, merely asked her how.

Her eyes vanished into pools of wrinkles as she smiled. He thought she looked very like a cheerful prune. "Not by storming gates and attacking cities," she said sagely. "We'll do it the kender way. All I need is the Royal Loyal Militia."

"What Royal Loyal Militia?" Tylocost protested. "Most of your people deserted long ago."

Casberry looked askance at him, saying to Zala, "Slap him again, honey."

In spite of herself, Zala laughed. Tylocost kept a wary eye on her.

"Not one of my Royal Loyals has deserted!" Casberry proclaimed. "They're about, even if your dull senses can't see them. They're looking around, listening. All I have to do is call, and . . ." She waved a hand. "Come nightfall, we'll free your father and Lord Tolandruth's big wife."

"We?" said Tylocost.

"Certainly. What kind of queen would I be if I sent my brave troops into peril alone?"

The Silvanesti imagined the gnarled old queen, decked out in one of her astonishing outfits, entering Caergoth in her sedan chair and proclaiming, "Make way for the Queen of Hylo!" He shook his head to dislodge the ludicrous picture.

To his amazement, the queen appeared to have been telling the truth. Although she made no proclamation, nor sent out any heralds, kender began returning to the hidden camp. Over the course of the day, they arrived—alone or in small groups—bearing whatever odds and ends they had 'found' while wandering. They filed past their monarch, and Casberry greeted each by name. She asked particular ones to volunteer for the mission to Caergoth. All agreed cheerfully, without hesitation or questions.

"They're quite fearless, aren't they?" Zala said admiringly.

Tylocost, perched on a nearby log and studying a sketch map of the vicinity, muttered, "Fools are never afraid."

Casberry explained the job to her hand-picked group of forty and told them to gather at sunset on the hill where Tylocost had first surveyed the city's defenses. The kender troop asked no questions, so the meeting was brief. Then they drifted away to do whatever it was that kender did.

Excited by the prospect of freeing her father, Zala knew she must try to rest. The upcoming night likely would be long and strenuous. She spread a blanket under a willow tree, lay down, and covered her eyes with one arm. Not ten breaths later, she felt someone approach.

"I must speak with you, lady."

Helbin. Not moving, she said, "So speak, and be quick about it."

He said nothing, but she could hear him fidgeting and shifting his weight. With a sigh, she opened her eyes and sat up. Immediately, he sat down on the end of her blanket.

"Take me with you to Caergoth," he whispered.

"Why?"

"My spells are gone, and I must contact the empress!"

His desperation was so great, she grew curious. "What do you mean, gone? What happened to your magic?"

"It's been negated. I don't know how. I must consult my colleagues in the Order in Caergoth. They can send a message to the empress, apprising her of my position. I must go with you."

He saw the denial in her face even before she spoke. Leaning closer, he said, "Please, you must help me! You must understand that more is at stake than the life of your father, however dear he is to you! The fate of millions depends on my communicating with the empress!"

"You're a learned man. Can't you just"—she waved a hand—"restore your ruined talismans and trinkets?"

"That would take too long!" he exclaimed, then grimaced, trying to contain his impatience. "The magic mirror alone must be consecrated during a conjunction of Solin and Luin, which won't occur again for forty days. I am reduced to purely mortal means. You must help me! Name your price, I will pay it!"

Beyond the wizard's shoulder, Zala saw Tylocost approaching. He carried a cloth-wrapped bundle in the crook of his arm. When he saw Helbin was with her, he stopped.

"Fine. Be on the hilltop with the kender at the appointed time," she muttered to the wizard. "Now go!"

"May the gods bless you!"

"Save your blessings till after you hear my price."

Looking slightly alarmed, Helbin withdrew. Tylocost came forward.

"Everyone's paying court to you today," he said. "Was Master Helbin pleading his suit?"

The suggestion was so absurd Zala laughed. The sound drew a quick smile from Tylocost. Kneeling, he held out the bundle he carried. "This is for you," he said quietly.

She unwrapped the oblong object warily and was taken aback when it was revealed to be a sword—a truly fine short sword, with damascened blade and a hilt handsomely chased with silver filigree. It must have come from the treasure trove.

"Why?" she asked, looking up at him.

The elf had difficulty answering. Finally, he said, "In a crowded city street, a short blade will be more useful than that saber you carry." Standing quickly, he added, "The kender have similar weapons. Good luck tonight!"

He strode away. Zala studied the weapon. The blade was leaf-shaped, designed for close-quarter stabbing. A small pale amethyst was set in the pommel. Under the circumstances, it was a thoughtful gift, not to mention an exquisitely beautiful one. Was Tylocost trying to apologize for his past behavior? Or did his gift mean something more?

She forced herself to put the weapon aside and lay down again. Sunset would be here all too soon, and she needed to sleep.

In spite of her best efforts, Zala's mind would not be stilled. Her thoughts went round and round as she tried to make sense of the elf's motives—and her feelings about him. She got no rest at all.

❦ ❦ ❦ ❦ ❦

The sun shone through gaps in the low-hanging clouds, sending scorching beams down onto the Ergothian army. The Riders of the Great Horde moved forward slowly, armor clanking, horses breathing hard in the heat. The enormous earthen mound of the bakali fortress reared up ahead of them. There was as yet no sign of the lizard-men themselves.

Ackal V, atop Sirrion's ruby-red back, rode in the center of his army, surrounded by scores of warlords, aides, and his personal escort of one hundred archers. Heralds bearing the standards of sixty-six hordes were arrayed around the emperor. Most of the hordes were from the northern and western provinces.

Prince Dalar rode on a war-horse beside his father. The boy's legs were barely long enough to allow him to sit astride the great charger. He swayed in the saddle, from the precariousness of his position as well as the heat. Sweat trickled from beneath his miniature helm.

A horn bleated. Dust swirled as a courier galloped up. A member of the emperor's entourage met the rider and relayed his message to Ackal V.

"Your Majesty! Marshal Tumult has the enemy in sight!"

Havoc Tumult, Marshal of the Seascapes Hundred, was leading the advance guard. He had some of the best remaining hordes under his command, including the Wind Riders, who were peerless scouts; the Red Thunders; and the Bulls of Ergoth, no man of which could be shorter than two paces tall. Riding straight toward the enemy's stronghold, Marshal Tumult had come upon a sizable body of bakali, arrayed in circles to resist cavalry attack. He now awaited his liege's orders on how to proceed.

Ackal V considered how to respond. It was typical of the bakali to offer a sizable force as bait, to lure the Ergothians into a trap. They'd played this trick over and over.

"My compliments to Marshal Tumult," he finally said. "Tell him to keep the enemy in sight, but do not engage." To another warlord he said, "Who has the forward elements of the right wing?"

"Lord Janar, with the Deathriders."

"Bring him to me."

While he waited for Lord Janar to ride back to him, Ackal V ordered the army to halt. Sixty thousand warriors reined up their steeds and waited, restive in the face of the enemy.

Janar and his retinue arrived in the inevitable cloud of dust. They saluted with drawn daggers.

Ackal V raised his voice for all to hear. "My lord, there is your goal." He pointed to the mud-colored mound rising above the trees. "No matter what happens, to me or the rest of the army, you are to breach that stronghold, and destroy anyone and anything in your path! Do not look back, Janar— fix your eyes forward and smite the invader!"

The emperor's loud commands agitated his horse, but he controlled Sirrion's prancing with ease. "That is your task. Succeed, or never come before me again!"

Lord Janar's round, sunburned face tightened. He saluted again and galloped away with his retinue.

Once they were gone, Ackal V turned to his nearest aide. The emperor was smiling. "Inform Lord Tumult he may attack," he said. "Remind him of the tactics we set forth in our last council of war." The messenger departed.

"Cornets!" the emperor shouted. "Sound the call to battle!"

Five hundred trumpeters raised brass horns to their lips and blew the age-old sequence of notes. A concerted shout went up from the Great Horde.

Ahead, in the advance guard, a corps of archers rode out from Havoc Tumult's ranks. Once within bowshot of the bakali circles, they dismounted, braced their bows, and commenced bombarding the lizard-men. A concerted hiss rose from the bakali, and as one they raised their shields skyward to ward off the lethal rain of arrows.

Tumult sent forward two hordes, the Bulls of Ergoth on the right and the Silver Skulls on the left. They formed into narrow columns just four riders wide and trotted into the gaps between the bakali defensive circles. As expected, the lizard-men on either side of the advancing Ergothians lowered their shields to close in. When they did, more dense flights of arrows rained on them, felling many. Up went the shields again, and the bakali awkwardly tried to attack the horsemen while still protecting themselves from the arrows.

"Spearmen!" Tumult shouted.

The Red Thunder Horde had been armed with long spears

in place of their traditional sabers. At the marshal's command, they charged forward, spears leveled at the bakali trying to crush the Bulls of Ergoth. A terrible chorus of screams arose when the two forces collided. Bakali shields and axes were no match for iron-tipped spears, and the first two ranks went down like wheat before the scythe.

At that moment, something happened that had never happened: the bakali formation broke. The southern side of the circle, inundated by spearmen, disintegrated.

Shouting their emperor's name, the Red Thunders galloped into the open field and fell upon the bakali circle from behind. The Silver Skulls and Bulls attacked from either side. In short order the enemy was annihilated.

Word of this success reached the emperor's entourage and cheers erupted. Ackal V seemed unimpressed.

"One company destroyed," he said coldly. "Now kill the rest!"

On the right, Lord Janar's Riders crossed a shallow stream and climbed the opposite bank. A hidden ditch tripped the leading horses. Their riders were thrown onto a hedge of sharpened stakes. Janar held up his own horse by sheer strength and pushed through the obstacle, advancing more warily now. The bakali fortress was no more than half a league ahead of him.

Company after company of armed lizard-men poured down the ramps leading to the earthwork structure. Sunlight and humidity gave their green hides an iridescent sheen. Even at this distance their pungent smell seared the nostrils of men and horses alike. The animals rolled their eyes and champed their teeth. Warriors cursed, hawked, and spat.

Once the remainder of Janar's force was through the ditch and stakes, he cried, "No quarter!" In companies of two hundred, his men charged.

Men and lizards met halfway between the ditch and the fortress. Ordinarily, twenty thousand Riders at full gallop could trample any number of enemy foot soldiers into the dirt, but the bakali set their clawed feet in the dry earth and took the full impact of the Ergothian charge like a cliff facing a crashing sea. Sabers rang off their helmets, their shields, and their thick, scaly skin. In turn their axes and spears wrought much damage among Havoc Tumult's men. As the front ranks were reduced to bloody wreckage, the following companies charged home.

In time, a raging sea can wear down a stone cliff. So it was with Tumult's companies. Little by little, they pushed the bakali back. The price was high; blood, both crimson and purplish red, ran thick over the parched soil.

Ackal V, watching from a knoll in the center of the battle-field, had not yet committed his left wing to battle. He was holding them in reserve, ten thousand warriors led by a young Daltigoth warlord named Vanz Hellman. They sat on their horses, motionless as statues, waiting for their emperor to summon them to battle.

Ackal V fed more and more warriors into the battle's center, shifting his hordes sideways and forward like pieces on a game board. When the bakali formed a tough defensive position, archers and spearmen scourged them until saber-wielding Riders could break them.

Against fierce resistance, the Ergothian center slowly advanced. The casualties were appalling, especially among the sword-armed hordes. They had to close in to fight, and the lizard-men exacted a terrible toll.

The center pulled abreast of Janar's Riders, then ground ahead. The bakali stronghold was closer now. Built of logs and mud, it resembled a great hornet's nest fallen to the ground. The fetid, telltale reptilian odor wafted strongly from open holes in its sides. The smell was strong enough to reach the emperor, overcoming the odor of horses, sweating men, and spilled blood.

"Lord Janar falters," said one of the emperor's aides, pointing. "The enemy has him stopped!"

Janar had found himself facing a solid wall of green, scaly skin and bronze armor. Bakali continued to spill from the mound in great numbers, filling in the ranks ahead of him until his way was blocked completely. Many were only half-equipped, gripping a sword or axe and wearing the usual ring-mail coat, but lacking shield or helmet. Although strangely uniform in height, the lizard-men varied in appearance. Some had yellow horn ridges on brow and upper lip, and large, domed heads covered by small green scales. Others, lacking brow ridges, had smaller craniums sheathed in iridescent, pale green skin. They stood shoulder to shoulder, horned beaks gnashing, hacking away.

Janar was wounded but still fighting when a message arrived from Ackal V: Press the enemy harder. Voice cracking from the strain, the warlord urged his men to even greater efforts. He knew the consequences of failure.

A shrill screeching sound filled the air. It came from the summit of the bakali fortress and echoed eerily from the dark tunnel mouths. Hearing it, the lizard-men engaged with the Ergothian center ceased fighting and drew back. Before the surprised Ergothians could pursue, a new terror appeared.

Holes opened up in the ground amidst the ranks of Ackal's hordes. Lids of packed earth, mud, and twigs exploded upward, revealing the entrances to several large tunnels. Armed bakali poured out of these holes. In the blink of an eye, hundreds of fresh enemy soldiers appeared in the midst of the Ergothian center.

Horses reared, throwing Riders to the ground. Ackal V, his son, and his personal retinue were inundated by furious bakali.

The emperor drew his saber and cleaved the skull of an axe-waving foe. As he fended off billhooks and poleaxes, his war-horse lashed out fore and aft with massive iron-shod hooves. Dalar could not hold on and shrieked in terror. Ackal V hacked off the clawed hands grabbing for his son, grasped the neck of the boy's hacketon and lifted him onto Sirrion's back.

A bakali thrust a long spear at Dalar, now seated in front of his father. Ackal V lopped off the spearhead, but the wooden shaft caught the emperor in the throat. Choking and furious, he put the point of his saber through the lizard-man's eye. Blood sprayed over the ashen-faced prince. His father cursed and shoved the dead bakali off his blade with the toe of his boot. Warlords in his retinue finally cut their way through the throng of lizard-men, surrounded their liege, and fended off further attacks.

243

All organization was lost as more bakali poured out of the hidden tunnels. Ackal's well-planned attack degenerated into a vicious melee.

"Your Majesty!" cried his cousin, Hyduran Dermount. "Summon the reserve! Send for Lord Hellman now!"

In answer Ackal V struck the gray-bearded warlord on the jaw with the hilt of his saber. Hyduran fell backward off his horse.

"No man gives me orders!" Ackal V roared. "We came here to kill bakali. So kill them!"

Several warlords suggested he and the crown prince should remove to safety, but Ackal V refused. "Better to die in battle than yield to these lizards!" he told them.

Six hundred paces away, Lord Janar likewise was battling for his life.

The blond warlord, who'd been a shilder with Tol at Juramona twenty-five years before, weighed sixteen stone and was known for his robust constitution. Four times wounded, including a deep stab in the thigh, he still sat tall in the saddle and bellowed encouragement to his men. When he noticed that the outpouring of bakali from the stronghold had thinned, Janar called for the rearmost horde in his formation, the Thorngoth Sabers, to ride wide around the bakali line. Under cover of the heavy dust clouds hanging in the air, the Sabers pulled out of line.

That order was Janar's last. An thrown axe connected solidly with his forehead. He swayed in the saddle, and fell. Unconscious by the time he hit the blood-soaked ground, he was hacked to pieces by five bakali who muscled through the press of horsemen to reach him. They in turn were slain by vengeful Riders.

The Thorngoth Sabers found the edge of the bakali phalanx and rode wide around it. Hooting and screeching, the lizard-men turned to meet the new threat. The lead Riders steered around their slower, clumsier foe. Agitated, the creatures thinned their line further in an attempt to contain the Ergothians. Their line was four ranks deep, then three. When it thinned to only two bakali deep, the Sabers wheeled in unison and charged.

For one brief, gory moment the bakali line held. Then it shattered. Bakali, minus limbs or heads, flew aside as the Sabers burst through into the open. Leading the charge was young Estan Tremond, son of the governor of Thorngoth. Estan wore his golden hair long, like his father, and it flew behind him as rode hard for the ramp leading into the fortress.

The pressure on Janar's hordes slackened. A shout went up. The Ergothians had flanked the bakali line. They were nearly to the mound. For the first time the lizard-men wavered.

Moments later, the same hesitation struck the bakali fighting among the Ergothian center. Their usual cold-blooded prowess faltered. Anxious looks were cast back at their threatened fortress.

The emperor thrust a clenched fist into the air. "Now is the time!" he declared. "Send word to Lord Vanz to bring his men forward. He will strike the enemy on our left, as we contain them here!"

Six couriers carried the message, to ensure it would reach its intended recipient. Only two made it through the confusion and carnage. The first courier found Lord Vanz sitting on horseback in the shade of an alder tree.

Only twenty, Vanz Hellman was already an imposing figure. A descendant of northern seafarers, he was dark-skinned and very tall. When his hair had begun to thin two years earlier, he shaved his head and kept it so. He wore no mail beneath his cuirass, so his bare arms, impressively muscled, showed clearly under his turned-back mantle.

The courier galloped up to him, gasping out his message: "My lord! His Majesty commands you to advance!"

"Thank you," Hellman replied. His voice was low and very deep. He remained motionless on his white horse, giving no orders.

As the puzzled courier prepared to repeat his message, the second messenger arrived, face bloody, right arm hanging limply at his side. He relayed the emperor's order and received the same calm acknowledgment.

Lord Vanz called for a draft of wine.

More than a league away, the Thorngoth Sabers gained

the foot of the enemy's ramp. The thick walls of the bakali mound were heavily plastered with mud and leaves. The ramp spiraled upward, growing narrower as it rose. Scores of round openings dotted the walls next to the ramp. None were defended.

The Sabers sensed a trap, but urged their horses onto the ramp anyway. When they tried to turn the animals toward the first of the yawning holes, the horses balked. Ergothian war mounts did not shy from the clash of iron or the smell of human blood, but none could be made to push through the vile, throat-clogging odor emanating from the entrance to the bakali stronghold. Their riders were forced to dismount and proceed on foot, sabers drawn.

Within was a winding gallery fitfully lit by the streams of sunlight coming through the entry holes in the walls. As more Riders arrived, they followed their comrades inside, leaving the lowest-ranking among them outside to guard the horses.

There were only two choices, head up or down. As the stronghold was broader at the base than the summit, it made sense to seek the enemy below. Armor jangling, Captain Tremond and his men descended the curved gallery. The interior ramp was wide enough for them to walk five abreast.

A single guard appeared, wielding an axe in each clawed fist. He held them off for some time, skillfully dodging saber thrusts and whirling his twin blades with such force that a single hit severed heads or limbs. They finally overwhelmed him by sheer weight of numbers. After severing his hissing, spitting head from his torso, they continued downward.

The evil stench grew stronger as they descended. So did the enervating heat and humidity. Some warriors, veterans of many battles, became so nauseated they collapsed. Comrades with stronger stomachs kept going.

The curving gallery ended in an open chamber. Pine and cedar knots burned fitfully in the gloom, casting just enough smoky light to reveal the room's vastness. It was forty or fifty paces across, its domed ceiling supported by trees ripped from the ground and installed with their branches and bark still on. The chamber was lined from wall to wall with thousands of oblong yellow-gray objects, each about the size of a small wine cask.

Tremond poked the nearest of the objects with his sword. The leathery skin yielded. Instantly he realized what they had found.

"Corij preserve us!" he breathed. "It's a hatchery!"

The bakali eggs were layered four or five deep. There were easily a hundred thousand of them in this single room. They accounted for the terrible smell, as well as the heat and drenching humidity.

An Ergothian slashed the nearest egg. Its pliant shell split and thick green fluid gushed out, as did an amorphous-looking dark mass—an immature bakali. Several soldiers gagged at the sight, but most, following their comrade's example, began slashing at the eggs. Soon the soldiers were ankle-deep in yellow-green slime.

Tremond halted his men's frenzied retribution. At this rate they would drown before a thousand eggs were destroyed. Something stronger was needed.

Torches burned in the curving gallery behind them, but the eggs were soft and moist, and the air heavy with damp. It would be impossible to get a blaze going without copious amounts of oil or some other fuel.

"The trees!"

The cry had come from a warrior who carried one of the axes taken from the bakali guard. He stepped out onto the uneven surface of the egg trove and picked his way toward the center of the chamber. There, he drew back the iron axe and began to hack at a tree trunk. Wood chips flew.

Chest working to take in the humid, harsh air, Captain Tremond thought briefly of home, of the fresh breezes that blew off the bay in the mornings. Then he shouted, "Everyone! Cut down those posts! All of them! Right now!"

A soldier with gray in his beard caught his young captain's arm. "You know what will happen when we cut through those supports, don't you?"

"Yes," Tremond said evenly, "we'll save the empire."

The imperial reserve shifted restlessly, ten thousand warriors on ten thousand horses waiting for their commander to obey the emperor's order to advance. So far Vanz Hellman had drunk a cup of wine, watched the injured courier carried away, talked idly with his officers, and removed his mantle in the heat of the day.

After his mantle was carefully stowed in a saddle bag, Hellman sat up straight and wrapped the reins around his hands.

"The hordes will advance by columns, to the left," he said quietly.

Heralds relayed the order as trumpets blared. At a trot, the left wing of the imperial army moved up on the west side of the bakali position. The leading elements of Hellman's hordes found numerous concealed traps—pits, ditches, deadfalls of huge logs. Each was marked and circumvented. Had the hordes galloped straight ahead, they would have suffered grievously from the traps.

"My lord, how did you know the obstacles were there?" asked Hellman's second-in-command.

"Because I would have put them there, if I were a cunning lizard."

Their approach was so deliberate and calm they surprised a phalanx of bakali formed behind a screen of trees. The lizard-men were standing in neatly ordered rows, axes and billhooks resting on their shoulders. Hellman's Riders appeared beside them as if by magic. Reptilian faces were not expressive by human standards, but the bakali's astonishment was plain.

Vanz Hellman's powerful voice burst forth. "Give them iron!"

The Ergothians sabered hundreds of the enemy before they could shift formation and raise their shields. Lord Hellman, in the front rank, put down a bakali with every stroke. Because of his unusual height, he wielded a specially-made saber, its blade a span longer than any other sword on the battlefield.

Although surprised, the bakali did not break. They fought, isolated into bands of six, eight, or ten, until all were slain.

None attempted to surrender. The Ergothians were not taking prisoners anyway.

Hellman's hordes cut their way to within sight of Ackal V's position in the center of the battle. One of the emperor's aides pointed out the towering ebon warrior to the emperor.

Ackal V, still clutching his son to his chest, wheeled his horse about. "About bloody time! Did he come by way of Ropunt Forest?"

The emperor's ire could not dilute Hellman's accomplishment. His warriors, fresh and eager for battle, were cleaving the enemy in twain. Ackal V, breathing hard, allowed his bloody sword to hang idle from his hand for the first time in ages.

A tremendous crack split the air. Heads whipped around, wondering if the sound heralded some new bakali trick. Shouts went up from the warriors fighting around the emperor, and thousands of blades, formerly engaged in killing, rose skyward, pointing at the bakali stronghold.

The great earthen mound was collapsing. Its roughly conical peak dropped several paces. Black dust spurted from the open tunnel mouths along its sides. From the embattled lizard-men came a hair-raising, ululating cry, a sound not of anger or bloodlust, but of wrenching despair.

The walls of the mound split apart and fell inward. The pinnacle, which had once reared so high, plummeted into the center of the stronghold. With a prolonged roar, the entire structure gave way, hurling broken logs and dried mud for hundreds of paces all around.

# Chapter 18
## A Knowing Child

The sun was setting on a sweltering day. It dipped behind the smooth walls of Caergoth, lending to the cool white stone the sheen of old gold. Humid and heavy, the day had passed quietly. The Juramona Militia and the five hundred Riders acting as cavalry escort guarded the treasure and kept out of sight.

Tylocost remained on the hilltop for most of the day, his face shaded by the wide brim of his gardener's hat. He did not speak. Now and then he plucked a stem of grass and chewed it thoughtfully.

On the other side of the hill, Zala and Casberry completed preparations for their foray into the city. The forty kender chosen by the queen had left to enter the city in whatever way they could. At the appointed time they would join up at the prison cages in the center of Caergoth. In spite of his urgent pleas to be taken into Caergoth, Helbin had never shown up. He likely had developed cold feet, Zala thought. She was glad. That was one less worry on what would probably be a dangerous night.

Zala, with her glean, could enter the city by the gate. Casberry declared herself too old to climb high walls or wriggle through drain pipes. She wanted to accompany the half-elf, and pondered how she could accomplish this since the glean covered only Zala herself.

Her solution to the problem caused Zala, in spite of her nervous excitement, to break out in laughter.

Casberry dispatched Front and Back, her sedan chair bearers, to find her a wheelbarrow. While the men went off to search the treasure trove for such a thing, the queen and the half-elf put together their disguises.

Zala was to be a peasant woman. The queen happily rooted through the numerous chests of her "royal luggage" to find an appropriate dress for her. A lady's gown of green velvet was just Zala's size, but much too fine. It would draw attention, and they certainly didn't want that.

The dress the kender queen finally produced was a patched and well-worn homespun garment. Zala pulled it on and put her arms into the long sleeves. She squirmed a bit, trying to accustom herself to the garment's unfamiliar feel. Its full skirt covered her legs and the trousers she had flatly refused to remove, and transformed her into frumpy shapelessness. Her hair had grown in the weeks since she'd left Caergoth, but she tied a grimy kerchief over her head to make certain her ears remained covered.

Casberry stripped to her white linen smallclothes, carefully folding each piece of her flamboyant attire and stowing it in her sedan chair. In moments, she completed her own transformation, and Zala was left to stare at her in openmouthed astonishment.

The kender was clad in a dirty green dress. Around its neck and hem were the remnants of embroidered flowers and bumblebees. A matching bonnet covered her head and cast her face into deep shadow. In one hand, she held the final piece of her disguise—a decrepit cloth doll. Casberry, who must have been at least a hundred years old, was dressed as a human child.

She grinned widely, showing many ancient yellow teeth. "I'm your darling baby!" she declared.

Zala began to laugh. Casberry joined in, her high-pitched mirth sounding like a cat yowling in pain.

Front and Back returned at last with a two-wheeled pushcart. Zala and Casberry put their weapons in and covered them with blankets, then Casberry climbed in.

The sun was nearly gone; only an orange sliver remained above the western hills. Zala wanted to tell Tylocost they were leaving, but the elf was nowhere to be seen.

"He's sulking," said Casberry, arranging herself in the pushcart. She cocked a sly look up at Zala and added, "He wants something he can't get."

Zala frowned, but before she could say anything, Casberry began issuing orders to Front and Back. They would tell Tylocost of the rescue party's departure.

On the way to the city, Casberry regaled Zala with ribald stories about her travels through the lands beyond the empire. Hearing these, Zala decided the kender queen was an unscrupulous old wench, but shrewd, brave, and without a doubt never, ever dull.

The paved road was empty when Zala wheeled the creaky barrow onto it. Few travelers dared move after sunset, fearing the wild animals and even wilder raiders who prowled by night. The Dermount Gate bulked large in front of them, blazing torches marking the entrance and the soldiers guarding it.

A figure appeared, instantly and without warning, on the grassy verge just beside Zala. She jumped in shock, her hand reaching for the sword she no longer wore.

It was Helbin, sweeping back the folds of the loose, dark cape that covered him from head to toes. He seemed to appear out of thin air.

"How'd you do that, Red Robe?" Casberry piped.

In reply, he drew the front of the cape up around his eyes. When the motion of the moving cloth subsided, he all but vanished. If Zala looked very closely, she could see the pale oval of his forehead.

"A cloak of invisibility, eh?" said Casberry, sitting up in the barrow. "I could've used one of those in Silvanost, a few years back. With garb like that, why do you need us to get you in?"

Helbin folded the cape's edges back and stood revealed again. "It's not a cloak of invisibility. Such garments are written of, but they're fiendishly hard to come across. This is a lesser artifact, a Mockingbird Cloak. It mimics the colors around it, hiding the wearer. It works fine as long as you stand still, but movement, especially against a changing background, renders its mimicry useless."

"Come along," Zala told him. "If I can pass as a mother, you can be a father." The queen of Hylo chuckled, but Helbin looked appalled.

Zala hung her head and slowed her footsteps. She didn't have to feign weariness. Pushing the barrow in the smothering heat was exhausting, and the sweat was streaming down her face.

A score of paces ahead, the soldiers heard the barrow's squeaking approach. Their desultory talk died. By the time the newcomers entered the torchlight, the guards were standing ready, swords in hand. Their vigilance made Zala sweat even more.

"Kind of late for travelin'," said a sergeant with brass chevrons on his helmet. "What's in the wheelbarrow?"

"Only my darling Cassie."

Warily, the sergeant parted the blankets. The queen of Hylo pretended to be asleep, sucking her thumb and clutching the cloth doll close to her cheek.

The soldier's eyebrows shot up, and he recoiled as if slapped.

"Sweet Mishas! That's your child?"

"Spitting image of her father, she is," Zala said, turning a glowing smile upon Helbin. The wizard shuffled his feet and looked at his toes. Fortunately, beneath his cloak he wore plain attire and not the robe of his Order.

The sergeant motioned a corporal over. This second soldier bent to see Zala's passenger and guffawed.

"Someone shaved a gnome!"

Indignant, Zala presented her glean. "This night air isn't good for Cassie. I must get her home."

Shaking his head over the young mother's homely offspring, the sergeant noted their entry in his log.

"You can go, once I search the wheelbarrow," he said, handing the log to another soldier.

Zala's breath caught. "Search? For what?"

"Contraband. Folks try to smuggle goods into the city every day, to avoid paying the merchants' tax."

Zala's terror did not show on her face, but her mind was racing. If the soldier found the swords hidden in the barrow, she and her party were doomed. Worse, if they looked closely at Casberry, they'd know for certain she was no child. The three of them would end up with the prisoners they had come to liberate.

The sergeant had only begun to feel among the blankets when he suddenly stepped back, a look of disgust on his ruddy face. He fanned his nose with one hand.

Helbin made a gagging sound, but Zala cooed loudly, "Poor Cassie! Do you need changing?"

"She needs burying!" the corporal replied catching a whiff.

The sergeant gestured vigorously for them to pass. "Go! Pass on, at once!"

Once in the city, Zala wheeled the barrow quickly into a dark alley and whisked away the blanket. Casberry sat up, tugging the bonnet from her head.

"Faw, what did you do?" Zala hissed, as Helbin continued to make retching noises.

"Kender learn many things, wandering the world. For example, a sprig of frogbone root, snapped open, gives off a remarkable stench." She held up a dry bit of broken twig.

"Throw it away!" Helbin gasped, waving a hand desperately. The queen flicked the offensive root into the gutter.

They shucked their disguises and retrieved their weapons from the barrow. Zala's cotton undershirt was thin and sleeveless, which felt good after the sweaty confinement of her long dress.

Helbin would have left them at this point, but Zala pulled him up short. He insisted he must go and find other Red Robes.

"No," she said flatly. "You'll stay with us until the prisoners are freed."

Away from the well-patrolled streets just inside the city wall, Caergoth was busy. Refugees and leaderless soldiers prowled the wide lanes seeking diversion. As there weren't enough taverns to accommodate the flood of newcomers, enterprising residents had set up pushcarts and peddled bread rolls, cold meat pies, and a variety of cheap drinks: raw young wine, cloyingly sweet mead, and fizzy beer. In some of the lesser city squares, where the press was especially thick, Casberry mourned the loss of her frogbone. Its odor would have cleared a path through the throng in no time. Helbin shuddered at the memory of the loathsome stench.

For her part, Zala paid close attention to the people around them. The general mood was one of disgruntlement. The refugees had been driven away from their farms, forges, and shops into a city that had no use for them. They wasted their days drinking, gambling, and fighting. Theft was common, as was Governor Lord Wornoth's harsh justice. For a first offense, a thief lost a finger. Second offenders lost a hand. Anyone caught a third time lost his head. Many heads decorated the high wall of the citadel.

Soldiers in the crowd were bitter. As Riders of the Great Horde, they were used to sweeping all enemies before them. Now, having been defeated by a swarm of barbarian nomads, they were reduced to cowering inside stone walls. It was no life for a warrior. More than a few times Zala heard Wornoth cursed as a miserable coward. The emperor in far-off Daltigoth had forgotten his loyal hordes, so they rotted in the peasant-choked streets of Caergoth.

Zala and Casberry kept Helbin between them, to be certain the wizard wouldn't be tempted to use his Mockingbird Cloak to evade them. Casberry sampled a pocket or two on the way, but found the pickings uninteresting. The refugees were as poor as they complained they were.

Luin's Field was lit by clusters of torches, set around the vast cage complex in its center. Pairs of guards on foot stood watch by each set of torches, while mounted warriors circled the fence. The smaller cage by the temple of Corij, which held the condemned, was better illuminated. In addition to the torches, bonfires burned at each corner. Zala doubted anyone in the cage could sleep with the glare of light and constant noise.

She wondered how they were to get close to the prisoners. Helbin offered to go, but the half-elf quickly vetoed that idea.

"You don't know my father, or the Dom-shu," she pointed out.

"I know Miya, wife of Lord Tolandruth."

An argument threatened, but Casberry put an end to it by giving Zala a shove.

"Get under that cloak, girl, and both of you go!" she hissed, then turned away, melting into the shadows beyond the firelight.

Helbin was slightly taller, so Zala stood in front of him while he drew the Mockingbird Cloak around them. The intimacy inside the cape would have been disturbing had she been sharing it with Tylocost or Lord Tolandruth, but Helbin radiated nothing but indifference.

"Walk very slowly," he whispered. "The cloth must have time to adapt to its surroundings."

At a snail's pace they moved toward the condemned cage. The ensorcelled fabric gradually took on the bloody orange hue of the bonfires. Peeking through the open slit in the front of the cape, Zala saw the dark outlines of sleeping prisoners inside the pen, which smelled worse than she remembered.

When they were near enough, she parted the cloak. As loudly as she dared, Zala called her father's name.

"Shut up," said a voice from the mass of unmoving captives.

"I must find Kaeph the Scrivener!"

"He's here. Keep talking so loudly, and you'll be in here with him."

Helbin whispered, "Is that Miya?"

One of the shapeless mounds stirred. It was indeed Miya. Moving slowly, as though languid with sleep, she sat up. Although she acted sleepy, her voice was clear and her ears sharp.

"There are two of you," she said.

"Yes. We're here to get you out."

"Just two of you?"

"No, there are forty kender here, ready to help."

Miya stiffened. "Forty kender? May the gods have mercy."

She leaned forward and prodded the figure in front of her. He snorted and woke, grumbling noisily. Miya clapped a hand over his mouth, and hissed, "Quiet, all! Guards!"

A pair of foot soldiers approached. Their hobnailed boots struck in unison as they marched along the length of the cage. Zala drew the edges of the cloak together again. She and Helbin stood motionless.

". . . out of beef, they said," one guard was saying. "So I put my knife to the innkeeper's throat and told him if he didn't have beef, he could give us his daughter!" His partner joined him in rough laughter.

The men's voices drew closer. Zala held her breath and wondered if they would bump right into her.

As the men passed, one brushed lightly against Helbin's back.

"What was that?" he asked, stopping abruptly.

"What was what?" said his comrade.

"Something touched me."

Zala flexed her fingers around the grip of her short sword. At close range, she could take both men down, if they weren't wearing heavy armor.

"There's nothing here but stinking prisoners. Come on. We're off duty."

In spite of his comrade's urging, the first guard drew his saber and swept the air around him. The flat of the blade struck Helbin in the back. The wizard stumbled forward, throwing Zala against the bars of the cage and out of the cloak's protection. Instantly she was revealed, and out came her sword.

Both guards shouted, tearing the cloak from Helbin's back. More soldiers came running in response to their yells.

"So much for being rescued," said Miya sharply.

"Wait," Zala hissed. "We're not done yet."

The Ergothians quickly ringed the wizard and huntress in a wall of swords and halberds. An officer on horseback demanded Zala lay down her weapon. Instead, she cut the air with her blade. The soldiers started to close in.

Miya and the Dom-shu rushed toward the bars, shouting. The sudden movement distracted the guards. Zala thrust the pommel of her sword through the bars to Miya. "Free yourselves!" she said. "Run, wizard!"

Helbin tried. He got about ten steps before soldiers tackled him, knocking him down on the grimy pavement. Zala proved more elusive. When she felt fingers snag the back of her undershirt, she spun, gripped her pursuer's arm, and used his own momentum to send him flying. Then she took off in a new direction.

The houses along the eastern side of Luin's Field had been turned into barracks for hundreds of soldiers. As Zala raced down the street, she heard shouting from within the barracks, followed by a furious pounding. Sparing a glance in that direction, she saw that every door was blocked with timbers, piles of masonry, casks, or barrels. Further on, she passed a solitary figure leaning against the columns of one of the fine houses now home to part of Caergoth's garrison.

Queen Casberry. She and her kender troop had been busy. They had blocked the barracks' doors.

The commotion near the prisoners' cages had become an uproar. Zala's sword had been passed back among the ragged Dom-shu and vanished. The guards who hadn't chased Zala demanded it back. Miya's reply was brief but pungent.

The sergeant of the guard summoned a squad of archers. Soon, ten bows were leveled at the foresters, standing shoulder to shoulder just inside the bars. Other prisoners scampered out of the line of fire.

"Give up the blade!" shouted the sergeant.

"Come and take it, grasslander!" Voyarunta bellowed back.

The Ergothian raised his hand. Ten bowstrings creaked as they were drawn back.

"Will you murder us all?" said Miya. "I am the wife of Lord Tolandruth!"

The archers glanced at their commander. "You are all condemned prisoners of the empire!" said the sergeant. "Yield the blade or die!"

Uncle Corpse pushed his daughter behind him. "Enough talk! Dom-shu, time to go!"

The tribesmen rushed the bars, smashing into them with all their weight. Bows twanged, and arrows flashed in a short flight to meet the oncoming wall of flesh.

Governor Lord Wornoth's factotum was a plump, fussy man named Tello. He arrived at his master's bedchamber to find the doors already closed. Squaring his shoulders, Tello lifted his baton of office and rapped on the portal. A loud voice beyond the door yelled at him to enter. He did so, and the servant behind him scurried in to light the room's lamps.

Wornoth sat up in bed. Although he was not an old man, the strain of ruling the second city of the empire in Ackal V's name showed in his hollow eyes, sallow complexion, and thinning brown hair. Tello pretended not to notice the young woman lying next to Lord Wornoth, her face buried in the bedclothes. She was not, he knew, one of the governor's wives.

"Tello, if the bakali aren't at the gates, I'll have you flogged for this interruption!"

"My gracious lord," Tello said, putting his soft hands together and bowing. "The prisoners in Luin's Field are rioting!"

"Sweet Mishas, you woke me to tell me that? Tell the guards to quell any disturbance. When they're done, tell the captain to give you forty lashes!"

Tello bowed again in acknowledgment of his master's judgment, but added, "There is more, Lord Governor. We have captured one of those who was trying to free the prisoners. It's the Red Robe Helbin, my lord."

Wornoth's annoyance vanished. "Helbin! Where is he?"

"In your audience hall, my lord, under heavy guard."

The governor slid out of bed. A lackey hurried forward to hold his robe. As Wornoth tied the sash around his waist, he told Tello to rouse the garrison.

"Have them clear the streets," he commanded. "Anyone caught helping the prisoners escape is to be killed on sight. I will see Master Helbin at once."

"Very good, my lord."

Factotum and servants departed, and Wornoth's bedmate exited through a door concealed in one of the room's walls. Wornoth donned his rings of office and hung the heavy governor's medallion around his neck. The golden emblem of the House of Ackal felt cold against his skin.

So, the Red Robe deserter had been caught. The emperor's pleasure at this news would be great—as would his gratitude.

He went to the small gong by his bed, intending to summon a scribe to take down an immediate dispatch, but he paused. Perhaps it would be better to find out exactly what Helbin knew first. Great discretion had to be exercised in dealing with any important person from Daltigoth, especially Ackal V. Although the emperor had issued a death warrant for the wayward wizard, it was entirely possible Helbin was acting on the emperor's behalf, and the warrant was only a ruse to confuse Ackal V's enemies.

Wornoth rubbed his forehead. Countless possibilities chased themselves around in his brain. He could feel a major headache beginning, just behind his eyes.

🦉 🦉 🦉 🦉 🦉

Dirty and exhausted, Tol and a twenty-man escort rode into Tylocost's dark, fireless camp. They had covered the distance between the Isle of Elms and Caergoth in less than two days. The Army of the East, moving more slowly, was strung out behind them. Its full strength would not arrive for another day, possibly two.

The Juramona Militia cheered Tol's arrival. The noise brought Tylocost out of his tent, and he bowed to his captor-commander.

Drink was brought. Tol gulped cider as Tylocost apprised him of the discovery of the Dom-shu prisoners and Zala's father.

The wooden cup fell from Tol's gloved hand. "Miya is here? And Chief Voyarunta?"

"So I am told. Is Kiya well? I'm surprised she isn't with you."

Tol said only that Kiya was well and was coming later with Egrin and the main body of the army. In truth, she had been profoundly affected by her experience at the Isle of Elms. Tol had told her to remain behind and watch out for Egrin, and she hadn't objected. Oddly, she seemed sad, as though the slain nomads were her own kin and not the enemy.

Tylocost had little faith the kender could prevail against an entire city garrison, but Tol didn't share these sentiments. The kender, he said, could be a valuable asset to Zala—if the erratic little folk remembered they were on a rescue mission and not in Caergoth to "find" interesting things.

Tol glanced at the eastern sky. It was well past midnight, but daybreak was still marks away. Nevertheless, he made his next decision quickly.

"Muster your troops, General. We go to Caergoth."

"My lord? You intend to force an entry with only five hundred Riders and a few thousand foot soldiers?"

Tol smiled grimly. "I don't plan to force anything," he said. "The governor will invite us in."

# Chapter 19

# Whirlwind Harvest

The Caergoth archers loosed a single volley into the rebellious prisoners. Three of the Dom-shu went down, and Chief Voyarunta received an arrow in the upper thigh. Grunting, he broke off the fletched end, pushed the shaft on through, and yanked it free of the hard flesh of his leg.

The Dom-shu, with other prisoners, formed a human ladder pushing against the fence. Miya and a dozen captives climbed the tangle of limbs to the top of the cage. Their swift progress unnerved the archers, who shifted their aim to pick off the prisoners as they reached the top of the spiked fence.

They never let fly the second volley. A barrage of brickbats and paving stones struck them, knocking some flat and spoiling the aim of the rest.

The sergeant of the guard whirled to see who dared interfere with his men. On the steps of the Temple of Corij were more than a dozen short figures. He took them for children until several in front bent over and bared their bottoms. All heckled the soldiers in loud, high-pitched tones.

"Kender!" the sergeant bellowed. "You men there! Get those stinking—!"

A heavy weight landed on his back, driving him face-first to the pavement. It was Miya. She stepped off the unconscious man and said mockingly. "Thank you for breaking my fall!"

Although Chief Voyarunta's leg was bleeding, he had taken

his place among his men at the base of the human ladder. When he saw his daughter outside, he shouted for Zala's short sword and tossed it to her through the bent bars. She caught it deftly and hurried to free him and the rest.

Luin's Field was in full uproar. Buoyed by the success of the Dom-shu, the rest of the captives were storming the fence. Guards rushed from one point of crisis to another. Prisoners threw rags and blankets over the spikes along the top of the barrier, climbed over, and dropped to the ground. Kender darted through the confusion, tripping soldiers, or pelting them with rocks. Mounted warriors tried to charge the escapees, but instead found themselves fighting to control their horses as kender menaced the animals with stolen torches. No horse would charge into fire. The riders were set upon by throngs of prisoners, dragged from their mounts, and stripped of arms.

The sole entrance to the condemned prisoners' cage was on the opposite side from the Temple of Corij. Miya fought her way to it through the mob. It was secured by a crossbar as wide as Miya's waist, and kept in place by a thick black chain. No one had dared climb the gate. It was studded on both sides with sword-sharp bronze barbs.

Miya regarded the gate helplessly. The short, thin sword in her hand was of no use against either the massive crossbar or the chain.

"Need help, lady?" said someone, tapping her elbow.

She turned. Four soot-stained kender stood behind her. The one who'd spoken added, "I'm Curly Windseed, at yer service, and this is Cuss, Juniper, and Fancy."

"Get this gate open, quick!" she told them. The prisoners had to be freed before the city garrison arrived.

"Sure. Fancy, you got that bar?"

The tallest of the kender pulled a thick metal rod from his collar. It was a straight iron prybar, and evidently had seen a great deal of use. Fancy put one end in the chain and proceeded to wind the bar around and around, binding the chain in the process.

"Lend a hand, big lady," said the smallest kender, the one called Cuss.

With Miya and the kender pulling and straining for all they were worth, the chain finally snapped. Prisoners rushed forward, and the heavy crossbar was thrown aside.

Before Miya could move, a wall of escapees surged against the gate, swinging it open and almost knocking her flat. She held onto a gatepost while the torrent flowed past. Of the helpful quartet of kender, there was no sign.

Once the flow of prisoners thinned, Miya saw Zala run into the open pen, calling her father's name.

Miya yelled, "Your father's in the shanty. He was too sick to stay out in the open!"

Together they raced across the rapidly emptying compound. Zala's father lay under a makeshift lean-to. A gray stubble covered his face. His eyes were rheumy and dull.

"Papa!" Zala said, grasping him by the shoulders. "Papa, I'm here. You're safe!"

"Hurudithya," the old man whispered. "I knew you'd come!"

Miya looked a question at her, and Zala shook her head. "I was named after my mother," she explained. "I don't use often."

The clatter of iron-shod hooves warned them the city garrison was on its way. Supporting Kaeph between them, Zala and Miya crossed the empty prison compound and quickly moved out the gate.

The great square of Luin's Field was almost empty. The freed prisoners had not lingered, and neither had the kender. Miya helped Zala get her father to the steps of the Temple of Corij. Leaving them there, the Dom-shu woman raced back to the prison cage to look for her own wounded father. However, save for a few unconscious guards and slain prisoners, the cage was empty.

Miya called for her father, but her cries were lost in the growing thunder of approaching horses. She ran back to the Temple of Corij.

Zala and her father were not where she'd left them.

With a low cry of frustration, Miya dithered on the temple steps. Where was everyone? Where was her father?

A diminutive figure in a brown surcoat came down the

steps toward her. His head was covered by a brown hood.

"This way, friend," he said, holding out a hand. "Enter the sanctuary of Corij."

Corij, god of war, was served by a priesthood of soldiers and former soldiers. This little person could hardly be one of them. Miya spun him around and tugged back the hood of his vestment.

The Dom-shu found herself staring at a brown, leathery face seamed by hundreds of wrinkles. It was not a visage easily forgotten.

"Queen Casberry!" she exclaimed. Who wasn't in Caergoth tonight?

"You better lift those big feet!" the old kender said, sprinting nimbly up the steps.

Casberry led Miya through the temple's open portico. Burning candles lit the dark interior and spread a musky scent. A crowd of people huddled among the thick columns. Among them, Miya was relieved to see, was her father, as well as his warrior escort, the half-elf Zala, and her ailing parent.

A genuine priest of Corij came forward. Although his long beard was gray, he was broad of shoulder and straight-backed.

"I am Almarden, high priest of Corij," he said. "I will guide you to safety."

Armed with a hooded lantern, Almarden led the way. The house of Corij was the largest temple in Caergoth. Parts of the complex predated the city itself. Through passages broad and narrow, straight and twisting, the priest never lost his way. The fitful light illuminated shadowy figures lining the passages. These weren't enemies, but suits of armor belonging to famous, long-dead warriors. It was customary for a family to dedicate a dead warrior's armor to the god of battle.

Fleetingly, Miya wondered whether Tol would have a suit of armor here someday, or an unmarked grave on the endless plains.

The high priest reached a bronze door and halted. Holding his lantern aloft, he whispered, "Outside is the Street of the Coopers. It runs straight down to the Dermount Gate."

Paul B. Thompson and Tonya C. Cook

"Thanks to you, holy one," Voyarunta said. "You are a true man, even if you are a grasslander!"

Behind the Dom-shu chief, naked blades gleamed. Determined not to be taken without a fight, the escapees had helped themselves to the weapons of the ancient heroes on display.

Almarden raised no objection, saying only, "May Corij and Mishas favor you. Good luck."

Voyarunta and his warriors moved out first, and the rest of the escapees followed them into the dark street of the barrel-makers. Queen Casberry had shed her priestly garb somewhere along the way. She tossed the high priest a cheery, "Thanks!" as she departed.

Last in line were Miya, Zala, and Kaeph. The old man was moving on his own now. To Miya's surprise, he and the priest of Corij embraced before parting. Zala, her short sword back in her hand, surveyed the street outside, then waved her father forward.

As Almarden gave Miya a saber, she asked, "Why do this, holy one? We were prisoners of your governor. Why help us escape?"

"The rulers of our land are not always just. When Queen Casberry came to me, my duty was clear. Corij will judge my actions, not Lord Wornoth."

Almarden watched Kaeph and Zala move slowly away. "Besides, what man could refuse to save his own brother's life?"

❦ ❦ ❦ ❦ ❦

"Enough."

Wornoth, seated in his governor's chair, frowned. Despite the best efforts of two brawny guards, Helbin still refused to say why he was in Caergoth, or how he had entered the city.

"Why are you here?" he demanded yet again. "Who came with you?"

Helbin lifted his bloody face. One eye was beginning to swell shut, so he peered at his captor through the other.

"I came with the Queen of Hylo!" he said, and no one believed it.

266

One of the guards raised a meaty hand, but the governor waved him off.

"I have a death warrant for you, wizard, signed by the emperor himself. Tell me what I want to know, and your death will be quick and merciful."

Helbin made as if to speak again, but a fit of coughing interrupted him. At Wornoth's direction, the soldiers dragged the wizard to a sitting position.

"Your days are numbered, savage," Helbin finally rasped. "The greatest warlord of our age is coming fast upon you. I may die, but you will not long outlive me!"

"What are you raving about? What warlord?"

"Tolandruth of Juramona."

Wornoth snorted. "Don't be ridiculous! The emperor banished him years ago."

Helbin's split lips moved in a ghastly smile. "Mark my words. He is coming."

The wizard's certainty, even after such a beating, rocked Wornoth. At his last encounter with Lord Tolandruth, the formidable warlord had threatened to kill him.

He declared, "Tolandruth is a condemned exile, and a traitor. If he dares show his face in Caergoth, his head will decorate the highest tower of the citadel!"

The wizard began to shake. Thinking him broken at last, Wornoth beamed. His toothy smile froze when he realized that Helbin was laughing, not weeping.

Wornoth snapped, "Take him away! Carry out his sentence at once. I've no time for his foolish threats!"

The soldiers dragged Helbin to his feet. He realized the time had come for a last, desperate act. He had a single spell remaining, one he'd prepared before leaving Tylocost's camp. He wasn't certain its effects were reversible, but trying it was better than death—he hoped.

He pushed a parchment-thin wooden chip out between his teeth. Through all his rough treatment, he had kept the chip hidden beneath his tongue. The sigils on its face were clear and sharp, not eroded by blood or saliva.

Wornoth immediately spotted the chip. Certain it was magical in nature, he shouted for the guards to stop the wizard.

He was too late. Helbin bit down, snapping the chip in two.

In the next instant, the wizard began to writhe as though in terrible agony. As the guards drew back in fear, the ragged silk of his crimson robe shredded and long, black feathers pushed through skin and cloth. Helbin's sandy hair fell out, revealing a mass of flame-red skin. His head shriveled. Gray eyes darkened and shrank. His swollen, bloody mouth elongated into a hard yellow beak.

In the space of half a dozen heartbeats, man transformed into vulture—a monstrous, black-plumed creature fully as tall as Helbin had been. The vulture spread its wings and uttered a single, sharp screech. The cry was deafening.

Terror-stricken, Wornoth tried to climb over the back of his tall, heavy chair. He shrieked at his men to kill the monster.

The closest soldier tried to bring out his dagger. The vulture's hooked beak raked a bloody line across the man's face, from right eye to chin. The soldier threw his hands over his eyes and fell aside, cursing.

The way was open. Talons slipping on the polished marble floor, the huge vulture scrambled away, wings flapping.

The guards in the audience hall had only spears and sabers, no bows. They could not hem in the flailing creature. The vulture reached an open window and leaped onto the wide stone ledge.

Casting one last black-eyed glance over his humped shoulder, the vulture that had been Helbin the Red Robe let out a piercing scream and leaped into the air.

Wornoth rushed to the window, following the vulture's flight. Dawn was breaking over Caergoth. When the black curl of the vulture's wings finally vanished, the governor turned his gaze downward. The sight that met his eyes sent an icy shaft of fear through his gut.

An army was mustering on the plain outside the city. A sizable army, it bore before it the standard of Juramona.

❦   ❦   ❦   ❦   ❦

Hundreds of miles away a pall of dirt and smoke hung high over the collapsed bakali stronghold. Two days had passed since the end of the battle, and still the dark cloud remained.

Few Riders of the Great Horde knew what the great earthen mound contained, but the despair of the lizard-men over its fall was powerful. A great blow had been struck against the invaders.

Even so, the bakali's withdrawal, though swift, was in good order. Under the cover of roiling clouds of dirt, they had formed into three compact columns. They retreated swiftly northwest, toward Ropunt Forest. Caught off guard by the sudden change of fortune, and utterly exhausted, the imperial army did not try to stop them.

Ackal V had his victory, but it was not the crushing triumph he'd expected. Half his army was dead or wounded. An entire horde, the Thorngoth Sabers, had perished in the collapse of the bakali mound. The battlefield was heaped with the dead and dying of both sides.

A prolonged blast of trumpets had summoned the surviving commanders to attend upon the emperor. Servants spread a gold and scarlet carpet on the blood-soaked ground, and Ackal V's portable throne was set up. Prince Dalar, looking wan and limp, was delivered to his father by two brawny Riders who had been guarding him. The boy was required to stand at his father's right hand.

There weren't many warlords left to answer Ackal V's summons. Many of those who finally gathered before him were swaying on their feet from exhaustion or wounds. All were streaked with gore, grime, and sweat.

Vanz Hellman was in remarkably good condition. Although his armor bore the marks of many blades, his face and bare arms were unmarred. Ackal V ordered the towering warrior forward, and Hellman went down on one knee before him.

"What is your will, Majesty?"

Even restrained, his voice rolled out like thunder.

"My will is to have your head on a pike! Why didn't you come immediately, when I ordered you into battle?" Ackal said.

"I did come, Your Majesty. My hordes broke the lizards' resistance."

"You delayed responding to my command!"

Dalar flinched at his father's shout, but knew better than to retreat a single step from his prescribed place.

The kneeling warlord pressed a hand to his heart. His gesture of sincerity seemed somehow mocking.

"As commander of the reserve, sire, I had to judge the best time to strike. I waited until the lizards were deeply committed against Your Majesty's position, then I attacked."

"You hoped they'd kill me first!"

"No, sire!" Hellman said instantly. "I acted to insure victory. I am Your Majesty's most loyal servant."

Ackal V regarded Hellman through narrowed eyes for a long, heart-pounding moment. It was a ruthless warlord indeed who dared dispute with the Emperor of Ergoth, but Ackal V could not deny that Hellman's final charge had been perfectly timed. The carnage around them was testimony to that.

Ackal V did the one thing that made even the bravest of his commanders tremble, Vanz Hellman included. He smiled.

"Very well. I am sure of your abiding love for the throne of Ergoth. As a loyal servant of the empire, you will gather what remains of the army and pursue the lizard-men." The emperor's tone was almost genial. "Harry them out of our realm. Drive them into the sea, and spare none, do you hear? I want to hear of nothing but mounds of bakali skulls from here to the Seascapes!"

Hellman stood. His demeanor remained calm, but sweat trickled down his smooth, dark face. He vowed he would carry out the emperor's command.

"See that you do," Ackal V said. "Your life is pledged against your success."

Hellman and his retainers withdrew. Other warlords were called forward to give accounts of their losses. The death rate was unusually high—neither the Ergothians nor the bakali had shown mercy to those who fell. When a handful of survivors from the right wing of the army told of the discovery of eggs inside the mound, it became clear why the lizard-men had fought with such tireless abandon.

The emperor commanded the priests and clerics from his entourage to come forward. These learned folk were led by a priestess of Zivilyn named Talatha.

Although the eldest of the group, Talatha was not yet middle-aged. She wore her dark hair tightly confined in a long braid, and her moss-green robe was simple and shapeless.

Ackal V wanted to know why the bakali had fought their way to the heart of the empire to build their nest, when they could have done so anywhere.

Talatha cleared her throat and replied, keeping her eyes lowered, "Great Majesty, I believe they were compelled to do so by their own natures." She held a hand out, and a lesser priest put a thin scroll in it. "This document is from the time of the Dragon Wars. It speaks of the life cycle of the bakali. After many generations, the lizard folk are driven by instinct to return to the breeding ground of their ancient ancestors."

The emperor's brows rose in surprise. "That's a revelation. Why was I not told this before?"

His words, spoken gently, drained the color from Talatha's face. Nervously, she fingered her gold medallion of faith.

"The, uh, document is a most obscure one, Your Majesty. No more than a gloss, pasted onto a larger scroll in the temple library, it was discovered only this day, during the battle, as we searched for the meaning of these events."

Ackal V made no reply. Instead, he called for wine. He did not offer refreshment to anyone else. Talatha and her colleagues remained still, gazes deferentially on the ground. Only after he'd drained his golden goblet twice did Ackal dismiss Talatha. She led her people away in grateful haste.

The emperor addressed his warlords again. "We must make absolutely certain all the bakali eggs were destroyed. I don't want to have to fight again when the creatures' progeny hatch out among us!"

The bakali stronghold would be excavated, he decreed, and every egg found inside destroyed. Ackal did not specify who was to undertake this prodigious task, and the commanders began to shift uncomfortably and mutter among themselves. Would the emperor really set his noble warriors to digging, like so many slaves?

# Paul B. Thompson and Tonya C. Cook

Ackal V laughed, a short, harsh sound. Cuffing his son, he said, "See, Dalar, how the mighty lords of Ergoth tremble at the thought of a little labor!" The boy managed a weak smile at his father's wit.

The warlords were visibly relieved by the emperor's next orders. All warriors not going with Vanz Hellman were to organize into bands and sweep the countryside. All peasants, farmers, or stray travelers they found would be drafted into work gangs; any who resisted would be put to death. These gangs would dig through the bakali mound.

"One thing more."

Ackal V sat back, gripping the arms of his throne. "The tradition of my ancestors demands that I, as victor, raise a mountain of our defeated enemies' heads here on the battlefield."

He paused to send a cold glare across the assembly, then added slowly, "This task you will conduct yourselves. It is the duty of the Great Horde to offer up the enemy dead to their emperor."

Not by word or look did the nervous warlords betray their distaste for the gruesome task he had set them.

By sundown, the emperor's order had been obeyed. Two great pyramids of death rose beside the fallen mound. One was made of bakali heads, the other of decapitated corpses.

❦ ❦ ❦ ❦ ❦

Valaran stood alone in the palace solarium, before a magnificent wall of firetongue orchids. Bright red in daylight, the stamens of the orchids glowed in the dark like hot coals. Filling a corner of the sunken garden with color, the rare flowers were a pet project of Ackal V's youngest wife, Lady Halie. Only eighteen years old, Halie was an extraordinary beauty, with thick red-gold hair cascading well past her waist and eyes as violet as the twilight sky. She was the emperor's current favorite. Valaran knew her husband. He could not be swayed by mere beauty. Halie's loveliness was coupled with a quiet, obedient disposition—just the sort to find favor with Ackal V.

272

Valaran had come to the solarium to read. This morning that simple act, which had sustained her soul for as long as she could remember, brought her no peace. She couldn't concentrate. As daylight brightened the isinglass panels above her, she abandoned the marble bench to walk the path that wound through the garden.

If only Dalar was here! Were she certain of the boy's safety, she could revel in her daydreams of Ackal V hacked to pieces by lizard-men. Instead, all such thoughts ended the same way: Dalar shrieking in hopeless fear, Dalar set upon by bakali, Dalar lying dead on a distant battlefield . . .

She smote a clenched fist on the low wall beside the path. She would not give in to mindless fear. She was a woman of reason and intellect, a Pakin. Her husband might be evil, a brutal tyrant, but he wouldn't allow harm to come to his son. Succession was intensely important to him.

If only her other nightmare could be rationalized away so easily.

*White robes flapping in the wind. The old woman screaming, growing smaller and smaller with distance. A heart-stopping impact.*

"Your Majesty! Your Majesty!"

Valaran flinched at the unexpected interruption. A lady of the court was rushing toward her. Flushed with excitement, her starched headdress askew, the woman dropped a quick curtsey, her slippers skidding on the white marble.

"Majesty! Talatha, priestess of Zivilyn who accompanied His Majesty, has sent word to the College of Wizards," she panted. "The emperor has achieved a signal victory—the lizard invaders are defeated!"

Valaran said nothing. In fact, she was so pale, so motionless, so long silent, the lady-in-waiting grew concerned.

"Your Majesty?"

"Praise the God of Battle," Valaran finally said, her voice toneless. "The empire is saved."

# Chapter 20
## Weapon of Choice

**P**ale predawn found Tol riding slowly down the ranks of the Juramona Militia. Tylocost rode beside him. Egrin and the mounted hordes were on their way, but with Miya at risk inside the city, Tol could not wait.

He directed the men to straighten their line, to hold shields and spears up. It wasn't going be easy to intimidate the governor of Caergoth with only two thousand foot soldiers and five hundred Riders. Wornoth commanded at least twenty-thousand seasoned troops. Still, knowing the governor for the weakling he was, Tol felt it worth the risk to try to bluff him into releasing his prisoners.

The militia was deployed across the face of a low knoll east of the city. At their backs, scarcely a quarter-league away, flowed the Caer River. Instead of their usual close ranks, the men were positioned in open order, like spots on checkered cloth. Shields were held out on their left and spears to their right, as they tried to take up as much space as possible. From the high walls of Caergoth they might appear as though twice their number. The demi-horde of Riders Tol held in reserve, just behind the knoll.

Tol and Tylocost turned their mounts about and rode back toward the center of the line.

"What if the garrison sorties?" the Silvanesti asked.

"We'll have to hold them off till Egrin arrives."

Tylocost's disbelief was silent but unmistakable. Tol

nodded to some veterans he recognized in the ranks, then said, "What's the matter? Don't elves like to gamble?"

"In point of fact, no. We find the human love of hazard inexplicable. It's an extravagance we prefer to avoid."

Tol chuckled. As a general, Tylocost was famous for taking enormous risks. At the Battle of the Capes he defeated an Ergothian force eight times larger than his by dividing his army. The Ergothian commander, Lord Lembroth, could not attack one of Tylocost's divisions without exposing his flank to the other. Lembroth's nerve failed utterly after the elf repelled attacks on both forces. Lembroth lost his army and his life.

Tol was taking a terrible risk today. The treasure recovered from the nomads lay unguarded in Tylocost's hidden camp. Egrin, with thirty thousand Riders, plus Hanira's Tarsans, was at least half a day's march, perhaps a whole day's, away. If Wornoth sortied all his hordes, no one in Tol's small army would live to greet Egrin.

Tol and Tylocost took up positions at the center of the line. The sun had cleared the knoll behind them, its light streaming across Tol's army and onto the walls of Caergoth. Lookouts on the walls would have that glare in their eyes. So would Riders emerging from the gate on this side of the city. In a situation like this, any advantage was welcome.

Signal flags went up from the towers along the wall. Horns sounded, muted by distance and thick stone walls.

Without further ado, the eastern gate opened and a double line of horsemen emerged. At the same time, a small band of people on foot, drably dressed in brown and gray, rose up from the tall summer grass near the city wall and started running toward Tol's position.

"Stand ready!" Tol boomed. "Close ranks at my command—and not before!" To the elf: "Can you make out who they are?"

Tylocost stared across the distance, concentrating. Fine lines grooved his forehead and the corners of his close-set eyes.

"Twenty or so kender."

The kender troop moved across the open field. The horsemen—several hundred Riders of the Great Horde—

drew sabers and spurred forward. Their targets were the kender, not Tol and his troops.

The kender kept together until the horsemen were almost upon them. Then, as though in response to some silent signal, the little band scattered, each kender heading in a different direction. As the Riders swerved to chase the various foes, their disciplined line was reduced to confusion.

Tol laughed. Tylocost pushed back the brim of his gardener's hat and muttered a phrase in his own language.

"I'm beginning to see why you recruited them," he said. "They're damned infuriating, aren't they?"

"Best skirmishers in the world. Fighting a band of kender is like trying to count dandelion seeds in a gale!"

After several embarrassing collisions and much disorder, the Ergothians sorted themselves out. By that time the escaping kender were filtering through the open ranks of the Juramona Militia. Tol called out to one familiar face.

"Curly Windseed! Where's your queen, and the humans she went to save?"

The brown-haired kender scrubbed his nose. "They lit out for the other side of the city. Nice of you to meet us, by the way."

Tol saluted the brash little man. "My pleasure. How was the city?"

"Crowded."

From one of his many pockets, Curly pulled out a bandanna to wipe his nose. Assorted trinkets—bracelets, rings, coins, and even a tiny silver cup—cascaded to the ground. Quite unabashed, he stuffed these back in his pockets and followed his fellows over the hill, angling north by northwest.

"The treasure's that way, you know," Tylocost said.

Tol sighed. "I know."

The pursuing Riders, once more arranged in two neat lines, trotted through the high grass to within bowshot of the militia. One, bearing the emblem of a herald on his helm, detached from the rest and rode directly to the two mounted men. He hailed them, asking who they were.

Tol responded in ringing tones: "I am Tolandruth of Juramona! In command of the Army of the East!"

Although disconcerted by Tol's name, the herald looked askance at the men ranged behind him. "Army of the East? This, uh, rabble?" he said.

"This is only the vanguard. We've come from the Isle of Elms, where we defeated the Firepath nomads and slew their chief, Tokasin."

"Huh! What do you want here?"

Tol had been pondering that very question. He wanted his people back alive—Miya, Zala, Queen Casberry, and the rest of the Dom-shu. However, his men expected more. So did the landed hordes who had given their sabers to his service. The nomad menace was over. Although the bakali were still a threat, the true danger to the empire, he admitted to himself, was Ackal V.

"I have come to accept the surrender of Caergoth," he said after a long pause.

Decades of experience allowed Tylocost to mask his astonishment. The herald had no such reserves to call upon. His jaw dropped open.

"You have taken up arms against the rightful emperor of Ergoth!" he sputtered. His horse pranced nervously, and he jerked on the reins. "You dare to threaten rebellion against His Majesty Ackal V?"

Slowly, Tol drew Number Six and rested the blade across his thighs. His voice once more boomed out, rolling across the quiet field.

"The rest of the army, thirty thousand Riders, is coming. I have no wish to shed the blood of loyal warriors, so all those who wish to may leave the city. The governor and his councilors will remain to face the justice of the people they have wronged. I give you two marks to comply, then I will take Caergoth by force."

The herald could scarcely credit his ears. Was the man before him insane? He stared at Tol's grim face, finding no answer there, nor in the annoyingly superior expression on the face of the ugly Silvanesti who rode at his side. The men at his back wore equally determined looks.

The messenger shut his mouth with a snap. "I regret your coming death, my lord. I served with Lord Urakan in Hylo, seventeen years ago." Directing an angry look at Tylocost, he added, "Your choice of allies these days shows how grievously you have lost your way."

He yanked his mount's head around and cantered back to the waiting Riders. Even across the distance it was plain they were astonished to learn Tol's identity and message. At length they formed up and returned to the city.

When they had gone, an odd ripple in the grass presaged the arrival of Queen Casberry. The green stems were taller than she.

"Your Majesty! Are you alone?" Tol said, looking anxiously behind her for signs of Miya and the rest.

"No kender is ever alone," she said. Casting a glance over her shoulder, she added, "The rest of the party is coming along shortly, but they're not alone either—if you know what I mean."

Tylocost drew Tol's attention to traces of dust rising in the air. It appeared Miya and company were being pursued.

"You enjoy this sword stuff so much, I leave the rest to you." Casberry strode past, head held high.

At Tol's order, a hundred men formed in close order before him. He dismounted and handed his reins to Tylocost.

"Stay here. If the garrison comes out, call up the Riders, and stand and fight."

Although plainly unhappy with the decision, the elf nodded grimly.

Tol and the company of soldiers jogged away. They descended the slope of the knoll and veered northward, eyes fixed on the plumes of dust moving toward them. On their left, along the wall of Caergoth, the flapping of signal flags tracked their progress.

All of a sudden they found what they sought. Some forty people were struggling through the grass, hampered by the elderly and wounded comrades. Zala carried an aged, unkempt man on her back. Her father, Tol reckoned. The man whose life he'd guaranteed.

Taller than the rest was Voyarunta. On his thigh a hastily arranged bandage was soaked with blood. He was supported by his younger daughter.

Relief flooded through Tol and he shouted Miya's name.

"Husband!" she cried, her strained, sweating face breaking into a smile. "Make yourself useful!"

When the pursuers came galloping over the rise, they were surprised to find, not unarmed, ragged prisoners, but armed infantry ready to meet them. Tol's men had formed a hollow square with the escapees inside. The leading Riders hesitated, and the whole troop milled about for a moment. Re-forming, they charged, waving sabers and shouting. The Juramonans, hardened by screaming nomad attacks, stood firm, and the Riders pulled up when they saw the militia wasn't going to break.

Taking advantage of their indecision, Tol ordered, "By section, close ranks and advance!"

The men on the far side of the ring moved in to fill the gaps between the men on the engaged side. Then, with spears ported under their arms, the whole troop advanced on the horsemen.

The startled Riders stood their ground, hacking at the spearpoints with their sabers, but the compact band of foot soldiers kept coming. Horses lost their footing in the confused press and toppled, throwing their noble riders. Alarmed, the captain of the Riders called for retreat.

Tol let them go. Eight Riders had fallen, either wounded or unconscious, but the Juramonans hadn't lost a man. The militia backed away as the escaped prisoners scurried to safety.

Tol caught up with Miya, still supporting her injured father. He asked why she and the other Dom-shu were so far from their forest home.

Frowning at his gruff tone, Miya looked up at her father. "See? He is an ungrateful wretch! How's Sister?"

He said she was fine, and coming with Egrin and the main body of the army. Relief flooded Miya's face.

"Praise Zivilyn! She left the village with her burial beads, you know."

Tol stopped in his tracks. He hadn't known. When a Dom-shu warrior came of age, he or she was required to weave a headband that would be worn only when the warrior expected to die in battle. When Kiya had left her people to become Tol's hostage and wife, her beads had remained with Voyarunta. To have brought her death raiment with her on this journey was an ominous sign.

Drums clattered and horns blared from the distant city. The southwestern gate—called the Centaur Gate for its representation of a tribe of galloping centaurs wrought in fine bronze—swung open. Horsemen six abreast trotted forth. Soon two hordes had deployed across the paved road leading southwest to Daltigoth.

More horns proclaimed the emergence of a third horde, and a fourth could be seen mustering inside the barbican. The presence of four thousand Riders meant Wornoth was no longer concerned about a handful of fleeing prisoners. He intended to kill Tol. Militia and escapees alike quickened their pace.

Tol finally noted the absence of Helbin, and Zala said he'd been captured. This likely meant the wizard was dead.

The group was moving as fast as they could. A flight of arrows arced up from the battlements of Caergoth and descended. The missiles fell far short, but the Ergothian hordes started forward in pursuit formation. On foot, and burdened with weak and wounded people, Tol's band couldn't outpace horsemen. The first Riders caught up with them, then passed by on either side.

There was no choice but stand and fight. He pushed his group hard until they reached a spreading oak, the largest tree in sight. The militiamen deployed in a circle around the tree. The escapees clustered around its base. Zala, Miya, Chief Voyarunta, and the Dom-shu warriors borrowed swords from the spear-armed militiamen and formed a tight group around Tol.

Without preamble or any call to surrender, the Ergothians attacked. They came straight in, and ran onto a wall of spears. Recoiling, they left a dozen dead and dying. Again they surged forward, on two fronts, trying to pinch the small band in two.

One Ergothian pushed his horse through the melee, thinking to come up on Tol's blind side. Miya shouted a warning. Tol whirled, and his attacker's blade met Number Six with a clang of iron on steel. Disengaging quickly, Tol sliced the saddle girth. Rider and saddle crashed to the ground. Tol thrust home through the armpit gap in the Rider's breast-plate.

After more furious fighting, the Riders withdrew. The reason quickly became clear—Tylocost was coming. The remainder of the militia was marching in two compact blocks, bristling with spearpoints. Behind them, cantering quickly, was the demi-horde of Riders Tol had left in reserve. The Caergoth hordes circled the slow-moving militia, looking for a weak spot to exploit. Doggedly, the two phalanxes came on. As Tol's mounted men drew near, the Caergoth hordes pulled back.

"Their hearts aren't in it," Miya observed. Sweat plastered her short hair to her face, and she was breathing hard. There were no soft Dom-shu, but six years as a village mother had ill-prepared her for fierce combat.

As he watched the Caergoth Riders withdraw a short distance, Tol suddenly frowned. Riders of the Great Horde retreating after only a brief engagement with foot soldiers? And withdrawing in the face of a force of Riders only a quarter their strength? Understanding struck him.

"You're right!" he declared. "Their hearts aren't in it!"

Tol called for his cornet. A young fellow, once a journeyman brewer from Juramona, arrived and was told to blow "Parley." The brewer didn't know how, so Tol sang the four notes for him. The cornet repeated the notes properly and Tol slapped him on the back. "Get up that tree and blow until I tell you to stop!"

The lad clambered up the oak, assisted by the strong arms of several Dom-shu. After lodging himself in the high branches, he put the brass horn to his lips.

He had sounded "Parley" several times before the imperial horsemen took note. Silence fell as the hordes re-formed their lines. A delegation of eight horsemen advanced from the Caergoth contingent: four horde commanders, each with his standard bearer. Tol recognized those standards. The Lightning Riders, the Bronzehearts, the Caer Blades, and the Iron Falcons had served under him in the war with Tarsis.

The leader of this delegation also was known to Tol. A barrel-chested warrior with a forked black beard, Geddrig Zanpolo, commander of the Iron Falcons, was a formidable fighter and widely hailed as a brave warrior. His famous beard had been grown, it was said, to hide the deep notch cut in his chin by a wild centaur. Disarmed, grievously wounded, Zanpolo had slain the centaur bandit with his bare hands.

Tol decided to go out alone to meet the delegation. Such veteran warriors of the Great Horde would not talk to him were he accompanied by women, foot soldiers, or foreigners. He reckoned he could trust the honor of the warlord of the Iron Falcons.

He left the shade of the oak tree and walked out into the midday sun. He headed uphill through the trampled grass to a small ledge of weathered sandstone. This put him at the same height as the approaching mounted men, so there he waited.

Eight riders drew up in a line before him.

"My lord," Zanpolo greeted him. "I was told you led this motley army. I am sorry to see it!"

"Save your sorrow. You see before you the advance guard of the Army of the East."

"I know of no such army. Who created it? Not the emperor."

"We created it ourselves. Nomads had burned and looted half the eastern provinces. Were we to sit idle simply because the emperor could not be bothered to defend his own people?"

"I wouldn't," Zanpolo admitted.

"This parley is illegal! We cannot treat with a proscribed man!"

This outburst came from a younger warrior at Zanpolo's left, the commander of the Caer Blades. He added, "By rights, we should take his head and present it to the governor!"

The young warlord's hand moved to rest on his sword hilt, but Zanpolo growled, "This is a parley, Hallack. I'll cut down the first man who dares draw a blade!"

Tol relaxed. With this proof of Zanpolo's honor, he decided to make the appeal he'd been rehearsing in his mind.

"Warriors of Ergoth," he said loudly, for all to hear, "you

know me. Some of you fought with me against the Tarsans. Ten years we fought together, boot to boot, shoulder to shoulder. We were not city soldiers then, living in warm barracks and eating in taverns. For a decade we rode together, sleeping on the ground, eating from the same pot.

"After the war was won, our late emperor, Pakin III, died and I was recalled to Daltigoth. So were many of you. There, while serving the new emperor, Ackal IV, I became involved in the machinations of the rogue wizard Mandes, who had done me much wrong. He was driven into exile and began a campaign of evil against the empire. I convinced His Majesty Ackal IV to let me bring Mandes to justice. This I did."

The Riders, except for Zanpolo, showed signs of impatience. They knew this story. Tol's next words erased their boredom.

"It was the worst mistake of my life. While I was away from Daltigoth, Prince Nazramin usurped the throne." Anger bloomed on Lord Hallack's face. Tol pinned him with a glare. "Yes, usurped," he repeated. "Through the use of evil magic, Nazramin drove his brother mad, then had him deposed and murdered.

"When I returned from dealing with Mandes, the new emperor stripped me of my titles and authority, and had me beaten nearly to death. He could hardly allow the champion of his late, unhappy brother to go free, so he had me proscribed.

"For six years I have dwelt among the foresters, my friends the Dom-shu. There I learned again how decent and honest people behaved. We've long despised the tribes of the east as savages, but they treated me with fairness and generosity."

Tol's expression grew hard again. "Then the bakali and the nomads invaded the empire. Ackal V made only half-hearted attempts to defend the east, preferring to hold back the Great Horde to defend Daltigoth. With what result? Murder, pillage, fire, and waste! Juramona and a score of lesser towns are in ruins. Farms have been burned, herds scattered or slaughtered. Orchards have been left to rot, mines and markets are empty. Tens of thousands are without food or shelter. In the east there was no law, no order!

"Egrin, Raemel's son, came to me in the Great Green and convinced me to return. I hammered together the Juramona Militia, which you see accompanying me today. We fought off armies of nomads while Egrin summoned the landed hordes from all the eastern provinces. Together, the militia and landed Riders drove the nomads out of the empire, slaying two of their great chiefs in the process."

Zanpolo nodded, breaking his stern silence. "We heard as much, from prisoners," he said. "We did not know you led the landed hordes." A trace of a smile crossed his lips. "Though I should have guessed."

"This is irrelevant!" snapped Hallack, unable to contain himself any longer. "This man has been condemned by the emperor himself! It is our duty to arrest him and deliver him to the governor!"

"Our duty," Zanpolo said quietly, "is to the empire."

Tol looked his old comrade in the eyes. This was exactly what he'd been hoping to hear!

"I have thirty-two hordes in the Army of the East," he said. "With the garrison of Caergoth added, we'll be strong enough to defeat the bakali and save our country!"

"And what about the emperor?" asked Zanpolo, after a pause, black brows lifting.

Choosing his words with utmost care, Tol said, "An emperor who does not defend his country should not be emperor."

"Treason!"

Lord Hallack erupted out of line, drawing his saber. Tol stepped back, reaching for Number Six, but before he had done more than grasp the hilt, Zanpolo spurred his horse forward. He caught Hallack's sword arm in one hand, and with the other, backhanded him across the face. The harsh blow sent the Ackal loyalist flying from his horse. Out cold, he rolled over and over in the grass, down to the foot of Tol's perch.

Zanpolo looked at the other two warlords, who sat calmly, hands folded across the pommels of their saddles.

"Moristan. Caminol. What say you?"

Moristan, commander of the Bronzehearts, inhaled and exhaled slowly. "For six years," he said with customary deliberateness, "I've done nothing but collect taxes and chase unworthy bandits. When the nomads invaded, Wornoth kept us here to defend the city, even though the barbarians had no way to breach the walls."

Caminol's response was more succinct. "The Lightning Riders serve the empire, not one man," he said, nodding to Tol and the other two warlords.

"So, what will you have us do, my lord?" Zanpolo asked Tol.

Hope surged through Tol's weary frame. "Take Caergoth, first," he said. "Will the hordes inside resist us?"

"A few young hotheads might, and Wornoth's guard. No one of consequence."

"Then let's enter now. The governor will think we have surrendered and you have captured us!" The three warlords agreed.

Tol hurried back to his people, still clustered around the oak tree. When he told them what had transpired, they were incredulous. Except Miya.

"That's Husband," she said, shrugging. "Throw him in a pit of snakes, and he'll make friends with all the vipers!"

The Juramonans formed two columns, one behind the other, and set off toward the city. Tol rode at the head of the foremost column. At Zanpolo's order, the unconscious Lord Hallack was draped over his horse and the beast's reins given over to one of his men. Word flashed like lightning through the Caergoth troops: instead of fighting Lord Tolandruth, they were going to follow him!

Riding close to Zanpolo toward the city gate, his men chanting his name, Tol was filled with emotion. His mind whirled, but not with battle plans. He couldn't stop thinking of Valaran as he'd last seen her: her face white as the ermine robes she wore, green eyes spilling tears onto winter-pale cheeks.

*Whatever happens, you must live—because I will return.*

That was the promise he'd made her on the snowy field outside Daltigoth. With every warrior he gained, every battle he won, he was coming closer to fulfilling that oath. Yet no battle, no honor could make him complete until he held her in his arms again.

# C h a p t e r  2 1
## The Anvil

ol's entry into Caergoth was more confusing than glorious. Zanpolo chose to return the same way he left, via the Centaur Gate. The gate opened readily enough, but the soldiers there were plainly puzzled to hear the returning warriors shouting the name of the man they'd been sent to destroy.

Zanpolo quickly ordered his own men to displace the city troops at the gates. No blood was shed; after a brief scuffle, the surprised soldiers found themselves imprisoned in their own barbican. Their compatriots, looking down on these events from the battlements, abandoned their posts.

"Little birds are flying away," Miya said, gesturing toward the fleeing men.

Tol nodded. The men would certainly carry word of his coming to Lord Wornoth. As there was no way to prevent it, there was no reason to worry about it.

The first city square beyond the Centaur Gate was known as the Starwalk. Its broad white pavement was marked with bronze stars, and black lines of basalt radiated from a common point not quite in the center of the square. The square was a public observatory. By standing on the lines or on the various bronze markers at appropriate times during the year, ordinary folk could mark the movements of the moons and stars.

This day, it was not being used for any lofty purpose. Like all Caergoth's public squares, the Starwalk had become a squalid shanty town crowded with war refugees.

Tol reined up. His Juramonans halted behind him. Zanpolo stopped his own horsemen and doubled back to see what was wrong. He found Tol surveying the smoky, fetid scene in the Starwalk with a scowl on his face.

Zanpolo grimaced with understanding. "I know," he said. "With a few hundred sabers I'd clear this trash out!"

Tol shook his head, but said nothing. He turned in the saddle to look back at the column winding behind him. There was Queen Casberry, once more in her beloved sedan chair, borne on the capable shoulders of Front and Back; Uncle Corpse and his Dom-shu, a bit worse for wear; and the half-elf huntress, Zala, who had refused all aid and still carried her frail father. Still further back, the ugliest Silvanesti in the world led a human militia comprising artisans, merchants, farmers, and herders. Somewhere in the city, thousands of men were wearing out horses to join Tol's army. Retired warriors, they'd left home and hearth and taken up the weapons they'd hung up years ago. In their company was the oddest contingent of all—soldiers of an army Tol had defeated, now led by a wealthy, embittered woman who had lost her own daughter in a struggle not her own.

All these people—all these *different* people—had come so far and done so much because of him. Their loyalty, their faith in him, had brought them from every corner of the empire and lands beyond.

Dismounting, Tol handed the reins to Miya, who'd been walking alongside.

"Watch out," she said, seeing the look in his eyes. "Husband's up to something."

"All of you stay here. No matter what happens, stay here till I call you," Tol said.

He walked into the maze of temporary shelters covering the Starwalk. The refugees moved out of his way. They knew to make themselves scarce when a warrior came near. They came from half a hundred small towns, from isolated farms, and from semi-nomadic camps. Not all were Ergothian. This human avalanche had been set in motion a thousand leagues away, by the arrival of the bakali and by attacks from plainsmen also displaced by the lizard-men. Most refugees regarded Tol blankly as he moved among them. If they did react, it was with fear.

Anger swelled in Tol's breast. This was not why he had become a warrior. Most Riders of the Great Horde, born into wealth if not outright nobility, considered this their due—daily tribute in the form of terror. But Tol had chosen the life of a soldier because it promised more than endless years grubbing in the dirt, herding recalcitrant pigs, and praying daily to the gods for sun and rain, but not too much of either. He'd led a full life, earned loyal friends, and loved an intelligent, beautiful woman. The time had come to pay for those past pleasures and glories.

Forty paces away from his waiting comrades he found a waist-high stone pedestal and climbed on it. An alabaster disk was inset in its top. From this spot, when the square was clear, one could mark the passage of Solin through the seasons.

Those immediately around him fell silent and regarded him uncertainly. The quiet spread through the square, with neighbor nudging neighbor and gesturing at the warrior standing atop the Solin pedestal. Tol waited until the silence was complete, then spoke.

"People, listen to me! I am—" An instant's thought, then— "Tol of Juramona. I bring you good news. The tribes who ravaged your homes have been defeated!"

There was no response. A baby began to cry. Several people coughed.

"You can go home! The nomad invaders are gone!"

The baby continued to howl. There were more coughs. A woman called out, "We ain't got no home! They burned it!"

"You can build another!" Tol replied. "But you must leave the city! It's too crowded for you to remain!" He was amazed disease hadn't broken out among the refugees already.

"You drivin' us out, m'lord?" asked a man standing nearby.

Exasperation sharpened Tol's voice. "No! I'm telling you, you can leave! The nomads are driven out."

"So it's safe?"

Tol's impatience evaporated. He answered honestly. "No, it's not."

The crowd began to mutter, confused and unhappy. Tol raised his voice again, saying, "But when were you ever safe? Were you safe when cruel warlords ruled over you, and a ruthless, mad emperor ruled them? You've never been safe, but the nomads have been defeated, and you must leave Caergoth. Here, there is only poverty and illness!"

Unfortunately, the wider import of his words was lost.

"The emperor is mad?"

"We was *never* safe? I thought the city wall was supposed to keep us safe."

"I told ya' they'd come to drive us out, and here they are!"

"*This* emperor is mad, too?"

"Let's get out 'fore they attack us!"

Some refugees grabbed their meager possessions and set out for the nearest gate. Others argued whether to stay or go. These grew so heated that Tol was jostled off the platform.

When he disappeared into the crowd, Zanpolo and his captains spurred their mounts forward. They separated Tol from the mob and ushered him back to his waiting people.

Zanpolo's bearded face wore a smile. "Clever stratagem, my lord! You've sowed the seeds of a riot," he said. "It will tie up Wornoth's loyal troops!"

Tol didn't bother answering. He hadn't meant to start a riot. He'd hoped to make the people understand they should reclaim their lives and not blindly follow the whims of emperors, warlords, or any of their lackeys. But the hopeless, helpless squatters didn't see him as "Tol of Juramona," born one of them. To them, he was Lord Tolandruth, Rider of the Great Horde, oppressor and protector. That he could be interested in their well-being was as unfathomable to them as the workings of the celestial map on which they squatted.

The noise around him quickly grew deafening. The unrest Tol had unintentionally incited radiated outward, spreading from the Starwalk through the clogged streets, to the next square, and the next.

"What did I tell you?" Miya shouted above the chaos. "When Husband acts, the world trembles!"

"This is crazy!" Tol protested. "I told them to go home and live for themselves. They think I threatened them!"

Tylocost said, "You did threaten them. You told them they weren't safe. Safety was the one lie they all believed in."

Zanpolo bawled orders at his men. Tol, feeling stunned and stupid, mounted his horse.

They headed for the citadel, sited atop the tallest hill in the city. Zanpolo's hordes banged their sword hilts against their armored chests. The ominous sound frightened the refugees and they shrank from the column of fighting men. The hordes cleaved through the crowd without bloodshed, as Riders swatted slow-moving squatters, or booted them aside.

At the Great Square of Ackal Dermount, near the center of the city, they encountered their first serious opposition. The square seethed with panicked refugees, and at the opposite end of the plaza were several hundred horsemen in the funereal white and silver livery of the Governor's Own Guard. Their sabers were out.

"Here's where we cleave a few skulls," Zanpolo said.

"Can we try persuasion?" asked Tol.

"Not with them, my lord. They take Wornoth's coin, even as the Lord Governor takes the emperor's. They'll fight."

Tol knew he was right. "Give quarter to any who ask for it, but we must reach the citadel before Wornoth seals himself inside."

Zanpolo rallied his own horde, the Iron Falcons, with a roar that made Tol's hair stand on end. With an answering bellow, the Riders raised their sabers high, then extended them at arm's length. Zanpolo called for a point charge. In the tight confines of Caergoth's streets, there wasn't room for a full-tilt attack.

The Iron Falcons bolted across the Great Square. On their flanks, the Lightning Riders and the Bronzehearts surged forward. The Juramona Militia broke out of marching order and formed a wall of shields around those on foot. Tol rode with Zanpolo.

Innocent townsfolk and terrified refugees raced out of the way of Zanpolo's charge. Some did not make it, and were trampled.

The Governor's Own men were confused. They thought Zanpolo's attack was directed at the refugees choking the Great Square. Their hesitation lasted only briefly, but it was long enough. If they had withdrawn immediately up the narrower side streets, Zanpolo's thrust would have been less effective. Instead, they took the full brunt of the Iron Falcons' charge.

Tol was bent low over his horse's neck, Number Six extended. A guardsman tried to deflect his point with the small iron buckler strapped to his left forearm. Dwarf-forged steel pierced the buckler and, propelled by Tol's strength and the horse's speed, drove on through with only a momentary scrape of resistance. As their horses collided, Number Six buried half its length through the man's neck. Tol recovered, and the guardsman slid lifeless to the ground.

After the initial contact, a brisk, slashing battle followed. The weight and power of the Falcons drove the Governor's Own men back to the walls of the House of Luin, the hall of the Red Robe Order in Caergoth. Stubbornly, the governor's men fought on.

"We can't spend all afternoon at this!" Tol shouted at Zanpolo. "Keep going here—I'll take my footmen on!"

"Can you really get through with that lot?" said Zanpolo, with a Rider's traditional disdain for foot soldiers.

"They got me here, didn't they?"

Tol broke off and rode back to his Juramonans, standing at the other end of the Great Square. All the civilians had fled and he made quick time across the empty plaza, sheathing his saber as he arrived.

Tol and the militia would head for the palace, with Zala leading the way. Her father, Voyarunta, and the other wounded would remain behind with the Dom-shu men. Miya, armed with spear and shield borrowed from a Dom-shu warrior, stood ready to go with Tol.

He gave her a surprised look, and she shrugged. "If you get yourself killed and I'm not there, Sister will skin me."

Tol's lips twitched at her reasoning, but he addressed himself to Queen Casberry, asking her to remain behind also.

The kender queen, dressed today in a sky blue tunic and

matching trousers, consented and immediately invited Voya-runta to join her in a dice game called Three Times Dead.

Tol divided the two thousand men of the Juramona Militia into four companies of five hundred. Each company would follow a different route through the grid of streets, marching parallel to each other and reuniting before the main gate of the Caergoth citadel. Zala gave them quick directions that would allow them to avoid the public plazas, where troops loyal to Wornoth might have congregated.

Tol's orders were simple. If challenged, the militiamen should fight. But if the opportunity arose, they were to offer opponents the chance to join them, and keep heading toward the palace.

The four companies set off at a trot. Tol, Miya, and Zala went with the center-right column. Tylocost accompanied the far left.

As they progressed, the streets grew increasingly narrow. Miya complained and Tol explained the constriction was intentional, to prevent large bodies of troops from attacking the governor's palace.

At one intersection they flushed out a band of archers. The militia company charged, but the surprised bowmen, armed only with mauls for close-range fighting, turned and fled.

After passing down another tight street, the Juramonans found themselves before the citadel's ceremonial gate. This portal, dedicated to Draco Paladin, was open, and some fifty soldiers wearing the governor's colors milled about it in confusion. As the Juramona spearmen emerged from the alley, the soldiers sent up a shout. The ponderous double doors of the gate began to close.

"Secure that gate!" Tol bawled, and his contingent rushed pell-mell for the portal.

Tol was confronted by a subaltern wearing a fancy gilded helmet. The fellow was half Tol's age, but wielded his slim blade with skill. Twice he scored, cutting a bloody line on Tol's right arm and left thigh. Tol tried to cut him with his stronger blade, but his strikes met only air. The young officer was never still for very long. He darted from side to side, avoiding every swing aimed at him.

A Hero's Justice

Sweat stung Tol's eyes. His breath moved up and down his throat harshly. He'd never been adept at fancy dueling, and as the contest dragged on, his years began telling on him.

Finally, his enemy's bright iron blade whisked over Tol's shoulder, snagging briefly on his earlobe. As blood spurted from the cut, Tol managed to seize the man's wrist.

"Yield!" he said. "Don't fight us, join us!"

The subaltern punched Tol in the chest with his buckler. Tol staggered backward. The tip of the young soldier's blade flashed toward his eyes. Reflexively, Tol threw his head back. A cut opened on the bridge of his nose.

Angry now, Tol gripped his saber in both hands. He made a whirling parry, binding up the officer's slender, straight blade. The fellow hit him again and again with the iron boss of his small shield, but Tol ignored these blows, concentrating on the motion of the blades. At the top of an arc, he flung his hands up, yanking the young officer's sword high. Disengaging, Tol drove Number Six at his opponent's heart.

The subaltern brought up his buckler. An iron saber would have been turned aside, but Tol's steel point punched through the shield's brass rim and kept going, running the officer through. Mortally wounded, the fellow stumbled backward, dropping his sword. He gaped at Number Six, its hilt nearly touching his chest. There was no pain or fear on his young face, only bewilderment. He simply couldn't understand how the saber had penetrated both his buckler and his damascened breastplate.

His eyes grew distant, and his lifeless body fell sideways, as Tol recovered Number Six.

"Husband, the gates!"

Miya's warning drew Tol's swift attention. The great portal was slowly swinging shut.

Her warning had been heeded by another as well. Out of the melee dashed a slight figure, sword in hand and a floppy hat on his head. Tylocost, running ahead of his men, sprinted for the closing doors. With the fleetness and agility of his race, he wove through the battle, avoiding swords and spearpoints with astonishing dexterity. Reaching the gate, he twisted sideways through the rapidly diminishing gap.

Tol was thunderstruck. He respected the Silvanesti's skills as a general and knew him to be brave in the casual way of most well-born warriors. But to fling himself, alone, into the midst of a host of enemies was unbelievably courageous—and reckless.

Yanking himself out of his daze, Tol shouted, "To the gate! To the gate! Never mind the guards!"

The Juramonans tried to comply, but only Zala was nimble enough to evade combat and rush to Tylocost's aid. Tol saw an unusual expression on the half-elf's face as she dodged and wove through the fracas.

Zala was worried about Tylocost.

The gates had stopped. When Zala arrived, the space between them was less than the width of her shoulders, but she pushed through.

For a few terrifying moments, she was blind as she left bright sunlight and entered the gatehouse's gloomy interior. When her eyes adjusted, she beheld four guards dead or dying by the windlass that operated the gate. Tylocost was battling three more, all equipped with polearms that badly outranged his saber. The thunder of footsteps on the wooden stairs behind them told Zala reinforcements were on their way down.

One of the three soldiers aimed a thrust at Tylocost's blind side. Lightning-fast, Zala drew a long knife from her boot and flew at the man. She turned aside the overhand chop from his halberd, saving Tylocost. The elf glanced at her, pale eyes widening, then resumed dueling with the remaining two guards.

Zala was panting from exertion. This was not her usual style of fighting. She could use a bow, or slay a charging boar with her sword at short range, but protracted battle, first outside the gate and now in the tight confines of the gatehouse, was foreign to her. Her opponent was an older man, his black hair flecked with gray, and he knew his business. He pushed her back with short jabs of the halberd's spearhead, then followed with broad sweeps of its blade. She couldn't reach him with her shorter blade.

*Clang!* The side of the axe caught her hand and sent her

sword flying. Before she could recover and bring up her knife, the veteran soldier lunged. His spearhead took Zala below the ribs. She gasped in shock, and fell.

Just then, Tol, Miya, and two hundred Juramonans burst through the gate, knocking the double doors wide. A tragic scene met their horrified gazes: Zala lay on her back, clutching a belly wound from which blood welled. Tylocost stood over her fending off two determined halberdiers. A third lay dead at his feet.

Miya screamed. As she intended, the sound distracted one of the halberdiers. He glanced her way, and instantly died at Tylocost's hand. The other went down beneath a swarm of Juramonans. Reinforcements coming down the stairs from the gatehouse above likewise met Juramonan iron, and after a brief combat, cried for quarter.

"Spare any who lay down their arms!" Tol shouted. "Search the citadel! Find the governor!"

More of the militia poured in to carry out Tol's orders, and Tylocost's saber clattered to the stones as he dropped beside Zala. He took her hand in both of his.

"Stupid girl," he said. "I didn't need your help!"

"They'd've chopped you to bits," she gasped. Her face was translucent as wax.

Miya's arms were crimson to the elbows from her efforts to stanch the flow of blood. She looked up at Tol and shook her head. Pain creased Tol's forehead, and he, too, knelt by the fallen huntress.

Tylocost saw none of this; his attention was focused on Zala, on the blood that continued to well from her terrible wound.

"You shouldn't be here. You're not a warrior!" he said, voice harsh with emotion.

"I'll soon be out of your way."

He squeezed her hand, and her fingers twitched weakly in response. Helplessly, he whispered her name, heedless of the tears that were falling. Her dark eyes stayed on his face. She blinked once, then her hand went limp in his. Tylocost gently closed her eyes.

"I'm sorry, Husband," Miya said quietly.

Tol touched her shoulder, but there was no time for more. Armed men were streaming past them.

"We must go. We must find Governor Wornoth," Tol said. "Tylocost?"

"I will be here."

Tol and Miya left the grieving general where he was. As they ascended the steps into the palace proper, Tylocost removed his absurd gardener's hat and placed it gently over Zala's face. He began to speak softly, in the melodic language of his people, offering an ancient prayer to Astarin.

🦉 🦉 🦉 🦉 🦉

Tol strode through the halls, boots thumping loudly on the carpeted floors. He'd been here before and knew the way to the audience hall. Close at his heels was Miya. Behind her, the crowd of soldiers gawked at the opulence. Wornoth had expensive taste, and had decorated the public halls of the palace with thick carpets, elaborate tapestries, and the finest works of the sculptor's art.

All resistance had collapsed. The only people they encountered were servants or courtiers, often burdened with loot liberated from the city coffers. If they dropped their booty and fled, Tol ignored them. If they tried to flee with their ill-gotten goods, Tol sent soldiers after them.

The doors of the audience hall were bolted. Tol stood aside, and militiamen hacked the polished darkwood panels with axes. In a trice they broke through.

Within, a fire blazed on the marble floor. Two men were feeding parchment scrolls to the flames. The shorter, younger man was Wornoth.

"Seize the governor!" Tol commanded.

Wornoth wore a dagger, but offered no resistance beyond abusive language. While attention was focused on him, the other man—a portly, yellow-haired cleric unknown to Tol—took a small vial from his gray robe and flung it at them. It struck the floor two steps in front of Tol, and shattered.

The very air shuddered. Everyone but Tol was knocked flat by an invisible blast. Even as they were falling, Tol rushed up to the priest and put the sharp edge of Number Six to his double chin.

"Any more magic, and I'll set your head on a spike!"

The astonished cleric surrendered but demanded, "Who are you, that the Hand of the Wind does not touch you?"

"Tol of Juramona!"

It was Wornoth who had answered his cleric's question. The governor's nose was bleeding and he glared in impotent fury at his captor.

"Traitorous barbarian!" he shrieked at Tol. "You'll die a hundred times for this outrage!"

Tol ignored him. The fire had been reduced to glowing embers by the Hand of the Wind. He raked the point of his saber through the hot ashes and came up with a large, unburned piece of parchment. It contained a list of figures. At the bottom was written, in a neat, scribal hand, "Collected from the squatters in University Square."

The governor was apparently trying to hide his misdeeds, not from Tol, but from the person he'd been cheating: his patron, the emperor of Ergoth. If Ackal V learned Wornoth had not been sending him the full amount extorted from the refugees, his fury at being cheated would certainly cost the governor his head.

Tol dropped the parchment scrap. "For failing to defend the people under your rule, I depose you, Governor," he intoned. "Once we sort out what's happened here, I'm certain we'll find other crimes to charge you with."

"You have no authority! You are a proscribed man!"

Number Six came up so quickly everyone in the hall flinched at the sudden flash of steel.

"This is my authority! The empire was made by the sword, and it can be unmade the same way!" Tol stalked toward the governor—

—and found his way blocked by Miya. Unlike her stalwart sister, she was no warrior. She did not raise her weapon or speak, just stood before him, golden-brown eyes brimming with sympathy.

Tol glared at her for only a heartbeat. Her action made him realize just how close he was to murdering the unarmed

Wornoth. The image of Zala, dead on the cold stones below, filled his head, and he was shaking with wrath.

Still staring at the silent woman before him, Tol growled, "Get him out of here! Put him and the priest in separate cells under close guard. And search the cleric thoroughly before you lock him up!"

The captives were removed. Tol turned away. He burned with the need to strike something. The governor's elaborate chair—the literal seat of power here in Caergoth—offered a handy target. He smote its heavy carved wooden back with Number Six, cleaving it halfway down.

"Listen," Miya hissed. "Do you hear? Temple bells!"

The deep tolling penetrated even the citadel's thick walls. Did they signify a new alarm, or a celebration of the city's downfall?

The answer came in the form of a messenger who burst into the hall. The man saluted Tol.

"My lord! Lord Egrin is here with the army!"

Miya and Tol looked at each other. The Dom-shu woman grinned.

"Sister missed all the fun!"

🦉 🦉 🦉 🦉 🦉

Bells were pealing in Daltigoth, too. The emperor had returned in triumph after destroying the bakali in one epic battle. His welcome was surprisingly muted. The streets were crowded, but the people were more relieved than joyous. The day itself was less than auspicious, too. Gray clouds towered overhead, and the air was heavy with a threatening storm.

Ackal V rode into his capital with Prince Dalar on the saddle in front of him. Arrayed behind the emperor were his surviving warlords, less than half the number who had departed Daltigoth with him not so many days before. Following them were those warriors who had distinguished themselves in the battle. Many were seriously wounded. There was an interval of space, and then a rider bearing the standard of the Thorngoth Sabers. The Sabers had performed so nobly in destroying the bakali mound that none of them remained to receive the honors they'd earned.

Behind the standard of the lost horde stretched a long line of wagons laden with booty taken from the defeated enemy. Here and there an article of gold gleamed, but for the most part, the caravan contained arms and armor stripped from the bodies of slain bakali. In addition to the usual ring mail tunics, there were bronze and iron plates that had been shaped to fit strange reptilian bodies. Everything was coated with purplish red bakali gore. The emperor wanted the people of Daltigoth to know what the aftermath of battle looked like—and smelled like. The grisly trophies would be dumped in the plaza before the great temple of Corij, as an offering to the god of war. When an appropriate amount of time had passed, smiths would collect the armor and melt it down. Bronze would be used for statues honoring Ackal V, iron would go to the imperial arsenal, and the blades and helmets would enter service again with the Great Horde.

Near the end of the long line of wagons, the cargo abruptly changed. The bloody armor was replaced by piles of leathery, yellow-gray objects, each the size of a smallish wine cask. These were bakali eggs, salvaged from the ruins of the nest mound. Tens of thousands of eggs had been destroyed by the collapse of the mound and, later, by conscripted laborers. At the last moment, on a whim, Ackal V ordered a few dozen saved. Some would be given to his scholars to study. The rest he intended to let hatch, if they would. A few lizard-men would make interesting slaves.

The procession wound through the straight, wide streets of the New City. The Temple of Corij, largest in Daltigoth, lay at the edge of the Old City, its sacred precincts surrounded by a low granite wall. The hammered golden gates depicted, on one panel, Ackal Ergot, twice life size, mounted on a rearing horse. Facing him, and equal in size, was Corij himself, on his divine war-horse Skyraker. Their postures made it look as though man and god were dueling. As the empire's founder had once vowed to fight anyone, even the gods, who stood in the way of his vision, the depiction was not entirely untruthful.

# Paul B. Thompson and Tonya C. Cook

As Ackal V approached the temple, priests of Corij drew the double doors apart. Elder clerics were already arrayed on the sacred steps. They had donned their priestly vestments of golden scale armor, but in place of the usual brown surcoats, they wore short tabards of Ackal scarlet. Gravely, they watched Ackal V enter the holy confines on Sirrion's muscular back, his pale, wide-eyed young son seated before him.

The emperor looked up at the temple's massive dome and squat columned façade, built of rose porphyry and red granite. He well remembered how the priesthood of Corij had loved his father, Pakin III. An old soldier himself, Pakin III gave generous grants of gold and land to the temple. Ackal V did not. He had better uses for his money. Still, one could not ignore the gods completely.

"O Corij!" he shouted, voice echoing against the hard stone face of the temple. "See the tribute I bring you!"

The wagons of wreckage rumbled forward, drawn now by teams of warriors. Although war-horses were allowed in the sacred precinct, lowly draft animals were not.

Ten paces from the temple steps, the first wagon stopped. A dozen brawny Riders of the Great Horde braced themselves under its side and heaved upward. Iron helmets, ring mail tunics, bronze cuirasses, and axes clattered to the ground. The empty wagon was hauled away and another took its place. Wagon after wagon discharged their cargo, until the noisome heap was as high as the emperor on horseback.

The high priest of Corij, a solemn, long-bearded oldster named Hycontas, descended the steps. Once a Rider of the Great Horde, he was a provincial from the empire's western reaches. His family were minor nobles, not particularly distinguished and only modestly well off. In Ackal V's eyes he was little better than a peasant.

"Greetings to you, Great Majesty, and to your honored son," Hycontas said. "It is a mighty gift you bring. The God of War has been well served."

"Yes, at last. I sent too many fools to do what I should have done myself." The emperor gave a tight-lipped, faintly mocking smile. "My apologies for the messy state of the offering, but time was short, and there's much still to do."

Hycontas bowed, his blue eyes sharp as icicles. "As Your Majesty says, but word has reached us the nomads have been defeated and dispersed back to their homelands."

Surprise showed briefly on Ackal V's proud face; he obviously wondered how word had reached the priesthood of the nomads' defeat. His usual sneer returned quickly and he said, "Those country hordes had better toe the line! I won't stand for any backcountry heroics!"

Hycontas bowed again. "Your Majesty rules with justice."

Ackal V studied him for any hint of sarcasm, but Hycontas's face showed only bland sincerity. The emperor wheeled his horse, turning Sirrion so tightly the horse's long, dark red tail whipped past the high priest's face. Hycontas did not react. For his part, Dalar had learned well his father's abrupt ways and was holding tight to the pommel.

"When the dedication to Corij is complete, send word to the Arsenal, and the tribute will be removed," Ackal V said over one shoulder, as Sirrion cantered back to the procession outside the temple wall.

Flies were gathering around the pile of gory trophies, and the sun's heat only strengthened the rank odor of bakali blood. Hycontas ascended the steps to escape the stench. As he did, a shadow fell across him, cast by a single, large black vulture circling overhead.

Messengers come in all shapes, the old priest mused.

# c h a p t e r 2 2
# A Place in the Shade

Once Governor Wornoth's capture became known, resistance to the Army of the East ended quickly. Only a small body of troops, the governor's private guard, was imprisoned in the citadel. The streets grew calm. People seemed dazed, like sleepers awakened from a deep but troubled slumber. Refugees streamed out of Caergoth, leaving by every gate to every point on the horizon.

Tol and Egrin, standing on a balcony of Caergoth's Riders' Hall, watched the lines of ordinary folk leaving the city. The view was of the Centaur Gate and, beyond, the road running southwest toward Daltigoth. It was late afternoon, and Tol could hardly credit all that had happened since sunrise, when Zanpolo had escorted them through the city gate.

"It's not wise to let everyone go," Egrin was saying. "Those leaving should be questioned. There could be deserters hidden among them—loyalists who'll carry word to Daltigoth about what happened here."

"Good. Saves me the trouble of sending word to Ackal V of our coming."

Egrin started to say more, but loud laughter erupted from the open doorway behind them. Tol smiled. "Sounds like the party is well underway."

"Something else we must keep an eye on," the old marshal said gloomily.

They went inside, entering the feasting hall that took up

the entire second floor of the Riders' sanctuary. As he had no intention of ruling Caergoth, Tol had set up his headquarters not in the governor's palace, but in the Riders' Hall outside the citadel.

A hasty banquet had been laid out, provided from Wornoth's impressive larder. The scene within was a merry one. Around the huge table were gathered Zanpolo, Pagas, Argonnel, Mittigorn, Trudo, and the other warlords who'd joined Tol; Casberry and her bearers; the Tarsans, Captain Anovenax and Syndic Hanira; Tylocost; Chief Voyarunta; and the Dom-shu sisters.

The reunion of Kiya and Miya had been memorable. Kiya, riding beside Egrin, had spotted her sister in the mob surrounding Tol at the citadel gate. She dismounted and shouldered her way through the happy throng of Juramonans and city folk, and came up on her younger sibling's blind side. Gripping Miya's shoulder, she whirled her around.

"Sister!" Miya exclaimed joyously.

Kiya slapped her hard across the cheek. The people immediately around them fell silent, stunned by the sudden violence.

"How dare you come here! Why did you abandon your child?" Kiya demanded.

Miya planted her fists on her hips. "Abandoned? Eli has more aunts than an anthill!"

So saying, Miya slapped her sister back, knocking the blonde warrior woman sideways.

A handful of militiamen stepped forward to stop what they were sure would be a fierce fight, but Tol waved them off. The sisters, each with the red imprint of a hand on her face, glared at each other, until Kiya finally spoke.

"Not bad—for a mother."

"Ha! You know our mother had a harder hand than the chief ever did!"

Voyarunta, standing only a few steps away, protested. The sisters simultaneously turned on him and said, "Quiet!" The Chief of the Dom-shu wisely obeyed.

The sisters embraced abruptly, each vigorously pounding the other on the back.

"By Corij, you stink!" Miya chortled happily.

"And you feel fat as a pig!" Kiya countered, laughing.

Now, when Tol and Egrin re-entered the feasting hall, shouts of greeting rose to meet them. The Dom-shu sisters, seated together, saluted them with a wave, and Pagas pressed a cup of foaming beer into Tol's hand.

Hanira, looking cool and elegant in a gown of pale green silk, called for quiet. From her place at the end of the long table she lifted her goblet and pronounced, "To the conqueror of Caergoth!"

Casberry and the Dom-shu raised their cups and drank, but the Ergothians present looked embarrassed.

Egrin spoke up quickly. "Begging your pardon, Syndic, but we're not conquerors. Liberators, yes, but Caergoth was and still is an imperial city."

"And anyone who uses the word 'rebel' had better be prepared to draw iron," growled Zanpolo.

Casberry snorted loudly. She now sported a multitude of gold bracelets and necklaces. These flashed brightly against her tunic of midnight black shot through with strands of crimson and gold.

"For victorious warriors you certainly know how to mince words," she piped.

Tol shook his head. "No, Your Majesty. Lords Egrin and Zanpolo speak the truth. We have freed Caergoth, not conquered it." He raised his own cup and amended Hanira's toast: "To success, and good friends!"

He sat at the head of the table, facing Hanira. Egrin took the chair on his left, and the Dom-shu sisters were arrayed on his right, as befit his wives. By precedence, Queen Casberry should have had Hanira's place of honor, but the diminutive monarch had chosen her location herself, the seat nearest the keg of lager.

They ate and drank heartily, and conversation remained jocular and light until mention was made of Wornoth, a subject Tol had been hoping to avoid. It was Hanira who broached the delicate subject.

"My lord, what do you intend to do with Governor Wornoth?"

Wornoth deserved swift justice for his many crimes against the people of his city and for his gross negligence in defending the empire. But the man was such a weakling Tol found it somehow shameful to order his death. Others obviously did not share his ambivalence.

"Hang 'im," said Pagas. The other warlords agreed.

"A dog like him doesn't deserve honorable death by blade," Trudo said.

"Wornoth will meet justice," Tol promised, hoping that would be the end of the discussion.

He should have known better. Like a ropesnake, Hanira preferred to surround and strangle her victim slowly, rather than grant a swift death from venom.

She tilted her head. Sunlight streaming through the windows lent a sapphire sheen to her black hair, piled high on her head for this occasion.

"What does that mean, my lord?" she asked, smiling sweetly.

"Gotta execute him," Casberry said, before he could respond. "He's a murderous toad, and everybody wants his blood. If you spare him, you'll look weak, my lord."

The warlords began enumerating the evils of leniency. Angered, Tol smote the tabletop with his fist.

"Have I said I would spare Wornoth?"

The diners fell silent, and Voyarunta said, "You are chief here, Son of My Life. Do as you think right."

Hanira sipped wine, preferring this to the beer the others drank. Her honey-colored eyes regarded Tol with amusement over the rim of her goblet. She said no more.

Tol firmly turned the discussion to other matters. "The time has come for some of us to part company," he said. To Casberry: "Your Majesty, I thank you for your help. Without you and your people, we wouldn't be in Caergoth right now."

"If your neighbor's house is on fire, better to grab a bucket than close the shutters." She cocked a knowing eye at him, adding, "But Daltigoth is a different proposition, eh? No place for kender in the capital?"

The shrewd little queen had put her bony finger on the

heart of the matter. The march on Daltigoth would be extremely dangerous. They had reached the gates of Caergoth unhindered by imperial forces because of Wornoth's timidity, and his unshakable belief that his garrison, in truth quite powerful, was not sufficient both to defend the city and defeat Tol. Ackal V would have no such worries. Once he realized Tol's army was coming, he would send the Great Horde to stop them.

Casberry asked how many warriors Tol expected to face. Argonnel answered her.

"The emperor has lost many men to the bakali, I've heard," said the commander of the Iron Scythe Horde. "But I reckon he can draw upon eighty to a hundred hordes."

Casberry reached for a grape. "Sounds like you'll need every friend you've got."

"No. None but Ergothians can ride with us to Daltigoth."

Tol's quiet, blunt declaration put an end to all merriment. Hanira dabbed her lips with a silken scarf—Ergothians knowing nothing of napkins—and said, "Are you certain, my lord? You're giving up much good help."

"It must be so. Your pardon, Syndic, but the presence of foreign troops would change the way our approach is perceived. Instead of patriots and liberators, we'd be seen as invaders."

"Rebels," rumbled Zanpolo. "Which we are not!"

"Victors can style themselves any way they choose," Hanira said. "Losers only die." She toyed with the goblet before her, turning it slowly in her fingers. "You know the Pakin Pretender is in Caergoth, don't you?"

Her words struck like well-timed slaps.

"What Pakin Pretender?" Egrin demanded. "The last claimant was slain twenty years ago, in the reign of Pakin III!"

"He had children, did he not?"

Trudo, eldest of the warlords, said, "Three that I know of. All daughters."

"The youngest, Mellamy Zan, is twenty-five. For the past dozen years she's lived in Tarsis. She's come to Caergoth."

Argonnel leaped to his feet, hand on his sword hilt. "You

did this, trickster! You brought the Pakin infection with you from Tarsis!"

Hanira looked up at the red-faced man. "Upon my word as a syndic of the city, I did not," she said.

Tol curtly told Argonnel to sit down. Once he had, Hanira explained that she'd placed spies among Mellamy Zan's followers soon after the Pakin princess arrived in Tarsis more than twelve years ago. The troubles in Ergoth had encouraged the new Pretender to leave Tarsis with a small entourage. She had entered Caergoth only yesterday, before Tol arrived.

"Where is she?" Argonnel growled. "Tell us where to find her, and we'll settle the Pakins for once and all!"

Hanira looked down the long table at Tol. "Well, my lord?"

All eyes turned to Tol. His gaze was locked with the syndic's. She knew his fragile alliance of disgruntled warlords could not hold against the threat of a new Pakin rebellion. She knew, too, he would loathe having to kill someone who had committed no crime, but who could cause untold trouble in the future. Hanira was positioning herself cleverly. If Tol asked, she could have Mellamy Zan assassinated. The gratitude of the warlords would be enormous. So would her influence in Ergoth.

But there was one fact about the Pakin Pretender that Tol knew he could use to his advantage. "A woman?" he said, forcing a patronizing smile. "One princess is not that important. Still, I'm sure there's room aplenty in the citadel for another prisoner. So yes, Syndic, I would like to know where Mellamy Zan is."

Her maneuver had failed. Hanira dissembled politely, promising to put the Pretender in Tol's hands.

Chief Voyarunta announced himself ready to return home. He'd seen quite enough of the grasslands and its cities of stone. He didn't say it in so many words, but it was plain he regarded Ergoth as immoral and decadent. The fighting was good, but there was too much plotting and treachery.

"And too many noisy women," he said.

"You fathered two of the noisiest!" Queen Casberry snorted. There was laughter while Miya flushed and Kiya scowled.

It was agreed, after more wrangling, that all Tol's foreign friends would depart before the final ride to Daltigoth. Hanira and her Tarsans would leave immediately. Voyarunta and the Dom-shu would remain until Tol left Caergoth, then they would depart. This would allow the chief's wound to heal before beginning the long trek back to the Great Green.

Around midnight, as the party was breaking up, Tol announced that the Army of the East would depart for Daltigoth in five days. The warlords were startled. It seemed a very short time to organize and equip so momentous an expedition.

In reply, Tol quoted one of Ackal Ergot's favorite maxims: " 'Suffer or strike, strike or be struck.' Until we know where the imperial hordes are, and what's happened to the bakali, we can't risk being trapped here. For all we know, the emperor could be at our gates tomorrow."

On that cheerful note, the guests departed. As servants moved in to clear the table and snuff the torches, Tol took Tylocost aside for a private word.

The elf had said little during the meal. His head seemed oddly bereft without his gardener's hat.

"You're not going to Daltigoth either," Tol told him. "I have another task for you. Find out from Syndic Hanira where the Pakin Pretender is. Get the princess—alive—out of Caergoth. Go wherever you like, but send me word of your location once you alight."

Tylocost's pale eyes showed a glimmer of interest. "What is your plan, my lord?"

"Only to avoid another civil war. Killing one princess won't solve anything. But—" He drew a deep breath. "But having a Pakin in reserve may add weight to my dealings with Ackal V."

Given the marriage habits of high Ergothian nobility, there were scores of Pakins scattered throughout the empire and border regions. Valaran herself was of Pakin blood. Killing Mellamy Zan was no answer; any of her kin could incite a revolt by claiming the throne, if they could gather enough followers. However, having the chief claimant as hostage might have a chilling effect on any warlords who backed her on Ackal V. With the Pretender in his clutches, Tol could use fear of a Pakin uprising to keep the emperor in check.

"You're putting a great responsibility in my hand," Tylocost said. "Do you trust me that much?"

"You're the man for the deed."

Tylocost bowed his head. "I will do as you bid, my lord."

All the nearby torches had been extinguished. A candle on the table reached its last mark and went out. The Silvanesti, silhouetted by the remaining light, said, "I must retire, my lord. I have a task at dawn."

Tol had an inkling what the task was. "Shall I come?"

"Thank you, my lord, but the rite is for Silvanesti only."

Though Zala had been only half-elven, in death such distinctions no longer seemed to matter.

❧ ❧ ❧ ❧ ❧

Four laborers, hired in Caergoth, dug a deep hole on a hilltop northwest of the city. It was the same hill on which Tylocost had observed Caergoth when he'd first arrived. The treasure caravan was long gone, safely stowed in the citadel.

Dawn was a pale promise on the eastern horizon as Tylocost paid off the diggers and sent them home. He assured them he did not need them to stay and fill in the hole "after."

The laborers' two-wheeled cart creaked away, and Tylocost was finally alone among the widely spaced oaks. The grave held two shrouded bodies. Zala would not sleep alone. Her father, Kaeph, had passed away not long after his daughter. His cough was pneumonia, and the Caergoth healers could not save him. He spoke only once, to ask for his child. Miya was sitting with him at the time. She assured him he would be with his daughter very soon. The Dom-shu woman spoke only the truth to the dying man.

Tylocost pressed his palms together and began to chant an ancient Silvanesti song. It was the *Wath-Ranata*, a hymn for those who perish far from the sacred homeland. He sang it for Zala. The gods would forgive him for performing the hymn in the presence of the human. Tylocost would not part father and daughter again.

The song was long. He sang it as the sun lifted itself above the horizon and washed the land with heat. Bluish gray clouds hovered in the west. The weather would be foul for the ride to Daltigoth.

The last words of the *Wath-Ranata* echoed over the green hills. Tylocost scattered green leaves and flower petals on the linen shapes nestled in the earth, then took up the spade the diggers had left for him. By the time the hole was filled, he was sweating and dirty.

His final act was to plant a seedling tree on the grave. Every Silvanesti wanted to rest beneath the boughs of a living tree. He'd chosen an apple tree because he liked the idea that Zala would one day bear fruit to all passersby.

The unsightly gardener tied his floppy hat on his head and shouldered his spade like a weapon. The urge to salute, although long-ingrained by decades of military service, did not intrude here.

Tylocost had not buried a comrade. He'd said good-bye to the woman he loved.

᠅ ᠅ ᠅ ᠅ ᠅

Ackal V stepped out of his bath. His arms, legs, and chest were mottled with bruises, some already yellowing as they healed. The blows he'd sustained from the bakali might not have brought him down, but they'd certainly made a bold impression. He hadn't availed himself of the imperial healers, and rarely did. He had little faith in their spells and nostrums, and feared enemies might use the opportunity to hex him.

From her marble bench a few steps away, Empress Valaran kept her eyes averted, studying the mosaic pattern around her feet. She was all too familiar with the sight of her husband unclothed. It was not a view she cared for. Dalar played at her feet, humming to himself as he pushed wooden warriors on horseback across the floor. Some of the toy soldiers were painted red, others gray.

A lackey held up a gray silk robe. Ackal V slipped his arms

in and tied the sash with a savage yank. Equal pique marked his movements as he took a golden cup of wine offered by another servant.

Valaran had brought him the unwelcome news of Caergoth's fall to Tol and the landed hordes. Ackal V cursed Wornoth in between gulps of wine, damning the governor for his lack of backbone. For squeezing taxes from peasants and keeping the high-nosed residents of Caergoth in line Wornoth was adequate, but faced with real opposition, he wilted instantly.

"How was it done?" he asked.

Valaran replied, "Accounts differ, sire, but it seems some or all of the Caergoth garrison went willingly over to the other side."

"I want their names, all of them! Their families will suffer for this treachery!"

Valaran nodded, but vowed to herself that none of the families would face the emperor's vengeance.

The emperor asked about troop strength. "According to my spies, he has twenty to thirty hordes," she replied. "If every man in the Caergoth garrison joins him, he will have fifty-four hordes."

In fact, the information she had received by messenger pigeon that evening gave the total figure of forty-four hordes. Valaran exaggerated for Tol's benefit.

Ackal flung the empty cup at the wine steward. The man wasn't nimble enough and failed to catch the heavy golden vessel. It clanged loudly on the tiles. The steward cringed, knowing he'd just earned a flogging.

"Even if he had a hundred fifty hordes, he couldn't break into Daltigoth!" Ackal V declared.

Their conversation was interrupted by Prince Dalar. He suddenly began hammering away at the ranks of toy soldiers with a brass rod. Red and gray riders alike went down under his blows, some of the figures splintering.

He'd never been violent with his toys before, and his mother spoke sharply to him. Ackal V laughed.

"That's the way, boy," he said. "In ten years you can do that to real enemies!"

Valaran stood abruptly. "Is that all you require, Majesty?"

"Yes, go. And send Tathman to me."

She wanted Dalar to come with her, but Ackal V told her to leave the boy where he was.

"I'll not have the crown prince subjected to the company of that vile mercenary!" Valaran said.

"That vile mercenary is utterly loyal—unlike you, lady."

She protested, but he stepped closer and took her chin a painful grip. "I know you would like nothing better than to see me dead, and the pig farmer standing here in my place," he murmured. "You can consign that dream to the vale of night. It's the farmer who'll be dead, and that handy trinket he carries will be mine. As you are, lady. Forever."

She pulled free of him, eyes flashing in anger, then the import of his words sank in. He knew about the Irda nullstone? How could that be? How long had he known? Awful thoughts formed in her mind. Was it possible he had known of her plot to bring Tol to Daltigoth, but had done nothing to interfere, just so he could get his hands on the nullstone?

He laughed and kicked Dalar lightly on the rump. "Go with your mother, boy," he said. "Tathman may not have eaten yet and I'd hate to see him dine on you!"

The five-year-old scampered after his mother, sending toy soldiers skittering over the tiles.

In the corridor outside, several lackeys awaited the emperor's pleasure. Valaran gestured to one, a lower chamberlain named Fudosh. She relayed the emperor's summons of the Wolf captain. Fudosh paled, but bowed and hurried to find Tathman.

When Tathman arrived, the emperor was seated at a stone table in his bath chamber, his head resting on his folded arms. His youngest wife, Lady Halie, was anointing his many bruises with a soothing unguent. She could apply the balm as well as a healer, and was far prettier than any acolyte of Mishas.

Ackal V did not look up until Tathman cleared his throat. Coming from a man his size, the sound was like a panther growling.

"Captain," the emperor said without moving. "Farmer Tol is in Caergoth."

"Shall I go there and kill him?"

Ackal's shoulders shook with mirth. "That's the spirit! No, that won't be necessary. He's coming here—with forty thousand warriors."

The leader of the Wolves regarded his master stolidly. "Better to kill him far away," he rumbled.

Ackal V glanced at his young wife. Halie knew Tolandruth only as a name. She wouldn't betray her husband.

He said, "I want this army of traitors to come as close to Daltigoth as they dare. I want them to think success is in their grasp. Then, and only then, I want the farmer captured and brought before me. I will make such a lesson of him that all those country lords will take up priest's robes!"

Tathman bowed his head, the long braid of his hair falling forward. "Your Majesty is most wise."

"When the time comes, I may ask you to do things you won't like," Ackal V warned.

"If Your Majesty commands, I will pluck out an eye and eat it."

This declaration, spoken with such conviction, made young Halie pause in her labors. The emperor shrugged his shoulders, signaling her to continue.

"Patience, Tathman. Your time approaches. The prospect of facing the legendary Lord Tol worries you?"

The question was a half-joking one, but Tathman's reply was deadly serious. "No, Majesty. He bleeds like any man."

The emperor smiled. Yes, he did bleed. Ackal V had seen Tol bleed. It was a memory he relished.

He ordered the Wolves back to the Inner City to receive instructions, training, and new equipment. When he explained his idea, Captain Tathman finally showed surprise.

"Objections?" asked the emperor.

"No, Majesty."

Once Tathman had withdrawn, Halie paused her ministrations to renew the balm on her hands.

"Is Your Majesty in danger?" she asked diffidently.

"No." Ackal put his head down again on his folded arms.

## Paul B. Thompson and Tonya C. Cook

"But if you speak of what you've heard here, I'd have to cut off your head."

His young consort smoothed the white unguent across his bare shoulders.

"I would never speak of it, sire. Better my tongue should be cut out!"

Now there was a possibility, Ackal mused. And Valaran liked to believe she was the smartest of his wives.

# Trial and Errand

The cells beneath the gray citadel of Caergoth were much like the city itself—wide, light, and surprisingly clean. Everything about them was double the norm: the width of the central corridor, the size of the cells, the height of the ceiling. The walls also were twice as thick as usual.

Tol and Egrin walked down the central passage, looking at the open, empty cells. Wornoth had sent all the prisoners to the big cages erected in the city's main square to make room for extra soldiers and supplies for the citadel. With the overthrow of the governor, the dungeon was empty. An unnatural quiet had settled over the place. Only a few of the candles in the wall sconces were lit, so Tol carried a lantern.

The four levels of the dungeon held only a solitary occupant. No guard stood at the massive bronze-plated door to the prisoner's cell, as the dungeon itself was considered proof against escape. Tol leaned into the deep doorway and rapped on the door to announce their entry. Once Egrin had thrown the heavy bolt and pulled the door open, Tol thrust his lantern into the grayness beyond.

It was a large room for a single prisoner, illuminated by a single candle. Cut into the far wall was a stone niche designed for a bedroll. Here, former governor Wornoth sat slumped. He did not look up as they entered.

"If you've come to assassinate me, I curse you both!" he said hoarsely, sniveling into the sleeve of his dirty robe.

# Paul B. Thompson and Tonya C. Cook

Egrin grimaced in disgust. "Sit up, man," he said. "Show some dignity!"

"We're not here to slay you," Tol said. "We've come to tell you about your trial." Wornoth lifted his pale face, blinking in surprise. "You will be judged by a jury of nine warriors, chosen by lot."

Such a procedure was unknown in Ergoth, where justice was dispensed from on high by imperial officials. At the pinnacle was the emperor, whose utterances were law. The marshals enforced this law, ruling over provinces known as "hundreds"—a term that had once referred to the number of warlords serving the marshal, but was now merely a geographical term. Each marshal was attended by wardens, whose number in each hundred varied according to the strength of the population. The Eastern Hundred, Tol's homeland, had one warden. Caergoth had four.

At the lowest level, justice was enforced by bailiffs. These were usually Riders of the Great Horde appointed for a specific purpose—to catch a notorious outlaw, or to investigate a murder in some remote corner of the realm. Tol had learned of trial by jury in Tarsis, where the procedure was common.

"I am the imperial governor, appointed by His Majesty Ackal V! All I have done, I have done in his name!"

"Make no mistake, Wornoth. You're not being tried for being a vicious, petty tyrant, though you ought to be," Tol said. "The principle charge against you is failing to defend the eastern provinces of the empire. By keeping your hordes in Caergoth, you allowed the nomads to ravage four provinces. Hundreds, perhaps thousands, of imperial subjects perished, villages were sacked and property destroyed by your folly. That is your crime."

Wornoth's face grew even paler. He whispered, "I did what I thought best. You can't condemn me for that!"

"It is not up to me to condemn you for anything. That's why we're having a trial. It begins at dawn."

Tol turned to go. Wornoth sprang from his sleeping niche and grasped Tol's knees. Egrin's sword was out in a trice, but alarm quickly turned to revulsion.

Tears streaming down his cheeks, Wornoth gabbled wildly,

"Please, gracious lord! Please, spare me! I made mistakes, yes, but I can rectify them! I can! Please! Please!"

"Get hold of yourself!" Tol said, trying to pry him loose. "For Corij's sake, be a man!"

"But I don't want to die! I did only what I thought my emperor wanted me to do! Please!"

Tol managed to shove him away. Wornoth fell backward and lay still, sobbing and pleading.

"You're going to Daltigoth, aren't you? I can be of use to you, great lord. I know much about the emperor's doings. I can tell you things!"

Egrin asked, "Would you betray your sovereign?"

"Yes! Yes! To spare my life, yes!"

Thoroughly disgusted now, Tol said nothing. He went to the cell door.

"You are being used, my lord!" Wornoth cried. "The emperor's hand has guided you to the very course you're now on! If you go to Daltigoth, you shall be destroyed!"

Tol ignored this feeble gambit, but Egrin lingered.

"Why would the emperor want Lord Tolandruth to come to Daltigoth?" he asked.

An ember of hope lit the prisoner's eyes. "Spare me, and I'll tell you!"

"Tell us, and we may spare you," Tol countered.

Wornoth got quickly to his feet. "You have something the emperor wants." He glanced at Egrin, uncertain how much to reveal. "A certain item of great value, which protects you."

Egrin looked blank, but the words rattled Tol. The nullstone. How could Ackal V have learned of it?

The worry on his captor's face warmed Wornoth like a draft of strong wine. He dried his face on his sleeve and fingered the long hair back from his forehead.

"The empress hired a tracker to find you, my lord. A half-breed woman. To ensure her loyalty, I was ordered to hold her father."

"I know. She's dead," Tol said flatly. "And so is her father."

Wornoth shrugged. "No matter. You're on your way to Daltigoth, unwittingly delivering the very prize the emperor covets." He leered at the warriors. "He dangles tasty bait before you, I know. The empress—"

Tol crossed the distance between them in three strides and seized the front of Wornoth's robe. Hauling the shorter man to his tiptoes, he snarled, "Your information is worthless! Baited or not, I am going to Daltigoth to see justice done!"

"Justice for whom?" Wornoth rasped. "You—or the empire?"

"Enough!" Tol shoved him away. "Your trial takes place tomorrow."

Wornoth had one last hand to play. From the folds of his robe, he produced a small iron key. He tossed it toward the doorway, where it landed at Tol's feet.

"A gift, my lord! That key opens my private archive. Learn for yourself how the emperor draws you to him like a fly into a spider's web." Wornoth managed a smile. "What does this buy me?"

Tol's dagger thudded into the straw by Wornoth's feet.

"If I were you, Wornoth, I would not wait for a trial. Hanging is tricky business. If not done right, the condemned strangles slowly." With visible relish, Tol said, "Count five ribs down on your left side. That's where your heart is—that's where it is on a normal man, anyway."

High-born Ergothians had a horror of being hanged like a common criminal. Mockingly, Tol added, "I doubt you have the will to cheat the hangman, but I give you the chance."

He and Egrin went out, and the sound of the bolt being thrown echoed in the cell.

When the warder arrived a short time later with the prisoner's supper, he found Wornoth dead. A war dagger protruded from his left side.

His heart was in the right place after all.

§ § § § §

At the head of her private army, Syndic Hanira awaited Lord Tolandruth's review. She'd found a magnificent horse in Caergoth, a night-black steed. Mounted on its back, Hanira, in cloth-of-gold raiment, her own black hair streaming loose to her waist, cut a dazzling figure. Dusk was an unusual time to begin a journey, but it was the time Hanira had chosen.

Most of the warlords still mistrusted the Tarsans, regarding them as foreigners and enemies, not valuable allies. None had turned out for her departure. Egrin had taken Wornoth's key and gone in search of his papers, so only the Dom-shu sisters and Tol were present. Tol was mounted, the sisters on foot.

"Give my regards to Lord Regobart," Tol said, naming the commander of the imperial outpost near Tarsis.

"I will convey your greetings." Smiling slightly she added, "I seldom see him, you know. I make him nervous."

"Small wonder," Kiya muttered.

Hanira urged her horse forward a few paces, until she was close alongside Tol. Her smooth expression altered for a moment. "Beware, my lord," she murmured. "You are galloping hard to a precipice. Daltigoth is a maelstrom from which you may not emerge alive."

She was the second person this evening to tell him that. Shrugging, he said, "I've managed to escape death there before."

Hanira clasped his arm, warrior-fashion. "Live, my lord. The world needs you."

At Captain Anovenax's order, the Tarsans wheeled left and trotted away. Hanira turned her ebony steed smartly on its hind legs and cantered after them.

The Dom-shu were not impressed, muttering aloud that the Tarsan syndic was a "conniving wench," among other things.

"She seeks some advantage," Miya insisted. She knew the art of dealing better than anyone. "If you succeed, her position as your friend and ally is stronger than ever."

"But what does she want?" Kiya mused. "Not Husband as mate, I'd wager."

Miya shook her head. "She wants to rule Tarsis, that's what I think. With Husband's help, she could get rid of all the princes and syndics, and reign as queen of Tarsis."

"You two are so wise!" Tol snapped. "Hanira didn't have to come to our aid. She paid for her good deed with her own child's life!"

## Paul B. Thompson and Tonya C. Cook

Chastened, the Dom-shu sisters apologized and left him. He had given them the task of organizing supplies for the ride to Daltigoth.

As the dust kicked up by the Tarsan cavalry settled, Tol stared southwest—the route they'd taken along the banks of the Caer. In the distance, lightning shimmered across the deep purple sky.

The sisters had unknowingly touched a sore spot. Tol wasn't certain they were wrong about Hanira. But at that moment, he felt she had as much chance of becoming Queen of the Red Moon as Queen of Tarsis.

🦉 🦉 🦉 🦉 🦉

Valaran held the tiny slip of parchment to the lamp flame. It curled and blackened as fire consumed it. She had read the message three times just to be certain she'd not imagined it.

Tol was coming.

She'd managed to place a spy close to him, and now knew even what road he would take. The fear that had been her constant companion for so long faded somewhat. For the first time in a very long time, Valaran allowed herself the luxury of wondering what he was like, whether he'd changed.

Almost seven years had passed. In that time she'd borne a child, learned to govern an empire, and survived the cruel machinations of her unpredictable husband. And she had killed an old woman.

In spite of her room's warmth, Valaran shivered. She'd learned much in seven years. What had Tol learned?

🦉 🦉 🦉 🦉 🦉

Wornoth's opulent quarters had been ransacked by servants and palace guards when the city fell. Fine tapestries had been torn down. Furniture too heavy to move had been chopped apart by swords and axes. What remained of Wornoth's personal treasure had been stored in the dungeon below, for safekeeping, but random coins were scattered across the ruined, dark blue carpet like a rain of gold. Egrin was disgusted as much by the waste as by the unseemly extravagance of the governor's rooms.

Searching through the destruction, he found several strongboxes, broken open and empty. The iron key fit none of them. Not until Egrin reached Wornoth's bedroom did he find what he sought.

The bedchamber had received the same treatment as the rest of the rooms. The white walls had been stripped of tapestries and paintings, the furniture hacked by sabers, the broad mattress cut to ribbons. Heavy sculptures had been toppled and lay in pieces amidst shredded blue silk bed curtains. Eiderdown stuffing covered the floor and clouds of fluff swirled upward, disturbed by Egrin's passage.

His toes bumped something solid as he reached the great bed. Egrin knelt and carefully brushed away an eiderdown drift. In the center of the wooden bedrail, he found a small slot, rimmed in black iron and hard to spot. The key fit perfectly. A click, and a drawer slid smoothly out.

The secret cache held no gold or silver, but bundles of parchment tied with string and a thick-bladed short sword. Egrin opened one of the bundles and discovered a series of dispatches from the emperor to Governor Wornoth. The last few messages were terse and to the point: Where was Tol? Was he coming to Caergoth? What had Wornoth done to defend the city?

Egrin dug deeper into the bundle. The earlier communications were much longer and wilder, sounding like the ramblings of a deranged man. In them, Ackal V railed about treachery, particularly from wizards of the Red and White orders. The emperor insisted over and over to Wornoth that, above all other tasks, he was to keep an eye on the members of those orders in Caergoth.

The next discovery was much more upsetting—a packet of messages to Wornoth from various warlords. These outlined the warlords' struggles against the nomads and the bakali and requested that the governor send troops and supplies. As time passed and Wornoth sent neither, the requests became demands, then pleas. One dispatch from Bessian was literally spattered with blood. The invaders were closing in, it said, and the Ergothians could neither win nor escape; the governor must send aid. The governor of Caergoth, determined to defend his own neck, had done nothing to aid the dying hordes. This bundle contained no copies of outgoing missives. Wornoth had not even bothered to reply.

Coldly furious, Egrin put the pleading messages aside. The smallest bundle in the cache was not merely tied with string but also wrapped in a scrap of cloth. Egrin reached for this packet of letters, but it slipped through his fingers. He tried again. And again. And again. He glared at the bundle in perplexed confusion. No matter how hard he tried, he could not grab hold of it.

When Tol arrived moments later, Egrin told him of the strange small packet.

"I seem to have butter on my fingers. Can't pick this up!" the former marshal said, pointing.

Tol squatted by the open drawer. He reached for the packet. Although a flicker of heat played over his fingers, they closed infallibly on the letters. The sensation of warmth was familiar. Someone had put a spell on the letters, most likely to prevent them being tampered with, but the nullstone had negated the spell.

He handed the small packet to Egrin, who held it warily. This time it stayed in his grasp. The elder warrior muttered something about being old and clumsy.

"Rubbish, you're just tired," Tol said.

The cloth wrapping contained a dozen or so squares of thin parchment. The backs of the slips were scorched by heat, but lines of writing in unusual brown ink filled the other side. None of the messages was signed.

"Letters from spies," Egrin said.

The messages all were short, and most were demands for information from an anonymous correspondent. None concerned the nomads or bakali invaders. Some asked about the morale and loyalty of the imperial hordes in Caergoth and commented on the danger of sending troops beyond the walls and leaving the city "helpless and unguarded." Most sought knowledge of Tol's whereabouts; Helbin, too, was mentioned.

*I've had no word from Helbin in many days,* the anonymous correspondent had written. *If he comes into your hands, let me know at once. Protect him. He is a valuable ally.*

"Didn't Queen Casberry say Helbin had been captured by Wornoth's guards?" asked Egrin.

Tol nodded absently. They had looked all over for the Red Robe. There had been no trace of the wizard among the prisoners, either in the citadel or anywhere else.

"These messages are in Valaran's hand!" Tol exclaimed. Egrin's graying eyebrows lifted in surprise and Tol added, "Don't you see? Wornoth was playing both sides. He was spying for the empress, while ruling in the emperor's name." The duplicity of the man was incredible.

"Then why would he arrest Helbin? He knew they both served the same mistress."

Tol shrugged. "Maybe Wornoth was duping Valaran, betraying her trust to Ackal V. If so, the last thing he'd want around would be a loyal servant of the empress." Tol tossed the letters back in the drawer. "Helbin could tell us more. He's probably dead, but continue the search for him anyway."

He left Egrin to finish examining Wornoth's secret papers. Queen Casberry was departing, and Tol wanted to see her off.

Egrin waited until his friend and commander had gone, then picked up certain of the bundles again, riffled through them, and extracted a sheaf or two. These he burned in the flame of his lamp, watching the doorway all the while.

🦉 🦉 🦉 🦉 🦉

Tol, Casberry, and her bearers were just inside the north gate of Caergoth. Evening had come and Luin was rising, casting its pinkish light over the open landscape.

Tol asked the kender queen about her escort and received the breezy assurance that both Royal Loyals and Household Guard were "around somewhere." She had already turned down his offer of an armed escort, saying she might not be heading directly home. Kender were afflicted with wanderlust, and the queen was the most kenderish of them all.

Front and Back hoisted the heavy sedan chair onto their shoulders, seemingly without effort. As usual, Queen Casberry offered a steady stream of advice to the duo on the best way to carry the chair and, as usual, the men ignored her. Tol smiled. They were certainly an odd threesome.

When he thanked her again for her assistance, she patted him on the head. "You're a good fellow, for a human." Putting her little prune face close to his head, she added, "You're getting a bald spot up here, you know that?"

Tol cleared his throat and stepped back. He was past forty now, and it was true. Age was beginning to tell on him in many ways.

"Okay, boys, pick up your feet!" she said, and Front and Back headed for the open gate.

"Oh, your Majesty!" Tol called. "Where should I send the payment you were promised for your troops?"

Casberry lifted both arms and waved. Her arms, from wrist to elbow, were covered with gold and silver bangles.

"Don't worry, I've taken care of that!" she said, cackling.

The little party seemed so lonely, so vulnerable, Tol found himself following them out. The bearers kept to the center of the white-pebbled road, which curved away to the northwest. Before Casberry had gone a quarter-league, however, small shadowy figures joined her out of the darkness. Kender. More and more appeared as she progressed, falling in behind their clever, rapacious queen.

The cryptic phrase Casberry used so often—"no kender is ever alone"—was, Tol knew, true enough. He also knew the treasure recovered from the nomads was by now somewhat diminished. It didn't matter. The kender had earned their "found" valuables.

Tol walked back into the city, and the guards closed the gate. He rode through the darkening streets, now empty of the crowds of refugees. Trash blew along the wide lanes, last reminders of the thousands who had crowded into Caergoth to escape the chaos outside. On their own initiative, a brigade of street sweepers had organized to clean the city. Before long

Caergoth would once more be a byword for cleanliness in the empire.

Daltigoth lay forty leagues southwest, a ride of five or six days on the Ackal Path. Daltigoth was his journey's end. All Tol's goals were there, he reflected, with Valaran his prize. So wrapped up was he in thoughts of his distant love, that Tol didn't notice a caped figure emerge from an alley as he passed. But after a few paces, he said (without turning around), "Did you find her, Tylocost?"

The elf chuckled. "Your senses aren't bad for a human, my lord."

"Your sandals creak."

Tol had dispatched Tylocost to find the Pakin princess, Mellamy Zan, reported by Hanira to be in Caergoth.

"I found her," Tylocost said, putting back his hood. "I believe she will accept my protection. Her advisors were against it, but she overruled them. She seems remarkably intelligent and accomplished—for a human."

"Remember where your allegiance lies, General."

With irritating Silvanesti aplomb, Tylocost inclined his head gracefully. "I remember, my lord."

Tol offered his hand. As Tylocost clasped it, Tol said, "Thank you. And now you're free, General. You are no longer my prisoner."

Tylocost's eyes widened. "But so much remains to be done!"

"I know, but I also know that I may not return from this last ride. You've done amazingly well by me, and I'm grateful, so I give you your freedom." But he tightened his grip until Tylocost winced. "That does not excuse you from the duty I expect you to perform."

"Of course not. I would wish you luck, my lord, but you seem plentifully supplied already, so I'll give you a warning instead: be certain of nothing." Pale blue eyes bored into Tol's brown ones. "You stand in the center of events so complex and loyalties so tangled that even I cannot see all the threads. Make certain your will is as hard as that steel blade you carry, and trust no one."

Smiling a little, Tol asked, "Not even you, General?"

The elf's expression was grim. "Not even I."

Before Tol could say more, Tylocost was gone, melting into the darkness. Instinct told him he would never see the Silvanesti again.

It was very late when Tol retired to his room in the Riders' Hall, but hardly had he lain down when someone slipped into the room.

"Peace," said the figure, and he recognized Kiya's voice. "I wish to sleep here tonight."

He was dumbfounded. Not in twenty-odd years together had they ever been so intimate, despite Kiya's status as his wife.

He stuttered rather incoherently for a moment and she hissed, "I've not come to seduce you! My father snores so loudly, I can't sleep in the room he shares with his men. Move over, Husband."

He complied, but felt oddly shy. Kiya lay down with her back to him and muttered, "Don't get any strange ideas." There seemed no safe answer to that, affirmative or negative, so Tol said nothing.

He was just dozing off when someone else entered the room. "Husband, I—Kiya! What are you doing here?" Miya demanded.

"Trying to sleep! Shut up!"

"Both of you shut up," Tol growled. He was exhausted, and in no mood for sisterly wrangling.

Miya elbowed her way in next to Kiya. "You think I can sleep with Father's snoring? And I'm certainly not leaving you two here alone." Kiya told her she had too much imagination.

With the two tall forester women in the bed, there was scarcely room for Tol. He slid off onto the flagstone floor. While the sisters sniped at each other, he claimed a blanket and curled up beneath it.

Twenty years together, and now his wives wanted to sleep with him. The prospect was so daunting he vowed to get the final drive to Daltigoth underway as soon as possible.

The day dawned cloud-capped and windy. Before sunrise, the Army of the East marched out of Caergoth and formed on the great road to the capital—the Ackal Path. Virtually every Rider in the city had joined Tol, giving him a total strength of forty-four full hordes, six demi-hordes, and the two hordes of Juramona Militia, the only foot soldiers in the Army. There was great disaffection among the imperial warriors for their poor treatment by the emperor and the emperor's deputy, Governor Lord Wornoth. The proud Riders were ready to march on Daltigoth and present their grievances to Ackal V in the most direct manner possible—at sword point.

Even so, it was a tenuous coalition, held together by anger and injured pride. The Riders of Caergoth and the provincial Riders of the landed hordes would fight if contested, but privately Tol wondered how they would respond if the emperor sought to appease them. That didn't seem likely. Ackal V was clever, but he was not the sort to placate anyone, even with a sword at his throat.

The first rays of sunlight had just touched the tops of the city wall when the last men fell in place. Each horde commander rode out to meet Tol, who waited in the center of the road on a new mount. The Riders' stables had yielded up a fine dappled gray war-horse.

Tol greeted the horde commanders by name and assigned them their places in the march. Two wings of twenty hordes each would ride west, each wing flanking the imperial highway. The bulk of the army, and the baggage train, would proceed on the road.

"If we are challenged, do we fight, my lord?" Lord Wagram asked.

"We're not going to Daltigoth to attend a festival!"

There was much smothered laughter at Zanpolo's quip. The legendary warlord was mounted on a large horse as black as its rider's forked beard.

Wagram reddened, demanding, "Do we attack imperial troops on sight then?"

This was a legitimate question, one Tol had long been considering. "No, my lord. If any hordes confront you, try to parley and convince them to join us. If they spurn your advances,

ride on. If you're attacked, fight back. But don't start battles
yourselves. Our quarrel is with Ackal V, not every Rider in
the Great Horde."

Another of the Caergoth warlords, Quevalen by name,
asked, "What exactly is our quarrel, my lord? Wornoth has
paid for his perfidy. Are we to depose the emperor, or merely
seek redress for our many grievances?"

Tol wouldn't impose his private vengeance on every man
in his service, but neither would he deceive them.

"Ackal V seized power illegally from Prince Hatonar, his
brother's heir," he said. "And I have evidence he was behind
the illness and death of his brother, Ackal IV."

He sought the eye of every warlord before him. "We seek
the ouster of Ackal V and the restoration of the imperial
throne to the rightful heirs of Pakin III and Ackal IV. The
new emperor will see to it our grievances are heard." Again,
he stared at each of them, slowly turning in his saddle. "If
anyone here cannot accept this, let him depart now without
blame."

There was restive movement, especially among the younger officers, but none broke ranks.

"Remember, my lords, no one here is a rebel. We do not
seek to overthrow the empire. We mean to save it!"

He put heels to his war-horse's sides and set out at a trot.
Egrin and Pagas came close after, then the warlords of the
landed hordes—Argonnel, Mittigorn, Trudo, and the rest.
Soon the whole army was in motion. The noise of massed
hoofbeats was thunderous.

In the rear, at the head of the baggage caravan, Kiya slapped
the reins against the backs of her four-horse team, setting the
animals into motion. Miya, sitting next to her on the wagon
seat, finished tying a scarf over her head and signaled to the
teamsters to follow.

"Can he do it?" Miya asked.

Kiya squinted against the rising dust. "Husband *is* doing
it."

# Chapter 24
## Chance's Choice

The Army of the East rode ready for combat, but the first two days of the journey passed without hostility. The countryside, which had been emptied of people by the parallel invasions of bakali and nomads, had sprung to life again. As Tol's army passed out of the Caer Hundred into the Heartland Hundred, strange things began to happen.

Ordinary folk, who normally wouldn't have come within a league of an armed horde, turned out by the hundreds. Word spread that Lord Tolandruth was leading the hordes to Daltigoth to set things right, so cautious observers left their hiding places and came forward to cheer. Nor did they come with empty hands.

The bountiful countryside between Caergoth and the capital had not been ravaged in the recent invasions. No nomads had made it this far west, and the bakali had passed far to the north. With high summer upon the land, the fertile heart of the empire was bursting with plenty. Even the drought that gripped the Eastern Hundred had not affected crops here. The peasants brought fruits, vegetables, and smoked meats. Before long, Riders were festooned with bags of grapes, onions, melons, and carrots, and even several live chickens, their feet lashed together.

Kiya and Miya, having gotten the baggage caravan started, left it to join Tol at the head of the central column. A farmer's wife rushed up to Miya, shoved an enormous ham into her arms, and hurried away, all without a word. While the Dom-shu sisters were amused by the joyous reception, Tol found it unsettling.

Miya, staggering along with the ham, said, "They're happy, Husband! They know what you're going to do!"

Egrin remained dour. " If we fail, the results could be grave for those known to have given us aid."

As it developed, there were other, more immediate considerations. Gifts of beer and wine began to arrive, and the Army of the East grew merry indeed. Lord Argonnel cantered over from the right wing, where similar conditions prevailed.

"My lord, this must stop!" he said. "Discipline is failing. If the emperor attacked now, our men would flounder under an ocean of foodstuffs!"

"But the people love us!" Miya replied. "And it's for them you're doing this, Husband!"

Argonnel was right, but Miya had a point as well. How could they extricate themselves from the flood of well-meant gifts without alienating the good people of Ergoth?

It was Kiya who showed the way. Two children approached her, each bearing pots of berry jam. Even the tough warrior woman couldn't bear to wound them by refusing, but her hands were already full. Exasperated, she held out a bag of grapes.

"I can't take anything unless you take something in return!" she declared.

Laughing, Tol made Kiya's frustrated bargain a general order. No one in the army was to accept another gift without giving something back. He also ordered the pace of the hordes quickened. This would make it harder for the peasants to reach the warriors.

By the third day—halfway along in the journey to Dalti-goth—the bounty of food and drink had greatly subsided. Near the border of the Great Horde Hundred, in which the capital lay, it ceased altogether. The farmers were no less glad to see the Army of the East, but the influence of Ackal V's spies was greater. The first scouts were seen, watching Tol's hordes advance through the lush orchards and verdant pastures east of Daltigoth. Riders from Zanpolo's Iron Falcons tried to flush out them out but failed to catch them. The spies were mounted on fleet, carefully chosen horses, and they knew the countryside well. Tol took Zanpolo's failure in stride.

"If you can capture a scout, fine, but if not . . ." Tol shrugged. "We want everyone in Daltigoth to know we're coming. The time is fast approaching when all must choose—as you did, Zanpolo—whether to be with us or against us."

The first clash came soon after.

At the intersection of the Ackal Path and the Mordirin Way was a customs house. Here, imperial officials levied tolls on caravans passing east or west, and north or south. Comprising a stout stone building and a wooden tower enclosed in a stockade faced with sloping walls of earth, the customs house seemed an unlikely spot for a showdown. But as Riders from Mittigorn's Black Viper Horde approached, a shower of arrows greeted them.

Mittigorn sent word back to Tol, then dismounted sixty men and proceeded to attack. After storming the grassy scarp, the Vipers fell upon the occupants of the stockade. Much to their surprise, they discovered their opponents were not imperial warriors, but ordinary footmen armed with bows. Twenty-two bowmen and the customs officer constituted the entire garrison.

Tol arrived with his warlords and the Dom-shu sisters. The captured bowmen were sitting quietly on the ground, hands clasped atop their heads. Not so the customs officer. He was stretched out facedown, wrists lashed together behind his back, held at sword point. Both face and fists bore the bloody evidence of his resistance.

Ignoring the fuming customs officer for now, Tol addressed the leader of the bowmen, a man with a city haircut and light sandals on his feet. "You, stand up. What's your name?"

"Fengale, my lord." He spoke like a city man—pronouncing "my lord" as "ma ludd."

"Why are you here, Fengale?"

The sergeant shrugged. "One of the emperor's chamberlains hired us to defend this post. We arrived here only last night."

Kiya wondered why Ackal V would deploy hired soldiers when he had plenty of warriors at his command, but this was no mystery to Tol. The emperor had withdrawn all his hordes, concentrating his warriors closer to the city. What Tol couldn't fathom was why Ackal V had bothered to defend the customs house at all.

He turned his attention to the customs officer. Two warriors dragged the fellow forward. He fought and cursed the whole way.

"Traitor! Rebel! Your head will feed the crows for this!"

Tol waved a hand. "Yes, yes. Who are you?"

The officer couldn't break the grips of the burly Riders holding him, so he settled for stating loudly, "My name is Hathak. Captain Hathak, of the Imperial Customs Service!"

"Well, Captain Hathak, what's so special about your house?"

The petty official made a great show of not understanding, and Tol added, "We aren't fools, Captain. There has to be a reason the emperor wastes even a small number of troops defending a solitary customs house." To Mittigorn he said, "Have the house searched thoroughly."

Mittigorn's men carried out the order enthusiastically. Partitions were torn apart, floorboards pried up, and soon enough a shout of triumph rang out.

Two chests of gold coins (ironically stamped with the profile of Ackal V's revered father, Pakin III) were found secreted under the floor of the house. In the rafters the men found sheaves of spears, bundles of shields, and sabers. All the metal implements had been dipped in wax to keep away rust, and all bore the stamp of the imperial arsenal in Dalti-goth. Some were of recent make, others were older weapons.

Tol studied the cache carefully, all the while wondering why the weapons had been secreted here. A commotion outside interrupted him, and Miya appeared in the customs house door.

"You'd better come!" she said gravely.

Outside, they found Kiya standing over Hathak, once more facedown on the ground. The Dom-shu woman had her sword out and was glaring at several Riders standing nearby.

"They started beating him to make him talk," she reported. "I put an end to it!"

Tol looked to Mittigorn and the warlord, still mounted, shrugged. "One way or another we have to find out what he knows, my lord," he said.

Tol looked from the bloody, bound prisoner to Kiya's proud, angry face. Distasteful though it was, he asked Mittigorn, "What did you learn?"

"Not much. We were interrupted," Mittigorn said dryly.

Hathak had revealed that the gold was from tolls collected over the past half-year. The arms had been delivered to the customs house and hidden before the hired bowmen arrived from the city.

Tol gnawed his lower lip. He needed every bit of information he could lay hands on.

"Take Hathak inside," he said to the waiting warriors. As they hoisted the fallen man up, Tol said to Mittigorn, "Find out what he knows."

Miya gasped. Kiya grabbed his arm and demanded, "You're going to let them torture that man?"

He broke her hold and seized her wrist. "Do you think this is a game?" he asked harshly. "We're not fighting nomads any more. The emperor would not place money and weapons at a lonely outpost for no reason. I have to know why he did it!"

Like most foresters, Kiya would gladly fight and kill any opponent who challenged her, but the idea of beating information out of a helpless captive made her furious.

"If you do this, you're no better than him!"

Kiya jerked her arm free. She swung onto her horse and galloped off, not back to the column, but westward, away from the poised army. Tossing an anguished glance at Tol, Miya followed her sister.

Tol stalked back to his own horse, his entire body radiating anger. He told Lord Mittigorn to seek him out once they had the truth from the customs official.

The commander of the Black Viper Horde acknowledged the order. He was unmoved by the drama with the Dom-shu sisters. He didn't expect women (and barbarian women at that) to understand a warrior's duty. However, his equanimity was shaken when Tol ordered him to disarm and release the bowmen.

Dark eyes widening, he asked, "Is that wise, my lord?"

"They're only hirelings. We don't have time for prisoners, so take their bows and turn them loose. That's an order!"

Mittigorn snapped to attention in his saddle. "Yes, my lord."

Tol cantered back to the waiting column. The sky, which had been an unblemished blue all day, was clear no longer. On the northern and southern horizons white clouds were piling up.

🦉 🦉 🦉 🦉 🦉

When Miya lost sight of her sister around a bend in the road, she urged her mare into a canter. Bands of light and shadow flickered across the Dom-shu woman's face as she rode along the cedar-lined road. The air was hot and still; only the wind stirred by her passage made it bearable.

Rounding the curve in the road, she saw that Kiya had stopped where the lines of trees ended. The road there sloped downward, running straight and true into a breathtaking vista of green pastures and arrow-straight rows of fruit trees. An equestrian statue by the road marked the border of the Great Horde Hundred, the exact center of the Ergoth Empire.

Miya drew alongside her fuming sister. Neither of them spoke, they merely stared out at the bountiful countryside spread before them. Kiya's hair had come free of its confining thong and fanned out over her shoulders. As a child, Miya had been jealous of her sister's blonde locks, thinking the color much prettier than her own. Now, the sight of her sister's unbound hair suddenly reminded Miya of the white burial shrouds used by high-born Ergothians. She shook her head, dislodging the thought.

"Husband didn't have much choice," Miya finally said. "The tax collector is a coward, anyway. He'll probably talk if they only threaten him with violence—"

"Do you see them?" Kiya whispered in a strange voice.

"See what?"

"The clouds, Miya. Look at the clouds. Do you see the faces?"

Miya shaded her eyes, obediently studying the sky. Towering over the valley below were great masses of clouds, their bottoms flat as marble tiles. They were intensely white in the glare of the summer sun. Clouds and valley formed a vast panorama unknown in the close confines of their forest home. Beautiful in its own way, Miya admitted, but she didn't see any faces.

Miya said, "All I see are clouds, Sister."

Kiya frowned. As before, at the Isle of Elms, she saw rows of people, their faces without expression, staring down at her. She was not given to seeing portents and omens around every corner. That she was seeing this, and Miya was not, must be significant. The silent watchers must be a warning.

The sound of voices behind them brought their attention earthward again. The Army of the East was approaching. Many Riders were pointing at the sky and exclaiming.

Tol and Egrin, leading the central column, cantered up to the Dom-shu women. As they arrived, Egrin's gaze strayed to the clouds and he jerked his mount's reins. "Draco Paladin preserve us!" he whispered. "Who are they?"

As it transpired, about half the army could see the vision. The other half saw only clouds. Tol saw nothing but summer thunderheads. He asked Kiya and Egrin what the cloud-people were doing.

"Nothing, they just—" Kiya shrugged. "They just gaze at us."

The faces, she told him, were distinct but without detail, like simple representations molded in clay. Their expressions seemed frozen and did not change.

Although unable to see the apparitions, Tol could certainly see how the aerial spectacle affected his friends. Their awe was disconcerting. He didn't fear magic himself, not as long as he had the nullstone, but bitter experience had taught him spells could have a severe effect on those around him.

"It could be a warning," Miya said, unconsciously echoing Kiya's earlier thought.

To break through the army's immobility, Tol resorted to his loudest battlefield voice.

"All right, men! If you're through gawking, let's ride on! Close ranks!" he boomed. "Form up, I said!"

Egrin and Kiya shook off their wonderment and the column set out. Heralds galloped out to the flanking hordes to urge them into motion as well.

"It must be a trick," Egrin insisted, chagrined at the effect the vision had on him. "There are plenty of wizards in the Tower of High Sorcery willing to do the emperor's bidding."

The explanation was a sensible one, but Kiya was not convinced. For the first time she recounted the similar vision she'd had at the Isle of Elms.

Tol was intrigued, but before he could question her further an all-too-familiar hum filled the air. A wave of arrows clattered onto the road in front of them.

"Ambush!" Miya cried, as her horse reared in fright.

"Forward the vanguard!" shouted Tol. The front ranks of the militia jogged forward, shields upraised. They flowed around the four riders as a fresh shower of arrows arrived.

Tol sent Egrin back to bring Lord Pagas's Riders forward. As the old warrior galloped away, Tol and the Dom-shu sisters dismounted.

"There! The arrows came from there!" Kiya shouted, pointing ahead to a drainage ditch on the left side of the road.

Tol tossed his reins to Miya and drew Number Six. Kiya likewise gave her mount over to Miya.

The foot soldiers gathered around the younger Dom-shu and the horses, spreading out to cover the shoulders of the road as a third and fourth volley hissed overhead. A few men, careless with their shields, went down with arrows in their necks or shoulders.

Shields raised, the Juramona Militia followed Tol and Kiya off the road toward the unseen archers. The Ackal Path was built on an earthen causeway, some two paces above the surrounding farmland, and the soldiers skidded down the mossy slope. Behind them, the rest of the militia advanced straight down the road.

Tol estimated they faced about a hundred bowmen. He had five hundred men in the vanguard. Through the line of shields ahead of him, Tol glimpsed the archers as they peered over the top of the drainage ditch. At his order, his men lowered spears and charged down the embankment. Reaching the rim of the ditch, they pulled up short, astonished by what their eyes beheld.

There were indeed one hundred bowmen in the ditch. But behind them, concealed by a thick line of berry bushes, were imperial Riders, several thousand in all. Gasping, Kiya uttered a single pungent curse. Tol couldn't improve on it.

The vanguard attacked the archers, and a brisk battle ensued. When the rest of the militia reached the crest of the road and saw the hidden hordes, they immediately halted and took up defensive squares across the Ackal Path, calmly sorting themselves into formation.

The lightly armed archers broke off the unequal struggle in the ditch, and fled. Tol withdrew his vanguard, keeping the gully between his men and the poised hordes. As he was pulling back, two of the hordes charged the militia on the road.

The sight of the bellowing Riders, thundering forward on massive war-horses, was guaranteed to strike terror in the hearts of men on foot, but the charging hordes had never before faced foot soldiers trained by Tol. Certainly the Juramona Militia felt fear, but they stood their ground.

The hordes smashed into the foremost square, almost sweeping it away in one go. Plunging horses bowled over the men on foot, despite the walls of spear points they presented. The rear face of the square, unengaged, wheeled around and reinforced their comrades. Blood flowed on the Ackal Path, and Tol quick-marched the vanguard to support their comrades. Using tactics he'd invented long ago, his soldiers slung their shields on their backs, gripped their spears in both hands, and raced headlong at the engaged horsemen. Footmen weren't expected to attack riders, but the Juramonans knew how. As they attacked, they shouted the most famous battle cry in Ergoth.

"Juramona! Juramona!"

The Riders trapped between the militia squares and Tol's

charging vanguard broke off fighting and rode out of reach.

The Juramonans barely had time to draw breath before two fresh hordes bore down on them. Hastily they formed a new square four ranks deep. The Riders trotted along the outside of the square, hacking the spearheads jabbing at them. Fighting was at arm's length as the Riders surged around the militia, but once they realized the Juramonans wouldn't be easily broken, the hordes withdrew a short distance to rethink their strategy.

Around him, Tol heard the labored breathing of his men. Kiya had sheathed her sword and taken up a spear from a fallen soldier. She wiped blood (not her own) from her hands so she could better grip the spear. Again there was little time to rest before battle was renewed.

From between the reformed ranks of mounted men bowmen emerged—seven hundred of them. The enemy's plan was easy to discern: unable to force open the dogged militia squares, the imperial commander would use archers to thin the Juramonan ranks until his Riders could smash through.

The first arrows were falling when trumpets sounded on both sides of the Ackal Path. Tol recognized the calls. One was from Zanpolo, with the left wing of the army. The other came from Pagas and the horsemen attached to Tol's center column.

The ground shook with the thunder of galloping horses. Zanpolo's twenty hordes met the imperial Riders in a cherry orchard, and a furious cavalry fight erupted on Tol's left. Rank upon rank joined the fray. Tol guessed the number facing Zanpolo at ten hordes. The emperor was reckoned to have ninety more hordes at his disposal, better than twice the size of Tol's army. So where were the rest?

The militiaman beside Tol fell dead, an arrow in his eye. Tol put Number Six away and snatched up the dead man's spear and shield. He couldn't see Miya anywhere, but spotted Kiya's long blonde hair streaming below her helmet. Shouldering in beside the Dom-shu, he rammed his spear over the heads of the soldiers in front of him, impaling an enemy rider through the thigh.

Lord Pagas and his landed hordes joined the fray, hitting

the emperor's men on their left. Pressure on the infantry lessened as Pagas's Riders swept through the bowmen, cutting them down. Freed of the deadly hail of arrows, Tol ordered his spearmen forward.

Locked together by their overlapping shields, the phalanx of spearmen lurched into motion. Like some fearful spiny beast, the squares of infantry crept down the road. The hordes hovered but kept their distance.

The causeway descended to ground level, exposing the sides and rear of the militia to charges. At Tol's order, two blocks of spearmen swung right and left, forming a wedge behind the leading company. When a horde sallied out of the orchards on the south side of the road, the militiamen, moving in unison, whipped their spears around to cover that side. The massed movement was so startling (and menacing) that the imperial force pulled up short. Again and again Riders were thrown by the footmen's actions. Faced with an attack from elite Riders of the Great Horde, foot soldiers were supposed to run away, or toss down their arms and plead for mercy. The Juramonans did neither.

Pagas re-formed his scattered men. Egrin was with them, the high comb topping his marshal's helmet rising above the squat, round helmets worn by Riders in the landed hordes. At a walking pace, the Army of the East pushed ahead. Ackal V's men slowly gave ground, uncertain how to best them.

On the right, the north side of the Ackal Path, a low stone wall marked the boundary of a large pasture. Some of Pagas's men steered their horses around the obstacle, while others urged their animals to jump over it. Confusion resulted, and before they'd regrouped, three imperial hordes came roaring across the pasture, sabers forward. Frustrated by their abortive fight with Tol's infantry, the men vented their fury on Pagas's disordered men.

Tol bawled new orders to the militia. Companies of spearmen halted, ponderously swung to their right, and headed toward the boiling cavalry fight. Arrows sailed in from imperial troops. One skipped off Tol's helmet, throwing him off balance. Kiya looped an arm through his and kept him on his feet.

Pagas's horde fractured in half. The tough old warlord whose valiant battle against centaurs had earned him a bashed nose and a high-pitched voice was engulfed by younger, saber-swinging foes. He gave as good as he got for quite a while, but finally too many blades flashed around Pagas, and he pitched from his horse.

Egrin, trapped in the other half of the Plains Panther horde, tried to break through to the fallen warlord. Pagas was trying to rise on hands and knees when imperials closed in and trampled him under in a blur. Immediately the cry went up that Lord Pagas was dead.

Undaunted, Egrin and a wedge of horsemen plunged into the enemy riders, forcing them away from where Pagas lay. Unfortunately, it was soon clear the cries were true: Pagas was slain.

Armor clanking, sweat running down every face, the militia was about to close on the cavalry duel when fresh imperial hordes galloped up behind them. With this new threat at their backs, the Juramonans had no choice but to face about. Tol shouted for the nearest company to attack.

"Egrin!" Kiya shouted.

Her cry brought Tol whirling around in time to see the man who had been like a father to him inundated by enemies. A saber blow sent Egrin's helmet flying, though the old warrior skewered the Rider who'd landed the blow. Even as he recovered his weapon, however, four more warriors thrust at him. He parried the first attack, the next, and the next—then a saber tip caught Egrin under his sword arm.

From his vantage fewer than thirty paces away, Tol saw the strike clearly. The imperial Rider who'd landed the blow stabbed Egrin again, and the old warrior collapsed sideways off his mount and vanished among the churning horsemen.

Breath caught in Tol's throat. He felt as though the thrust had pierced his own flesh. He began to shout at the top of his lungs. Later, he would have no memory of what he'd said.

Kiya stared at him in shock. She'd never before heard such language from her normally even-tempered husband.

Tol drove his company forward, but the infantry could not catch the horsemen. The horde that had slain Pagas wheeled before the militia's rush and rode easily out of reach.

The bodies of the two warlords lay within paces of each other. Pagas lay on his stomach in the trampled grass. He had suffered a score of wounds. Egrin's only visible wounds were the jab underneath his sword arm and a shallow cut across his throat. After falling from his horse, his great stamina had allowed him to pull himself to a seated position. He was slumped forward, head hanging down. His right hand still gripped his saber.

With the militia encircling him, keeping watch for enemy attack, Tol knelt by Egrin. His hands shook as he dropped his spear and tilted the old marshal's head up. Hazel eyes blinked at him.

"Egrin!" Tol cried. "Egrin, can you hear me?"

He blinked again, and managed a barely perceptible nod, but he couldn't rise or speak.

"Husband!" Kiya said urgently. "We need you—the battle goes on!"

Tol gently laid the marshal on his back and stood, positioning himself so his shadow covered Egrin's face.

"We'll hold here," he said, wiping sweat and tears from his grimy cheeks. "We can't advance without more cavalry support. Ackal's men would chew us up."

With trumpet calls, the trailing hordes of Tol's army were summoned forward. Last to arrive were Mittigorn and Argonnel, hurrying from their position at the customs house. When the full weight of Tol's forty-four hordes was in place, the imperials began to withdraw.

Miya rode out of the ranks of Zanpolo's men. Tol took the reins of his gray war-horse from her. He was trembling so with battle rage and exhaustion, he missed the stirrup twice before finally setting his foot in and swinging into the saddle.

"Have the healers see to Lord Egrin," he said. "There's a man's weight in gold for those who save his life!"

He gathered his reins, ready to gallop after the retreating imperials, but Miya took hold of the gray horse's bridle. "Wait, Husband," she said. "Let your warlords chase the enemy. You should stay here."

He yanked his horse's head to the side, breaking her grip, and snarled, "No! Not enough blood has been shed—not nearly enough!"

Miya was appalled by his bloodthirsty words, and by the ugly emotions that twisted his face. Kiya, mounted as well, steered her smaller plains pony in front of his muscular war-horse, blocking his attempt to ride away. He shouted at her to move, but she refused to budge.

With a hiss of steel, Number Six came free of its scabbard. Tol raised the saber high.

Miya cried out, but Kiya said calmly, "Will you kill me, Husband?"

Crimson shame washed over his face as he lowered the sword. The three of them stood frozen in place as the hordes of Mittigorn and Argonnel swept past in a swirl of dust and pounding hoofbeats.

It was Tol who finally broke the terrible moment. He bowed his head and covered his burning eyes with one hand.

He'd lost comrades on every campaign he'd fought. It was never easy, but the sorrow was lessened by knowing they died well, fighting as honorable warriors. Yet he felt no such comfort in this case. If Egrin died . . .

Tol shuddered. Egrin was more than his second father. Tol had known his real father for eleven years. He'd known Egrin nearly three decades. Not only had Egrin opened up an entirely different world to Tol and taught him how to be a warrior, the former marshal had showed when it was best *not* to fight. Egrin had taught him what it meant to be an honorable man.

A strong hand clutched his arm. It was Miya's. She said his name, and the awed tone of her voice penetrated his grief. He looked up and beheld an amazing scene.

To the west, where the imperial hordes were retreating, clouds were descending onto the battlefield. Tol saw no faces in them, just billowing masses of white vapor sinking to the ground. They filled the open space between the withdrawing imperials and Tol's pursuing hordes. The green pastures and leafy orchards were slowly swallowed up by a wall of dense mist.

"The emperor's covering his tracks!" said Kiya.

Wearily, Tol sheathed Number Six. "The battle is over today," he said. "When the clouds disperse, we'll resume the march. This was just a skirmish to delay us."

Miya was incredulous. How could he call today's bloody encounter a skirmish?

"We faced no more than ten hordes today. Ackal has ninety more. Imagine today's battle increased ninefold."

Miya shook her head. She followed as Tol rode back to check on Egrin.

Kiya never noticed them leave. The low-lying cloudbank was staring at her—its contours holding the same implacable faces she had seen before. After a moment the faces dissolved, leaving only featureless fog.

🦉 🦉 🦉 🦉 🦉

Within the Tower of High Sorcery, the assemblage of wizards formed a great circle, hands clasped. As they ended their joint incantation, sighs and groans of exhaustion filled the vast hall. Older mages tottered to benches along the wall and collapsed. Young and old alike flexed fingers grown stiff from a half-day's concentrated effort.

By projecting their collective consciousness into the air above Lord Tolandruth's army, the wizards could study its progress. The veil that had formerly cloaked the bakali and nomads was gone. None of them knew why, although there was much speculation. But they had been able to follow Tolandruth's progress since his defeat of the nomads at the Isle of Elms.

Merkurin, chief scribe of the White Robe order, finished his description of the battle and signed his name to the scroll with his customary flourish. The document, covering Lord Tolandruth's movements for a single day, was over ten paces long. While his colleagues conjured, an image of what they were seeing appeared in the air over their heads. Merkurin, outside the great circle, wrote down all he saw. The process was exhausting for everyone, and made more so by the distance from which they had to operate.

# Paul B. Thompson and Tonya C. Cook

Merkurin rang a small bell. An acolyte of the Red Robes hurried to him. The chief scribe rolled his report and sealed it. Handing it to the young woman he reminded her, "For His Majesty. No one else is to see it."

She bowed her head. "Yes, Master Merkurin."

The emperor would soon have his report. Merkurin hoped he knew what to do with it.

# Chapter 25
## A Hero's Justice

Drums rolled, echoing off the walls of the Inner City. The imperial Household Guard was drawn up in a hollow square, swords bared. Outside the ring of armed men stood the assembled warlords of the empire—those remaining who were still able to reach Daltigoth at the emperor's command. They solemnly watched the spectacle unfolding before them. Every window in the palace and Riders' Hall facing the plaza was filled with spectators.

Within the square of guardsmen nine men stood in a line. Warlords all, the nine were bereft of arms and armor, clad in ordinary trews and linen shirts, the garb of condemned men. Their hair and beards had been shorn away.

Also within the square was Ackal V, seated on his golden throne. Prince Dalar stood by his right hand. The heir to the throne wore his own suit of armor, cuirass and helmet wrought in thin, brightly polished brass.

The condemned men were the commanders of the hordes who had been ordered to stop Tol's advance on the capital. Their leader, General Meeka of the Golden Ram Horde, had protested that he had not had sufficient men to stop Lord Tolandruth, well known as an accomplished strategist. His use of Tol's old title had cost Meeka his life, and insured the emperor's rage against his subordinates. Meeka was beheaded forthwith, and his horde commanders likewise now faced the emperor's wrath.

"You have been found guilty of cowardice," Ackal V declared. "By law and custom set down by my glorious ancestors, you should all be executed, and your property forfeited to the empire!" He paused for effect. "But I am disposed to be lenient. Only two of you shall die. I leave it to you to choose who shall lose their heads."

The nine neither spoke nor moved. Their eyes remained fixed forward, staring beyond their angry liege.

Ackal V flushed. "Choose two, or all will die!" he shouted.

The warrior at the right end of the line, a cousin of the Tumult and Dermount clans, stepped forward. "I will die to spare my comrades, Majesty," he announced.

Immediately, the man next to him stepped forward, saying, "So shall I!"

In turn, each of the others took the fatal step toward the emperor.

Ackal V leaned to the right, murmuring, "You see, Dalar, what I must work with? They fight poorly, disobey me, then offer their necks out of pride. What can I do?" He sighed loudly and sat back. "Very well. Your emperor grants your final wish. Kill them all."

The warlords outside the ring of guards stirred, shouting, "No!" and "Spare them!"

Ackal V glared at the assembly. "The Inner City wall has room for many heads!" he said loudly.

Dalar flinched at his father's injustice, but for once the warlords did not. New cries went up: "Shame!" and "Where is honor?" The plaza reverberated with the noise.

Nonetheless, the emperor jerked his head, and his executioner strode toward the waiting prisoners. The swordsman's bare chest rippled with muscle as he lifted his weapon high.

Without hesitation, the Dermount cousin went down on his knees. The two-handed blade severed his neck in one stroke. In spite of the outraged shouts from the assembled warlords, the next prisoner knelt immediately, and was dispatched with equal swiftness. The executioner traveled efficiently down the line, until all nine men were dead. Their blood flowed together in a great spreading pool, staining the mosaic of the constellation of Corij that decorated the plaza's center.

A prolonged groan went up from the warlords of Ergoth. They pressed forward, jostling the Household Guards holding them back.

"Justice is done," Ackal V declared.

He rose and commanded Dalar to accompany him. Outwardly nonchalant, he crossed the square to the palace. A double line of guards formed a path for emperor and heir, and more soldiers jogged down from the palace to reinforce their comrades.

A loud metallic clang behind him made the emperor pause on the first of the palace steps. He looked back. A warlord's personal dagger had landed on the pavement several paces away. Not a direct threat to Ackal V, the symbol of the warlord's rank had been hurled over the heads of the massed guards in a show of contempt and defiance.

As though a dam had burst, the single blade was joined by others. They spun through the air, jeweled pommels glittering, a veritable deluge of flashing iron clattering and skidding over the ancient mosaic.

Ackal V's studied nonchalance vanished. Face contorted with fury, he snatched Dalar's hand and stamped up the stairs. All present knew that retribution would be swift. No one insulted Nazramin Bethen Ergothas Ackal V with impunity. No one.

The emperor was almost blind with rage. He shoved aside any servant unlucky enough to cross his path. In the antechamber of the throne room, his chamberlains huddled out of reach and uttered soothing phrases.

"Stop that chattering, you imbeciles, or I'll have your tongues out!" Ackal V roared. The men instantly fell silent. He paced back and forth, unconsciously dragging the little prince along with him. "The arrogance! The conceit! I'll have them exterminated! Every one of them!"

"Who then will fight for you?"

Valaran, dressed in a gown of imperial scarlet, stood in the open doorway to the throne room. Her chestnut hair, free for once of the tall headdress required by fashion, hung loose down her back. Surrounded by ladies dressed in muted hues, the empress seemed a great summer bloom fallen into a bed of pale spring blossoms.

Her appearance elicited squawks of dismay from the chamberlains. The men immediately cast down their eyes, looking away from the empress's bare face.

"Why are you out of your quarters, lady?" her husband said icily. "And without a proper covering for your face?"

"Apologies, sire. I feared a riot and came with all haste to extricate Your Majesty from danger," she replied.

His laughter was short and harsh. "With what troops, lady?"

Valaran gestured to the women around her. "Troops enough, Majesty. Few warlords—even arrogant, conceited ones—would raise a sword against unarmed women."

This was certainly true, but when she held out her arms and Prince Dalar ran to her, Valaran's true reason for defying law and custom became apparent. The empress had left her sacred enclave to save her son.

Ackal V's attention returned to the original source of his fury. "This would not have happened if my Wolves had been here!"

Accompanied by a large entourage of priests, courtiers, and the emperor's elderly cousin, Lord Gothalan, the Emperor's Wolves had departed the night before. Their mission was known only to their patron.

Ackal V spoke to a nearby officer. "Tell the captain of the Householders to clear that insolent trash out of the Inner City."

The soldier saluted and started to leave, but the emperor wasn't finished.

"Have the daggers gathered up. And send the chamberlain of clans and heraldry to me. I want every blade identified." A slow smile curved the emperor's lips. "I intend to see to it each one finds its owner again."

❦ ❦ ❦ ❦ ❦

A small band of horsemen topped a rise in the Ackal Path, skidding to a halt. Before them, golden in the light of the midmorning summer sun, was the greatest vista in the empire: Daltigoth, capital of Ergoth.

On the left, the Dalti Canal ran parallel to the road, its waters jade green, its shimmering surface undisturbed by boats. Commerce, disrupted by the twin invasions, had not revived in the face of the Army of the East's advance. Peasant farmers and the usual stream of travelers flowing to and from Daltigoth were conspicuously absent.

Between the canal and the road was a line of tall, weathered statues commemorating rulers of past ages. Tol, leading the group of horsemen, noted that the headless figures of Pakin Zan and Ergothas III still stood, just as they had many years ago, when he'd first come to Daltigoth. An image of Ackal IV had been raised since. It was half the size of the other colossi, an indifferent likeness carved in soft limestone. Given the winter storms common to the Great Horde Hundred, the statue's features wouldn't last ten years.

The small hill on which Tol and his companions had paused was called Emperor's Knob. Legend had it that Ackal Ergot had stood here when he first surveyed the site of his future capital.

Tol drank from the waterskin Kiya handed him and reflected on the passage of time. When he'd last stood here, the land around Daltigoth had been gripped by winter, with deep snow blanketing the pasturelands to his left and the great orchards to his right, under a leaden sky. Now, the fruit trees were densely green and the pastures thronged with shaggy, red-coated cattle, the emperor's own herd.

Although still more than two leagues away, Daltigoth filled the view from horizon to horizon, from the canal in the east to the peaks of the Harkmor range, to the south and west. The great city wall rose like an impenetrable cliff face. Beyond it, and taller still, the wall of the Inner City enclosed the imperial enclave of palace, Tower of High Sorcery, and Riders' Hall.

It seemed impossible that they could overcome such a vast and imposing place. All Ackal V had to do was shut the gates, and the Army of the East would be powerless.

"They said we couldn't get into Caergoth either," Kiya said, reading her husband's thoughts. She took the skin back from Tol and drank deeply.

Young Lord Quevalen muttered, "Why do we sit here alone? Where are the imperial hordes?"

It was a trenchant question. In the two days since the battle that had cost them Pagas and gravely wounded Egrin, the Army of the East had encountered no serious opposition. A handful of patrols, a few bands of hired archers was all the resistance they'd met, and all were quickly swept aside. Where were Ackal V's vaunted ninety hordes?

Under duress, the customs officer Hathak had revealed that forces loyal to the emperor were gathering secretly behind the Army of the East. Minor crossroads north and south of the Ackal Path were the rendezvous points. Riders of the Great Horde had been sent out disguised as commoners, and only awaited word to take up hidden weapons and strike Tol's men unawares from behind.

Hathak obviously believed what he told them, but after some rumination, Tol decided he did not. Since entering the Great Horde Hundred, they'd seen no more than two dozen farmers. Where were all these supposedly hidden warriors? Where were their horses? He felt the story had been planted by the emperor to keep them off balance, to keep them looking over their shoulders rather than straight ahead. His warlords agreed with this sensible assessment.

Since the army's arrival at Emperor's Knob, scouts had returned with other news. The city gates were shut tight, but there were signs that large numbers of mounted men had crossed the West Dalti River not more than two days ago—headed *away* from the city.

Now, as they stared at Daltigoth in the distance, Tol and his warlords were discussing this peculiar development.

"They mean to outflank us," Mittigorn said. "With our attention fixed on the capital, the emperor's hordes can sweep 'round behind us and catch us in a noose!"

Two Riders from Zanpolo's horde arrived, interrupting the debate. With them was a stranger mounted on a sturdy cob and bearing a standard. The plain white disk on its top was not a horde symbol Tol or his warlords recognized.

"My lord," said the young man. "I am come from my master, chief priest of Corij, of the great temple in Daltigoth."

The assembled warlords muttered among themselves. Tol leaned forward on the pommel of his saddle. "Does your master have a name?"

The herald swallowed, glancing at the bored warlords at Tol's back. "Xanderel, my lord. My master is Xanderel."

"What word does the august Xanderel bring to us?"

"He seeks an audience, my lord, to discuss the grievances that have brought you here."

Mittigorn and the other commanders of the landed hordes were delighted by the news; they believed the emperor was making overtures toward peace. The Caergoth lords, however, did not trust that interpretation.

"This is not Ackal V's way," Zanpolo said firmly. "Negotiate? This emperor only negotiates at the point of a saber!"

"This time he's not dealing with foreigners, nomads, or lizard-men," Trudo countered. "We're warlords of the empire. Why not treat with us?"

Zanpolo shook his head. He was certain this was a trick.

Tol agreed. Ackal V was capable of the worst double-dealing. The whole situation smelled worse than a thief on a gibbet.

According to the herald, the parley would be attended by priests from the temples of Mishas and Draco Paladine, as well as a guard escort of one hundred Riders.

"A large retinue for a few priests," Zanpolo remarked, as all eyes went to Tol.

He replied after only a brief hesitation. "We will meet your master Xanderel, at sunset, at our camp on the plain, a half-league north of the Dragon Gate."

The delay plainly puzzled the herald, but he nodded assent and cantered away. As he was going, Miya arrived. She'd been helping nurse Egrin. The old marshal was conscious and improving, but had no use of his right arm.

Told of the proposed meeting, Miya sided with the landed warlords and saw the parley as a good sign. Her sister, predictably, sided with Zanpolo and the skeptics.

"It's a trap," Kiya said darkly. "Priests mean magic. Don't trust them, Husband!"

Lord Quevalen, who knew Daltigoth well, disagreed. "The priesthoods are not happy with the emperor," he said. "He taxes their holdings heavily, and it is well known that he slights the gods."

Argument ended as work on the camp took precedence. Tol had delayed the parley for that reason. If Ackal V intended a surprise attack while Tol was talking with the delegation of priests, he'd find a fortified defense waiting.

As work progressed, Miya entered the tent she shared with her sister to find Kiya already there. She was sorting through her scant belongings and had divided everything into four small piles.

"What are you doing?" Miya asked.

Kiya pointed to the first pile, which contained two good knives, a helmet, and a ring mail shirt. "This is for Eli, when he's old enough," she said. "That"—a pile of doeskin shifts, leggings, belts, and such—"is for you, Sister."

Ignoring Miya's demand for an explanation, Kiya pointed to the third pile, comprising personal items such as her tribal fetish, a carved ivory comb, and a nicely beaded vest.

"For our father," she said.

She pivoted to point at the final pile, which contained her sword, scale shirt, and greaves. Miya let out a horrified yell.

Kiya's long horsetail of blonde hair was gone. Her hair now ended raggedly at the nape of her neck.

The elder Dom-shu sister laid the thick hank of hair, tied with a leather thong, atop the last pile. "This," she said evenly, "goes to our husband."

Dom-shu warriors only cut their hair before a battle they did not expect to survive. The hair was offered as a sacrifice to Bran, god of the forest.

Miya grabbed her sister's hands. "What are you thinking? You've been gloomy ever since I found you at Caergoth!"

"You found me? Since when does a rabbit track a fox?"

Miya bit off a reply, refusing to be baited. "Why are you in such a hurry to die?"

Brown eyes finally met brown eyes, and Kiya said, "Because the final battle is near. I feel it."

Miya felt it, too, but not for herself or Kiya. Her chief worry was Tol. "Will Husband survive, do you think?" she asked in a low voice.

Kiya frowned and said, not unkindly, "If a mountain fell from the sky, that man would survive it."

A skirl of horns interrupted them, announcing the arrival of the delegation from Daltigoth. Kiya rose and buckled on her sword. "You watch the guards, Sister," she said. "I'll keep an eye on the priests. Agreed?"

For the first time in many years, Miya felt like weeping. Under her sister's stern gaze, she struggled to swallow the lump in her throat.

Kiya spun her around to face the door flap and gave her a rude shove. "Hurry up. Ever since you became a mother, you've gotten so fat and slow!"

Miya forced a smile and replied, "I'm not fat. I'm only rounded. You're sharp angles all over. No one would want to hug you!"

It was a lie. She pulled Kiya to her, and they embraced.

❦ ❦ ❦ ❦ ❦

The delegation from Daltigoth arrived as the sun was disappearing behind the city. The priests filled four horse-drawn wagons. They were accompanied by a dual line of horsemen. Torchlight showed the escort to be a rather nondescript group, wearing indifferent armor. They looked like provincial levies. Tol's warlords had expected to see imperial Riders, men they knew, but these horsemen were strangers.

Seven priests descended from the first wagon. All were clad in long white robes, topped by brown, hooded surcoats. All but one were quite tall. That one, the eldest judging by his yellow-gray beard, wore a golden circlet on his head. He was supported by a priest with a clipped brown beard who wore a white turban.

The remainder of the clerics, twenty-three in all, wore robes of sky blue for Mishas, or silver and white for Draco

Paladine. They arranged themselves respectfully behind the seven priests of Corij.

There was a tense moment as five hundred spearmen of the Juramona Militia moved in, interposing themselves between the priests and their escort. The priests talked amongst themselves, ending their whispered conclave when Tol and his warlords approached.

Tol greeted the elderly man with the circlet, and asked, "Do I have the honor of addressing Xanderel, high priest of Corij in Daltigoth?"

The old fellow bowed. "I am he."

"I am Tolandruth of Juramona. Welcome."

"Thank you, my lord. Shall we retire to your tent to speak?"

"No. Anything to be said will be said out here in the open, for all to hear."

Xanderel looked distinctly uncomfortable. He insisted they remove to a more private location, but Zanpolo interrupted.

"Speak, priest, or depart!" the forked-bearded warlord snapped.

Xanderel flinched and glared at Zanpolo. Recovering his equanimity, Xanderel produced a slim scroll from his sleeve. "Hear the words of His Imperial Majesty, Ackal V," he intoned.

Once again, he was interrupted. A lone figure limped out of the shadows. Head bandaged and right arm in a sling, Egrin looked pale as a specter.

"You should not be up and walking!" Miya exclaimed, hurrying him.

"I have a right to be here," the old marshal rasped, looking to Tol.

Hiding a smile of pleasure, which he feared his old mentor might misconstrue as amusement, Tol said, "You're welcome, my lord. Always."

Egrin shuffled through the crowd and stood at Tol's right hand. Tol told the priest to continue.

Xanderel began to read the parchment he held.

" 'To those warriors gathered outside the gate of my city, I, Ackal the Fifth, sovereign lord of the Empire my forefathers made, send you this greeting.' "

Weak though he was, Egrin shot a penetrating look at Tol, who nodded. The emperor did not call them an army—an army suggested a legitimate body.

" 'Since returning to Daltigoth in triumph, after leading my imperial army in battle to destroy the bakali invaders, I have learned that certain eastern warlords banded together to fight the nomad tribesmen who entered my realm to plunder and pillage. Though not under imperial command, these eastern warlords did manage to drive the savages out of the empire, and for this I commend them.' "

A murmur went through Tol's followers. A promising beginning.

" 'Yet this was not enough for some malcontents. Guided by malice and greed, these warlords forcibly entered the imperial city of Caergoth, damaged my property, and wrought violence on the person of my governor, Lord Wornoth. These and other crimes are fully known to me.

" 'Now these malcontent lords have come to Daltigoth, not as humble petitioners to my imperial majesty, but in arms, as rebels.' "

Loud denials came from Mittigorn, Argonnel, and the rest, and Xanderel paused in his reading until the protestations subsided.

" 'Despite this treason, I, Ackal V, forgive you.' "

More shouting. Xanderel plunged on, reading faster. " 'I forgive all your transgressions against my majesty, including bearing arms against my loyal hordes. Further, I will meet with all those warlords from the east who so desire it, to further mitigate the grievances they imagine they have against the throne of Ergoth. All this, I, Ackal V, do grant, if—' "

• Here it comes, Tol thought.

" '—the living body of the criminal Tol of Juramona is delivered to me this night.' "

Xanderel lowered the scroll, his hands visibly shaking. The silence was so complete, the faint crackling of the numerous torches seemed loud.

None of the warlords wanted to turn Tol over to the emperor, but the offer of a full amnesty, backed by a personal hearing of the complaints that had brought them here, was extremely tempting.

For his part, Tol was impressed. The emperor's strategy was cunning. Smiling wryly, he turned and said to his followers, "Well, must I leave now, or may I pack my bags first?"

He never heard the dagger being drawn. The tall, turbaned priest standing beside Xanderel drew the blade from inside his robe. Without sheath or scabbard to scrape against, it came out as quietly as death. The Dom-shu sisters, standing just behind Tol, saw the blade glint in the torchlight.

"Assassin!" Miya shouted, as Kiya reached for her saber.

Xanderel and four of the clerics threw themselves to the ground. The rest of the delegation produced daggers or short swords from beneath their robes and flung themselves at the nearest astonished warlords. Their mounted escort drew sabers and attacked the Juramona Militia.

When the turbaned priest, drove his long dagger straight at Tol's throat, Miya yanked Tol backward and Egrin interposed himself. He seized the assassin's wrist with his good left hand. As they struggled for the dagger, the priest's turban fell away.

Tathman!

Tol instantly recognized the captain of the Emperor's Wolves, despite his trimmed beard. Number Six in hand, Tol shouted for Egrin to get clear, but the old warrior would not let go Tathman's dagger hand. Lacking a weapon and hampered by his injury, Egrin kicked hard at the other man's shins. His hobnailed boots cut through the priestly robes and drew blood.

Tathman punched Egrin in the face. The old warrior's head rocked back, once, twice, three times. Still, his iron grip did not falter. With a roar of fury, Tathman chopped at Egrin's arm with his fist and finally broke free. Immediately, he slashed downward at Egrin's face.

Tol caught Egrin and spun his friend into Miya's arms, then turned to deal with the emperor's favorite killer.

Tathman fended off Tol's cuts and thrusts, retreating back toward the wagon that had brought him. His fighting style was peculiar: He seemed more intent on cutting Tol than impaling him.

On one pass the iron blade hissed close by Tol's face, and he suddenly understood Tathman's intent. The edge of the blade was coated with a yellow substance.

Poison.

Tol risked a fleeting glance over his shoulder. Egrin lay on the ground, his head and shoulders in Miya's lap. His eyes were closed, and the cut on his face was bright red and inflamed.

Something deep inside Tol exploded with anger. With repeated thrusts of Number Six, he forced Tathman back until the big man fetched up against the wagon box. Around them, warriors and false priests fought, cursed, and shouted, but neither Tol nor Tathman said a word as they lunged and feinted. Tol's steel saber finally got through, slicing the captain's robe and revealing a gleam of metal beneath.

The poisoned dagger whisked by Tol's eyes. He recovered and slashed hard at the vile weapon, scoring a bloody cut on Tathman's chin. Down came the dagger toward Tol's scale shirt. Backing a step, Tol turned sharply and drove Number Six into his foe's unprotected thigh.

Tathman grunted, and backhanded Tol with his free hand. The blow rocked Tol, and he staggered. A red haze clouded his vision, but instinctively he raised his saber to protect his face. Tathman's dagger's struck his handguard. Tol swept Number Six down and felt his blade strike flesh. His vision cleared. Tathman was clutching the base of his neck with one hand, blood welling between his fingers.

The rest of the assassins had been subdued in the meantime. Several warlords, including the redoubtable Zanpolo and white-bearded Trudo, had fallen to poisoned daggers wielded by Tathman's confederates.

A company of militia ran up with spears leveled at Tathman. Panting, Tol waved them off. He and the Wolf captain stood, gazes locked.

Tol slashed at Tathman's already wounded shoulder. The big man parried, parried again, then made a backhanded swipe at Tol's eyes. Tol brought Number Six up to his cheek, edge outward, and the blade cut deep into Tathman's wrist. The Wolf captain groaned loudly as the tainted blade fell from his nerveless fingers. Still he did not go down, but only staggered back. His right wrist, partially severed, was held tight against his body; his left hand gripped his bleeding neck.

Tol struck again. Tathman received Tol's saber through the knotted muscle of his upper right arm. Howling, Tathman fell.

Incredibly, the villain was not yet finished. After a brief struggle, Tathman made it to his knees.

Up went Number Six. Tathman raised his face and peered at his foe through sweaty, bloody strands of hair. There was no pleading in his eyes, only burning, unquenchable hatred.

The steel blade flashed down, and Tathman died.

Tol hurried to Miya. She held Egrin tightly, both of them shaking from the force of her grief. Egrin's eyes were closed.

"He's not breathing!" Miya sobbed.

Tol seized Egrin's hand, saying harshly, "Don't go, old man! Our job isn't done!"

His plea was in vain. Egrin Raemel's son was dead.

Tol rose, stumbling slightly on shaky legs. Kiya, standing behind him, gripped his shoulder. Her face was wet with tears.

Looking to Lord Quevalen, who stood nearby, Tol asked, "Are any of the assassins alive?" Hearing that half the delegation and its escort still lived, he added coldly, "I want their heads. Now."

The Wolves were stripped of their clerical vestments and marched away. The genuine priests pleaded for mercy. Xanderel explained that he was not the chief priest of Corij. That distinction belonged to his master, Hycontas.

"Our part was forced, great lord!" the elderly priest babbled. "Our brothers in Daltigoth are being held hostage! They will be slaughtered because we have failed!"

Tol was not impressed. Xanderel or his fellows could have warned him. If they had, Lord Egrin would not now be lying dead. He ordered the priests stripped. None bore the distinctive chest tattoo of a Wolf—a crimson Ackal sun above a wolf's head—so he spared their lives.

A wagon was brought forward, and the severed heads of the Emperor's Wolves were piled inside. Clad only in their linen loincloths, the terrified priests were forced to sit atop this gruesome cargo.

Xanderel's terror set his teeth to chattering. "My lord, you can't mean to send us back this way!" he stuttered. "The emperor will surely put us all to death!"

Even through the hatred and anguish boiling in his heart, Tol knew the priest spoke the truth. He stared at the terrified men for a long moment, panting slightly from the force of his emotions.

"No. No one else will die in my stead. I will face Ackal V," he said at last. "Alone."

Quevalen and the other warlords protested vehemently, vowing Tol would be killed long before he reached the Inner City. A few threatened to stop him bodily, but the sight of Number Six, still reeking with Tathman's blood, dissuaded them.

He turned to take leave of the Dom-shu sisters. Respecting their privacy, the warlords drew off a few paces.

Miya still held Egrin's body, with Kiya kneeling beside her. Joining them, Tol took Miya's hand and pressed the Irda nullstone into her palm. "Keep this for me, in case I don't come back."

"No, take it. It will keep you safe!"

"I won't need it to do what must be done," he said firmly. "And I won't risk it falling into the emperor's hands."

Her fingers closed around the braided metal circlet. Face distorted by unaccustomed malice, she whispered, "See justice done, Husband! If it takes every piece of luck the gods owe you, see it through!"

He squeezed her hand tightly. "I will, Wife."

When he stood, Kiya rose as well. "I must come with you," she said, hand on her sword hilt. He looked her in the eye, and nodded. Miya bowed her head, weeping all the more.

Tol left Mittigorn, eldest surviving commander, in charge. The warlords, shocked by the emperor's treachery, were equally dazed by Tol's decision, yet as one they saluted their peasant general.

Kiya and Tol climbed onto the wagon's plank seat. To supplement her sword, Kiya brought along a bow and a full quiver of arrows.

Of their own accord, the men of the Juramona Militia gathered on either side of the palisade gate and raised their spears, as Tol drove the wagon and its grisly cargo past. He looked left, then right, acknowledging their salute, then fixed his gaze on the distant Dragon Gate ahead.

The night air was warm and stiflingly still. Sweat was trickling into Tol's eyes. Every small jolt of the wagon felt like a blow. His hands were clenched around the reins of the two-horse team. The priests behind him were quiet except for an occasional whimper or moan. The only other break in the silence occurred when, after a particularly hard jolt, the large head of the Wolf called Argon rolled over and thudded against the side of the wagon. The sight was too much for a younger priest, and he was sick over the side of the slowly moving wagon.

The torches flanking the Dragon Gate came into view. Their light played over the reliefs that surrounded the monumental portal: the hero Volmunaard's battle against the black dragon Vilesoot. The images seemed alive, moving and shifting in the orange glow.

The gate was open.

Tol pulled the horses to a stop. Both the entry gate—an opening large enough for two riders abreast—and the great ceremonial portal stood wide. The latter yawned like a primeval cavern, black and endless. Twenty horsemen riding boot to boot could fit through it. No guards were in sight.

"This isn't right," Kiya muttered.

"It's perfect." Tol snapped the reins, setting the horses in motion again.

They passed through the broad tunnel of the gatehouse and into the city proper. The streets were devoid of people. The windows of every house and business were shuttered. No light showed. Wind stirred along the stone canyons, pushing rubbish before it. Somewhere a dog barked.

Against the cloud-streaked night sky, the Tower of High Sorcery glowed like a pearlescent lamp. Its light gave the Inner City wall and palace towers a gray, insubstantial look, as though they were edifices of fog. Kiya recalled the cloud faces that had watched her from the summer sky. She lifted a hand and touched her burial beads, tied around her neck. If Tol noticed, he did not say anything.

Following the route he well remembered, Tol guided the creaking wagon through the empty streets.

At a square just outside the Inner City gate, they found two thousand Riders, bearing the standards of the Scarlet Dragon and Whirlwind hordes, waiting for them. The Riders sat in close ranks, their horses snorting and bobbing their heads in the humid night air.

Tol halted the wagon. Four men in officer's garb left the front ranks and rode forward.

"My lord Tolandruth!" The one who hailed him was about Tol's own age, with a close-cropped blond mustache and pale blue eyes. Tol didn't know him. "I am Gonzakan, warlord of the Whirlwind Horde."

"Ah. You have come to arrest me."

The officer frowned and leaned forward in the saddle, as though trying to see better. "I did not picture you arriving by wagon, my lord. What cargo do you carry?"

"The Emperor's Wolves."

Astonished, the four warlords rode closer. They swore eloquently.

"The Wolves never looked better!"

"By Corij, he got Tathman! And Argon!"

"He got them all!"

The blond officer addressed Tol in an awed voice.

"We know your errand, my lord."

"And you mean to stop me?" His fingers tightened on the sharkskin grip of Number Six.

"No, my lord."

Tol's eyes narrowed. He suspected a jest, but Gonzakan quickly explained. After the emperor's execution of nine blameless commanders for failing to stop Tol earlier, the warlords of the Great Horde had come to a momentous decision:

they would no longer defend Ackal V. They were not acting to save the empire, but out of a sense of collective dishonor. For years Ackal V had tormented his people, from the highest priest to the poorest peasant, but Ergoth had known tyrannical rulers before. He had ordered his hordes to fight hopeless battles, but that was a Rider's lot in life, willingly accepted. To fall in battle was expected, hoped for. However, a pointless, dishonorable death at the emperor's own hands could not be tolerated. By unanimous assent, the Riders had abandoned the emperor to whatever fate Corij decreed for him—fate in the form of Tolandruth of Juramona.

Tol was stunned. What of the Household Guard? The Horse Guards? The imperial courtiers?

"Some have resisted," said Gonzakan. "They are being dealt with. Since you've disposed of the Wolves, no one now stands between you and the emperor."

Valaran is mine!

The thought made Tol shiver, in spite of the night's heat.

Kiya leaned close. "Let's go, before the dream ends and they change their minds!" she whispered.

Tol dropped the reins. Jumping down from the wagon, he told Kiya to wait there. Like a sleepwalker, he passed between the lines of mounted men, crossing the broad square under the eyes of two thousand warriors.

Iron scraped. A warrior in the front ranks drew his saber and raised it high.

"Tolandruth!" he shouted.

Two thousand sabers thrust up toward the starry sky. "Tolandruth! Tolandruth!"

The Inner City gate was open and unguarded, but the imperial plaza wasn't empty. Dark stains covered the mosaic. Farther on were several bodies, shapeless mounds illuminated by the glow of the Tower of High Sorcery.

He found more broken weapons and blood on the palace steps. There'd been a brisk fight here, but the Householders had been swept aside.

Once Tol had seen Emperor Pakin III stand on these steps, bathed in the adoration of his loyal subjects, Tol included. Now there was only the sound of the night breeze and Tol's own harsh breathing. Only one of the iron sconces by the palace doors held a lit torch, and the double doors themselves were ajar. A brass lamp, stamped flat by a heavy boot, lay in the doorway.

The imperial palace felt like a cemetery—potent with the feeling that people had once been here, but now were gone. Tol finally encountered living occupants, small knots of courtiers or servants hiding in alcoves and whispering. More than once he heard his name spoken with the sort of frightened reverence usually reserved for forces of nature. Fire. Flood. Plague. Tolandruth.

The audience hall was barred to him. Its floor-to-ceiling double doors did not yield when he leaned against them. Tol smote the panels with the pommel of his sword and shouted. Ruddy light bloomed in the thin gap between doors and floor. A heavy bolt clanked. The left door swung inward.

Tol lifted Number Six, prepared to face a reserve contingent of Wolves or even Ackal V himself. The face that greeted him was pale, hollow-eyed, and indescribably lovely.

"By all the gods," Valaran breathed, lifting her oil lamp higher. "It *is* you!"

Tol's breath caught and held. She was thinner than he remembered, her chin sharper, and her cheekbones more prominent, but her eyes were still the clear, bottomless green of fine emeralds and her hair a warm, deep chestnut. She was clothed in white, with a delicate tracery of crimson thread decorating her gown's close-fitting bodice.

"Valaran." How sweet it was to speak her name aloud! "Valaran," he said again. "I have come for you."

She moved back a step so he could enter. She swung the ponderous door shut and threw the bolt. Without warning, Tol suddenly found her in his arms, her face buried in his shoulder. She held him tightly, her body shaking.

"I have worked so long for this moment," she said, lips close by his ear. "So long and so hard, and I thought many times I'd failed. Yet here you are!"

The catch in her voice touched him deeply. Her scent filled his head, making him dizzy with desire. He lifted his hand and carefully rested it on her shimmering hair.

Paul B. Thompson and Tonya C. Cook

"I swore I would return."

A small laugh, faintly edged with hysteria. "I know."

They kissed, tentatively at first, then with increasing fervor. He had nearly forgotten his rage and his mission, until Valaran drew back and said, "Come, my love."

She took his hand and led him down the carpeted path that ran the length of the long, high-ceilinged audience hall. Only a few candles in the room's numerous candelabra were lit. Most of the enormous iron racks were overthrown, candle wax spattered over the floor. Elegant chairs were overturned, tables smashed.

Valaran led him to the rotund body of a man, clad in fine burgundy velvet, lying facedown on the marble floor. A wide bloodstain spread out from the man's head.

"One of his most loyal chamberlains—Lord Fedro," she said. "He killed him himself."

Tol wondered what had happened here, but was given no time to ask. Valaran drew him onward.

The far end of the hall was brighter than the rest of the cavernous room. The throne of Ergoth was flanked by flaming braziers. The seat was vacant.

"Dal! Dal!" Valaran called with quiet urgency.

A small boy emerged from behind the throne and ran to her, clutching her gowned legs.

She smiled, laying a hand on the child's thick mop of black hair. "This is my son, Crown Prince Dalar of Ergoth."

The child had his father's high forehead and sharp features. His eyes were Val's, emerald green and enormous in his pale face.

Tol nodded awkwardly at the boy, then looked beyond him. Protruding from behind the throne was a foot clad in a crimson slipper. It twitched. Tol strode around the imperial seat to find the emperor lying on the floor. His robe of gold and imperial scarlet was twisted around his legs and torso, as if he'd been thrashing about on the floor. His eyes were half closed, his fingers twitched convulsively, and he was mumbling into the carpet.

Taken aback, Tol said, "What happened to him?"

"Drugged." Valaran shrugged at his shocked expression,

364

adding, "I put a sleeping draught in his wine. With the Wolves gone, and him so preoccupied, he didn't notice until it was too late."

Tol rolled the semiconscious man onto his side. Ackal V reeked of sweat and sour wine. A bloody dagger lay on the rug beneath him—the same blade, Valaran said, that he'd used to slay his unfortunate chamberlain.

He felt Valaran's hand on his shoulder. "Everything is ready," she murmured. "The Great Horde has forsaken him. The Household Guards are beaten and scattered. His Wolves are gone. I knew they couldn't kill you! No one remains to defend him."

Tol stood. Valaran put her arms around his waist from behind. She pressed the trembling length of her body against his.

"This is the reason I lived, for this moment! I tried to kill myself, but he stopped me. Then there was Dalar—another reason to live until you came back to me. I dreamt of this, Tol, awake and asleep, for nearly seven years! Only one deed remains. Just one act, and I am yours forever."

He felt the feather-touch of her lips against his neck. "Kill him, Tol."

Tol looked down at his enemy. There was no one in the world he hated more than this man. Haughty, cruel, vicious Prince Nazramin, who had murdered his own brother to steal his throne. No one deserved death more than the man who had worked such evil against Tol, from the moment they'd first met up to this night.

Yet Tol did not move.

To hear the woman he adored say, "Kill him, Tol," as easily he had said, "I love you," was more than Tol could bear. The touch of her lips had sent a wave of desire through him, but those words brought a nauseating rush of revulsion. His sword arm seemed turned to stone.

"Tol, my love, what are you waiting for? Kill him!" Valaran said, more loudly.

Prince Dalar was watching them, peering around the golden throne of Ergoth. What did the boy make of this? Tol wondered. What did he think of his mother, kissing this strange, savage-looking man and demanding that he kill Dalar's father? The child's wide-eyed gaze only deepened Tol's revulsion. He shook off Valaran's embrace, stalking away. She followed.

"Where are you going, Tol? This is the culmination of our dreams! We've waited so long for this night! Finish him! No one will weep for such a monster!"

The gods alone knew how much Tol wanted to kill Nazramin! When he'd been driven out of Daltigoth, broken inside and out, it was the hope of Valaran's love and the dream of Nazramin's death that had kept him alive. He had always imagined killing his enemy, but in some honorable fashion. Never once had he considered slitting the throat of a helpless, drooling drunkard.

Valaran circled the throne to stand by Dalar, who clung to her hand. The great chair stood between her and Tol. "Don't be misled by pity!" she insisted. "Great men are not moved by such feelings. You are the finest warrior of the age! Look at what you've done: slain monsters, bested wizards, conquered nations! Your deeds will live forever! Only one challenge remains. You must complete the saga of Tolandruth of Juramona! Kill the emperor, and both my love and the throne of Ergoth will be yours!"

Valaran's face was no longer pale, but suffused with blood and contorted by hate. The woman he loved was suddenly a stranger to him. Was this the woman of his dreams?

He had to clear his throat twice before words would come. "I never wanted that," he told her. "The empire would be destroyed. Riders and nobles would never tolerate a peasant on the throne."

She made an impatient sound and waved his objections aside. "Any who objected could be put down! You have an army, don't you?"

Taking up her husband's dagger, she offered it to Tol.

"Don't worry, my love." Her voice was soft, caressing. "You can rule as regent until my son is old enough to reign for himself. Teach him to be as honorable and forthright, as you are." She extended the blade closer. "How else can we be together? I've lived half my life as wife to men I did not love, and lover to a man I could not have. Do you know what that's done to me?"

Sadness welled inside Tol. Pity and regret were so strong that speech was difficult. "Yes, I can see," he whispered.

The emperor's mumbling grew louder and Valaran's voice rose as well. "Take the dagger, Tol! Kill him! You must! Kill him, Tol!"

He took the heavy golden blade from her hands. It would be easily done. A simple thrust would end Ackal V's life, as it had ended Egrin's. A cold shock of pain hit Tol as he remembered: Egrin was dead, killed by Ackal as surely as if the emperor's hand had held the poisoned blade.

"Egrin—" Tol's voice broke, but he forced the words out. "Egrin died tonight, killed by Tathman with a poisoned dagger. And Zala, the half-elf huntress, she died in the fight for Caergoth."

She blinked at him, not understanding, and he added, "Helbin was your ally, too. He has vanished, you know, and is probably dead."

Valaran turned to stare at her husband. He was stirring more, his mumbled words becoming clearer. Raking her fingers through her long, loose hair, she said, "You're a warrior, Tol. Haven't you lost comrades before?"

The polished blade in Tol's hand was stained with the blood of the slain chamberlain. Tol hadn't known the man. He might've been a cowardly toady, like Wornoth, but he hadn't deserved to die like that, his throat slit by the very master he served. No one deserved that. No one.

Enough! He threw the dagger to the floor. It skidded across the marble, coming to rest by Dalar's foot. The prince picked it up.

"It's done, Valaran. I'm done. And I'm going away. Far away from here." He held out a hand. "Forget the emperor and come with me."

Emerald eyes huge, she recoiled. "What are you saying? Go away? I am Empress of Ergoth!"

"All I care about now is you. Come with me, Val. You and your son."

He could see her breast rise and fall with her rapid

breathing. She stared at him, brows knotted in thought. "This is a test. The gods are testing me. That, or else you're mad." She gripped her throat with one hand and uttered a short, sharp laugh. "Worse, you're a coward! Your enemy lies at your feet, and you won't finish the job! What did all your friends die for? Why did you come here?"

"I've done everything I could to save the empire. I won't stain my soul by killing a helpless man, Val. Not even for you."

He walked around the prostrate emperor. He was halfway to the doors when Valaran acted. She snatched the dagger from her son's hands and raced after Tol, white gown flying.

"You can't leave!" she cried. "The emperor must die, don't you see? Our lives are forfeit if he survives. He'll hunt you down, torture you to death! And me! He'll kill me, Tol! He'll kill me with his own hands!"

He turned in time to catch her in his arms. Her heart was beating wildly, and ribbons of chestnut hair fell wildly about her face. She radiated fear and fury in equal measure. What he did not sense in her was love.

For more than six years he had survived for one purpose—to be reunited with Valaran. That dream had taken on a poignant reality as he witnessed the suffering Ackal V had inflicted on his people. Now, at the very moment of his triumph, Tol realized his dream was nothing more than that, without substance, without reality.

He was so very weary, in body and in spirit. "Kill him yourself then," he said.

Fury blazed from Valaran's eyes. "Do you think I can't? I've killed, Tol, for *us*! Winath—" She bit off the name, choking back a sob, then insisted, "But the gods would curse me for killing my son's father!"

He let her go and walked away, out of the palace and out of the Inner City. In the square beyond, the Riders, whispering among themselves, watched him depart, alone and unhurried. Kiya still waited for him. She'd secured two saddle horses and was mounted on one of them. Without a word, he took the reins of the other and swung into the saddle.

Ignoring the questioning hails of Lord Gonzakan, Tol and Kiya cantered away.

Outside the Dragon Gate, Tol paused. Directly ahead, the eastern sky was brightening. Sunrise was not far off. Tol dismounted beneath the imposing reliefs of Volmunaard and Vilesoot and drew Number Six. He jammed the steel blade into a chink between two massive stones, putting all his weight and strength behind it. The saber bored into the mortar to half its length. With both hands Tol pushed down on the hilt. Number Six bent and bent, farther than any iron blade ever could. Just as he began to think the dwarf-forged metal would never yield, it snapped off a span above the hilt.

He returned the stump of the famed saber to his scabbard and swung up into the saddle again.

"Are we done?" asked Kiya.

"We're done."

They rode out into the new day.

# Monuments

They laid Egrin to rest in Zivilyn's Carpet. It was Tol's idea to bury him in a peaceful place, amidst a monument of flowers for a man whose life was war. Tol and the Dom-shu sisters made the journey alone. Tol dug the grave, while Miya sewed a deerskin shroud for her friend and Kiya stood watch with her bow. No one followed them.

By the time preparations were complete, sunset had come. Whippoorwills made their mournful calls from the forest. The meadow itself was quiet, and above it, the clouds crimson and gold.

As a last gesture, Tol tucked the Irda nullstone into Egrin's hands, crossed on his chest. "His valiant spirit will guard it now," he said quietly.

With the grave closed and the earth replaced, night was upon them. The sky had cleared. Red Luin and white Solin sailed the starry sky, casting their light upon the scene. The time had come for the sisters and Tol to part company. Tol had made a difficult choice: solitude.

Miya's eyes kept turning to the Great Green, the dark forest beckoning her home. Eli awaited her in her father's village.

"Where will you go?" she asked Tol. Coloring, she added, "I'd like to know, in case I ever need to find you. Is it to be Tarsis?" Despite their recent troubles, she knew Hanira would always find a place for Tol.

He shook his head emphatically. His presence in Tarsis would be a provocation. If Ackal V's successor didn't demand his head, Hanira would certainly try to involve him in one of her complicated plots. He'd had enough of war and politics for the time being.

"Some place quiet," he said.

Miya embraced him with fervor, and whispered, "There's always a place for you by my fire."

He smiled. "I am grateful for that," he said, and held her tightly for moment.

Kiya, her stoicism firmly in place during Egrin's burial, began to cry. She asked Tol no questions about his future plans. After kissing him on both cheeks, and cuffing the back of his neck, she headed for the forest.

The Dom-shu had no need for horses, so Tol and Miya unsaddled the sisters' animals and set them free. Tol had not ridden the gray war-horse here. Like the sisters' horses, his mount this day was a plains pony. After a moment's reflection, he set his animal free as well. He would seek peace as an ordinary peasant. That's where he had come from, and that's where he belonged. No one would search for the vaunted Lord Tolandruth among the humble folk.

A last word to Miya and he set out, striding through the waist-high summer growth.

Miya remained by Egrin's grave. She watched Tol diminish with distance, until he was lost among the wind-tossed flowers.

❦ ❦ ❦ ❦ ❦

The empire endured. The tumultuous events set in motion by the twin invasions of Ergoth did not end when Tol left the capital, but plunged inexorably onward, like a growing avalanche.

In the confusion following Tol's departure, Ackal V perished. The exact cause of his death was never established. Common rumor had it he killed himself rather than face Lord Tolandruth's vengeance. His son, Prince Dalar, was proclaimed emperor, and a council of four warlords declared themselves the boy's regents. Two of them hailed from the Army of the East, Mittigorn and Quevalen. The others were Daltigoth lords, Vanz Hellman and Rykard Gonzakan, the warlord with the blond mustache who had met Tol in the plaza before the Inner City.

The regency of the four warlords ended in less than a year, however, when a new threat arose in the east. A fiery young claimant to the throne of Ackal Ergot, Pakin princess Mellamy Zan, raised her standard on the open plain. Taking advantage of the same discontent that had led so many warlords to rally around Tol, Mellamy raised a sizable army and marched on Daltigoth. Her advance broke apart the alliance of the four regents.

Mittigorn, who was from the east, was accused of secretly sympathizing with the Pretender and executed. Youngest of the regents, Lord Quevalen was maneuvered out of power, leaving two strong generals to vie for sole control. Vanz Hellman, popularly called the Hammer of the Bakali, held his own until fortune forced him to take the field against Mellamy Zan's army. The Pakin Pretender had a supremely talented general at her side, a mysterious figure who never appeared in public without a mask. A few folk thought her brilliant commander was Lord Tolandruth himself, but no one who actually saw the masked general believed that. The Pretender's commander was slender and elegant, with a polished voice and elaborate manners. Tol of Juramona was none of those things.

Mellamy Zan's army crushed Hellman's hordes at the Battle of the Caer Crossing. Hellman was slain, and Rykard Gonzakan became sole protector of the underage emperor. However, soon after Gonzakan's ascension to power, Emperor Dalar, who had never been crowned, vanished from history. His fate is unknown, and in time he disappeared even from the roll of Ergothian rulers. He was no more than ten years old.

Mellamy Zan reached the gates of Daltigoth. In a masterful bit of negotiation, a peace parley was proposed by the Red Robe Helbin, who had emerged from hiding after the death of Ackal V. The wizard was a profoundly changed man.

Known before for his fastidious style and calculating brain, now Helbin was colder and coarser, with shaved head and a strange taste for raw meat.

Helbin's plan called for Mellamy Zan to marry the Ackal heir, a nephew of Ackal V, thus uniting the warring Pakin and Ackal clans. However, unbeknownst to her supporters, Mellamy Zan had formulated her own plan. Realizing the nobles of Ergoth would never accept a woman as their ruler, she secretly applied to certain illegal sorcerers for a rite of transformation. Only days before her scheduled marriage to the Ackal heir, Mellamy Zan became Mellamax Zan, Pakin prince.

All Helbin's careful work came to naught, and Mellamax did gain the throne of Ergoth for one hundred days until General Gonzakan gathered Ackal loyalists and deposed the Pakin emperor. Bereft of power, unable to keep the dark, mysterious bargain she'd made with the sorcerers, Mellamax once more became Mellamy. She fled to Tarsis, where she lived in eccentric splendor until assassinated by agents of Regent Gonzakan.

Empress Valaran did not long enjoy her freedom from her vicious husband. Lord Hellman wooed her, but she rejected his advances and ended her days a lonely prisoner. Confined to a rocky promontory overlooking the western sea, Valaran was consigned in the same stone keep that once held the deposed Empress Kanira. The governor of her prison was changed twice a year to prevent any one man from falling under the sway of his beautiful, clever captive.

Valaran adapted to life in her remote prison. Her main expenditures were for parchment, quills, and ink. She wrote eighteen additional books before her death: histories, commentaries, and learned discourses on natural philosophy. Her most famous title was *The Life of Lord Tolandruth*, which predictably was suppressed by the Ergothian regent. Still, copies were smuggled to the capital and circulated in secret, copied in back rooms and cellars. The biography was popular in foreign lands, too, particularly Tarsis. Over the years, many errors—both accidental and intentional—entered the text. Much of what later generations read about Tol of Juramona were copyists' tall tales.

## Paul B. Thompson and Tonya C. Cook

The mind of the former empress remained acute to the end of her life, it is said. For forty-two years she dwelt in captivity, although as she once remarked to one of her governors, she had in fact been a prisoner from birth—thirty-seven years in the Inner City, forty-two in Kanira's Keep.

Her only protest against her fate was a symbolic one. She refused to cut her hair. By the time she died, it swept the floor behind her. Although no longer its original warm chestnut shade, the pure white fall was still breathtakingly beautiful. On her deathbed Valaran made only one request: she asked that her hair be cut close to her head and sent away for separate burial. Not to Daltigoth, city of her ancestors, Valaran asked it be interred in the rebuilt city of Juramona. Her last jailer, a young warlord named Gabien Solamna, faithfully carried out the wishes of the former empress.

Uncle Corpse, long-lived chief of the Dom-shu, met his fate while hunting. An enormous boar, the largest ever seen in the Great Green, turned on the hunters pursuing him and gored the old chief. Voyarunta managed to thrust his spear into the beast's heart. Man and boar perished side by side. The Dom-shu didn't practice blood succession. A new chief was chosen from the leading men of the tribe.

Miya and her son Eli lived quietly in their forest home, the old woman much respected for her many adventures. Eli, inheriting his father's facility with his hands, spent six years among the dwarves, learning metalworking. He introduced both iron and steel to the forest tribes.

Kiya married a Dom-shu warrior name Voraduna, a stocky fellow with black hair and eyes, half a span shorter than she. They were together many years, until during a minor fight with the Karad-shu Kiya stopped an arrow. Mortally wounded, she asked her husband not to leave her to the mercy of the enemy. He gave her his dagger. The Karad-shu did not get any prisoners that day.

Hanira, Syndic of Tarsis and mistress of the guild of goldsmith and jewelers, never married again. She lived for twenty-four years after the death of her daughter, Valderra, and when the gods claimed her she was reputed to be the richest woman in the world. It took a hundred laborers three

374

days to empty her personal hoard of coins from the vaults of Golden House.

❦  ❦  ❦  ❦  ❦

The forty-three years of war and dynastic struggle that raged after Ackal V's death were known collectively as the Successors' War, because each faction put forth new heirs and new claimants to the power of Ergoth as soon as the previous pretenders perished. It was a war of cities and sieges mostly, and the countryside was spared heavy damage.

The eventual victor was Pakin IV—not an Ackal, but a true descendant of the great Pakin Zan. When his armies were sweeping through the Eastern Hundred, one of his scouts became separated from his horde. Confused (one hill looked very like another to the city-bred Rider), he rode down cart tracks and cow paths, searching for his comrades. He could get no help. Frightened peasants fled at his approach.

Early one spring morning, the lost scout came across an old man working a field. The peasant saw him coming but didn't run away. The Pakin warrior rode up slowly, hailing the farmer in a friendly fashion, and offering a silent prayer to Corij that the oldster could tell him where in Chaos's name he was.

Stooped and weather-worn, the farmer looked up at him. "Greetings, my lord," he said readily enough.

"And to you, good man. I'm lost. Can you tell me where I am?"

"This is the Jura Hill Country, my lord," the peasant replied, leaning against his hoe.

"I know that!" Striving to control his exasperation, the young warrior added, "Where is the nearest town?"

"The village of Pate's Knob is half a day's ride that way." The old man pointed due east with one large hand.

"No, no. Where's the nearest real town?"

"That would be Juramona, my lord. Three days, north-northeast."

Relief spread across the rider's face. He grinned, teeth white against his grimy, sun-baked face.

# Paul B. Thompson and Tonya C. Cook

"Juramona! That'll do. We took Juramona ten days ago!"

" 'We?' "

The proud Rider straightened his back. "The loyal hordes of our rightful emperor, Pakin IV!"

Pursing his lips, the old man nodded slowly. He unhooked a heavy gourd from the cloth sash around his neck and offered it to the Rider.

The warrior took it gratefully. After the first swallow, his eyes widened. Instead of the spring water he'd expected, it was filled with potent cider.

The farmer chuckled at his expression. "That will light a fire in your veins, eh, my lord?"

"Indeed! You must have a leather throat to drink this stuff, old man!"

"I'm used to it." The farmer took the gourd back and drank two quick swallows of cider before hooking the gourd on his sash again. "So, the Pakins took Juramona. By storm or by siege?"

"By storm. We scaled a section of wall by night."

"Mmm. Not like the old days."

Warmed by his unexpected libation, the Pakin leaned comfortably on the pommel of his saddle and asked what he meant.

"Juramona used to be a more formidable place. In Marshal Odovar's day, no one could have scaled the wall and survived."

The name of the long-ago marshal meant nothing to the twenty-four-year-old warrior. "You sound like you know what you're talking about," he said. "Were you a soldier once?"

The old man plied his hoe again, loosening the soil along a row of onions. He shook his gray head. "No, my lord. Just a poor farmer."

The Rider turned his horse in a half-circle, toward the northeast and Juramona. He took a single coin from the purse at his waist and tossed it to the elderly farmer.

"Thanks for your help, old man—and for the drink!" he said, and spurred away.

The farmer let the coin hit the ground. It was a newly

minted silver crown and bore a glowering profile. The latest Pakin Pretender must be doing well enough if he had time and money to strike coins.

Raising his hoe, Tol cleaved a dry clump of soil into bits and raked them over the coin. He had no need of it. The directions were free, and so was he.

# Strife and warfare tear at the land of Ansalon

## FLIGHT OF THE FALLEN
### The Linsha Trilogy, Volume Two
### Mary H. Herbert

As the Plains of Dust are torn asunder by invading barbarian forces, Rose Knight Linsha Majere is torn between two vows— her pledge to the Knighthood, and her pledge to guard the eggs of the dragon overlord Iyesta. To keep her honor, Linsha will have to make the ultimate sacrifice.

## CITY OF THE LOST
### The Linsha Trilogy, Volume One
### Available Now!

## LORD OF THE ROSE
### Rise of Solamnia, Volume One
### Douglas Niles

In the wake of the War of Souls, the realms of Solamnia are wracked by strife and internecine warfare, and dire external threats lurk on its borders. A young lord, marked by courage and fateful flaws, emerges from the hinterlands. His vow: he will unite the fractious reaches of the ancient knighthood— or die in the attempt.

### November 2004